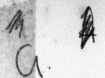

WHEN COLTS RAN

Also by Roger McDonald:

WHEN COLTS RAN

ROGER McDONALD

VINTAGE BOOKS

Australia

A Vintage book
Published by Random House Australia Pty Ltd
Level 3, 100 Pacific Highway, North Sydney NSW 2060
www.randomhouse.com.au

First published by Vintage in 2010

Addresses for companies within the Random House Group can be found at
www.randomhouse.com.au/offices

National Library of Australia
Cataloguing-in-Publication Entry

McDonald, Roger, 1941–.
When Colts Ran / Roger McDonald.

ISBN 978 1 86471 041 0 (pbk).

A823.3

Cover photograph titled *Yarning Mode* by Jeff Carter
Cover design by Sandy Cull/gogoGingko
Internal design by Midland Typesetters
Typeset in 12/15 Bembo by Midland Typesetters, Australia
Printed in Australia by Griffin Press, an accredited ISO AS/NZS 14001:2004
Environmental Management System printer

10 9 8 7 6 5 4 3 2 1

Peaseblossom Ready.
Cobweb   And I.
Moth   And I.
Mustardseed   And I.
All   Where shall we go?

– *A Midsummer Night's Dream*, Act III, Scene I

ONE

CLOSE TO MIDNIGHT BOYS THREW back bedsheets and sat in a window chasing coolness, cupping cigarettes in their palms, hanging over boarding house balustrades. The night was blackout black as they whispered a vow – if any of the younger boys narked, they would kill them.

The four monkey-scrambled down a fire escape and off through descending leafy streets. The first was Kingsley Colts accompanied by stray cats at ground level, flying foxes overhead. When Colts ran the ghost of himself led on, always too far ahead, always out of reach – a boy counting telephone poles and lumpy cracks in the bitumen in lucky odds and evens.

Squawks and crashes of fruit bats in the figs were the only sounds except for the wet slap of sandshoes. They passed Royal Sydney Golf Club and came to the seawall at Rose Bay, sharing another fag, shielding it under their shirts. They could do nothing, it seemed, without a puff.

Breasting water, they sidestroked to a moored launch with their clothes fisted above their heads. There was a low humid sky, the feel of rain. Once reed beds grew in the bay, dugongs fed in the shallows, lights of fishermen were fireflies and the smell of bushfire smoke drifted over the water. Now military craft choked the harbour: torpedo boats, destroyers, gun barges, ferries converted to barracks, tethered Catalina flying boats. Outlines of shipping rose and fell. Sentries watched but the low-slung launch with its rumbling inboard motor slid past unchallenged.

'So much for national defence,' said Colts, eyes down at water level sweeping the dark. It was the way his guardian, Major Dunc Buckler, snorted the phrase.

'Colts,' the others growled back at him, 'shut your bloody cakehole.'

Colts stood in the scuppers spreading his arms in the dark, creating a willing target.

They travelled the length of the harbour past Garden Island docks, under the walls of the tram depot at Bennelong Point, below the high span of Sydney Harbour Bridge where they circled awe-struck and idled the motor. Nobody saw them or cared enough to shout warning – it was perfectly infuriating to be so powerfully ignored.

Since the Japanese war started Colts hadn't seen Dunc Buckler, only had letters with marginal cartoons of soldiers around cooking pots, men shooting crows with guns that went *pop*, drawings of box-shaped Blitz wagons in the background, their radiators geysering steam. Buckler was posted to the interior of Australia, where there weren't any bullets flying, but that would change when the army bosses got smart about him and stopped belittling him with the real war going on without him.

The boys tilted their heads back.

'Look at that, willya?'

The bridge's arch bulked over them, riveted in grey. They stood in the wallowing hull, backs turned to each other, aiming out in the water as far as they could reach. Mist trailed down and stroked their faces. To see a road and railway high in cloud was to be drawn to a life reversed from the one they knew – where authority would flow to their knuckles, money to their pockets and distances unravel under their boots.

Colts whispered he wanted to scramble up the granite piles and crawl over the half-moon of towering steel protected by radiating spikes. 'Bullo to that,' said the others, ready to chuck it in. Colts passed round a corncob pipe stuffed with bitter shag. His temerity was exhausting. Old boys of their school had won medals in Libya, in Greece, had fought in Malaya, their names asterisked on the honour board in gold. *Let me go free*, Colts prayed to the gods of civilised restraint who bound him. Everything was in his circumstances, all that mattered was blocked wishes. *Get it over with, Colts*, he said to himself.

A fourth-former, Wayne Hovell, came to the housemaster's door, knocked, twisted his toes with caution, half wanting to be out on the water, wild in the dark and forgotten, the other half waiting for the harbour to go up stupidly thanks to Colts. Slope-shouldered, with a distinctively protuberant breastbone and a habit of tucking in his chin then jerking his head forward to make a point of incontrovertible rightness, Hovell was nick-named Chook.

He spoke his moral duty. 'There's something up, it's stupid, it'll go all wrong, it's that, it's that –'

'Who are you talking about?'

'Colts. He's a bigger noise than Tojo.'

The housemaster went to the side garden wearing a spotted dressing gown, holding an umbrella in the downpour. Old Gargler slapped at mosquitoes against skinny calves that were pitted with shrapnel wounds from the First War job. Colts the moral blur. Hovell the wielder of conspicuous truths. The master knew which he liked better, but Hovell would be Head Boy soon enough.

'Colts?' he addressed the leading shadow coming home in sodden shirt and shorts, a boy with bony knees, wrists too large for shirt-cuffs, floppy hair of bedspring curls, eyes of bottle-brown making an appeal of tainted innocence.

'Sir.'

'Brains?'

'Of a bird, sir.'

'Of a brainless bird, Colts.'

Old Gargler steered the boys into his study, whippy cane at the ready. They emptied their pockets of tobacco tins and pipes. Colts stepped forward untangling fingers from his hair and smearing clammy palms down the sides of his shorts, wondering who'd narked. Old Gargler was against boys nose-picking and combing their hair in class; for the rest he was mostly onside.

'Ready?'

'Sir.'

Extending his arm, Colts rotated the cup of his right hand and stretched his palm obligingly. Victims of firing squads culti-vating martyrdom displayed such pride, and Colts flinched but did not cry out.

Gargler gave them his lecture and they listened with grave attention. 'You could have been killed, aargh. How would the school have explained it? Aargh. You. Colts. What about Major Buckler? Imagine the shame, aargh.'

Colts tried but it was too hard, really, and he could only grin. Wait until Buckler knew what they'd dared. Colts wouldn't write any letters, he'd tell Dunc Buckler himself – follow the wheeltracks, cross the desert, climb the last sandhill, find the bush camp and be hailed for pluck and humour. That was the wish, although who knew how it would happen.

4

Tired as he was, chastened as he was, and as flaming lucky, Colts slipped around warning fourth-formers to say their prayers. 'You're dead in the morning,' he said, twisting ears and giving Chinese burns as a taste of things to come. 'You're maggot-meat, green mutton, duck-guts – you're skinned.' The one in particular, Chook Hovell, he kept his eye on, followed after lights-out, tackled on the flagstones of the deserted quad. Hovell fought back using fists like hammers while Colts knelt on his rib cage. Thumping and pounding, he couldn't keep the kid down.

'Say quits.'

'Like buggery I will.'

Colts stood back and gave a kick to Hovell's weaving head that landed somewhere around the ear. After that jolt, Hovell drew raggedy breath but stared at Colts harder, cleaner, fiercer than before. A stare that said, *I know better what a bloke should do.*

'It was me told Gargler,' he said, getting up on all fours.

'Berrk, berrk-berrk, bk-bk-bk.'

'I'd do it again.'

Leering down and calling Hovell a matchless prick, Colts chose to follow through to an ending, because once committed to an action there was no other path to follow. The coup de grâce was a tap to Hovell's jaw with his toecap, hardly more than a gentle lofting motion, though it awfully sounded like a crunch. Regrettable, but there you were. No such thing as Marquis of Queensberry rules on a dark night, and guess whose quotation that was.

On the trip they'd made in the last month of peace, Colts and Dunc Buckler came to the wide grassy curve of a thousand-acre river paddock. It was more beautiful in that arid landscape than a lord's neglected parkland. With the truck unpacked and the camp site arranged, Colts came out from behind a tree flexing his bowling fingers and asking Buckler if he'd like a knock. Buckler found himself holding a bat. Seeing how useless he was made Colts laugh.

'Give up.'

He'd never joked like that with his guardian before. It was like getting his stripes.

They unrolled their swags each side of the fire and lay propped on their elbows drinking burnt coffee mixed with sweetened condensed milk. It came from a tin cracked open with a tomahawk. In the morning they stamped their feet and warmed their hands at the embers. Emus came stalking towards them, attracted by Buckler standing near the truck and waving his grey felt hat. He was a square-built, dark-complexioned man, scowlingly handsome, full-lipped with a sensitive, almost offended twist to his smile. Colts often practised the look in a mirror: '*Imshi Yallah*,' he hissed at Johnny Turks attacking him.

Later in the day Buckler sat on the running board and balanced his Remington typewriter on a log. Bruising his fingertips, he generated the feeling of opposition he needed all the time. Authorship was good for that, he said.

'What are you writin'?' said Colts when he was back from potting rabbits with the .22 and Buckler was still at work, only pausing to brush away flies.

'Never ask. It's bad luck to tell.'

When Buckler took a walk Colts looked anyway. Lifted a stone and rustled the loose pages with his long fingertips to find it was all about the would-be soldier, the sensations he would feel in battle. Buckler was the living ghost of old mates, the sworn defender who spoke for the dead. They'd spent their quota of flesh at Gallipoli and in France, and he lived the full nine lives making them right.

'I'm calling it *Infantry Fighter's Handbook*, if you want to know.' Buckler shaded a hand across the page, stopping the boy from reading on. 'The army chiefs don't want it published; they don't like the truth.'

The few bits Colts read – 'A normal reaction for a man and not a coward's is to soil himself under fire' – only confirmed Colts's view that to be chosen by Buckler was the pinnacle. Shit-scared was how Colts felt often, but you could still be the best in Dunc Buckler's books in that condition.

It was Saturday cricket a few days after the night adventure. Colts took the new ball. Utilising a deceptive angling action, his fingers plucked at air, shimmered air currents where swallows flew – screwed blindness into a batsman's stare. He was inspired by Randolph Knox, Captain of School and the First XI when Colts was a long-eyed thirteen and followed Knox everywhere in a worshipful gang. The ball nipped through a player's defence and deftly removed the bails. With every delivery the umpire sucked his pencil but nodded play-on.

Colts's odd wrist action, almost a throw, produced its share of full tosses and wides, giving Colts three wickets for twenty runs that day. Old Gargler said if he could find the length it might be Colts for the NSW Colts. More was involved than competence with a ball, however. There was the matter of moral character to be measured. The school only did what it could with what it had. Old Gargler liked Colts but had no final answer when it came to character; sad to say, that was up to the Head, who arrived during tea, running a weary hand back through his silver hair. Word had reached him through an influential parent, Lady Margaret Hovell.

'Colts?' he called the boy over to the door of his car, declining to offer a seat, as he did to his favoured ones. 'Do you know what you're up for?'

'Up for, sir?'

'Don't act the innocent, lad, it won't wash.'

Colts stood with his hands folded behind his back, hip cocked.

'No, sir.'

'Stand straight when I'm talking to you,' said the Head.

Colts obliged like a piece of string not entirely devoid of slack.

'Shoulders back,' snapped the Head, and Colts, just then, braced inside his thoughts, having had enough of it, sensing what was coming. With a bothered sigh he returned to his habitual lean against nothing, getting his limbs arranged like half-balanced sticks, his grubby blue felt cricket cap pulled down over one eye.

'Very well,' the Head hissed. 'So must it be.'

Boys gathered in closer, savouring an event. The match hung waiting. Colts stepped into a school story published on coarse wartime newsprint, where chums raced around behind a jolly old principal and lashed his ankles together with school ties, and everyone had a good merry jape as the chief went facedown in the turf, and later there would be forgiveness, raspberry buns, roast chestnuts, cocoa by the fire.

Colts scratched himself on the backside.

'Are you with me, lad?'

Colts said he was, indeed.

'Alackaday, Colts, I have written to your guardians, the Bucklers. You know the sort of letter I mean. I have penned only a handful of such missives in my long career.'

'Why me, sir?'

'We have a fourth-former in sick bay with a broken jaw, that is why.'

The Head scrutinised Colts, the sort of wheedler he'd expected to find in a colony bred from slum children when he came out

8

from Cambridge in '33. Headstrong in games but lacking in moral valour.

The matter of Colts's orphan state, ward of Major Buckler and his birdlike bohemian wife, Veronica, moved the Head's emotions only a little. Colts's father, gassed in Belgium, had died in the early '30s, and his mother passed away soon after. Call this a test for any boy, and sad, but with few families untouched by Great War tragedy – and the Head himself, though he never blew the regimental trumpet, taking a fair whipping on the Somme – there was no special pleading in it.

The recalcitrant Dunc Buckler had been sent his account for term fees, plus several reminders, responding with airy excuses from various dismal posts.

'I am ruling off the ledger, Colts. You are to return to the school, collect your belongings, and then a taxi will be called. I have telephoned Mrs Buckler, who is expecting you. After that, Colts, may the good Lord help you.'

Veronica Buckler held her brush high, standing on a fruit crate to reach the top of the canvas; instead of bringing the bristles down to make a streaked, deliberate smear, so familiar to her as to be a reflex of the spirit, she jumped back to the floor and took a fistful of rags made from her husband's old pyjamas and cleaned up.

The Head's phone call expelling Colts was a delicate condolence compared with more personally distressing news to hand. Her informant – 'so sorry being the one to tell you' – was a seedy young man Buckler had sacked, by the name of Des Molyneaux, assistant surveyor's clerk. There'd been two letters three months apart, the first a wages demand, belittling Buckler in the tradition of slighted employees. Veronica was appealed to as keeper of the books. She'd sent ten pounds.

Today's letter came in the same rounded, backward-sloping, resentfully particular hand. It stated for Mrs Buckler's 'private information' that Buckler was 'making a run', was 'released from ties', was 'consorting with freckled Irish barmaid types'.

Oh, the awful petty victories of the tittle-tat. So fleeting to the teller, so branded upon the told.

The venomous phrasing had Veronica recall a woman's name: R. Donovan, and Buckler's nonchalance around that name when they'd entered cheques-paid in the monthly ledger.

'R is for?' she'd wondered, as Buckler deprecated while colouring.

'Rusty – a charity case with a snotty-nosed kid sister in tow. They're on the wallaby.'

Closing her studio door Veronica turned the key and, tapping the window glass, looked back in. The old tom she trusted through a leather-hinged flap to rid the room of mice stared past her. It showed how little she mattered to creatures of instinct. Promises made, banns posted, ceremonies gone through, life lived, love played out – what a circus.

Her painting looked back at her, roughly right: a stone verandah, a distant view reflected in tin cans and acetylene lamps, veined eyeballs of a boy being attacked by a goat, its hoofs balanced on his skinny shoulders. In the opposite corner a woman in a torn raceday suit chewing on a feathered hen leg. Climbing around the frame a pumpkin vine and a pile of Queensland blues. Flying overhead a small bird of nocturnal disposition, the Australian owlet-nightjar, her figure or mark of integrity she sometimes thought. One had sung at her birth at two a.m. on a winter's night.

She called the painting *Goats* and the boy was Colts – the same bleak, smitten and fanatical concentration of gaze, the lick of devil's curls at the forehead, the mocking flat smile and the squared dimple on the chin with a pattern of goosebumps. The ravenous woman was Pansy, Colts's dear mother, locked down in pomegranate shades of oils, denied her fullest expression of love by early death. She'd enjoyed a day at the races, eating the raceday lunch of cold poultry, wearing a suit of fine-cut linen with a straw hat and fake cherries. Laughter always so quick. And then so finally gone. The verandah posts of the homestead framed the track to her grave on a rocky ridge. Small as a postage stamp, it was drawn in every detail.

Expecting the boy since the telephone call from the Headmaster, Veronica heard noises in the house and followed down to his room, watching from the door as he packed a kitbag with Buckler's initials stencilled in flaking black army lettering.

He was sniffling, crying, turning his face away.

'It's all right, Kings, I know everything,' she said in her whimsical, flutey voice so ill-matched to any sort of energetic undertaking or seriousness, although that was deceptive.

He didn't reply, of course. Worst thing known was to tell a boy what he felt, that he wasn't the first on earth to bust with a feeling. The offence was bullying a younger boy, inflicting physical damage. Veronica had little doubt that Colts was in the wrong. Intimidation was the counterfeit courage of sixteen. He'd learned it when younger, uncritical with awe: Buckler and his returned-man cohorts breaking up meetings, confronting strikers with clubs and following them round in cars, sending men to their houses when they weren't at home to wise up their wives. Buckler was no coward but his politics were craven. Here was Kingsley caught in the same old trap; you had to feel sorry for him.

They sat at the kitchen table while she spread pikelets with honey and poured tea. With just the pair of them it was all right like this – only when Buckler was present did Veronica feel barred from the boy's attention. Now under his burning gaze she felt herself exist.

They needed to be allies for a time. She could not do this on her own – pump out from the damaged heart what love she had for Buckler and save the boy from the vortex of second-hand experience, which Buckler had roused. Because of something Colts once said to her in a blessed moment of childhood innocence, she knew him as a seeking soul. Such figures walked through the world half in, half out. Could it ever be proved to Kings that the world was enough? Through despair of him, with paints to hand, she'd attacked him by the goat to bring him back – to show him what pride was doing and too much prancing maleness. Look into the goat's vertical irises and see Dunc Buckler staring back. A goat was a proud, foolish, selfish and beautiful thing. It had its own stink about it, too.

Compared with that man's rule, what a weak, blind, uninspirational impression Kingsley had of *her* love and its power – nothing seemed able to convince him otherwise except that she loved his sister Faye best when the two of them, boy and girl, sad orphans and cuckoo chicks in her nest, were the definition of love as much as dependents could be. They were the children she'd been unable to have with Buckler, who'd won their care in the toss of a coin over the claims of his Anzac mate, Birdy Pringle.

Going to the sideboard Veronica opened a drawer, taking out a ten-shilling note. It was a situation needing manipulation. Kingsley guardedly watched her; he was amusingly tight, hating to spend his savings, wanting more.

She surprised him by handing the money over. Was it to shut him up and send him away? If so, good on her, his eyes seemed to say. Pies, lemonade, ginger nut biscuits and tins of sweetened condensed milk. Just don't stroke my hair and tickle the inside corner of my lips and say you love me.

Later they sat listening to the radio, getting the tally of stab and feint on land and sea. Colts doodled down the margin of a newspaper map of war zones. Fear, isolation, loss and bravado gave national defiance a personal cast. Veronica looked over to see what Kingsley had drawn, glimpsing a sketch of their old horse-drawn caravan.

Interesting that, because the product of Veronica's own incessant pencilwork was a doodle of the same darned cart. So much for Europe in flames, North Africa scorched, Greece fallen, the victorious Japanese knocking at Australia's dunny door − it all came back to a woman, a man, a boy and a bleached sky beckoning their hopes. To a place called Limestone Hills in the Central West. To an old horse-drawn caravan on the Darling. Buckler had poisoned the mood of their happy lives, but Veronica had the energy to split the earth like a seed and gather the growth, taking back whatever fell tangled into her arms.

She found Colts looking at *Goats*, staring through the cobwebbed glass at her crowded canvas.

'It looks like scrambled eggs,' he said.

'It's you, darling. It's yours.'

She watched him deaf to the idea.

'Kings, I've decided. *Goats* will be yours one day.'

'Don't bother,' he said, fists clenched tight against his trouser seams, and she was satisfied because in denial he always went to the heart.

Colts left first, heading off when she honestly thought she had him. Give him twelve hours, eighteen at the most, to get to Limestone Hills.

The whole train was drunk and singing, rattling along, all seats taken, aisles blocked, corridors crammed, the engine far ahead and visible rounding a curve with the firebox flickering red. A boy with dark, alive eyes cupped a hand to rattling window glass and his hopes went out like a radio call, out to the stars and into the constellations. Are you receiving me, over and out. Wilco, wilco, wilco went the pounding engine on its iron tracks, making its way over the Blue Mountains and onto the slopes and plains under starshine.

A green jumper peeled back his thoughts. She was a young mother with red hair and white skin, her baby's fists in the way as Colts slid around to get a better look. When she saw him looking she stared back and he left his seat and stood in the corridor feeling beaten.

Before leaving home Veronica took a pair of scissors and rough-cut her hair short enough for regular basin washes. From a high shelf she took overalls she'd worn in her tomboy years, nipped to the waist and still needing no letting out. Barely eating, she was back to smoking, bundling hoarded tins of quality cork-tips. Following Colts mere hours behind, she took her husband's old Bedford, roll-starting it in the street – sitting on pillows with cushions at her back and double-shuffling the gears, wearing chamois leather gloves and looking exceedingly important, like a child. She had enough rationed petrol to get her to Limestone Hills, where she guessed there was more fuel stored through the reasoning of squirrel-minded Buckler.

When Veronica was Colts's age, before studying painting at East Sydney Tech, she'd gone with her dad to Riverina cattle sales. At sixteen she'd looked eleven, sitting up driving a one-horse dray. They'd returned droving store cattle over the dry ridges and steep gullies of the Dividing Range, taking weeks to reach home on the reedy lagoons and saltwater estuaries of the Isabel River emptying to the sea.

Now it was time to reclaim that capable part of herself

14

consigned to Buckler when they wed. She would make a loop of a thousand or even two thousand miles, if needed, attend to her questions of that goatish man and return to the sparkling estuary; its snapper, flounder, sweet prawns; its beaches eight miles long with curved waves thumping in hard from the Tasman Sea. There she would become whatever she might have been before Buckler claimed her. If Buckler came back with her, it would be on those terms, that she would be herself – except what those terms might be in the sense of an agreement she could not imagine. The whole circumstance made her sad from the wartime situation with cousins and friends dead or in Japanese hands to the sexual insult of not being wanted by the fool she loved.

Colts came to a cold siding and spilled out while the train barely slowed. Crawled under a wattle bush, shivering and damp. Drank water from a brass tap at a ringed water tank as the sun came up. Train-song was audible when he put his ear to the rails, the razor-thin hum of departing carriages. There he stood exposed, broken open, newly hatched, a sore-eyed long-necked boy in a rumpled army greatcoat.

Wrong place, wrong siding, he'd made a mistake in the half dark and stepped from the train a stop early. Limestone Hills siding was the next along.

Sensations poured in, not of Colts's own bothered self so much, now that he started walking and hoping, but of a time that was always there without him – a country place that was the truest part of him: the smell of dry grass and morning dust in his nostrils, the clamour of flocking galahs and the bells of topknot pigeons, with always the light lengthening, fingering through bushes and rocks, seeking, he sometimes imagined, the quartzite at the old cemetery where his mother was buried.

But he wouldn't think of that. Not in a thousand years. Not of the streaks of gold in the hard white stone.

The sun burnt off cool distances. Hills that seemed close weren't anymore – they were slammed away in hardness of light. Colts was part of this world as he walked, being swung by Buckler in a game of being let go, of knocking Faye flat as he rolled through the dry grass, laughing so much he spewed. How did you take hold of life again? What was the trick? When would it happen? Yell him the secret!

'Climb up, sonny, I'll give you a ride.'

A farmer going the same direction drove him in a sulky to a house along fencelines with tight, right-angled bends and stock laneways running with skinny sheep. The farmer said he wanted to improve a lot of things but there was the drought, the manpower shortage, all the odd-jobbers away in the army, men chewing sand in Palestine or studying Bushido in Changi Gaol, only oldsters left now, crocks and whatever greenstick boys fell from the sky. Looking sidelong at Colts when he said that.

In a yard protected by rolls of hessian, a leggy foal stood with its mother glistening with new life.

'She's one day old. I've been up all night,' said the man, easing the sulky to a stop, his cheeks colouring and something getting into his manner as he told Colts about the distances foals travelled following their mothers in mile after mile of loyal pursuit. They would never run as far again in all their born days with so little to fuel them. They had the whole greatness of their lives in them from the start.

'You'd know that.'

'Me?'

'Because you're a runner,' said the man a bit slyly. 'Streaky as bacon, speedy as a wheel.'

Colts turned aside, admitted nothing. But it was the greatest feeling a boy could be given – being known but not pinned down.

In the kitchen a tall wife greeted him and he was fed on mutton chops, eggs with hard skirts fried in fat, cups of dark tea with sticks in them. Toast was made by burning slices of bread on the hotplate of the wood stove. He was hungry and grateful, but he hated that kitchen. You didn't always have to do your washing up in a kerosene tin cut at the diagonal, saving the soapsuds for the roses, all eaten by bugs.

They asked his name.

'Kingsley,' he said after a struggle.

'Just "Kingsley"?'

'Colts.'

The two looked at each other and their eyes said, 'Limestone Hills, Dunc Buckler's kid.'

'What about a day's work,' said the woman, 'because we're a bit stuck.'

'Only if he's keen,' said the man, 'before he pushes along.'

'I'm ready,' said Colts, lifting his jaw.

The woman looked round startled when he came back into the kitchen to get his hat and heard her on the telephone asking for Limestone Hills, Mrs Buckler.

Through cleaning a feed bin and hauling heavy sacks of seed wheat onto a horse-drawn wagon, Colts's fingernails bled, his eyes ran red-rimmed and sore that day, and he developed a rasping cough. Through digging a post-hole to a depth of three feet, his hands were raw by smoko time.

The farmer was a First War man. 'You're looking for trouble,' he said as they yarned of the scrap, leaning on shovels. 'You're scared you'll miss out. You think fighting will give you that. Well, it might, so get on with it, son, and you'll soon find out.'

A rabbit plague was on and the man handed him a pea rifle. There were so many bunnies coming in for a drink they barely

17

stirred when Colts walked through them shooting from the hip, rippled hunched furry nothings with nowhere to go.

In the full day's work Colts understood something about labour that seeded a thought in his brain. The heave of a strainer post made its own dumb impact down the end of its hole and stood there throwing a hard shadow into the day.

When he came back to the house there was a figure on a motorcycle waiting. Not a male, he saw when he came closer, but a woman in trousers with a hat and the front brim turned up. He recognised the bike, too. It was Buckler's old BSA 250cc with sidecar from Limestone Hills, which Faye – hair flying back – had so loved to ride, spinning around like a willy-willy as Colts sat in the sidecar laughing and hanging on.

TWO

THEY HADN'T SPOKEN ABOUT FAYE but her presence was every-where at Limestone Hills. They reached there on dark. Mementoes of past holidays lay where she'd left them over the years – a play table made of twigs, arrangements of fossilised shells, a book with a gumleaf bookmark, *The Green Hat* by Michael Arlen with a sentence underlined and the word 'sigh!' pencilled in the margin. That night Colts carried a hurricane lamp, sweeping its bars of light into corners of his old room. It was a whitewashed cave with fig trees over the window, where a tawny frogmouth came and sat unblinking.

A smell of warm fat was in the air. There was a leg of mutton in the oven. Veronica promised the crunchy burnt outer slices he loved, which he called Vegemite. Faye always handed hers over when he wanted more.

The first time they were brought there it was as if Colts had been born there. A gate clicked behind them. Limestone Hills. Whatever feelings had filled his heart on the other side of four years old were left behind. Except there were scenes of them walking together. She had such dreamless eyes he couldn't find them ever again. There were rounded rocks like giant eggs in the bush behind the house, where she took him in his stroller. It was where she was buried: he knew that. His mother. Yet every surge of his feelings denied the oblong mound of earth that was stuck in his heart and would never shift. He remembered a room, how he'd looked into corners finding spider webs of interest, but not looked at her lying blue, pale and alone in a pleated nightdress. He must have looked, though. Otherwise how did he know it was her, dying, and he'd felt nothing? *Nothing*.

Standing at the edge of the dry garden at Limestone Hills, he'd eaten a fig. They grew wild there, fat and purple, splitting their skins with sweet red jam. He'd set off climbing the rocky creek, looking for goannas, hitting puffballs with a stick, the landscape fitting around him like a skin.

After his basin wash he lay naked on the starched clean sheets and touched himself. He gazed at the stars until he was no longer able to tell who he was and slid from the bed to the cotton rug on the cement floor and lay there with his eyes jammed open.

Even after Colts was too old for baby things he'd carried a tin truck and a stout, bedraggled teddy bear under his arm, and when the truck gashed his knee Faye asked the teddy to make him better, on account of the red cross stitched to its chest. The last time she did that he threw the playthings away, but she gathered them and put them somewhere safe.

Loose soil and road ruts baked in the sun were the material of his playground then, soil blunting his hearing as he wiggled a finger in his ear imitating the way men did, at the same time as holding their pipes. The grainy feeling of Limestone Hills dirt, the taste of it spat from his tongue, clinging to damper cooked in the ashes, dirt stuck to a boiled lolly taken from a paper bag, was the medium Colts was born into, as far as he could tell. A fly got stuck in his ear, sizzling deeper. That was the feeling too. He'd never get over it or past it either. The hum of the dry bush, crickets, Christmas beetles, cicadas.

Faye wasn't so smitten by their country life, but now, thanks to a passionate love match, lived on a mission station in the wild ranges of Western Australia, a place as rough and remote as any in the world, where there were only four whites – herself, her husband Boy Dunlap, a mission mechanic and a mission nurse – and a tribe of wild blackfellows who nobody except Boy understood. So Faye wrote in love and praise of Boy Dunlap and his anthropological religion.

In the returned men's magazine *Reveille*, Buckler wrote about missionaries – 'malarial young reverends, dithering sky pilots, poodle fakirs of the worst order, defeatist milksop hem-clingers living in the wide-open, undefended north of Australia peddling pork-pie caps and pipe-clay dreams to demoralised savages'. That was when Faye had informed him she was marrying one.

Before Faye left Sydney, Veronica had painted her bare-headed, gold hair a halo, in a white-spotted blue dress in the garden with a branch of wattle bloom dipped over her shoulder. There were many such paintings of Faye bundled up awaiting their future: just the one of Colts.

Faye's letters spoke of difficulties, hardships for which her whole life had waited. She had previously been too blessed – each had been by the guardian of their own sex, leading to opposite impulses. Faye turned outwards dealing with the world, believing she went inwards to God, while Colts battled the world clambering over material reality from where he lived too much in himself.

*

21

Next morning, looking up the track from the kitchen window, Colts remembered a great sight of Buckler – a man going away the moment he was seen – heading off with a handkerchief around his neck, driving a finger-slapper grader.

With its hard metal blade screaming against the earth, a grader had the power of returning without turning around, sending out sparks and the acrid smell of gunpowder rocks. It clanked under kurrajongs with leaves dusty in the heat as down it came into the dry creek bed and up again, scraping a path for farm lorries on limestone and quartz. A road was raised under the boy's eyes as Buckler banged the controls, flipped levers, spun handwheels in repetition. Colts drank crushes of heat and gulps of diesel fume and noise.

The homestead's tennis courts were built by Buckler from forty ant hills especially so young people and their friends could use them. The last time Faye was there Colts smashed, volleyed, lobbed and backhanded with an accuracy that wiped away smiles as the three of them played cutthroat. Buckler played to win but Colts toppled him. Faye wasn't so flash: she ran for a shot, concentrated on preparing a serve, laughed when she lost a point or received service badly, parachuted to earth after missing a high lob and stood there, giggling, just for the fun of it. That was Limestone Hills in the days when Buckler stayed put.

Swallows nested in the kitchen and the smell of the fat-stained boards and old iron cooking pots swam round the boy sitting with a breakfast cuppa and reading Joshua Slocum's *Sailing Alone Around the World* and waiting for his toast. Afterwards Veronica laid out harness along the verandah stones for soaping and mending.

He looked up at her.

'Those horses are immortal,' he said.

No need to ask which horses, or who coined the phrase. Buckler and his big-noting. They both understood where they were going, then, on this wartime excursion released from ties, what the first target of their march would be – a triangular paddock far away.

Dunc Buckler's Clydesdales were kept on that reserve of the Darling River, downstream from Wilcannia, two hundred miles away, eating thistles and rare green pick. They were as old as Moses, wiry whiskers on rubbery lips, shaggy hairs matted over their hoofs. They had the stars for company and visits from a swagman to see they weren't ever bogged, foundered or caught in wire. Veronica's old tin caravan stood nearby, shuttered tight against snakes and mice. A painted arch gave shade protection. Old George and Mrs Dinah, they were called, released to a life of greater ease. Last seen in '39, they'd snuffled their nosebags and ambled closer, giving Colts the feeling of hoofs about to stand on him, a delicious fear that he encouraged while curling his toes inside his boots.

The best idea was to take the truck but the petrol they found was almost all siphoned away, so off they set on the motorbike with a cluster of spare containers and a canvas waterbag. Colts took the controls wearing dust goggles, Veronica huddling in the sidecar protected by cushions. They had bags, boxes and bottles stacked, everything roped or wedged for the ride west, both intently hopeful of make or break. With stubborn ceremonial pride devoid of reason, Colts wore his cricket boots – a pair of once-white Niblicks bought from a man named Kippax in a store hung with bats and pads and pyramids of cherry-red stitched balls. Those boots charged to Buckler left a distinct impression of Colts in his footprints, heart shapes riveted with studs. He found patches of smooth sand and made perfect stencils of them as they went along.

The small towns they came to had one long road unravelled at either end by thistly stockyards, tin shacks and smoking garbage dumps, with a motor garage, a stock agent, a bank, a school, a police station, a pub with a long, high verandah, a few lank peppercorn trees, drifting dust, iron roofs catching glare and corrugated water tanks waiting for rain.

Talk was of bombs wrecking towns far to the north. Colts imagined Japs penetrating as far as these drought-stricken districts, peering into mirages, kicking at shadows under trees, attacking sheep.

The motorbike continued on its wrenching way, Colts erect at the controls, observed by crows and circling kites.

A dim, relieved shadow stole over the plains and stars pricked the sky. First night, they camped on a showground, second night on a claypan. Colts threw brush on a fire making a bright roar. He studied Buckler's letters under the lamp of constellations, their position markers dangling. The cartoon drawings in the margins of the letters he'd always believed would make indicators of Buckler's location, but the idea was hopeless. There was the fat cook, Abe, the skinny sergeant, Jack Slim, and stout Buckler himself under a big hat visible as a pair of boots and a pipestem.

Veronica said they were simplistic scribbles worthy of one-track minds and carried on scooping a hip-hole for herself in the dirt, laying a canvas over blankets to protect them from dew. Buckler had lived that way for years, carving bush tracks with or without her, often without her, living half their married life away and coming back into towns that weren't hers but, oh, he seemed to have made his own so cosily now.

Sounds in the night made Colts sit up from his blankets.

'Whaassat?'

Curlew, vixen, wild-pig-grunt, wandering cow, tawny frogmouth, earth-tremor, shooting star.

'It's all right, Kings. Nothing to fear. No reason to be. Look at that sky!'

Colts peered from his swag and saw her sitting in a light that seemed to shine from her like dew. Whatever he denied in himself spoke for him. She said, 'You must go back, one day, and visit your mother's grave,' and his answer was, 'No.' Pushing himself back into sleep, he woke again, and there was Veronica still going on.

'A beautiful young woman, gay, free, social, full of life, never put-upon, always willing, humorous, naughty, a fountain of laughter. My darlingest friend.'

The words laid onto him thickly. Her darlingest friend who'd introduced her to Buckler, and so on.

The hour before dawn was enchanted. Insects clicked and there was a regretful thrill in the last of stars as the old world, the night world, holding such sway over everything, was beaten back to its lair and Colts's eyelids drooped. He knew the day had truly begun when the first fly got in his ear and another one tickled his eyelashes.

The fire crackled and Veronica appeared at Colts's side with a mug of tea. When she brushed his tangled hair with her fingers he was too sleepy to knock her hand away. He fell asleep again. Or so he pretended.

Buckler said in a camp, stay in your swag, someone will bring you tea, stay longer you'll get the whole box and dice, the chops and eggs, fried damper. So it proved with Veronica.

At last they reached the bank of the Darling River, a scene of desolation. Bleached bones were scattered under trees. Hide and hair scrawled in shifting dust along sagging wire fences. Kangaroos and sheep lay dead of thirst at parched turkey's nest dams as windmills rustled and groaned. A plague had been through and the plague was a worse drought than the one they knew. Australia was a dry roasting bone of a country tossed away by time. At the corner of the triangular paddock where the roof of the old caravan was sighted, the carcases of Old George and Mrs Dinah were found, the two great horses stretched with dry hide where they had fallen into their last grins.

'It's not them,' said Colts, remembering love he had for named animals.

'Stop that always denying, Kings, it's wearing thin.'

He didn't reply, and she was left once again with understanding of him softer than thistledown in her bruised heart.

The only living creatures were goats – a herd of big-horned, dapple-bred animals making their way through dead trees on the riverbank, disdaining shortages and getting by on pride. Their smell was rank urine on a twist of breeze.

'My goats,' Veronica called them.

'You can have 'em,' said Colts.

'Your goats,' she taunted back at him, and he'd never tell her how when he'd looked through her studio window and seen that goat and that boy, how he'd loved himself in his collarless shirt and braces, chin up eyeing back at the painted eyes transfixing him. He'd been made a hero, taking that exchange of looks as an assurance of time at his feet like dirty clothes he'd never need to pick up.

The padlock on the caravan dangled open and tinned food left inside was gone. Piles of old newspapers were stained by marsupial mice, their nest of leaves neat as a whirlpool, but soiled. Veronica's painting of a lovers' arbour done the year of her marriage to Buckler, 1931, was blistered and cracked.

She cursed the swagman who was left to mind the outfit. Buckler had promised his care.

Colts went around cooeeing and then went to the waterbag and drank tepid, fibrous water.

Veronica found the swagman when she went to wash in the billabong. She covered her mouth. He seemed to have arranged himself with some deliberation in a cleft of eroded bank. Pads of dumped leaves matted his head and shoulders. The gun, what her father called a fowling-piece, well named, had fallen from his grip when the shell was fired, leaving his shattered face thankfully turned away. He was a clothed skeleton.

Colts heard her cry and came looking.

'Don't look,' she warned.

Suicide was expected of mad hatters and lonely figures in the bush, but the details were unwanted.

'A dead body,' Colts so very needlessly stated. His gaze, like a wary fly resisting its need, came and went but never too close.

Veronica spoke a prayer for the dead, in the same breath thinking such inert, angled limbs could never be imagined but needed to be studied in this lonely place, nose wrinkled against the stench. She wanted pencils she didn't have on her, and lucky for her shame. 'Hallowed be thy name, thy will be done . . .'

Colts stepped away from Veronica's side and peered closer over the bank. 'Ashes to ashes, that is for sure,' said the trembling boy. Dead men were a separate matter from the fine singing soldiers of human memory Dunc Buckler wrote about, yodelling and chucking grenades at Huns.

Veronica had no answer except to hope, as Colts once expressed it — a small boy longing for a mother's love — that they would all gather in heaven.

It was what he'd said one day, she insisted on reminding him, reducing them all to tears. 'Such a wise little man, so beautiful.'

'That's bunkum and bull, and you know it,' said Colts.

'You were seven, dear, almost eight, the age of divine reason in a child, and what can I say?' She reached for his hand. 'That you were wrong? You were not wrong. Heaven is a memory and a promise.'

'Bloody palaver,' he spat.

'Buckler's words,' corrected Veronica. 'What are yours?'

Colts had the motorbike running when Veronica came back. They had not unpacked. Now he switched the engine off and watched as Veronica stacked dry thistles and parched leaves under the caravan and hauled dead branches over and struck a match.

'What are you doin'?'

'Making a fire.'

'You're not going to burn it?'

He tried too late to stop her.

'That's ours!'

The flames drove him back with his arms crossed over his face. The fire wouldn't spread because there was no grass to burn, just bare dirt everywhere, although dirt itself might explode from the emotion he put into watching.

'Wait till I tell him!'

Veronica danced around the burning caravan waving her hat. 'Tell him, if you can find him,' she said.

The caravan speared through with sparks, flame spiralling at first and then going straight up and making a chimney roar.

Colts walked down the track away from the blaze, looking back to check on the caravan as he'd done when they last left, making sure the roof was still there, a sentimental tactic stamping images to recall when he was stuck back at school. The difference now was a smoking curve held by spindly uprights getting charred black and wrapped in sheets of flame. The corrugations rose like an aeroplane wing, wafting but never taking off. Through stacks of heat he saw Veronica going to the bike, and so he kept walking, turning his shoulder on her until she caught up.

He climbed into the sidecar and wedged himself steady with cushions. It was soon dark as she drove. The headlight flounced ahead like a dying torchbeam but always finding a tree or a bush.

'Can't you go faster?' Colts urged, but only because he didn't want her to know he hated being taken away like this, dependent, stunned. She kept stealing glances at him, easing her shoulders around and angling her neck as they drove, and wondered about a feeling, if it was true motherliness, which she had never strongly had. The boy had not screamed and threatened her so much as treated her, not coldly, but reservedly, saving passionate attachment for the real mother he barely knew and who awaited him six feet under, and giving his male ardour to that heroic goat, Dunc Buckler.

The ingratitude of children she was feeling anyway. That, at least, was an authentic touch of the parental fate.

In Colts's mind the triangular paddock by the river wasn't how they had left it, destroyed. The caravan was replaced by a shining turnout on four pneumatic tyres inflated hard, with new wood and bright copper nails, and those horses, Old George and Mrs Dinah, displayed freckled lips and foaming spittle as they had when hauling loads, great with leaning life and hoofs biting forward.

Just by Veronica lighting the fire and destroying the lot, the horses returned with their immortality intact. Colts wondered if Veronica knew the mare of the couple still wore a perky straw hat. And she did. And she did.

Later that night a town slept, tin roofs shining under a zinc moon, silent except for dogs jerking on chains and drunks under a tree on the track to the blacks' camp there, the riverbank plunging down a clay slide to cracked mud and smoky camp fires.

They went over the rattling-board bridge and slept by the roadside a mile out, returning next morning for Veronica to wash and groom herself on the riverbank, to bargain for rationed petrol at the town garage and speak to the police.

When details were given, the circumstances of the swagman explained, the long-faced sergeant said: 'I knew this was on the cards with that gent. I'll have to mention the fire you lit, Mrs Buckler. There might of been things of his in it.'

'There weren't things though.'

The Sarge lowered his voice.

'You must have had a reason for it.'

'Does the name Molyneaux mean anything to you?'

The Sarge angled his head. 'Yes. But he's deceased.'

'Mine's out this way working – a friend, an associate of my husband, a pale sort of young fellow, book-keeping on stations.'

'The Molyneaux I knew was Joe Mole, as we called him – the little skipper.'

'That was Des Molyneaux's father,' Veronica nodded.

'A brave man. There must be good in the younger version, then?'

'He keeps in touch by mail,' said Veronica emphatically, 'and doesn't always sign what he writes, leaving no return address.'

'That swaggie, the returned man, Major Buckler's caretaker –' said the Sarge. 'A sad case, came from a good family.'

'There was a steel plate in his head,' said Colts.

'Messines or Kemmel, I believe,' agreed the Sarge.

Then the Sarge's wife said, 'There's a postie in Broken Hill called Molyneaux.'

'Postie is a good one,' said Veronica.

'He delivers to my sister and plays the harmonica if she's feeling off.'

'That's him,' said Veronica, 'purveyor of questionable emotions.'

All she wanted was for Molyneaux to look her in the eye, confirm his queasy truth with bold assertion – 'making a run', 'released from ties' – and then she would seek counsel of an

30

Adelaide lawyer, an old friend, and find her way forward in the changed condition of her time on earth.

The police wife invited them through to the residence and gave them mugs of tea, thick-lipped government cups on heavy saucers with Anzac biscuits baked to toffee hardness.

Veronica asked for a road report.

'Same conditions as always,' said the Sarge. 'Dry. Not even a trickle, never a lick to lay the dust. The world's gone off its lid, you dunno what's coming next, only drought's a cert.'

The road west humped across ancient floodplains, making for slow going on corrugations through sand drifts. Up ahead a purple cloud hung in the empty sky. Most strange: it wandered north and south as Veronica tightened a handkerchief over her mouth and raised an umbrella against the naked heat. They crept forward, the motorbike steering crabwise in the dust. Sand trickled into Colts's boots and the front forks flummoxed in ruts. At some point the cloud made a decision, packed itself into an anvil shape, turned thick blue, swelled. Up ahead a wall of rain descended with a perfect sheen and roaring, and they couldn't run or retreat as it approached with its arms out.

Their cheeks turned white, their noses red, as rain gulped down their collars, wet their ankles, irritated their noses. They stood with the bike helplessly humble, submitting to a drenching for ten minutes. When the cloudburst stopped it left a departing drumming in the ears.

Everything was soaked, including the matches Veronica searched for in a box held under her chin until she found a few dry heads and took a Players from a tin of dry twenties.

Colts tugged at the handlebars while she puffed and he calculated filching one for himself from her stash. The sun came out but the bike was stuck. Sheeting leftover water created foaming rapids of grit. Near by the hump where they stopped it ran into cracks in the ground and disappeared with a hurried chuckle.

Veronica draped blankets over the handlebars. Colts, after sitting sidesaddle, fist under chin and brooding, tried walking but stilts of mud on his Niblicks toppled him. He used a pocket knife, paring slices of muck from the soles. With the boots hung around his neck, he rolled up his trouser legs and picked his way along the claggy track barefootedly.

'Where are you off to?' said Veronica — a funny old question, as there was nowhere to go except the far horizon.

'I'm looking for something,' said Colts, mud squeezing up between his toes, the firm consistency extruding narrow, sausage-like rolls.

'Not someone?' she said. Buckler was a presence between them: deflated to one, overblown to the other. She thought she smelt goats and made an association with the forthrightness of Buckler's sweat.

Colts couldn't tell her it was really those horses he was still looking for. At first they were blobs of mirage, then long-leggedly they broke off and he could almost see their blinkers. They fell back again into what looked like a four-wheeled mustering cart, a cook's turnout. But, shading his eyes to be sure, the sight fell back even farther into the wavering broken horizon and Colts was almost blinded. Thus a vision became real and he found himself bringing it to earth. Could be his whole life would be dedicated to a job of search and answer in the outdoor light.

There was a stand of mallee nearby, its shade like strips of metal where bark lay curled and black. There Veronica pugged around as Colts grew small. She gathered dead twigs and made a fire, using a dry page from her sketchpad to get it going. Feeding the flames with damp, dappled leaves until one took, she sneaked a look over her shoulder and noticed the motorbike had more of a lean, but didn't worry too much about that until a kind of sucking collapse came, and the bike slewed into the table drain. Though she wrestled to hold it steady and called for Colts, the angle increased and the motor sank in mud, ribbed cylinder vanes the gills of a suffocated fish.

Colts heard her but thought she was singing hymns, which she often did satirically: 'Rock of ages, cleft for me . . .' They always put her in good humour; there was nothing more definite when it came to promise than the worn old earth.

Veronica returned to her fire to dry her boots. As a young wife she had taken this very road west with Buckler to home-steads where she sat on sunset-blazed verandahs and sketched and painted while he politicked.

During those honeymoon years, in the dingo-howling dark of bush camps, Buckler had limbed from his stretcher and stripped off his singlet and undershorts. Dunc her darling dented soldier, he'd stood in the dim tent nakedly brushing off sandgrains and imaginary fleas, catching a lone mosquito in his fist and doing a meticulous dry wash, no hurry at all, careless of her watching as he gazed down his pale trunk and sun-reddened extrem-ities and wrinkled penis with an expression of detachment. Yes, she would have to say she still loved his indifferent, corporeal, tangible being, his form and representation of male embodi-ment. Given the chance she would keep him around the way she saved bottles and jars holding form. Then look for the slit of light from his eyes looking her way, and hold him off in order to have him whole.

Buckler had continued over the New South Wales border and into South Australia for his rendezvous with Birdy Pringle that time, when the decision was made to better their lives by taking on the two orphans, Faye and Kingsley. It had been the Bucklers or Birdy by the toss of a coin, which Buckler made sure was double-headed. It was all so strangely wonderful to look back on, it brought her to tears.

Now in that bare width of country Veronica blinked, aware of Colts standing nearby and behind him a mob of goats. They pattered in the mud with a startled whisper and when she turned, touching her lips and smiling, they gazed back at her. Every dappled colour of the yellow earth and of the blue cloud-scattered sky was in their coats, streaked browns and blue-greys, black-shellacked hides and washing-day whites as they propped, snobbishly eyeing her, all of maybe half a hundred balanced between curiosity and flight. Goats' heads lifted, their tufty beards angled, their haughty eyes gazing.

'Kingsley Colts,' she breathed, 'what have you brought me?'

'Brought? I followed them.'

'They've made a goatherd of you, then.'

'Like fun they have, they're hers.' Colts indicated a blob of haze. 'You won't believe it, she's coming over to help with the bike.'

'She?'

It seemed amazing in the circumstances, unless you knew amazement really, how it came in everyday moments. Two women owning the deserted country stripped of men and left in charge of the half-hatched.

A structure on four wheels lurched closer. It might have been the original of Buckler's horse-drawn caravan taken back to its primal sketch of converted dray with curved iron roof on tree-branch struts, only lacking two children, a boy and a girl, large-eyed with small hopeful faces peering over the side-boards.

'Who is she?' said Veronica as the contraption lurched in. A tray shelf held sacks and drums, and what looked like an old garden seat, plump with pillows, in the driver position.

'Some old dame,' said Colts. 'Struth. I'll tell you what, hold your honker.'

The woman wore a heavy unbuttoned overcoat steaming from the recent downpour, her sagging breasts in a yellow, mudstained dress. On her head was a straw hat, a piece of sodden vanity. Two fat-pinched bloodshot eyes, a spread blue nose, stained teeth bared in a grin.

'Where's the mon?' was her almost incomprehensible greeting.

Veronica was about to say there wasn't a man, but bowed towards Colts.

The woman began clambering down even as the horses heaved to a stop.

'Let me introduce myself,' said Veronica, foolishly formal.

The other only grinned.

Colts backed off, sensing it was him involved in the matter of introductions.

The old dame advanced in the mud, weaving the flaps of her coat and driving him as far as Veronica's smouldering fire.

'A shrewd little ken all, ken little?'

He laughed exaggeratedly, the way he did when an unfair accusation was made, which always had truth in it.

She extended a mottled pink hairless arm, thick as a joint of pumped mutton.

Colts stood fast; she meant to give him a game of knuckles. 'All right, missus,' he said, 'don't lose your wool' – and held his breath against the ammonia goat pong. As he pressed his fist against hers, shaping up, she splayed her fingers to baulk him, and he suddenly drew back.

'My strike,' she said, spittle frying on her lips, and rained blows that caused the fine bones along the back of Colts's hand to burn and swell.

For an old lump she was quick, rocking on small feet, well

balanced. He wouldn't like to be the goat she held against the killing knife, backed to a fence, blood and hairs on her coat.

Veronica intervened impotently, 'Stop this, really, I say there, what's in it?'

'A guid game never goes astray,' said the woman. 'The lady poets of Greece focht aye the foremost in their birthday suits.'

'Is that the Scots' accent I detect there, Mrs . . . ?' said Veronica a little bit gaily.

'Lizzie Walker, I have no mon's name.'

Spoken as if we're supposed to know her, thought Veronica, as Colts looked on from under his hat, nursing his carpal bones, surliness changing to a leer. To be famous in this country you only had to live there.

Somehow the three of them and the two horses dragged the motorbike from the mud. Veronica caught the giggles, Colts frowning at her. A man must be stern. They unbolted the sidecar and using ropes raised the bike in pieces to the back tray of the wagon and set off walking, the horses hauling in the dusk. It was not altogether understood, but slowly an impression was gained, that Lizzie Walker regarded the bike as salvage, a rightful prize.

Turning south following the goats they found elevated sandy ground just on dusk. Goats circled, firing pellets of black dung as the woman hopped around finding a nanny to milk. Colts collected sticks for a cooking fire. It was buck stew and not bad either.

Lizzie Walker raised a square bottle to the firelight after pouring a splash into her guests' mugs. She stirred the pot and spoke of her life. There had been men, but they couldn't hold her.

'The one was dim as a post from taking blows to the head. The other had fingertips like pebbles from pushing needles through leather. The drover, Bulleen, whose wee cat this was −'

'Cart?'

'Fezackerly. He was guid tae me but loved his stock more. A butcher mon had a way of twisting an animal's neck until it fell to the ground. Knew his way round bones and drank till his liver went phut. There was the bootmaker, he carried the clap. Curry, I gave a well-known jockey, mon burped like a frog, stank of bad teeth and was puir in the stomach unless he rode. Luton – should I mention names? Luton's hams were like a grasshopper's drumsticks from operatin' the pedal radio on guvvermint outposts and chasin' gins. See what's ahead of ye, laddie, if ye'd be a mon. See what ye're bound for, what ye'll be?'

Lizzie Walker was travelling hurt through a band of poor soil called Australia. It lent itself to that.

They reached the rail line at last, where a carriage served as the schoolhouse. The teacher's residence was a second carriage on termite-proof blocks under the bare sun. A few tin huts with canvas awnings ached with loneliness, slapping in the oven-wind, clinging to the edges of the iron tracks with desperate closeness. A boy and a girl, twisted with shyness, watched.

Lizzie Walker tramped along the railbed scavenging bottles thrown from trains and gathering papers blown from the railway camp. Her goats gambolled under an overhead water tank where there was a nibble of green pick.

'Puir railway children. They learn to put miles between them.'

Awaiting the train, Veronica had last words with the goat woman while Colts sat on the siding with the bags they'd sorted from their lot. It was a simple transaction without stated reason. Veronica stood upwind from her as they haggled it out. Then she rejoined Colts.

'How much did you get?' he asked, acting as if every oil-stained lump of metal Buckler ever kissed was tagged for his unique inheritance. 'You just let it go,' he accused her.

All Colts had was a blanket roll and a billycan like a swagman born to the track. Veronica hadn't much more. The boy's boots on laces hung around his neck, bumped against his ribs as he paced the siding, keeping clear of Veronica, looking for a smudge of engine smoke to the east that would take them farther west. He'd had enough of her and found a plank of shade, squatted and closed his eyes.

THREE

DUNC BUCKLER HAD TWO MAPS, one with place names and the other cross-coded with numbers. 'Use the first for bum fodder if we get sprung,' he instructed Jack Slim, his corporal.

'Shouldn't we just swallow it?' said Slim.

'First Jap we see, you start, Corp. Masticate into spit balls. Force 'em down. That's an order.'

They drove to places Buckler knew and the officer took tea with owners while Slim poked around sheds and listed machinery. Meantime Private Abe, their factotum, cadged them a boiling fowl or half a sheep, sometimes a wild duck on a scummy reach of station tank. Rabbits were plentiful with their small bones and stringy flesh, and just for variety's sake a haunch of dark-meated kangaroo might be spared from the dogs.

Buckler kicked tyres, made assessments of national value and recited the law of requisition to be applied in circumstances unpredictable but hasty if the Jap took the north. Such grandiose sheep stations they were – soil blown stripped, property names sand-blasted from galvanised iron sheets wired between posts on red sand tracks set back from rutted roads: Wonder Downs, Lily of the Valley, Hope View. A collection of tin sheds, the kitchens a bed of ashes.

In a high-stalking Chevrolet wagon crossing Australia slantwise, Buckler and his duo emerged from grey saltbush country into red sand mulga country, into broken golden downs of spinifex with purple ranges on the skyline.

They camped in dry creekbeds burning red gum logs, from which spiders and foxes, lizards, red-bellied black snakes, native cats and ground-nesting swallows emerged on the run. The road through the ranges revealed station after isolated station, the homesteads looking whole from a distance being built of stone, empty-eyed when the Blitz lurched closer, abandoned as the region returned to desert. An inventory was accumulated worthy of the industrial revolution: boilers, mine batteries, pumping engines, electric and motorised contraptions of many sorts. Stranded tide-wrack from a generation of defeated hopes, Buckler's own included?

He wouldn't say that.

It felt almost halfway across the continent to Jack Slim and somewhere short of no-place to Abe, who relished the going in his lip-smacking foreigner's way. Buckler believed the big Commonwealth offered such reffos the biblical factor, a parable of existence's last stab to the philosophical brain.

'We haven't even started yet,' promised Buckler, wiping his mouth with a kind of turbulent delight while his pair of six-bob-a-day tourists gaped. When the new moon dangling the evening star came up, his Byron rang:

> *The angels all were singing out of tune,*
> *And hoarse with having little else to do,*
> *Excepting to wind up the sun and moon,*
> *Or curb a runaway young star or two . . .*

And promptly Slim gave the next few lines, chapter and verse:

> *Or wild colt of a comet, which too soon*
> *Broke out of bounds o'er th' ethereal blue,*
> *Splitting some planet with its playful tail,*
> *As boats are sometimes by a wanton whale.*

Buckler couldn't keep anything from Slim. Veronica, damn her knowledge, and Colts kicked out of school were on Buckler's trail – the news in a letter dust-lined in his kit, forwarded from Brigade HQ and carried by the mailman until their paths crossed, he'd talked of it drunkenly while thrashing arguments with Slim. Women and children in the camp. History's tares and tatters.

Across the artesian basin, when they came to a steaming bore drain, Buckler declared a bogey, the bush bath and shave. They splashed in cattle troughs with bars of soap and face washers, Slim playing a boy's game – blocking the overflow and diverting it through the sand. Buckler left him for hours while he modelled canals, rivers and dams, singing and lost to himself on all fours with his balls dangling from his army shorts like a dog's.

'I've owned up to another kid,' supposed Buckler, who liked Jack Slim though couldn't get the measure of him exactly. Agreeable, jokey, smart-hitting the way they turned them out from Sydney University, which was to say with the shininess brought up, buffed with civilisation and then smudged a little in the colonial style. He worried that Slim was a card-carrying commo, but made allowances for youth and education – Slim telling about being kicked from school early, a time of hardship on the wallaby track before he studied at night and won a teaching scholarship. They were open with each other based on affectionate sincerity. On grounds of pinko conscience Slim believed it was all right to defend Australian soil, but as for expeditionary forces of the kind Buckler craved, forget them.

Up the back of the Blitz buggy they carted pots and pans, surveyors' pegs and crates of infernal tinned meat. They had bags of dried peas and a sack of Eyre Peninsula wheat, which Buckler sprouted with the exactitude of an agricultural ace. A winch and short-handled spades and a fury of digging got them out when they bogged in sand. There was always the stink of fuel drums, which Buckler twitched over draining, saving what they had, refilling the drums from station stores and leaving a voucher in promise. Under a blacksmith's shed he bolted a blade on the front with an arrangement of hinges, converting the truck into a push-puller able to clear the country of sticks, as he liked to say, boasting they might navigate the contraption on the diagonal, the full width of the continent if they pleased.

To which Slim said, 'It's never been done, except by Afghans on camels and by long-distance blackies carrying message sticks.'

'Don't try me.'

Slim strung an aerial between trees and they contacted HQ, reporting in code to their brigadier.

'That code name, Scorched Earth, dunno why, it fills me with hope,' said Buckler.

'You seem to mean that,' observed Slim, whose hobby on the track was working Buckler out. Their orders were to make an inventory of tools, motors, fuel in sealed drums and whatever they thought, when it came to it, useful if the army was forced to retreat on short rations through the arid zone, picking what it could from the skeleton of the land it called its own.

In the early weeks, when they'd first started, Slim saw the mailman hand over a packet of letters and Buckler bringing them to his nose, perfume-wafting-wise.

'Something sentimental going on,' Slim deduced, 'in the old father's trousers.'

Yes, Buckler was hooked. There was power in a name he couldn't help uttering: 'Rusty Donovan, I call her Red.' A great big idiot, he sighed over talismanic hieroglyphs — misspellings, ill-educated blots and scratches, the veined creekbeds of pressed rose petals.

Those were the times when away from the hullabaloo Buckler stumbled on something so beautiful it stunned him to humility — 'Men, come and look!' — a striped rock, a desert hakea blooming, the skin of a snake. His mind coiled round that Rusty Donovan and back at the camp he reached for his pen. A young married woman, her husband a violent man, Buckler had taken his chances.

Two weeks later they crossed paths with Charlie, the mailman, and Buckler looked sour. She'd thanked him for his trouble, prompt but hardly effusive like once upon a time, when she loved love.

But Buckler went on — hammering away at his heart, or was it his balls, in the instance of Rusty Donovan, formerly Mrs Hoppy Harris, formerly of Broken Hill, now of Adelaide.

A red track emerged from scattered bush either side of a T-junction heaped with windblown sand. The gaunt, burnt branches of a tree marked the spot with a piece of tin hanging from a length of wire. Buckler had been there years before heading west for a rendezvous with work and stamped his initials and the date, with latitude and longitude references exact, on the lid of an old kerosene drum and hung it up. The whole lot was still there, smoothly rusted and creaking like a gallows.

The jolting truck declared a fuel problem and choked to a stop. While Buckler bled fuel lines looking for the blockage, his pair crawled under the tailgate and snored.

Kangaroos in the heat of day as they raised their snouts were like shadowed human observers. They angled from the lying position and showed their perversely watchful faces. Then, in the same hypnotising way – right there on the track to nowhere – certain individuals emerged from the mass of land. A breeze kept the sound of a second vehicle to a murmur until dust made it obvious two miles away.

'Who's that?' said Slim, cranked up on an elbow.

'Must be someone,' said Buckler, shading his eyes to see the plume of an approaching transport.

An American Blitz wagon like their own but carrying a dozen men and boys stopped a short way off.

'I don't believe it,' said Buckler.

The young, slouch-hatted blackfellows were half-dressed in singlets and khaki shorts, toes hanging over the tailgate. Their leader, tantalising with native diplomacy, allowed a minute to elapse with the engine switched off before he stepped down. Then Buckler recognised him: the nuggety old soldier, Adrian de Grey, wearing corporal's stripes and in charge of a construction detail.

'Last place I'd expect to find a legend,' said de Grey when he eyed Buckler over.

'Ditto,' said Buckler, offering his hand.

In crisp army style de Grey ordered his boys to make camp and they jumped to the job.

That evening as the sun boiled into redness and the rickety shadows of mulga lengthened over a purpling plain, Buckler stalked imagined boundaries in his well-oiled and ferociously dusty boots. Away from the crossroads there was no edge. There were webs holding yellow coral-backed spiders in suspension between thorn bushes. There were dingo howls and shooting stars. In the coming dark he fancied meeting a man eye to eye and engaging him hand to hand, gristle to bone, clasp knife to scrotal sac. Slim worked it all out. The returned man's festering drive, the fascist solution of one and one, the disinclination to share what had been rhetorically bought by blood for the sake of the all. Knowing Buckler's attitudes, Slim didn't have to ask what de Grey was doing out this far on a mustering camp of Eureka. He said they were roo shooting away from their main camp but there was a definite impression of a meeting being sought. De Grey would be wanting to know what Buckler's troublemaking propensities were, around this unit he'd put together with pride and wariness of acceptance of colour.

Buckler came down the line and saw de Grey's boys turning away from him. So de Grey had said something about Buckler to his team, that he hated blacks.

That night, pressure lamps hissing, there were two camps under the stars. Abe cooked for both. Buckler looked over at de Grey's lot as they slurped on mulligatawny soup and chewed fresh damper from the camp oven. Dehydrated vegetables were served, mashed dried peas and sauerkraut, and a fatty cold mutton they hungrily eyed when Abe unwrapped it from a sugar bag and flourished his carving blade.

By the light of the camp fire Buckler gave de Grey a pointer on the nutritional shortcomings of his race: 'Abe is correcting it with his grub.'

De Grey curtly thanked him and went off into the dark to find his swag.

'Suit y'self, digger,' Buckler mumbled into his cocoa.

He worked on irritation, eyes sweeping the dark following infantry patrol routines unpractised in a while. Blow on certain resentments. Keep them bright. Watch men who moved as shadows. De Grey's band was rather too Australian for Buckler's taste, taking too much for granted. Look how de Grey came in from nowhere, he griped to Slim, his transport loaded with mere boys holding army-issue Lee Enfields. Buckler recalled de Grey's words back on the troopship *Taranaki* in '19, a pique against land taken without kindness from native inhabitants. De Grey already had his place in history, gloriously rained on him at Dernancourt and Villers-Bret. What more did he want? 'But the man's a fucking marvel,' Buckler conceded.

A cowboy song with a plaintive kick could be heard from de Grey's camp. It came with an eerie hum. Inland Australia was a country of spirits, make no mistake. Buckler surrendered himself to the second-rank listening. The blackies were plugged into spirit way up to their tangled eyebrows. The bush itself took on their shapes. When the songs ended Buckler heard them swishing a branch, calling and laughing. They never slept at night without brushing the sand around their fires for fear of the devil man. They worked it smooth as a bowling alley and Buckler thought they were dated but understood their urge. He'd do it himself against them because Adrian de Grey was smarter than piss – knew the outback was not quite the realm of the white man yet. You didn't have to ask him. It was still to be won. Otherwise he wouldn't be serving this time round making his push for possession wearing government-issue khakis.

In the night Buckler's thoughts went spiralling down until he groaned in his sleep, waking boys fifty yards away like a bull seal yawping on an icefloe. It was a wonderful concern, the army. You could be the definition of its meaning and for that very reason you were made a ragbag supervisor.

Next morning, talking of maps, de Grey showed Buckler a silk handkerchief with an excellent map of Australia printed on it with technical detail exact. 'What do you think of it?'

'Good.'

'Make of Nippon,' grinned the soldier.

'That good-looking kid in your lot,' said Buckler, 'the one who'd like to think I didn't exist, he's Birdy Pringle's Hammond, isn't he?'

'That's Hammond all right. Proved a bit of a runaway but we nabbed him good.'

Buckler's truck needed a tow and they chained it behind de Grey's. It was another day's drive to Eureka homestead where a blacksmith's shop and a mechanic on the payroll promised repairs. Faces grinned at Buckler's dependence while he jolted in the passenger seat and tried to doze with his arms folded tight. Only one face, that boy Hammond's, kept itself turned away.

They came out into a vast dusty bowl with ancient hills behind them, crossed sand ridges, skirted a salt lake crusted with red-stained rime, plugged on through saltbush and arrived at the station, which loomed in a mirage of galvanised iron pavilions long before they debouched like gypsies with the reek of diesel in their baggy trousers, and stamped their boots.

They crossed an open width of ground under the hot sun wearing their slouch hats with leather chinstraps fitted. When Slim observed Buckler and Abe marching in step beside him, he gave a skip and the three of them were crisply aligned.

Then behind them de Grey's boys fell in, and de Grey was heard grunting 'hep, hep, hep right hep'.

'Look at the half-arse army,' said a watcher in the shade, and Buckler couldn't help it, he bridled at any slur on the band.

Eureka was five million acres give or take a few hundred thou, epitomising the old continent worn down and reduced to whatever nutrition could be wrung out in the name of sheep.

It had a stone homestead with a wide paved verandah and a stone shearing shed architecturally huge under a sheet-iron roof. On average thirty shearers shore one hundred thousand sheep fed on saltbush that sprouted past all horizons. While a war went on somewhere, and our men were in it, a noted Australian battle was continued here between man and truculent beast, between men and men in the realm of boss relations. One of those fighters was Hoppy Harris from Broken Hill.

'Harris the contractor?' said Buckler, his mouth going a little dry.

'So you've heard of me?' smiled the hairy fellow oiling his handpiece.

There were only four shearers present, and the jackaroo Randolph Knox doing the work of ten, sweeping, skirting, fleece-rolling and pressing, wool piled on every side like mountain ranges. Harris roared over the engine noise, 'I can't speak to you now, you can see I'm fucking flat strap shorthanded. Unless you happen to know your way round a fleece, push off.'

Despite the forceful language Harris eyed Buckler neutrally enough, perhaps only indicative of what he reserved for everyone he met. But whatever went on under the look was perhaps something else, on the theory that men suspicious of each other in the realm of sexual betrayal were inevitably polite until tactics declared otherwise.

Buckler being of rank was welcomed a mile away at the big house where there were linen tablecloths, silver cutlery, napkin rings and a saddle of mutton accompanied by hermitage wine from the Barossa Valley, the bottles packed in sheaths of straw with the heads of wheat still on them. Buckler had sherry with the manager, Oakeshott. The jackaroo Knox entered wet-haired and breathless as the clock struck seven, and Oakeshott and his wife eyed him for manners and to be sure, when he was invited to remove his jacket, that his shirt was buttoned to the wrists, covering the yolk boils on his forearms from too much delving in wool. Randolph Knox had the biggest jaw Buckler had ever seen on a bloke, like a sack of marbles. They sat in chairs with carved backs. This Knox, Buckler realised, was the Head Boy of Colts's school, the former schoolboy cricketing great – how the mighty were averaged, Buckler reflected, removed from their marvellous contexts, smitten with boils and made into anxious apprentices.

That night the men took over huts almost empty of station workers. De Grey and his band had their blankets unrolled under the stars.

Oakeshott took Buckler riding early. He said he was tolerant of de Grey's coons for the sake of the war push. The two riders seemed to be going nowhere with the dawn light on their backs until they came upon relics undisturbed since the overland telegraph penetrated last century. Old huts with rifle slits, rusted horseshoes dangling from white-anted boards, eaten away iron pots, amber rum bottles tumbled in heaps.

Buckler said, 'Nothing to show the white man has any more claim on the dirt than the little yellow bastard brandishing his sword from Timor.'

'Except we're here,' said Oakeshott.

'*Je suis d'accord.*'

'And look at our field of fire. Three hundred and sixty degrees and cleaner than the veldt.'

Oakeshott was a noted woolgrower and eminent sheep classer with reason to reflect on achievement but personally liverish.

Each morning the jackaroos were given their day's jobs with barking precision. Stations were run as monarchies and, with his drooping moustache and silvered Pickelhaube haircut, Oakeshott added despotism. He wasn't an owner – that was a pastoral company in Adelaide with directors who interfered. What Oakeshott held was the hereditary impact he'd made on strong-woolled merino sheep over a lifetime of attentive breeding. When he retired his line would be spent unless he found a worthy successor. Young Randolph Knox, he confided, could be the one.

Back at the house tea and scones were served by Mrs Oakeshott's Martha, a girl around the age of Birdy Pringle's Dorothy, but luckier than her because she had these good people civilising her in a lace mob-cap and pinafore.

Over to the men's camp Buckler went to make himself felt. All was in order and he thanked Jack Slim.

'Bugger thanking me, it was de Grey.'

The truck was unloaded, gear stacked, and de Grey and his lads were at the shed with Harris, helping with the shearing now their own work was done, all except one worker – the lean boy who kept his distance as if by reverse magnetism. When Buckler walked around the end of the men's quarters verandah, the boy sloped off around the other so that Buckler only saw his legs. Then through a window Hammond Pringle could be seen sitting on a tool trunk cleaning his rifle.

Abe had the kitchen range going. In a side room Slim had the radio set up.

'You two have fallen on your feet,' said Buckler. 'I'd call it over-comfortable. Won't be for long.'

'What have you got for me in the way of loot?' said Slim. 'Anything special?'

'Oakeshott's a good man. I haven't pressured him yet.'

Slim said, 'It's all right supporting the war effort but better if your neighbour does it, and there are few exceptions to that golden rule not excluding managers protecting their patch for the sake of city slickers. Have I got that right, Major?'

'Something like it.'

'Here's my selection,' said Slim, handing Buckler a list he'd made after poking around in the Eureka sheds.

'That's not a lot either,' said Buckler.

'Prime stores,' agreed Slim. 'Pastoralists pay peanuts, but when it comes to gear they really know how to stint.'

'Get over the resentment factor, Lenin.'

'There's a lorry, a pump engine, and what about this adaptable trailer with fuel drums strapped on? I think we should grab it. Then we could really go the distance. De Grey thinks so too.'

'Who's running this army – corporals?'

'They say Hitler's one. We could go for weeks on end,' said Slim, 'just think of it.'

Buckler stared through the window at the half-dark boy sitting guard.

He went out to him. 'Everyone else is at the shearing, why aren't you lending an elbow, Hammond?'

It was said with a good smile. The boy scrambled to his feet.

'Wouldn't know what to make of a sheep,' he mumbled, looking down at the dirt.

'Say if it was buffalo hide?'

He looked up.

'That would be different, sure. No-one'd go up me for leaving cuts.'

'Seems just yesterday you were skinning them at ten.'

'I was, and younger. Pop had me working for it.'

Buckler peered inquiringly, sympathetically at the kid.

'Why didn't you say it was you, Hammond?'

'I've let ya down.' He lowered his head.

'Don't know anything about that,' said Buckler, who'd been sending school fees to the Marist Brothers, Townsville, on the quiet, and when it came to priorities, putting Hammond's share ahead of Colts's for the simple reason that Buckler thought Presbyterians, because he was baptised one, would stretch understanding further than would the Micks. A recent final demand showed he was wrong.

Buckler summoned Abe to bring them a smoko box. Hammond picked among the cupcakes and drank tea.

'You're a second-chance boy, Hammond. Give it another try, that's your luck. Us – me, your father, Corporal de Grey, all the good men who came through the first war show – we got it sorted out for you and Colts.'

The kid nodded. 'I know that bull. There was the time you crawled down a trench and tied a rope round his waist.'

Buckler said, 'Call it a trench, it was more like a river of mud. Then there was the time he lifted the spar off me, when my legs were jammed. Only they weren't crushed. Not quite. He got me back walking and I was right as rain. That was Messines.'

'I grew up on them bits. Like the time he felt the spent shell stroking his face. He talked about that. It landed like a ghost, he said. It would have been curtains in the mud, he would have been pushed in. The mud would have filled his face, but you had the jack and the length of four be two.'

'Can you imagine it?'

'Can't.'

'We knew worse, Hammond.'

'I know. He never shuts up about it.'

It made Buckler smile.

In the stillness came a pizzicato of crickets and men snoring with cello richness. Over several nights Buckler waited for the visit from Hoppy Harris. Percussion would come with the crunch of boots on gravel. At meals the atmosphere between them, their nodding politeness, started working on him through gaps of hefty silence. Someone wasn't eating. A fellow insomniac stood out in the dark smoking. Shape of that contractor under the stars.

Buckler didn't think Harris a man to negotiate or yarn. He was one who waited to strike a blow against the most satisfying material to hand, a wrongdoer in the flesh. Judgement circling closer tightened the fist and waited till work was done.

A principle of courage determined Buckler's mood as he considered the situation: don't get out from under it. Fall to the lowest plane of hope. There live or die as you did in her arms.

Around noon the following day Adrian de Grey left the shearing and Buckler failed to realise the meaning of the man's lorry heading a couple of miles out onto the flat. Later the sound of a plane taking off droned from the newly extended strip. Buckler felt wronged that de Grey was out there so smartly. First ever RAAF milk run down from the north, landed and then hurled into a hot sky and lost to Buckler's pride in greeting it as the most senior officer in a region the size of Great Britain, France, Germany and Scandinavia combined.

'Pilot Officer Tarbett asked where you were, could have fitted you in,' said de Grey later.

'What was he offering, a joyflight?' asked Buckler.

'A flip to Adelaide.'

'Bullshit.'

'Dinkum. They'll take anyone if there's a spare seat. There was a politician on board, Marcus Friendly, the federal treasurer.'

'Him,' said Buckler. 'I'd a' pushed him out the window.'

'Warner Tarbett's his personal pilot for the duration.'

'Ooh la la.'

So much for Buckler's importance. But he began making plans anyway, sounding off a bit, puffing himself up, indiscreet when tipsy on Jack Slim's hooch.

Harris watched Buckler from the tin cathedral where so many shorn sheep spilled from the board that clean, white, long-legged lines of South Australian merinos made fan-lines to the horizon. Talk about Buckler planning to shoot through for a week or so's furlough from the godforsaken continent's extremest gravel plain reached his ears. Awaiting the moment, Buckler kept seeing the man's wife taking him by the belt and leading him thunderstruck into a small back room, a broom cupboard would do for what was needed as he yearned for her with the hardness of a rock.

Dawn found Abe at Buckler's elbow with a cuppa in a tin mug and a fresh-baked twist of sweet dough on a blue tin plate. The flies got up a crawl on the offside of the flywire.

When Abe left there was welcoming silence except for their bump and buzz.

But soon Buckler heard a plane flying low in the rippling hard distance, thrumming and fading. It circled without landing. Buckler swung to the floor, his wide feet holding to the floorboards. The sound of a truck pulled closer, brakes grinding, door slamming, engine idling. Nibble of footsteps and Buckler lifted his nose from Abe's steaming cup. A shadow fell on the gauze.

De Grey, with an air of interest, stood at the door with his slouch hat tipped back from his forehead and the leather chinstrap looking chewed, eyes taking in the organisation and personal order of a longtime military mate.

'Tarbett aerial-dropped a fair bundle.'

De Grey deposited the mail with a lean of his arm and stood there fiddling with his hat. An envelope of hotel stationery topped the packet.

'Dunc, I've got a question.'

'Fire away.'

'What is it between you and the contractor? What's the poison?'

Mistrust the wide but trust the narrow, thought Buckler, assessing Adrian de Grey's honest features on this emotional text, the opposite of which too had often guided him as a man.

'Why do you ask?'

'Because of a feelin',' said de Grey, diplomacy dropped from his guard. 'Come on, it's bloody obvious.'

'That I know his missus,' admitted Buckler feebly.

'Yeah, but is that all?'

'That's enough,' said Buckler, holding de Grey's eye. 'If you ever met Rusty. Anyway, what's it to you when you're at home, Corp?'

'I could step in. You could give me a shout. Cover your back for you. Wouldn't want to see you damaged, say, by an iron bar at your age. There's those out there wouldn't agree with me,' he added with a scowl, 'them that have heard you say a black man is up for treason by living a life where he was born.'

Buckler felt shame inassimilable, and brushed a hand in front of his eyes.

'What's Harris said to you?'

'Nothin'. That's the point. I don't like camp fever.'

'Then do nothing. That's my point. Sweat it out.'

'Whatever you say, then,' said de Grey, stepping back out.

It seemed likely, from the letters Buckler had, that he was never to have a life absolutely and utterly his own.

FOUR

BEFORE FIRST LIGHT ON BUCKLER'S last day at Eureka, a rooster crowed from the pen where Abe kept his boiling fowl. There was an explosion of feathers, a screech, the sound of an axe then silence. Buckler half woke from a dream of stumbling over someone in the dark. Himself, he found, when he shone a torch on the face. In the dream he wrestled himself trying to get life back, whether with success he was unable to remember. But a sense of life stirred away below, sending out small white shoots, something like pea sprouts; they crunched under his boots, staining the heavy figure under him, leaving dangling webs of contrition.

Buckler awoke more properly with a grunt and looked around, cursing his luck if Harris came at him in his sleep. Wrote up his diary at first light including confounded dreams, just as he had with a stub of pencil under fire at Gallipoli on the famed 25th.

Buckler stepped outside for his wake-up piss behind the far end of the verandah, eyes screwed tight against the rising sun. Harris stepped up to him without warning, awareness of that moment was for later consideration – en route to Adelaide of all possible kismet-starred destinations.

The leaden finality of a blow. Buckler's pinpoint of consciousness knew only a darkening, a glimpsed hairy hand, a teeth-clicking jolt up the universe of skull.

Jack Slim detected imagined engines for an hour before they stirred the air from the direction of Oodnadatta. He looked at his boss with a lumpy gash on his head matted with blood and busy with crawling flies. Buckler was conscious after being out for the count and thought it a great fuss being made. The DH Dove bore down like a chunky blowfly, its fuselage pitted by gravel and the tips of its propeller blades flashing silver. Buckler was tied to a stretcher with troops attending, but all the same didn't like opening his eyes – could hardly do so – and spoke orders from the slurred corner of his mouth, of which nobody took notice.

They saw Harris's buckboard belting out along the flat. 'Gone for another year,' said Oakeshott, glad to have the shearing done before the mischief unfolded – Oakeshott not blaming Harris so much as rather putting it squarely on his friend Buckler's preposterous morality.

Buckler was threaded up and fitted into the body of the plane like a khaki grub. The pilot kept the engines turning while a nursing sister gave Buckler a veterinarian's dose of hypodermic solution. In a knapsack held crosswise over his chest he carried shaving necessities and personal papers, his letters, and a hastily scrawled note from Slim wishing him luck.

*

Thermals rose in the heat, the plane tossed about. When the air smoothed engine vibrations ached the roots of his teeth. It was amazing what the heart provided – amorous wants persisting after such a lesson. Where would they go after their hotel dinner? Upstairs to a room previously engaged? Back to her establishment? Down in the dirt of a public park, as had previously been imperative, like a pair of clean-lusting dogs? What would she be wearing? What perfume on her skin like animal sweat, bursting to flame under his touch? He trusted ardour never to look beyond the hour. There must be a reason for that: it meant so much.

They flew, Buckler calculated, over a place of charred sardine cans and bottle tops in ashes where he and Birdy Pringle had yarned, smoked and boiled the billy with a few meagre twigs back when Christ was a boy in short pants, when they had carried brushwood in bundles on pack camels. It was plausible the old-time tracks remained as fresh as when they first plotted the surface, deserts having such power of reminder. Those tracks would still be there in a thousand years. Anyone searching for mortal remains would know where to go.

The ego wouldn't shut up and would go on just as long. Each time Buckler memorialised himself it felt definitive. Original Anzac fighter. Protector of men back home. Thirties' lighthouse keeper against internationalist malice – all those warnings he issued evaporating in history's rush. Surveyor. Tanksinker. Road plantologist. Guardian of two and three. Parliamentary would-be. Soldier author. Husband and lover. Restive lover. Drunk.

It made him smile, which hurt.

None of the high points lasted. Just a feeling of survival as preparation. There he was in the Dove at six thousand feet, his racked shame gesturing to the nurse and being refused rum.

The pain returned from twisting about, the shot wearing off, and, my God, Harris had shown him – all that peering and skirt-lifting and notable excitement for a man of good age coming to an angry point of expression. He'd ceased knowing himself. But it couldn't be bettered either. Far to the east silver reflections in the blazing sky showed one salt lake after another, and in his mind he named them. Then he slept.

Upon waking he confused where he was with being hard-biffed with distinctive effect another time. Prior to his boyhood commission he'd been promoted and demoted a few times in France, locked in a small barred cell formerly used by Froggy farmers for storage of agricultural lime and guarded by a sadistic Tommy. It steeled a man for humiliations in life if it didn't break the spirit first. Birdy appeared one time and whaled into the surprised monitor with the lumpy hands of a farm boy. A good one was Birdy Pringle for taking specific redemptive action in a line of wrong. A matter of two men eye to eye, nothing wider, slogging it out. Though the ruckus that followed was an army blue in which Monash, no less, played the role of arbiter.

The hospital was near the beach. Hairline fracture of a man's skull was the diagnosis – severe concussion – he'd seen soldiers laughing and fighting with worse to carry on with, but didn't want Rusty to see him cut low. So he waited a few days before sending a note. Months of living on the track had engraved lines on his face that weren't there before. Dust spilled from his collars, sprayed from his socks.

An orderly informed him: 'Miss Donovan to see you downstairs.' It was not Rusty who came on the day but her kid sister.

At the hospital desk they said she'd gone to the corner deli.

Wavelets lapped on the sand, the sun broiled in the west. An explosion of pulse-rate threatened to choke Buckler, squaring his forage cap and dress khakis and taking controlled breaths to calm himself. Before he reached the corner shop with its flyscreen door and rickety verandah posts he saw the kid, Bernadette. She stepped from the shadows sucking a lollipop and propelled him to the intersection and a waiting tram. Buckler looked behind to see if a fellow officer caught him leaving on foot rather than in a staff car with divisional chevrons fluttering, as he'd apparently boasted by a manner of irritated authority brought down from the north.

He took a seat opposite the girl. They stared at each other, deciding what was up. The tram jerked into motion and began floating along. The conductor demanded tickets and Buckler paid. What a coach. What a come-down. It was how tinpot Napoleons arrived in their capitals covered in doubtful glory, escorted by urchins to the beds of their faithless Josephines. Or look at snub-nosed Bernadette and say it was how the righteous young discovered life, cheesed-off at their elders for reasons so obvious they could barely be given a name, except in this case – perfidious Buckler.

'Something eatin' you?' she said.

'Maybe.'

It wasn't so different from before, he told himself – buying time from nervous anticipation by sparring with a child. Those spells at the Hill when Bernadette brought love notes or carried them back innocently enough, as long as he gave her two shillings, a go-between skipping in scuffed sandals bearing Rusty's teasing put-offs and her mixed signals of sentimental wording decorated in purple ink. A few days when Bernadette had been content to knock around with him for the simple fun of it, when they'd played checkers and cribbage until they reached the time of day apportioned to a woman's unerring power. When curtains fluttered in the evening breeze and Rusty leaned with her perfect elbows on the sill, showing her flushed cheeks of excitement.

'You never told us about her, how beautiful Mrs Buckler was,' said Bernadette. 'We had the impression from the way you talked she was nothing much. Maybe an invalid or something like that, you big wart, but she's peachy.'

Buckler in foolish despair waited a long time before answering, 'Don't tell me she's here.'

'I won't if you don't want me to.'

The Adelaide streets were a furnace in the late afternoon. Off the tram and into the boulevards of protestant churches and wholesale merchants, they jumped like a large bug and a small bug into a fiery pan. Buckler felt sick at the thought of Veronica thereabouts and mistook every wafty woman of a certain artistic style as her lurking. They navigated stunned pavements towards Hindley Street until they came to a shaded, freshly swabbed pavement overhung by verandahs three-storeys high. Buckler gave the place an admiring glance: bluestone blocks, iron lace white-painted, brass nameplate shining (Licensee, Mrs H. Harris in gold lettering on a wooden plaque above the lintel), an establishment of undoubted good name.

He climbed solid steps and shouldered open engraved glass doors. Polished floorboards and oriental rugs, hallstands gleaming bright and the scent of fresh-cut roses enticing the traveller into a grottoed shade. He became aware of Rusty rather transformed, the perfect hostess watching through a hatch window.

'Dunc!' Her voice always seemed shy to him, provisional, with a smoker's burr. Its subtleties landing electrically on his tongue in the gleaming darkness with his eyes adjusting from the outside glare.

'Quite the establishment,' he said.

'Not all mine, heavens.' She laughed low, emerging into the room.

Hair up in a French roll, wearing a white silk blouse, a severe black skirt, high heels. First of his new impressions: the coolness of a counter-supervisor, white hand on shapely hip, green eyes upon him so resolutely truthful. They kissed, and there was a givingness in her manner, as if she were able, even now, to yield what she had without mucking about.

Not a good sign, though, because ill-suited to the circumstances. And yet roughly carpentered to his hopes.

Bernadette sat on a nearby chair and watched them. Rusty handed her a set of keys.

'Can you cope, sweetheart?'

Bernadette left the room.

'I wonder how he knew?' said Buckler, while Rusty examined his walloped scalp. 'In a situation, they say, a bloke's the last to know.'

'I'm so ashamed, Dunc, for getting you into trouble.'

'Then why start something?' he stoically maintained.

'I like the circus of a man going away, coming back,' she shrugged. 'I can be myself when he isn't there.'

So was Buckler the bloke still, who would do his lurking wherever?

'Your wife came with a lawyer, she held his arm while he looked around. I hated you for allowing it, for our not finishing when I said.'

Buckler couldn't remember Rusty asking anything so stark. She had merely cooled by mail. But he liked her implying he'd made it hard for her, as it gave him more reason to like himself.

As for Veronica, she was a storm beyond the windows, except that Rusty kept using the name, letting her in.

'The worst was meeting her – it can't go on now it's happened, Dunc dear, and we've met eye to eye.'

'That's only an excuse in a game one,' said Buckler, not exactly generously.

'You see, I liked her, so why wouldn't you?'

A woman handing a man's wife back to him.

'I liked your Hoppy too,' said Buckler. 'I don't think he minded me for who I am in myself, either. Just for where I came sandwiched in his life. So where does that leave us?'

Rusty played with an unlit Lucky Strike, and he wondered where she'd scored it.

Buckler loosened his tie and Rusty brought him a whisky. For herself, a hock and lemon.

They sat for a while in facing chairs in the cool, afternoon-deserted parlour.

'To what was.' They raised their glasses. 'Don't look so hangdog, Dunc.'

So quickly they'd schemed love in. He'd not needed a change of clothes whenever he returned to the Hill. A suit left was aired of naphthalene, a bottle of beer was on ice, corned meat sandwiches and hot mustard. Such earnest, devoted touches piercing him through. She had caddied for him at golf, running the scraper over the oiled sand greens to receive his putt and each step made over the blighted links was towards their love-making later. And a gift – a small parcel – of ruby cufflinks, jewels grubbed from dry hills up Dingo way where he'd found her and sis. Holding them to the light, seeing her fingers tremble as she tried them against her wrists. Then he'd know the night he was in for. Why that unprecedented feeling. Why that poignant premonition that culminated, he now realised, at this time, in this place over in the rough where Harris's drive had lofted him.

'Arriving with a lawyer was a nice touch.'

'He warned me off, lowering his eyes like a bull. I'm tired of it, Dunc,' said Rusty.

Not much later they went to her room because life, when on fire, ran back over itself sometimes.

*

Rusty kicked off her shoes, unpeeled her stockings, unhooked her skirt and shed a white petticoat, shaking out her great Irish hair, cool as the ghost of their too few encounters and free and as prodigally young as they kissed. 'This is goodbye,' she murmured.

Buckler thought as he loved her: *You worked and you drove and you hammered through fate, you swam to the stars, but if the patterns weren't yours, if the blessings of meaning bypassed you, then what were you to yourself, where was there left to go? Just the strike at beauty as you fell to earth – which had formerly saved you in rainbow patterns of oily mud and versions of sword dancing, against all odds.*

'I'm not safe.' Rusty pushed against him, held him.

Head hanging over the bed, Buckler saw a spider swinging between the uprights weaving a small web in the dust. *Brother*, he thought, the blood rushing to his brow.

Too soon Rusty untangled herself from the sheets, asked him to go, dressed and left the room. Buckler rolled over and shed hot tears into the pillows, a few rough sobs. Not like him at all, the scalding of sinuses, the stuffing up of nostrils.

Dear Rusty, he called to her in his mind, *you were the soldier's love, chosen to walk through the fire, not my fire as it turns out so astoundingly simplified down to this night, nor my struggle of a lifetime's continuance, my dreams on heaven's dust-scattered floor.*

Buckler sucked air into his pleura, encountering a cracked rib.

Then to Veronica the next day. She was wishbone-thin, sun-browned, the tips of her rough-cut hair turned almost white-gold from the sun. She was back to the independent and characterful stance of their early life together, in the '30s.

She gave an account of her ride with Colts on the BSA and

sidecar, Limestone Hills to the Darling River. She told him about the horses – dead – the swagman – dead – the caravan – burned. His mind on fluff she gave as a cause of death, dismay and madness. If a further example was needed, she gave the pungent detail of his BSA's new owner, a rank madwoman herding goats. At Broken Hill she'd found Des Molyneaux, who gave her Rusty Donovan's Adelaide address.

Their meeting was in offices of the legal sort, dark-stained wood and worn carpets, dim leadlight windows – lowered voices, curious restrained glances – the rooms of Bruce, QC. Man and wife were intruders upon each other's self-protection. It would be sentimental to say so, and hurtful, but Buckler wanted the best for her, and saw she might reach it without him – of necessity, if need be.

He was in battledress. She wore a cotton skirt and a high-buttoned blouse in the way she had of cultivating plainness, arguing against beauty but vital, like the female wren. His campaign ribbons and bravery decorations, hard-won, were rendered futile in her gaze.

'Look at yourself, you big soggy dope. I'm glad your greatest admirer can't see you; pull your guts in, you look like a generalissimo in corsets.'

'Where is he?'

'You'll find out soon enough.'

Buckler peered around the door, as if Colts might be lurking. The model for this meeting was married life – their reunions over the years, the arrival of Buckler late at night, the dust of Limestone Hills in every crease of his pants, Faye emerging from her bedroom wrapped in an Onkaparinga blanket, Colts stumbling from the sleep-out in his striped pyjamas. Buckler considered the whim of taking Veronica in his arms and begging forgiveness, or whatever a man did this end of a comedy situation caught with his duds down.

He'd always liked his homecomings. Veronica, the same as Rusty, had liked his goings away, his comings back. But only if they meant to him what they meant to her. Which they couldn't, on account of their gender. It was a goodbye kiss being male, living life to the limit as a bloke. You made a strike against yourself through the power of your truthful contradictions.

Veronica steered him to a room made available to clients and closed the door in the face of Bruce, QC.

'Why?' came her machine-gunned questions. 'Why did you stop loving me? Did you ever love me at all? When did this other life start – the secrecy, the betrayal of vows? I've met Mrs Harris – that Rusty.'

'How did you find her?' he challenged.

'My God, you want an assessment? As I imagined her. A bunch of American officers paying court and obviously, by the look of you, that's a surprise.'

They sat in Andrew Bruce's meeting room with the fathers of the firm in various photographic poses around the walls a tribute to strong-woolled merino enterprise. The Bruces were the princely owners of Eureka Station. Their sons went to Oxford and never came back, or dawdled a few years, living on dividends garnered between dust storms and turning themselves English. The photographs alternated donkey trains and camel teams hauling wagons of teetering bales to remote railheads. Watching from a rocky outcrop, a naked black man holding a bundle of spears.

Veronica told Buckler that although Molyneaux, formerly an acolyte, had betrayed him, Colts might still believe in him, though barely, as she thought he would soon grow out of him, according to the signs.

Buckler smiled annoyingly, his admiration having the quality of condescension. Her short, bitter account of their travels was as vivid as one of her paintings. He was not meant to feel blessed by her, but somehow he did, bending his thinning hair to her benediction. It was combed tight to his skull with a mixture of Bay Rum, which squeezed out in gold beads of sweat.

'Without you, Kings does his own feeling about everything. You should have seen him as we went along – a boy, a stung boy. In the mornings he's crouched over the fire with your old greatcoat dragging in the dirt. By nightfall he's thrown it off, making himself useful. Honestly, Dunc, you've come close to ruining him, just by your great example. Now he's got a chance without you.'

'He still wants to see me?'

'Of course.'

'Where is he, then?'

'On the grounds,' said Veronica, 'that you were stationed in the area, and one of his cricketing greats is there, Randolph Knox, he's agreed to being sent to the Bruces' pastoral concern, Eureka, to try his hand at jackarooing.'

'Eureka! When?'

'Left yesterday. Before I learnt you were here.'

And just as well, was the unspoken thought to that.

Buckler saw Colts in a jacket and tie, sweltering in that walloping great finishing school, Eureka homestead dining room, being handed a goblet of black wine by Oakeshott over a saddle of saltbush mutton, and having to choke it back.

'They've been advised he's ready to run, and if he does it's your concern. You'll have to deal with it.'

Buckler smiled and thanked her for the information, and they stood. Downstairs with the lawyer hovering they agreed they'd speak further. But neither honestly thought they would meet the next day or even long after.

*

Buckler set about getting a discharge from hospital and cadging a workable motor. A rendezvous with Jack Slim close to the Territory border was clinched by radio. Buckler went along, foot to the floor, getting away from Adelaide through the last abandoned farms, the sour washaways, the sheeted burrs and purple carpets of Salvation Jane, out past the gibbers and salt-white tracks of his home state and birthplace, sashaying north into the deserts and hotlands of sheep while he made himself right with the rocks, keeping an eye out for a boy who might just lurch from the scrub and flag him down.

FIVE

FROM A ROCKY HILL RANDOLPH Knox watched the road leading north and army trucks at intervals kicking up dust. The trucks floated into the sky in mirages, their dusty metalwork breaking into blobs of mercury shine. Engine sounds crossed the air from five miles away, looping and fading. Sometimes they knocked like a tooth being broken.

Randolph waited for the noise of trucks coming closer, belting across the gypsum flats to seek him, though why they would ever do so was a question he didn't ask.

Mornings showed wedge-tailed eagles in thermals, the ends of their wingtips trailing. A telephone wire on leaning poles sang a lonely tune as Randolph waited for Captain Oakeshott to call through after dark – two short rings, one long. Some of the seven nights Randolph was out there per month, reporting on broken fences and dead stock, fouled waterholes and broken windmills, Oakeshott missed calling. There was always the threat he would turn up unannounced at one outstation or another and give a reprimand of the sort that broke kids' spirits. Four years before, when Randolph had started, Oakeshott claimed he'd go loony in the boundary rider's hut and talk to his sheep. The manager didn't know Randolph then, whose reply was if you didn't talk to your sheep you got nowhere. Oakeshott denied it with scorn, but Randolph had only to listen: 'You're for the knife,' or 'Into the bucket of guts with you, my friend,' as down culls went, driven in a sad little mob into the dark hole of an old mine shaft one hundred feet deep.

Too hard by a long chalk was Captain Oakeshott; Randolph thought the pit a foul solution, indecent, lazy. But there was knowledge the man had around sheep and their breeding, the calculation involved in keeping them in good wool in dry country on the margin of the world's greatest deserts, and as much of that as could be imbibed Randolph Knox took in and made his own.

In the spare time, he was allowed reading or did leatherwork, making tooled belts and wallets with ram's horns embossed on them, the edges tightly sewn. He wasn't lonely. He liked his own company. Just sometimes he looked at his own shadow and wished it wasn't there.

It interested Randolph how Oakeshott was two people, one known to slaughter an animal in rage when it wouldn't do what he wanted, the other reflecting on watching bare-breasted lubras in Western Australia leaning over sheep and calming them by understanding, following the tip of the blade shears with their noses, and the sheep loving it so much that when they were shorn they didn't run away but seemed to want to come back again for another round of being nuzzled and clipped.

So everyone was two people, while Randolph's struggle was about becoming one person and sticking to that. Fair-haired, light-skinned, blue-eyed and of good strong build, Randolph Knox had one overriding physical fault – that jaw like a bag of marbles. It made him look as if he had a bad case of mumps all the time. His nickname at school was Bumper Bar. Being made Head Boy didn't overcome the humiliation of that.

Sitting on the hut steps with a .44-40 between his knees, Randolph counted out cartridges. It was the rifle that 'Won the West'. For a week there were ten slugs allowed. Eureka flour and tea likewise came rationed but, oh boy, dingoes needed to come up to Randolph's boots and make their crazy howling before he'd let fly and give Oakeshott the satisfaction of berating the waste of one shot. But that week he blasted at anything in a blowout marking his finish − bottles, tins, rabbits.

Home was a thousand miles east on a sparkling river, the Isabel, across from the Snowies on the other side, where Randolph saw himself returning with the sun at his back, droving a mob of his own, a royal progress up the home valley with cold thunderheads and blue distances. The mob would flow, bumping his horse's legs and funnel into a gate, pouring through into the evening paddocks, dust drifting as his father welcomed him without a word of praise, except he would mark the achievement with a broken blade shear driven into a tree.

Hours passed in such thought, daydreaming and planning before Randolph went inside and made himself ready for the night − into that one room of corrugated iron containing a wire-framed bed, lumpy mattress, blankets from the saddle roll and a smoking lamp by the light of which he read the novels of Sir Walter Scott. He dozed, and woke to see marsupial mice skipping across the pages. By the light of the guttering lamp he saw them enter the leg of his trousers, where they hung on a wall-peg, and reappear, tiny-whiskered friends peering over the belt buckle. Nevertheless, he threw his book at them. Then his attention was strained through to the first faint weak-ening of darkness when he regretted the night was over. He lived on mutton, dried apricots and roll-your-owns, at the start of a week routinely slaughtering an old wether, leaving the skin drying under stones. Cooked the best chops, salted a leg, fed his dog, scattered the offal and sat chewing till his jaws ached. The skins were his to sell, likewise any dead wool found on carcases thanks to which he was in good credit with a stock agent.

An older brother and uncles were away at the war, but Randolph was exempt by family agreement. Diversions were not in his nature. Those that were he wrestled and smothered down. By the sixth day he decided he'd earned a geek at a fuss though; and late that afternoon after checking miles of fence he rode the gypsum flats to look at the trucks closer. One came along and he was too far away to hail it, so turned around for the ride back. Thought he'd soon be at the hut, only down in the dry gullies dark came on. A horseman in that country was the hand of a crawling clock.

Light flickered in a ragged stand of trees; men were camped there mysterious as plotters in the borderlands of Caledonia. Edging closer Randolph saw the outline of their truck. Around a camp fire figures moved against the flames, tipping their throats back, hard voices grumbling. Obscenities Randolph had never encountered in his life exploded against the dark scrub and towards the commotion his sheepdog, Maisie, dragged herself on her belly as if roused by such words of sexual thrust.

Turning for home a second time, Randolph was baffled and supposed he was moving along a fence line rather than across it; couldn't get his directions fixed as eroded gullies trapped him and stars that were behind appeared in front. He gave up and returned to where cones of firelight hung above trees. Sparks flew as the soldiers added more sticks and Randolph scooped a hip-hole in the dust a way off, lying with his knees hooked to his chin, hand on his dog's muzzle to say *be still*. He felt crusty sleep gathering as the men by the roadside shouted and threatened punches and quietened. Later Randolph heard them lurching around in the dark, tripping over stones, cursing. It was cold. Maisie growled into her throat. Randolph would approach them in the morning hoping for breakfast.

Under a sky of pink, from under a rock like a lizard, Randolph Knox emerged. It was a morning stranger than he could have imagined, crumbly with dirt in the early light as he was, on all fours on gravel. To his wonder he heared the knock of willow, the cry of 'Owzat!' as crows flew up from the mulga.

Flies buzzed in the early heat. A ball rolled towards him, a scuffed six-stitcher slowing across stones and coming to rest at his toecaps. Pride compelled Randolph to emerge from the mulga dribbling the ball from hand to hand – a serious player who'd rejected a place with the NSW reserves for the sake of something more: to go jackarooing at Eureka, the farthest place due west where merino sheep ran, because the Knoxes of Homegrove raised merinos at the farthest point due east, and pride sat up for notice, spanning the map.

Two figures in khaki shorts, bare-chested, wearing unlaced boots and infantrymen's slouch hats took a moment to register the apparition out of the sun. Boys had jostled for places at the nets to watch Randolph's action and modelled themselves on him, muttering under their breaths as they faced him, 'Bend the front knee, get the weight forward, get the left elbow up, over the ball.' There'd been something appealing about Randolph as a boy, charming to dogs and strangers, yet so bloody ugly and grave, which Randolph strangled as he went through adolescence as a defence against being discovered in his deepest part. These were men, and he had the same defence against them.

The men ran to their fielding possies and waited half-crouched with their hands on their knees. One of them directed where the others should stand. They were having a go at him no doubt. The batsman squared up in front of a kerosene drum.

'Send 'er down . . .'

Rough ground slackened Randolph's pace, but not by much. The drum flew with a rattling crash – three batsmen in a row – and the players came forward to look Randolph over, disbelieving the sight: Stetson and skinny stockhorse, red kelpie and peeling nose blisters. They asked no questions, apparently stoking their conceit as he joined their breakfast fire listening to their talk. Bacon curled, eggs spat, baked beans sputtered. Randolph learned they'd been at Tobruk and were bitter fighters resentful at doing a cushy job while their mates took New Guinea and Yanks rooted their sheilas rotten under St Kilda Pier.

'Did you ever meet a lieutenant called Sandy Knox in the engineers?'

'An officer?' they spat.

'Missing in Crete.'

'Sorry to hear that, mate. No.'

Finally it was time to go. Throwing their kits on the truck they stomped around the camp site, hurling empty beer bottles into the bush and listening to the smash, stamping their boot-heels on empty cans of beef, which they flung discus-like as far as they could send them.

The truck crunched into gear and waddled along the road getting its links oiled. There it waited one hundred yards ahead with the engine knocking, and Randolph got the idea being offered. He turned the mare's head away, as if to indicate he was on the opposite tack from the one they wanted. They raced their motor and that was when Randolph acted, leaning his weight forward and nudging the nag around, cantering into the dust of the roaring truck. It wove and baulked until Randolph glimpsed an opening and galloped past, feet almost brushing the dirt, belly of the old bolter flat while the soldiers jeered.

Hauling up he watched that dusty, reeking, sunbaked mobile torture platform making its way gone. A game played out. Spectators and players heading their separate ways.

Back on the plain more trucks followed. They weren't of interest to Randolph anymore, mere grinding objects going past, growing smaller each time he looked back. Cresting the gypsum hillocks and walking, leading the mare tenderfooted over crystalline ground hotter than focused rays, he heard a higher, thinner whine.

They're comin' back for me, was the thought Randolph had, knowing he made a silhouette on the skyline.

On the barely visible track pursuing him was a low-slung utility vehicle, cack-coloured with army markings. Randolph leaned on his horse waiting for it to reach him. While still a way off the driver stopped and used binoculars, then came on as if making a decision, having identified Randolph or at least guessed who he wasn't.

The driver climbed out. It was Major Dunc Buckler returned from the grave where Hoppy Harris tried consigning him. Buckler hadn't shown much interest in Randolph the first time they met, except for the health harangue, eyeing off Randolph's boils, telling him what raw vegetables would do. Now Buckler made it seem like a meeting between mates — as if he hadn't crept through the hideous gullies ready to back up and disappear if Randolph turned out to be Oakeshott, branding him a lecher, or Hoppy Harris flexing for a second go.

'How are you, sonny?' — those bloodshot, intransigent eyes scanned Randolph's forearms, running over the now-puckered scabs.

So tell him what he wanted to know: 'I'm all cleaned up.'

'Good.'

''Cause I ate my greens,' said Randolph, giving Buckler pause to wonder at being mocked.

'Excellent.'

Buckler looked around the emptiness. 'Are you alone?'

'You could say that.'

They gathered a few sticks and piled them onto a claypan. Randolph squatted on his heels with his hat pulled over his eyes and rolled a smoke while Buckler did the work, lit the fire, got the billy boiling. A plaster remained on the back of his head where the shearing contractor had sliced him.

Buckler went to his tuckerbox and pulled out a tin of biscuits with chunks of candied peel in them, eruptions of crystallised cherries, rusted bubbles into which Randolph bit.

As Randolph kept dipping a fist in the tin Buckler invited him to keep it. 'You've got a sweet tooth, obviously, relish them.'

Buckler was working his way round to something he wanted. Hadn't come chasing Randolph shredding rubber and distributing largesse for no good reason.

'Oakeshott says you're the best young bloke he's ever had.'

'There's been a few,' shrugged Randolph.

Buckler didn't waste any more words then.

'Now there's another one, your brand-new first-year jackaroo. You'll meet him back at the homestead, he should be there by now, settling in, an old schoolfellow of yours but younger. I'm sorry I won't be there to introduce you, because he's my ward, a bit of a lost soul – Kingsley Colts.'

'Nobody lasts with Oakeshott.'

'You have.'

'I'm almost through and heading home.'

'Do something for me, Knox. Make friends with Colts. Don't be sour about him, he's a special case. Been brought up with old soldiers and women too much. Snap him out of it, bring him to earth. His father, Colonel Colts, was the original good bloke. Died before Kingsley knew him, I was the one stepped in.'

'Why not?' Randolph levelled.

'It's true,' Buckler said. 'I have my moments. But listen. No-one's as good as the person you make yourself.'

Randolph supposed not. It was a struggle though.

'He's had a taste of the outdoor life,' continued Buckler, 'on my soldier settlement block, Limestone Hills. Nothing he liked better than binding sheaves, following the plough, always first in the workshop to grab the wrench when I yelled out fetch one. Rode like a Mexican bandit flying off every second trot, but stuck to the mount he did, hates to surrender. Lately he's been kicking around the country on a motorbike, getting a mouthful of sand. Don't ask me why.'

'The idea with Captain Oakeshott,' said Randolph, 'is to do it right one hundred and one per cent of the time.'

'You might have to shepherd Colts a bit,' Buckler said. 'Horses, dogs — he's experienced enough with them — I'm not a sheep man myself, nor's he. Goats are his most recent livestock experience, ha ha, nothing too grand in that.'

Buckler scribbled a mailing address — Brigade HQ — and a radio code on a scrap of paper, which he took from his glasses case. 'None of it's his idea. Everyone's sorry about him. If he goes off the straight and narrow, this will always find me.'

Next day Randolph rode in from the boundary rider's hut through the heat of the day, watching Eureka outbuildings hover in the sky long before he reached them, mirages of rippled iron breaking and folding. From the weed and waste tracks of the station approaches, eaten over by stock, Randolph scanned the outbuildings for the presence of a newcomer.

And there he was, a slender youth escaping the afternoon heat in the shade of the jackaroos' quarters, poised over a game of solitaire tensely smoking a cigarette.

'You must be Colts.'

'So you remember me?'

A smile broke, light flooded his features. Randolph felt pleased, except for a little irresolute knot in the stomach holding him back from some bigger emotion he might feel, the intensity of friendship at first glance, a deeper attachment wanted perhaps too much.

'More or less,' Randolph hedged.

In fact he'd never forgotten young Colts at the school nets, no, not at all, the improver of merit in the Under-14As, determined to the point of tears to prove his worth. And that pure yearning look, nobody could shun the effect, least of all Randolph.

He led Colts around the quarters. 'Take this room at the end, move your gear, it gets the shade of the tank in the late afternoon. There's a doormat, a bedside cupboard made from a kero crate, the flywire's all right, anyway it keeps the biggest blowies out.'

'There's a suitcase under the bed,' noticed Colts.

'I'll get rid of it,' said Randolph.

Colts picked up a book and flipped the cover back.

'Is this your room?'

Randolph stared at him, 'No.'

But the book had his name in it.

A pattern developed when Oakeshott's work rule allowed. On the wide claypan between the big Eureka shed and the jackaroos' quarters, Randolph and the new first-year jackaroo bowled to each other on a makeshift pitch cleared of pebbles with an old fibre broom. It became a spectator sport for those who wandered past – cook, housemaid, yard man, and Ah Sup the Chinese gardener.

Colts enthused, remembering a day at Moore Park when there were twenty wickets on four fields and two hundred and twenty players in a schoolboys' carnival. Fielding at deep cover point he'd found himself alongside Randolph at deep square-leg in another game. Randolph said he only vaguely recalled the day but certainly he did – because of that serious, almost heart-breakingly earnest junior fieldsman in grubby whites, with the square dimple on the chin, and the way the dimple had smaller dimples in it.

When the mail truck arrived there were other jackaroos on Eureka, newcomers spilling out and staring around, adjusting to the dusty space. Two gawky pulled-from-the-gutter misfits who wouldn't last were caught entreating the mailman to take them back until Oakeshott cut in. The other two were stalwart sons of the land comfortable with starkness like Randolph and eager to be schooled by Oakeshott. Their names were Devitt and Poole. So they made a society but in later years whoever else was there in those last six months would slip from the surface of Randolph's memory – he would see only Colts.

They partnered at sheep work, one each side of a drafting race wrenching horned heads into line and shouting themselves into a rhythm of getting a queue of tightly pressed backs moving towards the gates. There Captain Oakeshott stood separating the spurned from the chosen, two-tooths from hoggets, ewes from wethers, wearing a grey dustcoat, a dented felt hat and smoking a pipe. Between Oakeshott and Randolph there was rarely a word exchanged; it was all speaking silences.

Sheep were the essence, that's why. Playing cricket was more just a trick, like the quandong seed Randolph rolled down the inside of his arm and produced in the open palm of his hand at smoko, or the tightrope walk he balanced in his dreams, thou-sands of feet above a deep blue sea.

Randolph gushed to Colts about sheep.

'They're only ground maggots,' answered Colts.

'But sheep's where things happen, success gets launched from the square of the yards, prizes are won. You take yourself to town for the Sheep Show and live it up at the Australia Hotel, and you're the same all through. People know who you are, there's no doubt in their minds. Sheep men with grime in their nostrils, mutton fat in their pores, they're the big names, only a bit down from God.'

'That's laying it on thick.'

'They have staples of greasy wool always tucked about them somewhere – in their pockets, between the pages of their note-books, in their saddlebags and caught in the hairs on the backs of their hands. You should see them.'

'I might, one day,' said Colts rather lazily, 'when I've done everything else.'

Randolph was intense, more than listening to himself, creating himself: 'The best blokes, at the breeding end, can hardly ever do the same thing twice without surrendering a quality they've bred for the first time round. It makes it hard to peak with an animal on most points. Sturdy on four legs like a low heavy table, my father likes to breed, packed with crimped fleece, lava flows of dewlap under the chin. I'm looking for a bigger, plainer animal. I like Oakeshott's Ironsides. That ram's ready for Noah's Ark come the second flood or Jesus of Nazareth, come the second coming – the Good Shepherd, they called him.'

'Get off your bike, Randolph.'

'Things have to add up. They've got to mean something.'

Randolph rolled two cigarettes and passed one to Colts.

'Shit scared is how a bloke feels,' said Colts, 'but you can be who you are and still be the best.'

Randolph looked at his young friend curiously.

'That's Buckler,' Colts admitted, colouring – the tags of the man who'd promised the world but abandoned him still coming to him. Defiance was what Colts had expressed when he agreed to Veronica's plan and caught the mail truck to Eureka on the grounds that he'd find Buckler's camp. Defiance was what he expressed being there when Buckler wasn't. It was the same defiance in looks but not in feeling.

'He won't say what he expects of you.'

'You feel it though,' said Randolph.

Colts faced the bouncers Randolph sent down. Struck on the arms, shoulders and head, he didn't complain. Likewise, he was hard on Randolph and kept the balls coming until it was time to clean up for tea.

Pre-dawn Colts was out catching the horses before Randolph was properly awake. If volunteers were called for chipping burrs in the holding paddocks, Colts went to it. If Randolph said he was off doing a job he found Colts willing to go one better; and he wasn't bad either, helping dismantle a windmill with the station mechanic, putting the parts back together, never wasting an effort, pacing himself, only needing to be told a detail to remember. All he wanted was more practice at sheepwork, and he'd get that. When Oakeshott assigned them to separate work parties, Randolph connived to get them back together again. It never took long.

After a while Randolph announced he'd extended his finishing date on Eureka another month, always worrying a bit that Colts needed extra shepherding before his farewell.

They rode out early with their fresh horses kicking each other and swishing their tails getting rid of flies. Colts wore a leather sweatband around his wrist, tooled by Randolph in a pattern of lizards and bush mice.

Randolph caught him turning at the sound of a motor at the rear of the sandhills by the salt lake, where the inwards track ran. At first he'd said the only thing keeping him at Eureka was that Buckler would be back. After a while he expressed his fury at being dumped. Randolph drew the story out. The only ones who cared had left him for the west and centre. His sister, Faye, was gone off as a missionary's wife; Mrs Veronica Buckler was gone to make Buckler pay for his sins; Major Dunc Buckler was gone pushing along north to find the war that didn't want him.

Buckler was hypocritical as all shit built up, said Colts, when he learned about Buckler's men and de Grey's boys heading off from Eureka together – he'd blocked Colts from going with him but travelled with a boy his age and toting a rifle too, Hammond Pringle.

Randolph knew enough to know that wasn't quite how it was. Colts was the one who broke out, got himself expelled from school and set off travelling inland spurning counter opinion. Lucky for him Buckler evaporated with his half-arsed army. You made objections to make a place where you could go in this life. Randolph saw it might be to Colts's surprise a place called Eureka.

Colts circled out looking for sheep dispersed in fives and sixes over wastes of saltbush stretching to a horizon of white dust haze and immeasurable glare. The animals scattered around one side of a clump but failed to appear on the other. Their fleeces were the same colour as the soil, a mustard grey. Randolph waited like a magnet a few miles away until the mob was mustered towards him, and they set off walking them.

'Listen, you're doing all right,' said Randolph, with the mob bunched and moving, and they could yarn as they switched away flies. Maisie ran away out, low to the ground like a dusty moving comma, keeping the sheep all in order. Randolph carried a small black-and-tan kelpie on his lap because her feet were sensitive to the hot ground, but later coming up to the yards when it was cooler she would do the job while Maisie stood back and rested.

'Eureka wasn't my idea – they duped me,' said Colts.

Randolph feared hearing him say it was a big mistake.

'It's all right, though,' Colts spoke into the angle of his chin and the shadow of his hat fell on his face.

Randolph whistled a tuneless tune as they advanced another mile or so. Then Randolph said strangely, after complicated thought, 'I'll never forsake you, Kings.'

Colts kept riding slack in the saddle and looking elsewhere, as if Randolph hadn't spoken.

After a while Colts said defiantly, 'If Buckler comes crawling back I'll tell him where to shove it.'

'Good on you, sport. Sounds like a fine idea.'

They rode along until Colts leaned across, making a sign of entwined fingers.

'Buckler and Hammond Pringle's old man, Birdy Pringle, who's white as you and me, were like *that* in the first war. They made a vow to look after each other's orphans if any came up. Each reckoned he was king pin and had the right. On the way back from France on the troopship they had an argument on principle. Birdy says he's killed, he can't get over it. Buckler says it's kill or be killed on the frontline, not murder as Birdy sweated it. They were demobbed and Birdy shouldered a swag in Port Adelaide and headed north on foot, he must have come through here, kicking Eureka stones, aiming for the Top End and a cattle run. When people asked what he'd done in the war he said nothin'. They gave him the white feather. You're like that.'

'Like what?'

'You give nothin' away.'

'I don't think so.'

'Why did he do it?' Colts spat a fly.

'Was he ashamed?' Randolph said.

'He was covered in medals. It didn't matter how many lives he'd saved, how many Turks and Fritzes he'd popped – he was beaten up. Then he married a gin, mission wedding and all. Buckler was not impressed.'

'Along came Hammond,' said Randolph.

'And Dorothy. They send us Box Brownie snaps at Christmas and cards rough-cut and glued with flour paste. Birdy sends a ten-quid note for the school year; he'll save his hard-earned money now. It might have been me and Faye living up there with them – halfies and creamies and full-blood boogies – under a bark roof with four poles, except for the penny Buckler tossed when our father died, to see which one would get us. Birdy never knew it was a double-header.'

'What about your mother?'

'Veronica?'

'No, your real mother.'

'I never had one.'

'That's a first.' Randolph let it go.

Each night they showered under the tank stand in sulphurous bore water, put on clean shirts, knotted neckties and buttoned their tweed jackets, no matter how high the thermometer climbed. Being trained for self-reliance they did their own sewing and mending, laundering their stiff moleskin trousers free of crushed dags and weight of dust in an outdoor copper cemented like a tomb. Woe betide the jackaroo who arrived late at the Oakeshotts' table with or without excuses. They were permitted to remove their jackets only after Mrs Oakeshott invited them. Following the meal they sat round the short-wave set while Oakeshott expressed tactical opinions. Sometimes London and Berlin were clearer than Radio Australia. At the distant end of the dial they heard Tokyo Rose broadcasting from Japan. Colts talked of enlisting as soon as he could, went around firing at shadows with an imaginary Tommy gun and mowing down Nips in the saltbush till Randolph told him to knock it off.

One Sunday Randolph and Colts spent the whole day searching for a sharpening stone Colts had dropped along the single-wire telephone line leading out to the boundary riders' huts. Oakeshott was a bastard, they agreed, for insisting on every meaningless tool being accounted for. But when Randolph said he still respected Oakeshott, Colts said he did too. If Randolph said he'd like to rocket to the moon and run sheep there, Colts would say, *wouldn't that be something*.

Everything hung on Colts as the keeper of Randolph's toothy smile.

SIX

FOUR MONTHS AFTER COLTS BEGAN at Eureka he flashed Randolph a letter. 'It's from my sister, Faye. There's been a ruckus. You won't believe it – Buckler turned up at the mission.'

'Struth.'

'You can't get there by road – there isn't one. They used pack-horses and took a fortnight from where they left their trucks.'

'Still hauling the water wagon they took from here,' supposed Randolph.

'Buckler used surprise because people always come by boat, not from inland, and guess who was there? Think of the last person on earth you'd expect to find, apart from Boy Dunlap and Faye and blackfellas and crocs.'

'Emperor of Japan?'

'Veronica. She left Adelaide, crossed the Nullarbor to Perth, caught the steamer to Derby, the lugger round the coast, the mission launch up the river and broke the regulations to get there. Buckler's bashing around in the bush, kicking over antbeds and shooting donkeys for meat and looking for some sort of weird thing, and he runs into her.' Colts spat it out. 'I was meant for that, I'm the one. Why not me? He can take them all and shove them as far as he can go up himself, and then the extra mile.'

'You'll get over it,' said Randolph.

'Get stuffed.'

Bad moods prevailed on Eureka. It was the time of year for regrets. Randolph wrote home and said expect him by Christmas.

Oakeshott blasphemed a prizewinning ram, Ironsides, bought by a syndicate of directors and foisted on him by the board. For three seasons he'd dreamed of dispatching the sire down the pit. The boys followed him around making notes in their blue-covered 1942 Jackaroo's Station Diaries. Randolph placed his hand on Ironsides' firm fleece, feeling the defined tips of each staple packed together like tiles on a roof, and when he parted the wool with his fingers it was clean down through with celestial whiteness and protected from the elements.

Ironsides' progeny were excellent sheep by any standard except Oakeshott's. He'd bred from the ram through spite to prove his point, but no longer would, he declared, and counted out four thousand ewes whose characteristics he damned as they jostled past him in the yards. Oakeshott counted by mentally scanning them one hundred at a time, coming up with a figure accurate to the last digit as they were drafted off. Whatever price they fetched would be a lesson to the directors, Oakeshott ranted, a statement that started Randolph's mind working. When an arrangement was made to run them into a mob of ten thousand being gathered on the Queensland side of the border, Randolph was given the job of taking the ewes to the meeting point with the drover, Bulleen. Colts went with him. Bulleen knew Randolph and liked him.

Around Bulleen's camp fire Colts described the other droving outfit he'd met, the dumpy goat woman jerking up and down on a wreck of a motorbike these days, most probably, and with a goat sitting in the sidecar. Colts fingered the small bones on the back of his right hand, still sore six months after his knuckling, and watched Bulleen's face break into a grin as he said what a small world it was: 'She used to be my wife, though we never made it as far as any church, boys.' He called her 'the old bat'.

In the droving camp Randolph wrote a letter to Oakeshott and gave it to Colts to take back. Enclosed was a cheque made out to the company and the signatory was Bulleen. However the true owner of the four thousand was Randolph Knox himself under an agreement with Bulleen.

Randolph and the drovers moved into country straddling dry watercourses coming down from the Cooper. Randolph on his way home at last, a drive that would last one hundred and twenty days and be compressed in feeling as if all those days were one. The sheep were spread wide yet could still be seen at a distance. At first they ran in every direction and had to be chased by men stationed around the mob at intervals. But after a few days they settled and Randolph walked among them with his sheepdog running across their backs. Most of the droving team were young station hands, like Randolph himself, working their way south. They were a half-brained bunch without much instinct for the life except they would use it to escape the country and get in the war from the first proper town they reached, whether Cunnamulla, Bourke or Dubbo. Randolph worked his dog as smartly as Bulleen used his; whenever there was a problem and the station hands found themselves in trouble they would say, 'Don't worry too much, Randolph will be here with his dog any minute.' Maisie the red kelpie bitch with prick ears turned a sheep so hard that the rest of the mob followed and saved everyone work. To block them and send them into a new direction, she ran several times back and forth across the face of the mob, and that was enough to turn them.

The densely packed sheep covering many acres moved like cloud shadow. The mob rose and fell with every alteration in ground level. When saying goodbye to Colts, Randolph had held back from asking him to break his commitment to Eureka and come a-droving. He wished Colts was with him, though, for the greatness of the ride. Wagtails rode along or flew from sheep to sheep chasing insects. At noon the cook's cart was always to be found under a tree. There were hammocks sewn from wheat sacks slung under the cart and the dogs rested in them when they weren't working. Those dogs were prepared to work themselves to death rounding up sheep, but they knew style and luxuriated when they had the chance. Before the trip was out Maisie would have pups to the best dog known to anyone, Bulleen's Target. Randolph would train them up and in time rail the best worker halfway back across Australia with a label on her collar for Colts.

When the cook's cart got moving again the dogs stayed in their hammocks until they were called. The cook made fresh bread each day in camp ovens and made his own sausages using sheep entrails for casing. Randolph experienced the idealism of pure emotion, a ladder to stars that winked and turned in contented circles. He overlooked the earth and was a portion of creation, experiencing himself as a particle in the existence of God, which he knew himself to be, but wasn't always so assured of it.

One of Oakeshott's maxims had been that no man should be allowed to overseer on a station unless he had done two years' droving. He thought Randolph would rejoin the company one day as overseer rising to manager and had been content to see him go on that basis. Whether Colts would stick was a question without answer. Randolph wrote to Buckler saying he thought he would, and now Randolph found himself engaged in a correspondence with a man who wrote back correcting his grammar and spelling mistakes.

Sometimes Randolph took Maisie and drafted off a bunch of his ewes where he could see them, just to watch them move past interestingly, in the pride of ownership, and give him the opportunity to consider what sort of foundation they made for the flock he was planning. He often found himself asking, what made a flock or a mob? What number complete to the eye? There seemed to be an answer to that question dangling beyond technical facts or personal experience – a form, a quantity of that form, created by happiness being a matter of light, movement and dust such as might be roused by a dusty planet rolling through the sky.

They were medium-woolled animals but very correct sheep, free-growing with long staple, well framed with three drapes on the fronts and an impeccable genetic background despite the way Oakeshott knocked them. Oakeshott had warned, 'Buy a ram to correct perceived faults and the chances are you'll be introducing new faults,' but the Adelaide directors with the little knowledge they had, feeling big in themselves and always going about getting second opinions, scientifically grounded, were intent on having a say. Oakeshott believed they were pushing his wool too far in the fine direction. Exactly that made the culls an opportunity for Randolph when the ewes were drafted out – their wool classed medium but the feel was softer. The Isabel district was all fine to superfine. There would be arguments with his father as Randolph introduced the idea of correlated mating: one sheep, ram or ewe to supply what the other lacked, distinct from the more usual mating of like with like. If he'd learnt anything from Oakeshott it was that stock naturally bred down whereas Randolph's father liked an even line in his paddocks, a tidy picture. The news Randolph brought with him – while the world at war had bigger intelligence to chew – was to have variety in your stock so that by selection you could breed up.

At the start of summer, Randolph and the stockman he'd engaged at Tumut came over the mountains on a track rarely used. They appeared at the headwaters of the Isabel bearing a weight of golden fleece on the backs of the four thousand. The behaviour of the ewes, long accustomed to travel, was precise as they came past the cemetery yard and moved steadily down the centre of the dirt road into the Knox paddocks, many with grown-out Ironsides' lambs at heel. Not a bleat did they sound.

When Randolph whistled Maisie the sheep stopped, and Maisie's run to the head of the mob was hardly needed. The sheep only trembled a little shaking off flies and blinking in the thin, hot, upland sun, awaiting the signal to move on.

Randolph saw his father coming from a fair way off, the lean man in the saddle with a contained way of riding grown from days of combing the hills, a short-handled spade tied to the saddle ready to dig out rabbits or consign clumps of thistle to perdition. His mother waited by the garden gate with a handkerchief to her cheek.

Colin Knox did not know where to begin with his second son. From information gleaned there had been the fragile belief, chosen as gospel, that Sandy was missing, not KIA, and would write as other men had on a Red Cross postcard even this long afterwards. The belief had sustained Colin, Edwina and Randolph for these past eighteen months. Australians were overrun on Crete, a Stuka attacked stragglers. Out of dozens of men exposed running, diving for cover, it was Sandy with his brilliance on the sportsfield and supremacy in the ram shed who was left in the open. He was not seen since. It was believed he'd gone ahead, hidden on a farm, found a cave or joined the partisans. That he'd been shipped to Germany finally as a POW was a good chance under the circumstances.

Now forget all that. Colin Knox and Randolph had never embraced but Colin lurched against his son for support. They both let the tears run. Nobody in authority told the Knoxes very much except for the brute fact conveyed by their parish minister doing his bereavement duty up the valley road from Isabel Junction – 'That Sandy would have felt nothing was a comfort,' he said.

Randolph learned details kept from his parents, those suddenly old, lost, strong ones. Sandy had been cut to pieces and went to his death screaming, a mate taken prisoner the lone witness. The mate was the one who'd written on a Red Cross postcard almost two years afterwards, on learning the Knoxes hadn't known. They learned that Sandy's remains were buried under a rock amid olive trees, weighted down by boulders on Crete.

Feeling came over Randolph as he wrote to Colts. It was possible Colts had never understood what Randolph meant or else chose not to react as he had when Randolph pledged lifelong fidelity so strangely. Each line of Randolph's letter burned but bereavement and shattered emotions could be used for excessive statements, and the recipient makes allowances. That was how Randolph dared a love letter anyway to a young man who offered no such strong feeling in return. The unanswered portion, the usual month or two coming, was Randolph's most heartfelt reply, while the answered portion – taking the identical time span, offering warm thanks for the brilliant pup named by Colts Cubby (Tiger's cub) and making sheep talk intricate as any breeder might wish – assured Randolph that friendship had not gone backwards at least.

For Colts had studied with Oakeshott at the wool table and in the joining paddocks and stuck to his post on Eureka, earning his stripes, as he expressed it, in the boundary rider's hut. He had been commended in the Manager's Report to the Board as Randolph himself had been commended in his time. Buckler wrote congratulating Randolph on playing a part in stabilising a runaway.

Then Colts's situation changed. Oakeshott dropped dead and Colts, just eighteeen, wrote from New Guinea. Apparently he was in some sort of small boat unit up in the Islands, Japs every-where but so were Aussies. Randolph feared he would never see him again, prayed for his safety and kept writing.

'I am very pleased with our rams this year of 1944 and even Dad considers them much better than we ever had before, the wool being deep grown thanks to the infusion of the bad Eureka blood, so called . . .'

'I went ashore for the heck of it,' Colts replied on Christ-mas Day 1944, 'carrying a swag of batteries from the beach up through some steep jungle, giving the boys a hand. It was a bright moon, we waited at the edge of a ridge until it set, no cigs, then walked through tall grass over the saddle. It was cool up there at four thousand feet. We walked, stopped, listened, keeping dead still we heard a crash. It was the sound of a wallaby in the bush at night when you know it's a wallaby but makes your hair stand on end. We tapped shoulders, the signal to move on, when the Japs opened fire. They'd never heard a wallaby taking off. Didn't know what a wallaby was. It was them and us, each end of the clearing. We didn't fire back, they never knew we were there. Bullets banged in every direction you can think of. I got one, but it's all right (left lung under armpit, if you want to know, clean healed thanks to miracle drug in powder form, sulphur).'

He didn't call out, thought Randolph. *He suffered, but wouldn't show it.*

As blokes returned from the war Colin and Randolph Knox were the first to find work for them, to settle them in. They located cottages and helped them win town acceptance. Quietly to himself Randolph hoped Colts would be one of them. He would not be the same – none of them were – and Randolph was ready for that. The war years put development on individuals. Some grew like trees by staying, though, and Randolph was one of those. To Randolph's outrage, bordering on disgust, he learned that his mother was pregnant at forty-four. 'Another Sandy,' Edwina Knox prayed.

The first mail ever to land in Isabel Junction postmarked 'Occupation Forces, Japan' arrived in the hands of Rose Demellick, mail truck contractor. She handed it over to Randolph like a blessed wafer while he repressed his disappointment. Colts had gone from active duty to an assignment with the occupation forces with the rank of sergeant, heading a bunch of older men, some of them sick from being first to enter the radiated zone of Nagasaki. They'd believed it safe because of intact architecture and an obliging Japanese businessman welcoming them to his soft drink plant where they had guzzled the wares.

Next Colts was learning Japanese and fascinated by the experience of being a 'conqueror on the q.t.' – *did that mean making free with geisha girls?* Randolph wondered – but expressed a wish 'to get back to the bush one day and take up a piece of dirt if it ever proved possible, and to get on with sheep'.

Randolph read the intention as a sworn statement of trust and relaxed his inclination to control the future too much. In appointing stud agents and allowing for offsiders, or even a

97

partner, he left a vacancy on the books, one of the dusty authors he favoured having somewhere quipped, 'What name doth best fit sorrow in young despair? – *Tomorrow* – What name doth joy most borrow when life is fair? – *Tomorrow.*'

Randolph had no interest in travel, except he intended visiting Crete one day and locating his brother's grave. Then he would continue to the old country as his parents had in the '30s, taking in Buckingham Palace and the Edinburgh Tattoo before settling in at Old Trafford and the Marylebone Cricket Club. Hopefully Randolph would cross paths with Colts if the latter still had the gadabout bug and they would follow the Ashes together.

Meantime Randolph planned new and better paddocks, laid out stock lanes, undertook advanced grazing schemes, rebuilt the ram sheds using second-hand materials, postwar shortages being what they were. Starting to make the cumulative changes in breeding that counted, he lifted himself into the almost meta-physical plane of stud masters. What had real existence for those beau ideals didn't exist yet – a sheep for local conditions refined on most points, and having whatever anyone said about the utility of the feature (in Randolph's persistent case) a progna-thous or royal jaw, defined as pride.

Randolph and his father rode the paddocks on prancing chestnut mares while the Isabel Junction stock and station agent, Careful Bob Hooke, puffed and swayed beside them on a fat-bellied pony.

'Sandy would have liked this' and 'Sandy would have liked that', said Careful Bob, who was with Sandy for a time in North Africa. 'How's that little Timmy coming along? Ain't he the dead spit of the other one?'

The other one was Sandy, and always would be.

There were universes of creation within sight of the old wire gate on the skyline, but just sometimes Randolph's personal lifetime struck like a blow and he was an irrelevance in the eye of nature. His father's favourite had been Sandy and his mother's now was Tim, born in '45 to replace Sandy plain and simple. Randolph felt a vacancy existed at the top of the family ladder where he should have been and Tim was meant to grow into it. Randolph would be old by then. If only he hadn't been born shovel-jawed Randolph, without much room for improvement, being considered a perfect enough all-rounder to satisfy under most circumstances, without the family getting too excited. Baby Tim was perfect, though.

Then Randolph stepped back from that feeling of panic in which nothing was promised, all was fixed, settled without him, and he was filled by a bounteousness of mood that needed an outlet proving he was better than shit. It was on such a feeling day that Homegrove Holdings sold Careful Bob Hooke a sweep of high mountain country called the Bullock Run, and Randolph, who had never looked at the untouched thousand acres before, went for a ride and believed his father had forfeited a paradise. It made him tense on the whip hand. When he showed his determination with management of the property he felt his father weaken, and his vocation was properly started.

Randolph stored Colts's letters in the old biscuit tin that Buckler had given him on Eureka Station in '42. It bore a design of embossed fruit in a silver bowl standing before a three-arched window and looking down on successive terraced ridges and greenish-yellow creek flats. Randolph could still taste the metallic, charred, candied cherries on the back of his throat and hear the last one rolling in the tin before Buckler rattled the invitation to have another and he took it out.

War it seemed had reshaped Colts not quite as expected. Missing from his attitude, it struck Randolph as he read and re-read the mail in the hallowed biscuit tin, was any trace of the exaggerated warrior urge derived from Buckler. War as a background to places, sights and sensations – that's what affected Colts more than the big drama he'd been raised on. Randolph prided himself somewhat paternally as one who'd turned the tide for Colts by making jackarooing possible, whereas the main cause probably was that Colts had suffered running supplies to the coast watchers – the shot he'd taken in the lung.

Something else, though. Randolph would never be able to explain how the knowledge of that shot, irreversible in damage wrought and not to be spoken about except in the code of men's soldiering, increased a sullen, selfish, brooding certainty of attachment in Randolph himself, a possessiveness towards Colts that soured his earlier feelings from supple to unyielding.

Randolph heard regularly from Dunc Buckler. The man's postwar obsessions dwelt on a world changed utterly from the one he'd saved, or attempted to save, as a Great War returnee and quarrelled with since. The big bogey was the Soviet Union getting the upper hand. Minerals were the alchemical key to victory – magnesite, mica, uranium, bauxite, asbestos and iron ore. Rare metals abounded in remote parts of Australia if only they could be dug out to benefit free nations in beating down Red cunning. Mention was made of those earths, very hush-hush – essential for jet plane alloys and who knew what, attractive to flying saucers wherever they came from, dancing into Buckler's consciousness on lonely roads as they appeared to fools the world over.

Stirred by Buckler's brainstorms, however, Randolph and his father invested in a revived mining company, Arcturus Metals N/L. Before leaving for the Centre on his first season's prospecting, Buckler called at Homegrove to show off the result of their interest (they'd sunk five hundred pounds into the plant). He arrived in an army surplus Blitz towing a pink plywood caravan.

And sitting up in that great, lumpy, left-wheel drive cab, on the right-hand side so that she seemed to be the driver, with Buckler only an appendage to the rig-out, was Mrs Veronica Buckler with a silk organza scarf tied over her yellow straw hat, tufted, sparrow-brown hair poking out in a cheerful way.

Introductions were made. She said, 'You're a bit unexpected, Randolph . . .'

It would be the jaw, because people always made oblique references to its oblique preponderance.

Well, so was she unexpected – bearing no resemblance to any brilliant artist type Randolph had ever imagined. She was a small woman in Land Army overalls with a perky smile and bright red lipstick. Maybe she talked too much, that was all, delivering her observations in an interested tone of voice without noticing that nobody had asked an opinion.

'Beauty is sooh dependent on an argument with perfection,' was one of her maxims. It made Randolph tug his chin in thought.

They crossed to the verandah for tea. Randolph took charge organising the whiskies and teapot and biscuits, leaving his mother to the business of getting on with Veronica. Edwina Knox was a handsome, forthright woman who knew all about art through taking adult education summer schools in Albury once Tim was old enough to be left. Veronica, in a thin piping voice, disputed art education at the popular level, saying it could never touch what painters suffered alone and condensed into visions. Edwina persisted, saying that knowledgeable people were always talking about Veronica as up there with the very best, and she would like to pick through her studio and bring her chequebook with her. Veronica clapped her hands and said she was won. While the men talked about minerals, the women walked around the garden arm in arm.

After the Bucklers left, Edwina told Randolph about the arrangements in Veronica's life, compromises based on failure and need, on convenience, submission, confusion or whatever. That Buckler was under Mrs B's thumb was deemed evident.

An amusing letter came from Veronica describing their travels. She'd set up a sun umbrella on a salt lake, on a rocky ridge, or on a sand dune, and paint; and when she wanted Buckler for some chore or other she fired a shotgun. Buckler would come in from wherever he was poking around with sample jars and testing kits and do what she wanted.

The war over, Japan occupied, the Far East travelled and known, the half-century year was almost upon them but Colts still hadn't yet come home.

After Japan he'd travelled some more – sailed in a ketch with two Canadians from Hong Kong to British Columbia, worked as a machinery rep in Canada and then as a truck salesman in America, shore sheep on a blizzardy mountainside in Wyoming, travelled to Mexico and arrived back via New Zealand. He was still only twenty-three years old at the end of 1949 and in the new year, to Randolph's satisfaction, took up the offer of working as the Knoxes' Homegrove stud agent.

The day Colts arrived at Isabel Junction on the all-stations Randolph couldn't sit still. He was the first one there, pacing the platform in the hot, empty afternoon. At last there was a distant whistle, the altered sound of wheels crossing the river bridge, and Randolph saw Colts leaning from the dogbox carriage and waving his hat from two hundred yards off. It was going to be all right, then, the mocking smile of the kid was still there, the old Eureka easiness was still in reach for both of them, thank God, as they shook hands, pulled off each other's hat, and crossed the road to the Five Alls Hotel to sink a schooner.

It was sales day and the bar crowded. Colts returned the shout and they got stuck into it, elbow to elbow. Standing close and summarising a good few years of work routines in the empty hills, Randolph heard a constant wheeze like a small bellows operating in Colts's one lung.

Two hard-living men set up in an old weatherboard house in a cluster of dwellings known as Woodbox Gully. Work was one thing, sport the other. Randolph Knox (capt.) and Kingsley Colts (vice-capt.) led the Isabel XI into a clean sweep of the regional cricket championships and went through into the NSW country finals.

The top end of sheep work was show preparation and rebuilding the stud along lines fought decision by decision in favour of Randolph. The routine end was crutching, paring feet against footrot, dipping, fencing, gate mending and rabbit and dingo control. The Anglican church held fundraising drives on Homegrove where parishioners beat rabbits to death against netted fence lines. Randolph fumed about the timbered country being a breeding ground for dingoes, and so Colts paid his keep by dogging, going around with traps and getting five pounds per scalp. After a year he began visiting distant parts of the state driving a utility truck and finding new clients for Randolph's rams advertised as Homegrove All-Purpose Doers. He made friends and began socialising away from Randolph's patch. His innovation was to carry two rams, San Pedro and Immaculate, in a crate in the back of the ute in order to show them off better than any catalogue description or photograph. When talking about themselves Colts and Randolph said they were old Eureka hands. That seemed to take care of many attributes they lacked in common.

Edwina Knox was a devoted horsewoman. With her band of alikes – men and women all long-faced as horses and wearing worn jodhpurs and old tweed jackets – Colts took rides into the untouched bush of the coastal ranges, which Randolph disparaged for its tangled uselessness. Tim Knox from a young age rode along, a boy senseless with adventure. It reminded Colts of his own young dream. It was how Colts became attached to the Isabel as wilderness and could name every bird, small marsupial, goanna and snake, and show Randolph creatures he didn't know existed that had lived under his nose the whole of his life, in logs or in hollows of trees. They passed up under the shadow of a cliff of rusty rocks, organ-pipe gullies and flatiron slabs said to be unclimbable, reaching three hundred feet in under the brow of Mt Knox. The great pile had never had a name, at least that any white man knew. Now they called it the Isabel Walls.

Incredible how time ran like water into the years towards thirty. Randolph watched rugby as Colts, grown rangy and headstrong, proved himself a player heedless of injury, managing on his one lung, always pushing himself, turning out for district games each winter. Sometimes Randolph spent weekends skiing with friends. Those friends wheeled down from Bowral and collected him in their Triumphs and MGs. They were never part of Randolph's world on the Isabel, for just as Randolph kept bloodlines distinct in fenced paddocks he kept his friends apart. 'There's goats and kings,' he said, leaving Colts with the feeling that he was in the former category, and that Randolph's friendship, so apparently unlimited in the way Randolph prickled with need, had limits.

The Knoxes affected a feudal relationship with Isabel Junction, calling the town the village to their Sydney friends when they entertained in their Point Piper flat or at Homegrove in house parties. As Randolph refined his life away from the stud into a social set Colts's friendships became locally rougher.

Colts enthused to Randolph about his Saturday afternoons on the Isabel blinding with cold, yellowed poplar leaves in the frozen mud of the playing fields, long blue shadows across the dirt roads on the drives home. It was when he got lucky with a 'local doer', as he called her, taking a hot bath at the Five Alls Hotel after a bruising, artless game. She was Sandra Turnley, the publican's daughter, who came in, locked the door and scrubbed his back in what he winked was a Japanese pleasure. It was how Colts became a Saturday night boarder in the Five Alls, his 'bolthole', taking Room 17 upstairs, the one with the fireplace in the corner and the narrow iron bed where Sandra Turnley snugged in.

After Rotary on Wednesday nights a group of returned men left Randolph feeling sidelined from the only Isabel Junction activity, apart from Anglican worship, that he regularly joined. When the meetings were over he shouted a round and headed home. His midweek drinking was done alone, under a gum tree, under the stars in the teeth of a gale as wind came over the Dividing Range like an endless, flapping, flaying bloody belt.

One day Randolph decided to say something heartfelt to Colts or explode with constraint. It might be asked: what was in Randolph that he needed to fix what was working, and giving him enough, little as it was?

After a typical silence at the smoko table, Randolph cleared his throat and remarked that he'd been ungenerous in not acknowledging how Colts, in his small boat experience, would have operated behind enemy lines in '44, not just that one time when he copped the bullet, but all through the twelve months of his New Guinea war service.

Ordinary enough to say, but did Randolph have to put his hand on Colts's wrist as he said it, taking courage to single out courage? For moments after he should have let go, he held on. It seemed to Colts that he suffocated from the arm up, small hairs prickling.

'Well?'

Colts responded that in jungle warfare nobody knew where enemy frontlines were, you moved through them constantly.

And from then on, simple as that, the friendship disappeared almost completely from their lives. Though as before, when something important broke through, neither of them could ever quite bring themselves to acknowledge its loss. More simply, Colts wondered what it was that had truly begun. Only from time to time did he find out. It was a few years before they had another conversation going further than a greeting. People watched them avoiding each other when they passed up and down the main street.

SEVEN

WHEN EDDIE SLIM WAS A BOY in the 1950s his father, Jack, recited a poem about a soldier who swam a frozen river to save his trapped platoon. It was printed in an anthology of the Left Book Club and translated from Russian, an episode in the Red Army's war against the Germans on the frozen steppes.

Jack Slim knew 'The Crossing' by heart. Their family friend, Uncle Abe, recited it in the original. To Eddie, the Red Army's exploits on The Steppes were more real than anything Jack had been involved in in the Red Centre, Top End and Kimberleys during the war. The setting was far from Australia, which as a battleground didn't count, yet to a kid in the haze of childhood stories, living on the saltbush plains and seeing corrugated iron water tanks as castles and knowing dark mulga scrub as a backdrop for imagination, there lingered a wish, and it seemed a good question.

'Was he Australian?'

'Was he what?' laughed Jack. 'Struth, little mate, screw your brains in, his name was Vasily Tyorkin. Does that sound dinkum?'

'Vaseline Tworkin . . .'

'Give it another try.'

'Is he still alive?'

'Like a colossus.'

Eddie crossed Vasily with Jack's commanding officer, Major Dunc Buckler, MC, whose mythical age of exploits was in the First War, while his Second was a joke with Jack, his offsider, getting the best digs in.

When Eddie was a bit older and understood things better it was no ordinary soldier but Uncle Joe Stalin in the poem, the swimmer who stepped ashore – big waxed moustache, grandfatherly eye, gigantic overcoat held ready to wrap around him, dripping with amazing icicles.

'Say it again,' said Eddie, pulling the quilt up to his chin and feeling blankets go tight as Jack sat on the bed and recited lines bringing the figure up and out from under the ice, staggering to the shore cramped, paralysed, frozen but grabbed and wrapped in a Russian overcoat down to his boots and given a big shake and then sent on his way to run like hell.

In 1953 the Slims moved one-teacher-schools five hundred miles east from Pooncarie to the Isabel River district under the Great Dividing Range. The Chev Fleetmaster was loaded for the move with pots and pans, laundry baskets, books and a stretcher mattress laid over the filled-up back seat where Eddie spent the trip in comfort, dipping into a paper bag of boiled lollies and licorice allsorts. He was a teenager now, fourteen, his world expanding just as he needed it, into mountain gullies and clear-flowing creeks.

It was a cool April night after brief rain when moths changed from grubs and crawled through cracks in the walls and burned in the tall glass chimney of the pressure lamp. The moon had a closer feel on the Isabel, sailing through tatters of upland cloud that might even have rain in them. Everything there had a stronger feel to it, better.

'Where've you been till you got this plum little perch?' said a young schools' inspector in those first months.

'Chewing sand in the desert, sonny, so you could get promoted,' said Jack.

He was his own worst enemy, a stubborn card-carrying commo but undeniably brilliant in the classroom, an inspiration to poor kids with no example at home. As author of rallying calls circulated by the Teachers' Federation he was hated by the Director General in Sydney, who kept him in the bush.

'Oh, being on the Isabel isn't bad,' agreed Jack, when Eddie was stirred by the place, saying he'd never leave it.

Tonight singed moths gave a charred, nutty aroma to the air and fell to their backs for an interval of sharp electric buzzing. Eddie scooped them up and busied himself with a magnifying glass while Jack looked on from the end of a table of rough-sawn pine he'd built in self-critical inspiration one weekend, and left unpainted.

'A good one, Ed?'

'Y'oughter see it!'

There followed a quick execution in a glass vial on a cotton pad of pure alcohol. Jack leaned close as Pamela looked over his shoulder and made encouraging noises while the legs of a scarab beetle struggled and went still.

Pamela avoided colliding with Jack in the small room. There was a charged space between them. All their attention fell on their son. Eddie liked the way they depended on him, when they fought, as the one subject they agreed on.

But they gave the feeling it would kill them if Eddie failed at whatever it was he was meant to do. This month Ed would be an entomologist, it seemed, next month – a geologist? He was at the moment when all was won or lost, according to Jack's wisdom. Now his rock collection was building outside, blocking the laundry sump, and his geology hammer with inlaid bands of leather was wrapped in tissue paper at the back of a cupboard, ready as a Christmas surprise. Trust it wouldn't end on a hillside somewhere, neglected and freckled with rust.

After the evening meal came the national news read by John Chance, heard with an attentive hush. Eddie lay on the floor with his ankles crossed, stretching closer, filtering static from heavy words and watching the green silk covering of the loud-speaker box vibrate.

Jack liked imitating the announcer's plum but not tonight; he raised a hand to bring on concentration. Valves glowed amber, batteries leaked power from a crusty set of wires; Stalin was dead; the name of his successor, Malenkov, came stumbling into the room as if the name of a self-server could enter where it pleased.

'Will it be all right?' said Eddie, angling a bony shoulder. He felt a panicky concern. The feeling was that America might take the opportunity to start a war against a weakened Soviet leadership.

'I'd say so,' said Jack. 'It'd better well bloody well ought to be bloody all right.'

The way Jack talked gave Stalin the power to rise from the slab, putting a stop to rot. Eddie had always lived in the shelter of that idea, but now the great man was stone-cold dead confirmed and world leaders were making their way to Moscow.

'They'll all be there,' said Jack with a narrow smile, 'singing "The Internationale" and looking for the chance to slip the knife.' He threw back his head as if he, Jack Slim, Australian country schoolmaster, was absent from the centre of world events by a mere oversight and the mourning Soviets, handicapped, would have to march their revolution on from the command end without him.

'Are they dreaming?' recited Eddie. 'Are they outta their minds, "is it hoarfrost on their lashes, are they seein' things, is there really something there?"'

'No, they're not seeing things,' answered Jack. 'A little *dot* has appeared to them far, far away.'

Eddie grinned. '*He's* the one to send for.'

'Send for old Vaseline Tworkin!' said Jack, parting the air with the Red salute. It was time for the State news, then, a tally of level-crossing accidents involving stalled cars dragged along railway lines by steam engines screaming with brakes locked. Then came the district forecasts and river heights. Afterwards Pamela moved to the bug-littered table with her sewing box and Jack swept the surface with his forearm, the gesture of a courtier making way for a queen.

Pamela opened her sewing box with a sharp snap. There was a reason for their fights but Eddie wasn't going to know it if she could help it. Kingsley Colts, who found, cut, delivered and stacked firewood for school and residence, was paying attention to her, awakening a liking betrayed by a blush.

'What's wrong with being helpful? You make it sound like a crime,' she said.

Pamela was making clothes for a needy family, the Maguires, a pair of khaki overalls with sharp, finger-cutting copper buttons. They were the same buttons she used on Eddie's trousers and shirts, and he hated the way they wouldn't ever properly fit and needed shoving in. Moving the lamp to one side Pamela leaned into a ring of light, sewing with quick strikes of the needle and snapping thread in her teeth. She had straight black hair cut short, shining dark eyes and a luminous pale forehead. Locals nicknamed her The Crow to disparage her disquieting beauty, which only *looked* fragile, as she went around relentlessly doing good among the most broken, hopeless and shocking cases. The little girl Maguire, when she came to school, had the mark of destitution and borderline starvation, threadbare outgrown clothing and nothing warm for winter. Jack sent her over to the house and Pamela darned her blouses. Rather than flatter more comfortable people with her friendship Pamela preferred driving down rutted tracks visiting these Maguires living in rags and scavenging at the dump. Then she would sit smoking and drinking tea with Colts, who appeared to have nothing better to do than drop by while Jack peered out the schoolroom window.

When Jack put his arm around her and kissed her on the back of the neck, she held still, then made a movement pushing him off.

'Jack, for heaven's sake.'

Jack went to the other end of the house and came back wearing his Harris tweed sportscoat, knotting a hairy tartan tie for his Parents and Citizens meeting at eight. He pinned on his Returned Soldiers' League membership badge, and altogether it was what he described as his camouflage for getting by in the world he was born into – foiling accusations of disloyalty among the small-minded and guarding his innermost convictions. At cricket Jack came number two in the batting order after Randolph Knox and put more into district events than the local MP because there was nobody finer in public spirit, more principled or devoted than Jack Slim. Everyone knew it and some even said it – this while the Director General withheld the city school he craved, the tougher the better in a working-class suburb.

'Time's up,' Jack said as headlights raked the windows and the firstcomer arrived to spread the supper table in the schoolroom adjoining the house. 'Mrs Dalrymple is here. The others won't be long. Got your tag written, Ed?' he said over the boy's shoulder.

'Almost.'

Later Eddie would pin the bug to a card, or maybe not. It

would certainly be Jack who wrote the Latin inscription, tired and watery-eyed after battling those who came to his meeting nights in confusion. Such fearful pioneers, he called them, and yet there was always one or a pair who made nights worthwhile. They were not always a couple – just the last time had been – one a man of the soil with strong ideas, the other a woman of passion who was invariably Pamela's threat. Jack drew them out from whatever circumstance he happened to find himself in. More often than not they were insensibly left wing or Douglas Credit loonies, and he ran an impromptu Adult Education class for them. When he returned from his meeting later he might or might not be tipsy, having shared a flask with his closest confrères. He might or might not have lipstick on his mouth, a hurled clench from his lady crush. 'I weaved and wove but Mrs Dalrymple got me, I couldn't duck it,' Jack might say. And Pamela, a little haughty, would almost certainly reply, 'Jacko, how am I expected to feel?' while Jack would respond with a standard materialist thrust: 'Feelings don't come into it, darling. Not of the finer sort when instincts raise their heads, ha ha.'

Eddie put a box of matches and a torch in his haversack.

'Going out?'

'Down to Bonney's.'

'Take the star map,' said Jack.

Eddie went to the drawer and fetched the folded chart of the heavens.

Pamela went to the pantry and found him an apple – 'I don't expect you've cleaned your teeth.' She kissed the top of his head, tugged his hair, twisted his ear and gave him a hug.

'Back by ten.'

'Let go of me, comrade,' squirmed Eddie. 'Won'tcha for once?'

She loved that little tussle leaving her helpless with longing.

*

Closing the screen door behind him, Eddie crossed through the side gate and into the schoolyard past the flagpole where the school's loyalty pledge was made; past the rainwater tank shining dull silver and heavy to the knock of knuckles; past the shelter shed of cream-painted tin where farm kids took their cold mutton chops and chunks of farm bread, their boiled eggs wrapped in newspaper and their salt and pepper in twists of greaseproof paper. The schoolyard felt alive to Eddie in the dark as he circled the big gum tree where he and Claude Bonney took their correspondence lessons and smoked cigarettes in school time. There was a low ding from the school bell as an insect struck – sometimes grasshoppers went loony in the dark or maybe it was a shell-backed beetle, hard as a pebble as it thrashed through the night towards the classroom windows where Mrs Dalrymple positioned the Tilley lamps. Eddie slipped closer and stood on a bench to see what the supper promised. Leftovers would be handed to Jack as of right and a portion brought home. The rest would provide school treats shared in the classroom until the last crumb was denied the hungriest mouse.

Mrs Dalrymple stood looking at her reflection in the window-pane, giving the neckline of her flowered dress a pluck and turning sideways to lift the back of her hair while moths pattered the glass. She was a sweet-smiling, plump-shouldered, soothing woman with blonde curls and blue eyes. She had large breasts (a 'big front', Jack called it) and wide hips but small wrists and fine hands, which she protected with leather gloves when driving and riding. Her husband, Oliver, was a thin, dark-browed farmer, an insistent bundle of nerves who consulted Jack with a sheaf of drawings about perpetual motion machines. Their son, Gilbert, freckled as a frog, skinny as a bean, was mad about aeroplanes and ran about the playground with his arms out stiff. Mrs Dalrymple, thrilled to escape such rattling inspirations for at least one night per month, had brought a plate of triangle-cut sandwiches and a tray of pikelets with jam and cream that were placed on the teacher's desk at the front of the room. Quickly, before anyone came, she took a pikelet from the plate and slipped it down like an oyster, wiped cream from the corners of her smile with the tip of a finger while still watching herself. Jack always said Mrs Dalrymple's bum was broad as a battleship – 'I like a good bum,' he said when Pamela raised an eyebrow. 'More bounce,' he winked at Eddie, 'per ounce.'

Eddie dropped from sight when Jack's footsteps sounded on the school verandah boards. Then he was out into the yard and into the open night, head tipped back and mouth open wide sucking oxygen. He ran along the ridge track with a pile of dark rocks outlined at the edges. 'Oh, the crossing! Oh, the crossing!'

When they first came there from Out West, the car so loaded with belongings it scraped gravel dips and threw sparks all the way, Eddie had run through dry grass up this hill, climbed in among these boulders and scrambled higher with the feeling of thistledown rising into the sky. A rock chimney made easy climbing. At the top wildflower seedlings grew.

There Eddie loved at first sight and forever the way the schoolhouse ridge dropped away to a sparkling creek, and how when he sped the full mile to the bottom there was the promise of getting back to the sky where the house parted the wind. The Dalrymple boy launched a glider, balsawood struts papered with tissue. It curved around, coming back into Eddie's outstretched arms because he got there first. At night from his bedroom window he saw the headlamp of a train and watched it streaming across the plateau, the carriages lit from within as if by Chinese lanterns. The red glow of the firebox flared ahead and the shriek of the whistle floated back and there was nothing, nowhere, no time on earth imaginable to Eddie that defined happiness and full contentment so completely as then. He would steal, murder and destroy to keep this feeling whole: and his only mistake was in thinking he was right in that, and deserved it.

While they were still Out West chewing sand and got the news of the transfer, Jack had talked of the drives they would take when they got to the Isabel. It was months before they'd made one. Maps showed the coast only fifty miles away but to get there and cast a line meant descending a maze of hairpin bends and driving back up to the cold country well after midnight. What Eddie liked on that drive was not the South Coast itself so much as the Isabel River going down. It had shallow stones of blue and rust, and high, steep sides, forest-edged cliffs with exposed tree roots dangling and goannas clinging to tree trunks with ribbons of bark stretching to ground level from big, white branches. This was the Isabel after it broke from the high plateau through a cleft in the ranges and came over waterfalls and through orange rock gorges sheltered by tree ferns. They stopped the car and Eddie threw stones at reptiles while Jack kept score, promising a penny per strike. When Eddie reached up to feel a sandpapery tail a goanna swayed out of reach, waddling vertically in defiance of gravity, angling its wrinkled neck and looking down at the boy from dragon eyes.

What Eddie wanted was to go back down there and walk along the riverbed, camping on sandy bends, and Jack promised they would. 'We can go anywhere we like, do anything we want, because we have only one bite of the pineapple, compadre, and if anyone tells us otherwise they can pull their heads in.'

Down at the coast they'd visited the man Jack said he liked telling to pull his head in most, Major Buckler.

'My fascist mate,' he called him, with puzzling affection for one so bent. Buckler lived in a small, pink, plywood caravan at the back of the house where his wife Veronica lived. 'She keeps him on a leash,' said Jack. 'Poor, sorry old bugger he strayed but she reeled him back in.'

Guarding Buckler's van, equipment, tools, generator set, water tanks and five-ton Bedford truck was the ugliest most ill-formed dog Eddie had ever seen. Patches of hair worn from its rump left bare, scabby skin. The Grabber was the name of the pooch. He was bred by a buffalo shooter, Hammond Pringle, said Buckler, whose Arnhem Land camp was described by no less an author than Ion L. Idriess and whose father was Buckler's First War mate, Birdy Pringle, made famous by broadcast interviews on the ABC, recorded on wire recording machines in the paperbark swamps.

A croc was the only known enemy of such a cur as The Grabber. It would scale a croc's tongue, said Buckler, run down its throat barking at tonsils swinging like the bells of St Mary's. Solid from a diet of stewing beef and stale bread soaked in milk, The Grabber's diamond-shaped head appeared to Eddie like part of its neck. The Grabber had a mean, sour, dusty smell and walked gingerly, as if stung. When he lay his head on Eddie's knee and his scalded eyes drooped, Eddie loved him.

The Slims went inside for afternoon tea but Buckler didn't join them. Through the screened kitchen door they could see him standing in the yard, smoking his pipe. Eddie was sent out with a mug of sweet black tea and a slice of fruit cake. Inside, Jack exchanged a few pleasantries with Veronica and then as soon as he could took his mug out the back, where Buckler filled it with rum.

The house had the clean, thick smell of oil paints and later, excited and putting their heads together about what money they had, Jack and Pamela made a choice from among a few small pictures. They reverenced the artistic vocation and would go without much to buy an oil painting by a name such as Veronica's was now becoming among select connoisseurs (or any old linocut by a CPA member).

A brackish arm of the Isabel River came up to a white beach at the foot of the garden forming a placid, tea-tree-stained backwater. Before dark Eddie swam there with The Grabber patrolling his elbow until moonrise hinted it was time to go.

Cars were bringing lastcomers to Jack's meeting. Headlights flickered and flashed closer. Where the road dropped, Eddie started running and tried to beat past them. At each cornerpost of paddock he paused and listened to the thump of his heartbeat and the chorus of frogs. When he reached the railway line the car lights were closer but sank from view in a ripple of dark. Eddie climbed through a barbed-wire fence, scrambled the embankment and made a right-angled turn, walking along the line to get to Bonney's. The headlights re-emerged and the glint of their lamps swept along the rails; Eddie slowed to a rolling gait on the raised railbed and saw the curving tracks illuminate towards him. At the last moment, as the cars came trundling past, he lay down to break his silhouette in case Jack was told. Then the cars went grinding up the ridge towards the school and he stood and kept walking.

Frogs. Crickets. Water. The railway trestle spanned clear reedlined pools. In the hot, dry summer Jack walked Eddie down there after school, reached in among the stones demanding quiet and tickled a trout. The two of them went climbing the hill with fish in a wet sack while Jack told his stories of being on the wallaby when he was Eddie's age, living off the beauty of the land and suffering people's hard charity, tramping from place to place eating rabbit stew and making johnnycakes and staying ahead of the wallopers. That was when Jack saw places he'd never dreamed he would see, taking him to the heights; when he'd had experiences no boy should ever have, plunging him to the depths;

when he got the idea that hunger and hardship, as he liked to say, had something to do with the country's wealth, and he joined the Unemployed Workers' Movement in Bourke, and was caught on the riverbank by vigilantes and sent packing. From conversations of the kind, Eddie developed not so much similar sympathies as a desire to grab experience by the throat and not miss anything to be had. This came out as mean greed in childhood play. At best, it came with a sense of limitless ambition, which Jack and Pamela liked hearing about, except they wondered: what sort of dreamer was he, with an account book for a heart, always wanting, but with a motive of resentment?

As Eddie worked his rhythm of stepping along the sleepers a song filled his head, saxophone wails, ripples of jazz and blues. His mind rang with the gramophone records Jack played on card nights – Leadbelly, Bessie Smith and the slave songs, the railway songs performed by venerable Negroes while Jack silenced the room with upraised fingers holding a cigarette between them and jerked his hand in time, conducting. The music was grooved in Eddie's memory but not to his liking: Jack shamed him, and to fight that shame, Eddie would shame Jack.

The shape of a low hill loomed ahead. From the angle Eddie looked it seemed the line buried itself, but then the hill broke open to reveal the high-sided railway cutting, leading through. Closer to the river bridge he put his ear to the rails, heard nothing but cold silence and knew it was safe to cross. Almost his favourite action, he'd found, was going across that railway bridge, slapping his hands from girder to girder. The river shone black with flecks of white current around rocks. Water, water in a dry year coming down from hills dense with timber, wrapped in mist, the home of black cockatoos and powdery snowfalls in winter. Eddie could never get over the enchantment of cold, clean water, and every creek he found he wanted to get up higher and find the rock where the first spring began and where the mud it oozed from led. Against the bank of a stream he imagined pitching his camp, pegging a claim and digging for gold. He would bathe in gold like Scrooge McDuck if he could.

The gatekeeper's house was on the other side of the bridge guarding the level crossing. It was where Claude Bonney slept on a verandah on a lumpy kapok mattress. When the night mail came through Claude blinked an eye, raised himself on an elbow and watched his father, Phil, walk to the old white gates and shoulder them closed. There was never any road traffic at that hour, and rarely at any other time either, and Bonney could be sure his father would stand to his post reliably. Yet he still watched over him. That was Claude.

Eddie gave out a whistle, scooped a handful of track-ballast and heard it rattling the verandah boards like nails. He shone the torch down the bank and saw his friend sit up.

'Claude, they've done for Uncle Joe!'

They sat on the embankment feeling in their empty pockets for tobacco.

'I heard,' said Claude.

'There's a handover,' said Eddie. 'A leader is just the voice of the masses, one's as good as another, but what's his name again?'

'Malenkov. Goodbye, Big Moustache. It's like the attention of a finger has wandered,' said Claude, 'and no-one's left to point.'

Claude Bonney was a big-headed, brainy boy with a thick-nosed look of inquiry and large hands that were always ready to fix Eddie's bike when it threw a chain and quick to mend a puncture. When Eddie sat under the schoolyard tree struggling with his algebra those same hands took up a pencil, reached across and corrected his mistakes. Jack, checking Eddie's work before it was posted off to the Correspondence High School, saw what happened but said little. It was another teacher's concern to bring his boy to the start line now. The Anglican vicar, Vince Powell, a former chemistry teacher, coached Claude and Eddie's science ahead of their grade. Next year Isabel Primary would be upped to an Intermediate High and Eddie wanted to stay on and go there and be with Claude.

Eddie had always fudged, to Jack and Pamela's despair, while Claude Bonney was one of their shiners. Maybe Eddie would learn from him. Maybe they should leave him to muddle through, if a transfer came about. They read Claude's class compositions and tried to explain to each other where his ideas came from. Of course there was always a shiner in the small schools they taught. The joy was in finding them, seeing it in the eyes of a dim farmer's kid, or in one of those people of the camp who Pamela looked to for the purity of giving. Eddie had the notion once that he was a shiner himself because Jack and Pamela had said so from hope and love. Not anymore as Eddie struggled over the most ordinary right word to convey an obvious thought, often just recited what Vince Powell taught him, and Claude Bonney's brain leapt about like a dog at the end of its chain.

'I'm desperate for a fag,' said Eddie. 'Where do we scrounge from?'

Claude knew all the places and uncurled a fist, showing a silver key. Eddie made out the embossed legend NSWGR and the indelible ink inscription on the leather tag, the words Railway Refreshment Room, Isabel Junction, No. 2.

'Property is theft,' said Claude.

'Where'd you hear that one?'

'Your old man.'

Starlight ran along the length of the key as Claude's fingers closed over it. He made a downward palming gesture, sliding it into his pocket. 'Give me the torch,' he said. Claude's every action had the feeling of mocking Eddie's unequalness to responsibility, even for a crime.

It was like that with Eddie's friends, parents, anyone. He gave Claude the torch. Lately Claude had returned the friendship favour with Normie Powell, the vicar's nine-year-old, a junior naturalist statewide schools' prizewinner. Eddie scorned the bug collecting and birds' egg blowing as baby minding. But he wanted advantage and went for the same pursuits jealously, with no feeling, only show.

Eddie and Claude walked along the side of the embankment towards the rail yards. Here engines uncoupled and shunted rolling stock with thundering crashes over a tangle of points. Two lines met and the Refreshment Room opened when trains came through. It was when Isabel Junction came alive and busied itself with an importance it had never known since goldrush days when sixty thousand miners lived under canvas and Chinese scroungers built water races that followed the hill contours for miles. There were still gold washings in the creeks and word of nuggets to be found in the hills by kicking a rock and finding it turned over with a gleam. There was hardly ever a rock anywhere that Eddie didn't kick.

Stock trains with their open-grilled sides were backed up to loading yards, and the stink of sheep and hot wool hung over the town. Sheep complained and bleated, at night cattle loaded for early departure bellowed. Even as far away as the schoolhouse Pamela heard them and, backed by Reverend Powell, went to see Careful Bob Hooke and made a complaint about the conditions they were kept in. Careful Bob asked Kingsley Colts to take action to see they were better watered, which he did.

Then there were the daily passenger trains. People in city clothes climbed out of carriages and stretched, looked around, took off their hats and mopped their foreheads, admiring the setting of poplars and lucerne paddocks on the banks of the Isabel River. Men strode across to the pub, 'the Five', and guzzled schooners as fast as they could before the whistle blew, when they grabbed lemonades and shandies for their womenfolk, who drained them and passed the glasses to Sandra Turnley, who came along the carriages shrieking for them and stacking them in tens, fifteens and twenties till they curved backwards behind her head like willow-wands. Other passengers walked the full length of the platform and down along the tracks towards the river where they stared under the bridge at the spirals of water flooding past. When everyone was gathered up and gone, the back of the train shrinking away, the knock of wheels faded mournfully. The dog at Demellick's store howled and Turnley the publican at the Five Alls bolted the doors with a loud clang and the Junction became neglected again, wind tossing the poplars and scattering leaves on the wide dirt road. Mrs Fripp, who managed the Refreshment Room, washed the teacups, wiped down the benches, inverted the urn, closed the cupboards and hung dust covers over the cigarette and lolly displays. She locked the double doors and went home.

Mrs Fripp kept the key, but there was a spare key and Claude hunted it down. It was hung with other duplicates on a rack in the mail van that came daily to a siding at the back of the station. That van had arrived and would leave in the morning. Time enough for Claude to slip it back.

The two boys in the shadows were almost there when Eddie heard the sound of metal on the ballast and looked down and saw the key lying at his feet. He waited for Claude to pick it up, but Claude stood waiting. Eddie would never be good enough to do wrong the way Claude did, as if it was the better side of good. When he picked up the key, the warm metal almost jumped into his hand.

All-night lamps burned in the junction box. The station cat ran along the platform. They followed the cat's shadow under the platform roof with its cast-iron verandah posts newly painted and crusted with a surfacing of soot. At the Refreshment Room doors Claude stood aside as Eddie fitted the key into the lock. The way the key turned felt loose, scuffed and worn over the years, and the door so easily opened that Eddie thought, as if answering an interrogation, *Well, that door opened all by itself, what was a bloke to do?*

Claude held his fingers over the torch bulb and switched it on. In the dim red light made by Claude's blood, Eddie detached the dust covers from their hooks. Behind the counter were displays of tobacco and cigarettes. 'You get those,' said Claude. 'Here's my order – Champion Flake, Dutch Pipe Mixture, Craven A's, Windsors. Take two of each. Cover the gaps. Get moving, light your farts.' So Eddie squeezed under the counter and filled his haversack. As he adjusted the tobacco displays, closing gaps, he heard a grunt behind him and there was Claude standing on the counter, reaching up onto a high shelf where chocolate boxes made a sequence of pyramids: Cadbury's Roses with MacRobertson's Milk Trays and packets of Fantales and Jaffas, which Claude held to his ear and rattled before making a choice.

They replaced the dust covers, took a last look around, listened to the silence of the outside and backed out the door to the platform. Claude turned the lock and led the way to the forward end of the station. They crossed the rails and walked around behind the junction box to the mail van on the side rail. Claude reached up and tried a curled brass doorhandle. The door creaked open and the sound of snoring came from inside. The boys looked at each other while Claude leaned against the door to close it again. Somebody was in there, long legs in a tangle of army blankets.

'It's Colts,' said Claude.

EIGHT

EARLY SATURDAY MORNING EDDIE Slim and Claude Bonney took their bikes and set off on a marathon of getting away. It was a week-end's ride there and back, where they wanted to go, on a dirt track with only the sometimes-glimpsed railway line for company.

They carried blankets in bundles roped over the bars, billy-cans tied to the frames. A bag of chops turned blue, they cooked them and tipped them into the fire. Bonney said, 'Leave it,' and the last sight they saw was a fringe of flame burning itself along a bare slope of withered weeds and dry thistles.

Up ahead a man ran the bare road getting closer. They saw him sink into gullies and reappear. Nobody ever ran through that empty landscape except one person – hardly anyone else was ever seen – and they tipped their bikes to the side of the road. From under the hill his noise ripped the air, breath taken through a narrow throat pipe into a bung lung. When he saw them he stopped, stood with his legs apart, head back, gulping. A Jacky Howe singlet dangled loosely from his shoulders and ribs, chest hairs showing. The boys smoked, watching him.

'Colts,' they said, in a tone implying he'd worked out another way to annoy them.

'Water,' he commanded, like a grinning skull. Bonney passed the canteen. When Colts finished drinking he thanked them. Eddie's eyes never quite met his. There was the shame of something like relationship. Sometimes Colts came on card nights and other times rang from towns miles away saying he couldn't make it, and Eddie watched his mother's face as his father related the word. Once Colts was even as far off as Bourke on commission from Careful Bob and he rang. When he travelled as train drover he slept in guards' vans and mail van bunks. Pamela said, 'That would be the life,' and Jack said, 'Dream.'

Everything in Colts's life was to do with sheep and he knew the lot. It made Jack smile. Eddie and Claude weren't rural like that. Colts eyed them over – they were smart-arsed boys in the country and Eddie a sly little shit.

'How's your woolly ones?' they said.

Colts said Australians had it easy, Icelandic sheepfarmers slept in ice caves, lying on beds of stone, and if they started freezing they rose and hefted fifty pound rocks in circles until they were warm enough to go back to sleep. Colts said running was what he did, how he did the hours he kept – driving, sleeping at the side of the road, driving on. 'You carry that stone with you.' He stared them out.

They watched Colts pounding back to his ute parked at a distant post. Bonney timed him at four minutes fifty-five the estimated mile. With one lung that took beating.

That night they slept in a travelling stock reserve guarded by mopokes hooting over starry distances. They were hungry and talked about the Lone Gum, a long-distance lorry drivers' garage known for mixed grills – platters of steak, chops, sausages, lamb's fry and grilled kidneys, and bacon thick as planks. It was another few hours' ride and they wanted their hands around hamburger buns, stuffing in strings of lettuce and beetroot dripping egg yolk; their teeth meeting the charred crunchy meat of the specialty rissoles cooked in a side kitchen by a kindly railwayman's wife, Mrs Carmichael. Claude declared he would have a chocolate eclair to finish up, and Eddie said, 'You've taken the words right out of my mouth, compadre.'

From the other side of a hill next morning as they were packing their camp, rolling their blankets back on the handlebars and dangling their billies, Eddie lifted his head and asked, 'Who's that singing?'

Claude angled an ear and was just beginning to catch it when they heard a low crump like a washing-day burst of wind. Cockatoos flapped past, shrieking, heat waves spiralled above the skylined trees.

'Somebody's copped it,' said Claude.

Fast-pedalling over a rise they saw the blue Holden burning before the fire had even turned black; the three sailors trapped inside with flame licking their bare heads.

They dropped their bikes, yelling who knew what, running with arms angled over their foreheads into the heat barrier. People were in that car rammed against the chrome bars of the seat backs. They were still alive. They were trapped. A part exploded. Smoke boomed, puffed, spread, blocked them. Claude turned his back and swore in a torrent of oaths while heat hammered his neck. Eddie covered his streaming eyes with his hands. The end of life would come as a curse, but expressed as a whim – a scatter of gravel, locked brakes. You could lie and cheat your way round everything but that.

When the smoke cleared the wreck was burnt clean, except for hummocks or hillocks of men with stripes of naval piping laid across the seat backs, still visible. It seemed they were hiding, that was all, ashamed and they needed some sort of encouragement to get up. Who could give it to them though? Swim the river, make the crossing . . . who?

This was only a second's glance but would last a lifetime.

Having dared look, the boys stepped forward to look as far as courage allowed into the blank horror. Nothing more stirred in the hot frame of the car, where stench of which description must be spared radiated on the attack. Claude turned away to be sick while Eddie walked to the trees at the side of the road dry-retching, and such trees they were – white, tortured, high-country eucalypts with bark like smoothly poured solder. Eddie put his cheek to a trunk and thought, *This tree will never burn*. He wanted to do nothing more ever in his life than had happened just before the moment when they heard the low crump in the distance and pedalled the hill to look. The moment before that singing: Eddie would live there and pull the blanket of sleep over himself.

When they came together again there was still no traffic and they began with the singing.

'It was "Home on the Range",' said Eddie.

'I don't think so,' said Claude.

'Well then what?'

'It was more like the wind.'

'They had their heads out the windows before they pulled them in, you could hear them, singing their heads off,' said Eddie.

'They were in angel drive coming over that hill,' said Claude, 'they must have been, and they lost their brakes and hit the gravel, and then it was curtains.'

A passing car doubled back, parked at an angle, waited with the engine running as white-faced passengers stared unable to credit what they saw. A man walked over.

'You kids saw it?'

'We was too late,' croaked Claude, while Eddie looked at his hands, turned them over and stared at the lines of life. He collected his bike from the ground, wheeled it well back, propped it against a tree. He sat on his jumper and scraped at the ground with a stick. Claude joined him and said, 'I think we're heroes.'

The police arrived and by then the Holden was a mottled shell, its tyres flattened, the feeling already cold as if this was a car in a dump except for the secret it held. People came past rolling their windows down. They rolled them up and accelerated away. Cloud gathered, came down through the trees, and before long there was fog wetting the bitumen and dripping from the tips of leaves.

The Reverend Powell stopped on his way back from a meeting of bishops, he'd been phoned – accident, highway – and he embraced the boys to awkward submission and bade them be worshipful in prayer. Eddie looked at Claude, and Claude looked at Eddie, and they kept their eyes open while he shut his.

The police spoke to a farmer, who loaded their bikes on a truck and drove the boys slowly along the highway. At the Lone Gum Garage they had heavy china plates put before them, holding everything they wanted, and this they ate, aware of themselves as objects of amazement. Mrs Carmichael stared from the servery window with puffy eyes. She came out with a steaming teapot. An arm around Claude Bonney, she would do anything for him. They talked and then she asked Eddie whether he would like an extra egg or another ladle of baked beans. He too, anything he asked, what would it be?

They heard the crunch of wheels outside, an engine left running. It was the Sarge from the Isabel wallopers, Timmins, who stomped into the room in three big strides and rested his hands on their shoulders: 'I came when I heard.'

Eddie and Claude squirmed under the touch. They looked down and found the pattern on the stained tabletop interesting.

'Somebody had to come,' said Timmins. 'In your case, Bonney, I can understand, a father with a job to do, a post to maintain. He can't watch your every move. But Slim, what is it with your old man? You do whatever you like, down to the river with a .22 shooting platypuses, and guess what, he would rather argue if it was platty pie than tell you to knock it off. Now you've seen something a kid shouldn't ever and there's just me to get you out of it.'

'We're out of it,' said Claude.

'I gather you saw the worst.'

'They're just material like you are,' said Eddie, not looking at the man.

'Smart-arsed, but I won't harp on that. I'll drive you back,' he added. 'But you'll have to leave your bikes behind.'

'No go.'

'Might you look a bloke in the eye, Eddie Slim, when he hammers work time over fifty miles of shingle to see you're all right? It's you I'm talking to, Hubert Opperman.'

Eddie looked at him. Claude stood and the two boys gathered their paper bags of sandwiches. 'We're all right to ride,' said Claude.

'Another thing,' said Timmins, 'seeing as I'm made to exasperate. Acting on information received I want you to take everything out of your pockets and empty your bags.'

They did what he said. The cigarettes told their own suspicious story, except they were only Craven A's, a cheaper sort, the rest being safely hidden. 'What else? Dig deeper, fellas. You know what I'm looking for – a big, fat, bugger of a key.'

Eddie waited for the telltale clink of metal to slap the table but Claude's pockets were empty. It didn't seem possible, because they had ridden their marathon with the aim of getting the key back to the mail van at Lone Gum siding, which spent weekends empty and unattended, creaking in the sun, awaiting its call to make the return loop at the start of the post office week.

No, it didn't seem possible, except that when they were on their bikes, freewheeling down a long steady hill, Claude said, 'When she finishes at the Lone Gum she goes down to the siding and cleans the trains.'

'You gave her the key?'

'Go to the top of the class,' said Claude. Eddie swerved closer and gave Bonney's back wheel a kick, but his friend didn't retaliate. He just started pedalling faster, and Eddie saw tears streaming back, streaking his cheeks in the slipstream while Claude screwed up his face to stop them. This made Eddie feel released and it all poured out, sick saltiness dredged from the messiness of the scrub at the side of the road and from the grim sky and the muddy, pebbly creekbanks where they stopped and splashed their faces in green weed drifting down from cow paddocks. It seemed like poor sort of country this far from home − dead, lifeless, everything coming back the opposite from how it looked going out. But when you numbed yourself pedalling it seemed to melt into your bones and you were as hard as the hills ahead.

When Eddie arrived home it was almost sunset and his father sat among the rocks overlooking the house, watching out for him. He'd have a list of misdemeanours as long as his arm and say nothing about it. Eddie rested on the handlebars and recovered his breath. He looked back the way he'd come and it was beautiful again, the creek under the railway line glinting mauve. Eddie knew that Jack had been watching him for miles, attention all screwed on him as he rode closer in his little plume of dust. But Jack grinned as if he only then realised Eddie was there, got to his feet and said, 'Hungry? We're having cheese on toast and we're playing five hundred tonight.'

'You're on!'

'She locked me out of the house,' said Jack. 'I came in with my tail between my legs.' *So their fight is over*, thought Eddie. 'What about you, any news?'

'Nothing much. Just a massive long ride, and we saw –'

'I know what you saw.'

'Mister Colts running his guts out, and –'

'Colts! He does that.'

'And three sailors in a car,' finished Eddie.

'I know, I know,' said Jack, watching as the last edge of sunlight slipped under the western hills.

Jack carried Eddie's bike across the road and helped stow his knapsack. Pamela ran a bath, the chip heater thundering and always threatening to explode. Eddie was too tired for cards as it happened. It was a night for thick toast running with melted butter, for bowls of soup made from barley and mutton bones. All the colours in the bowl were gold – the fat, the barley, the onion shreds.

When Eddie was half asleep, crawled into bed, Pamela stroked his forehead and tucked his hair behind his ears. There was the shriek of a train whistle but Eddie stayed put and didn't jump to the window. Pamela stood and watched the winking lights travel across the plateau. She pulled the net curtains into a bunch under her chin. 'Oh, it's a stock train,' she said, as if it was something royal.

They were still young, Jack and Pamela. In their life there was time for another life, and later that year Eddie learned that for all the trouble Jack had with the Department the move to Sydney was going to happen. As Jack ruefully announced, that was what happened in schoolteacher families; the frustration broke and the move came and the schools they left sank into the grass.

Eddie knew he would count himself out when it happened. Pamela would be for him. He would stay on the Isabel. She said, 'Yes, it's better here.' He would go to the river and cross the bridge hand over hand: 'Claude!'

'*Who's that calling?*'

As if he wouldn't know it would be Eddie, heartbroken, without knowing why.

Eddie could see them waving goodbye from the loaded car. Then he could see them coming back in the school holidays, getting off the train, Jack wearing a white canvas cricketing hat and carrying a trout rod, Pamela coming along behind, walking almost backwards along the platform because she would be helping someone – an old lady, a small child – carrying their bags for them and neglecting her own. Or not Jack at all – just Pamela. Just her.

Eddie's mind went from place to place as he drifted off to sleep, but never too far. Never as far as Lone Gum Garage, that was for sure, never so far again. There were plenty of places left along the river and up the purling creeks where banks of peaty soil held worms ready for the hook, dragonflies hovered and platypuses nosed along. When fires lapped the hills they burned in the daytime, flared, yet all was well, because at night mountain fogs came over the saddles and damped them down.

After a while people would forget who had lived on the ridge up there. They would hardly recall the small school, the brass bell, the flagpole, the water tank, the backyard dunny that Jack Slim dug ten feet deep every year in a new position, the shelter shed of flapping tin where farm kids took their lunches. They would even forget that old Eddie Slim had ever lived there.

But they would know old Eddie himself, Eddie believed. He saw himself coming back. There he would be heading down from the hills to get his weekly supplies at Demellick's store. Up in the hills he'd have an underground mine with a stout door and a brass padlock on it. Deep in the earth he'd go crawling along and chipping away in the darkness finding gold.

NINE

FRED DONOVAN, SON OF RUSTY Donovan, hotelier of far-western New South Wales, was a stocky boy, nimble on his feet, always running to catch up with older boys, clowning to get attention.

Typical fatherless son of a flash woman, you might say Fred was, until the day a stranger appeared dropping him at school, and his teacher put her foot in it, saying how lucky Fred was being brought to school by his grandfather.

Not so fatherless, then, after all, was Fred. Except there was an understanding, rigorously applied, that the relationship between them must not be admitted on either side.

That older man, military of bearing, came and went over the years, staying at Rafferty's Hotel with commercial travellers and railway engineers, school inspectors, clerks of the court and Group 11 Rugby League players locally employed as a condition of their transfer. Shearers and contractors stayed at the National, near the railway line. Hoppy Harris came that far east twice yearly shearing and crutching but never spoke to, or of, the woman who'd shamed him. Just sometimes he drove past Rafferty's to get a look at a boy who wasn't his.

The corridors and dining rooms jostled with father-figures but that bloke of grandfatherly age, Dunc Buckler, was the one: seemingly made of compressed rubber, with kindly, somewhat offended eyes, white teeth, minted breath and carrying a small japara bag stuffed with dried fruit, nuts and candied ginger. Fred played up and down the stairs, using the first-floor landing as a stage, getting Buckler's attention, having something to show, folding and unfolding paper parachutes and raining them down, laughing the whole time, being instructed by the old bloke's cheery, you might say loving, yet somewhat defensive encouragement. With its many rooms – warm in winter with fireplaces on the landings, cool in furnace-breath summer under shadowing ceiling fans – and enough decent permanent boarders to outweigh dubious casuals as an influence on a kid, Rafferty's seemed a good enough place for just about any lively boy's upbringing.

'But good enough for my son?' said Buckler aside to Rusty when the routine of visits was well settled.

'Don't question it,' said Rusty. 'Ever.'

She considered banning him just for saying it. Or slapping his face. There was support for her rule from the quarter of Mrs Veronica Buckler, who tolerated Buckler's visits for the reason that boys should know their fathers. Some who didn't were lost in this life, and don't say who. Don't say Colts the step-ghost of this boy on the other side of these lives split down the middle.

In 1953, when Fred was ten, Buckler had confided to Rusty that he might sell Limestone Hills and buy into a pub – they'd each have shares. Rusty said, 'Splendid, have you told Mrs B?' That was enough to silence him. It worked like the waddy she kept under the bar and sometimes used on blokes (or threatened to). The town was the third of six where Rusty would run hotels into her seventies. She wouldn't take money from Buckler. Her savings went to a fund for Fred. Buckler kept a Commonwealth Bank book for him, she allowed that. There was a handsome Greek courting her with princely discretion. He never showed up when Buckler came. He'd lost his money gambling – the café, the block of flats, the Armstrong Siddley motor car, all gone. Just a silver-haired foreigner's consideration for a woman's needs left to give.

Learning early to put on the dog, Fred Donovan was Peter Pan in the school play – and Buckler was there. He was district Empire Day speechmaker – Buckler sends a proud letter. Winner of the cross-country event in the Near West Interschool Athletics – a telegram is delivered congratulating Fred. At Christmas there is always a book. *Deerfoot in the Mountains*, *Nemarluk the Warrior*, authored by that old fraud Idriess, the flyleaf containing a homily in Buckler's scrip, signed off with his elaborate copperplate B.

For example: '*Reading Makyth a Full Man – Bacon.*'

Fred stared at the advice, turning it around in his head until he was old enough to realise that a book and a plate of bacon wasn't meant. Nevertheless, he would trudge down to the hotel kitchen, tired from play and happy, a book tucked under his arm, and sit up at the big steel counter while Mavis the cook fed him bacon crackling. She never had to ask what he liked shredded and crisped into the crusted sauce of his macaroni cheese: just put it before him.

Buckler showed Fred a white scar on the back of his head, shaped like a half moon. Hair wouldn't grow there. 'I came through two world wars without a scratch – look what a nine-stone redhead caused,' he said. 'A chain of events rounded off by a bloke with a two-by-four hardwood plank, "like a hammer on the red son of the furnace" as Dr Johnson said.'

Fred Donovan saw early that life was a construction: people

laid it down for themselves, then walked that path as if it was all news to them. In Fred's life entrances and exits were made according to certain conventions. Never, not once, did he doubt that Buckler was his father. But he never asked beyond what was given.

Letters were allowed. Buckler was to come to Fred, not the other way around. Christmases on the Isabel Estuary were never to happen. Veronica herself had no interest in meeting him. She had done enough, tolerated enough with stoicism, humour and forgiveness. This would be going too far.

As an aid to precocious wisdom Fred read Buckler's *Up Against It* (Angus & Robertson Pioneer Library, 1935) finding it a drama from the time of Troy, it had such whiskers. Buckler said Troy gleamed over the hill from a stinking gully filled with Australians. Anzac Cove was an amphitheatre, where they'd performed their piece with candles guttering and homemade bombs rattling off. Buckler never said much about it. In a play you strutted the stage, the rest was hidden. Fred's stage was Rafferty's: rooms for the various acts, doorways, proscenium arches, cellars and under-floor spaces, trapdoors, ropes, pulleys. When he left home he took that with him in his head – the enormous house that a pub was then.

Always well liked even though wearer of the badge of the boaster, as a boy Fred Donovan was Fred of the mashed mouth, split lip, chest of bruises from being knocked down, springing up, taking more. 'I betcha, betcha anythin' I can . . .'

Fred unmatched in the playground Monday mornings, acting out scenes from Ransome's Flicks where he huddles front row, dress circle, mouth open gaping light, as many times as he can get to go, Rusty always letting him, crushing a ten-bob note into his hand: 'Shout your friends . . .'

Red Indians crawled in dirt and Fred was them, the whole tribe of them, from chief what's-his-name in headdress to halfwit injun Joe. A gangster sat on the lid of a garbage bin, smoking a cigar made from gum tree bark, Fred gravelling his orders. Then there was Shakespeare, school showings at the flicks, ranks of them marching down there at eleven a.m., of which Fred could barely understand a word, except Shakespeare's words crammed into him like fire.

Best tree climber, too – unquestioned victor in that – and one who liked on Sundays to disappear, get away from the mob, take himself off carrying a hip haversack into the rocky hills west of their town, red-baked stones the size of motor lorries and torpedo boats, mournful casuarinas catching the wind at the rim of the western plains and howling like sirens in an air raid.

There was a picnic once when he'd shown a girl, the prettiest in his class, all the best places. She'd climbed where he climbed, grubbed in the bark where he grubbed, shared his egg sand-wiches and squashed sponge cake. With her Fred experienced love so intense it rushed after she was gone into the quartz veins of the rocks like a ribbon she left. Sometimes he'd breathe on a rock face for the life there, and watch it glisten to his call.

In a sandy-floored overhang Fred made a day camp and lit a fire. It was a sheltered gully, just a slit in the plain but remark-able where a ghost gum (as he called it) sent roots into moisture. Towards evening he started climbing, following the light. Found himself edging higher into the bare forked limbs, and where else to go but up?

Standing athwart a branch, swaying with his shirt flapping, he wondered what it was like to be the first person ever to come this way, finding these lands. How would he be as a spear-carrying Nemarluk such as Idriess wrote about, keeping an eye peeled for goannas and kangas?

As light faded Fred shifted his gaze a fraction down, into an old dead socket of the tree. A noise alerted him and a scrab-bling shape appeared, a small, round-eyed, delicate-nosed ball of fur hauling itself out of the shelter and coming warily into the evening light. A rat? A freak rat?

A membrane stretched from its armpit like Superboy's cloak – revealing a flying marsupial, a squirrel glider, a story for that girl he wanted to like him, if only he could grab it up, make it seen and felt. Then something happened that made him covet the creature more, yet stayed his hand. The glider scuttled along a branch and spread those delicate membranous wings. Fred blinked, having heard of possum gliders, and imagined them into his heart, as he did with all life that climbed and flew – moths to the light, hawks on air currents, eagles circling, pilots, mountaineers getting to the top. But to see one, and then have the creature implore as if to say *fly* – shining a last glint of those amorous eyes – well, there was nothing for it then except to follow.

The summer Fred was sent away to boarding school, aged thirteen, involved a size of rock, Buckler said, big enough for a boy greedy for superlatives to get his hands on. He'd caught Fred's word 'mountaineer' in a run of gushed, unreal ambition from the mouth of the mouther-off.

'I'll show you something on your way to barracks, it'll knock your socks off. She'll cut you down to size, Sir Edmund.'

The move took time to happen, waiting until Rusty relented her long-held opposition to sending a nominal Catholic to a toffee-nosed Anglican school. Buckler said it was either that or the Presbyterians up the hill, overlooking the Rose Bay reach of Sydney Harbour, but he'd dirtied his boots on their flaming kilts years back and they'd turned up their noses at him. The brains behind everything and the purse-holder supreme was Veronica. So the choice of school, in reality, was made by the woman whose name was never mentioned. It came down to obedience;

Veronica's absence, her disdain of Fred had the strongest hold. Years later, at her funeral, he would sit anonymously in the back row of the church and silently mouth wry words of thanks.

They loaded the Humber and Rusty hugged Fred to the point of never letting go. A big loop of country was involved, hundreds of miles, driving first to Dubbo where Buckler visited old mates and then turning south. They had until the first week of February when they'd swing north and put Fred into school. Fred kept his eyes on the horizon looking for the surprise Buckler said would be unmistakeable when it loomed from the shimmering flatness. But wait, wait, he said, wait. The day after the day after tomorrow or the day after that you'll see it.

Fred's love for Buckler would never seem more fixed than on the grey sweatband of his hat, the dottle he flicked from his tooth-scarred pipestem, the timeless waits he demanded by the hot, midafternoon roadside with Fred playing marbles while Buckler snored in the back seat, one leg hooked over a suitcase and his white, blue-scarred shins naked above his socks. His Australia was everything worn out and second-hand, out of date, his stories went backwards through two world wars to a time that didn't interest Fred all that much. What Buckler gave him, a clean gift, was his future.

From dim haberdasheries in country towns they bought items from a school list sent by House Matron: underpants too large and belted with thick elastic that Bucker said he'd grow into, singlets of coarse, itchy weave, wiry socks, overlarge Dunlop Volleys. Buckler kept a food pouch on his lap and trickled nuts and raisins across to the passenger side as he pointed the wheel and rumbled along hardly ever faster than forty miles per hour. If Fred wanted chewing gum, Cherry Ripes or Coca-Colas, he connived them. Rusty had stuffed his pockets with banknotes enough. But Fred made sure from consideration that Buckler didn't see his choices downed, except for a Coke, about which

Buckler had gained the idea from a wartime grudge against Yanks, was a love potion on the level of Lucky Strikes. So Fred got him one, and watched him fondle the squat dewy bottle then gulp it back, followed by a spray of disgust.

Fred loved that old man in all this, however, and had the feeling that his own role even as a boy was to protect him, to somehow enclose him away from the world as it was, or had become while Buckler had his attention fixed elsewhere. Why this should be so when Buckler was the greatest self-styled boaster that ever gave a detailed opinion of himself at full bore, Fred hardly knew, except that the louder Buckler carried on about something, the smaller and more limited the world seemed to get around him. He just couldn't see it so somebody had to.

The routine in that week out of time was they'd share a room in a hotel, Buckler would contact old mates, Fred would go to the flicks, whatever was on. He'd pretend to be asleep when Buckler came in, shoes dropped to the floor, a round of beery belching, and after the first fart if he gathered for another (the warning was a heave of his twanging bedsprings as he raised his haunches) Fred would sit upright in his narrow bed against the other wall.

'Faugh!'

Buckler would hold back, but give a homily on the benefit of keeping the gases moving. Same thing in the car.

'Was that you?'

'We just passed a dead cow,' Buckler said, rolling his driver-side window up while Fred rolled his passenger-side window down.

He never phoned ahead but would cruise into farmyards and blow the horn. Sometimes only a few fowls would scatter, no barking even of an old dog, and an old woman or some kind of gaunt stranger would appear, blinking in the haze, and tell Buckler that he was too late, that the bloke he wanted had passed away. The great thing Buckler had with the living was that he cheered them up. They got their smiles out, after some decades of keeping them locked, gave them a shake, worked muscles around their crusted, oxidised, acid-foamed lips. They turned to Fred, nerve-shattered old doubtfuls, long-damaged past repair and faced with the peerless, ageless bounce of Buckler. They'd ask, 'How does he do it?'

'It's his nuts,' Fred would say, an answer he could tell delighted Buckler right down inside deep, where he couldn't ever acknowledge that it quivered. His nuts bound them: one and one and Rusty forever. It was something that Mrs Veronica Buckler could only ever think about.

At the end of one long, hot, endless day they arrived at the national capital, with its monuments – Parliament House, War Memorial, Civic Centre – held off in dry grass paddocks, separated from each other by what seemed like miles of open country, dry-grassed, and Buckler himself, to Fred's way of thinking as he aimed the Box Brownie, a monument too, truer than all of them – face twisted, bitter switching to benign, hands on hips like angled tree branches grown crooked in bad seasons but with a hopeful expression on his dusty claypan of a dial.

'Say cheese.'

'Cheese,' said Buckler.

'Stand up straighter,' bossed Fred, but Buckler only propped himself the other way over. He needed to hold on to something – a cigarette, a lamp post. He was getting old.

'Get on with it, Frank Hurley.'

Next day when Fred collected the prints Buckler had the hunched look of an old wallaby seized in the bones from too much low browsing.

Before Canberra Fred had never thought of any man-made place on the face of the planet as coming into existence from nothing. The towns of his childhood simply were.

'They had a good idea here,' said Buckler. 'It was one of your Coca-Colas and his lady wife camped down on the flats that dragged us around to their thinking. They drew a picture we couldn't see ourselves. They got the one thing right in this country that brands this country like nothing else does – space. They put space into a town. There's a lot of space between every-thing here, and that's the idea. It's a fact if you've got space, you've got time. The old darkies knew that and lived their lives over many generations, setting off on journeys only their grandchildren or great-grandchildren would complete. It's why we've got to watch out for them. Look at all the time in the way the country's worn down. It's the air you breathe. You're part of that while you're in it. If you don't know where you are, you're standing in it.'

Buckler left Fred to himself next day. In the camping ground he made a friend, a boy his own age. The friend's sister lent him her bike, a girl's bike. The two mates spurted dust and rode away out into the country for a day. They took oranges and a paper bag of mixed lollies. They didn't even ask each other's name they were so in agreement over what boys did.

Up on a ridge was a building site, deserted, but with all the gear waiting as if the men had just walked off an hour ago. Timber shavings were fresh on the floor and the rafters, open to the sky, blood-red sap. The site was across the Federal Capital border, in New South Wales above the railway line. It was on farmland, on a rocky ridge.

There weren't any tools but there were loose nails, and a few bricks and stones. Fred started hammering nails in an upright, using a rock, and his mate with equal sweat and seriousness stood back from a cement mixer standing idle and hurled bricks into its open maw, keeping score of hits and misses.

'What's this wall made of?'

'*Mud.*'

They jerked their heads around and saw a man get up from under a tree where he'd been camouflaged in dappled shade, up from a card table with sheets of drawing paper held down by an ink bottle. He wore a blue-striped shirt and a bow tie, had hair flying out like Harpo Marx.

'*Mud*, now quit that!'

They dropped what they were holding.

'That's right, mud. Don't you like a mud house?' he said. 'That's why you're trying to knock it down?'

'We never meant nothin',' said Fred's new friend. 'It's an all-right humpy if you ask me.'

'What about you, Tub?' the man shaded his eyes and looked at Fred.

He hated that nickname – Tub, Tubby – the way it was pulled from the air. It seemed too accurate therefore cruel or funny leaving Fred no gas to breathe unless he reacted by striking a blow. He wasn't fat, it was just that sometimes he got into a way of eating, sitting around reading and thinking and daydreaming and putting on weight. Rusty liked it, he was fun to push, pinch and tickle, but she asked Mavis the cook not to feed him up so much.

'Come on. I won't bite you. Tell me what you honestly think.'

'Your house is a heap of crap.'

'Come over here, Tub,' said the bloke. 'Leave your girl's bike where it is and give me more of your infernal opinion.'

Fred hadn't looked at the house properly but now he looked. He jutted his jaw.

'Who'd build a house like this? Rough-hewn, I'd call it, an offence to finished standards. There's no words for it.'

'Now there's a pompous arsehole,' said the man to the other boy.

'He's a bit like that,' said the boy, kicking the dirt with his bare feet.

The man led them round the house, which changed before their eyes as he spoke.

'Some of my builders think like you, Tub, that they are beyond the pioneering habits of their forebears, leaving timber as it was dragged from the wilds: slabs of ironbark, pillars of yellow box still with scabs of bark on them, knotholes exposed, insect scribbles in the wood. When people left the bush it was for something better than a ramshackle proposition made of mud. Right?'

'S'pose so,' said Fred.

'Next thing I'll be wanting a bark roof and a dirt floor. That's what they say.'

He showed them the plans. Each huge sheet of the heavy paper had a variant number and angle of view but the same name: 'The Friendly House.'

'Why's it called that?' the boys asked. They'd changed in these few minutes from grubs to something better, maybe more human, even intelligent, and were at the bloke as if they'd known him a long time, and everything about him was all right. Fred thrust his hand into the lolly bag and took out teeth, the prize of the packet, and held them out to the bloke.

'Marcus Friendly, he's either hated or loved,' said the bloke, accepting the gift and biting off a lump of molars and pink gums.

'My father votes for him every time,' said the other boy, standing up straighter.

'Yours, Tubby?'

'I don't have a father,' said Fred, loyal to the unspoken pact of Buckler's part in his life and avoiding mention that Buckler hated the name Marcus Friendly and everything Friendly stood for as a Labor Party head.

'I'm sorry to hear that. You don't have a father.'

'Well, not really.'

'Hmm,' said the bloke. 'My name's Warner Tarbett.'

They gave their names. Fred's mate was Col.

'When I first met Friendly,' said Tarbett, 'he told me that architects were the greatest damned fool wasters of a man's time. I said you'll have to put up with me being cranky a lot and I'll fly you upside down till you learn better. I was his pilot during the war. They gave Friendly an Avro Anson and I was his Man Friday. He was like a father to me.'

'They were the flying brick,' said Col.

'Ansons were but I flew that brick all over the country from Tassie to Darwin and up to New Guinea. When it wasn't Friendly it was army bigwigs.'

'It was Friendly's plane that was bodgied in Moresby in '44,' said Fred. 'The plane's airspeed device was blocked by chewing gum, and water was found in the gasoline.' Fred stared at the architect.

The architect stared back at him. 'That's not widely known.'

'It was in *People* magazine.'

'Not the chewing gum.'

'You could work it out, anyone could,' said Fred. He felt himself turning red. You might know how a plane worked but the gum was one of Buckler's hush-hush tales from his right-wing mates who'd had sons in the forces. They were an underhand lot, disposed to dirty conduct. Buckler said so himself, yet saw their uses. Whoever did it had wanted it blamed on the Yanks. They'd used a stick of Beech-Nut gum and left the wrapper.

'They said it must have been a Yank,' said Fred.

'But Friendly got on with the Yanks,' said Tarbett. 'No malice there. However . . .' he bored his eyes into Fred's skull. 'There's a mean as acid Australian way.'

'What's that mean, "Australian way"?'

'The dinky-di dimwit, the dried-up mental type, son of the acidulated soil. He's a mighty fool who wears khaki like he wove it, then back home he's part of the country – oh, too right he is – right down to the twisted meaning he gives to everything. The mighty me. Yeah, that's Australian all right – a big dead gum tree dried out and hanging on for no reason.'

They went back to looking at the plans. It delighted Fred to see something emerge three-dimensional from flat – it was like seeing the house flying apart in the *The Wizard of Oz*, now coming back together.

'Some people hear a piece of music and that's it for life,' said Tarbett. 'Some read a poem, or see a picture, they hear talk of a certain slant, words, great words, and that's their tuning fork. What's it with you two weasels?'

Col said, 'I like trucks.'

'Fred?'

He couldn't say, but with him it was playing parts. Fred liked the way Tarbett was done up flash and didn't mind if he looked a galoot. He was an authentic show-off. Yet when Fred reached down into himself to say it was showing off or acting a part or making something real from nothing that he liked, he couldn't pull anything out except, 'Dunno,' but said with just enough understanding in his look that Tarbett nodded, and changed the subject.

'I've drawn the house down to the last nail,' he said, 'including the doorhandles. Friendly's on the site most days looking over my shoulder. He's sick today. Marcus Friendly was born in a bark hut. He's lived in railway barracks all over the joint. The only house he's ever owned is a workingman's cottage. The last few years he's lived at the government hostel in a room where you can't swing a cat. Why does he need a house at all? Because he's sick, he's dying, and the country won't give him a bloody thing, so I'm getting what the country won't give him all together and I'm giving it to him. The tree, the mud, the rock. It's like his face, it's craggy. It's real. It's true. You're all right, Fred, I think. Col, you're solid. But you wouldn't have the bloody slightest idea what I'm talking about.'

'We would,' they said.

'Then put what you've got in this tin here. Every penny counts.'

They reached in their pockets, Col had a penny and Fred pulled out a pound note.

'Jesus, sonny, that's too much,' said Tarbett.

Fred folded the note over and pushed it in.

'Now piss off. I've got work to do,' said Tarbett.

The last part of the drive was south, a few hours on a dusty road, then a turn-off and a winding two-wheeled track getting close to the climax Buckler promised.

Fred saw nothing resembling what might be given the name cliff, bluff, precipice, boulder or whatever, whether high or low, man-made or natural, and asked Buckler for a clue telling him what to look for such as would knock the socks from his boyhood hideout. All he could see were low hills and sheep paddocks. At a turn-off they entered a forest.

'Animal, vegetable or mineral?'

'Ethereal.'

They came to a shuddering halt at a point where Buckler said that if they went any farther they'd fall over an edge. The Humber Super Snipe looked strange in tall, bark-peeling timber.

Here they were at three or four thousand feet, surrounded by forest except for a hazy gap in the trees. Any moment a bunch of axemen would emerge and Buckler would ask what regiment they'd been in, and they'd stare at him, working him out as some sort of living ghost.

'Look away off there, what do you see?'

'Trees,' said Fred, searching east through the hazy gap over wild country that fell away below them, forested gullies and hills rolling into a line of distant bushfires. 'I see the horizon, no, it's a thin dark cloud.'

'That's the sea,' said Buckler. 'Forty miles away as the crow flies.'

Fred took Buckler's binoculars and staggered with the weight of them. Held them to his eyes, seeing a cream of white on a reef, a long breaking wave or a boat's wake, proving it was water. He handed the binoculars back.

'Now turn around,' said Buckler. 'Look up.'

It was like being struck on the head by a low branch, by an obvious thought, when Fred looked up, for what he saw just made him feel stupid; it was so big and in his way the whole time. How could he have missed it? A crag, a shadow, a bulk. A great lean of knobbly dark sandstone – a cliff – it rose in a tremendous slope, vertical stacks tufted with dry grass and with whole trees growing out of chimney cracks and finally, away up, just showing as a cluster of boulders hundreds of feet above their heads, attracting wisps of cloud and soaring wedge-tailed eagles; yet somehow ending, not in the sky, not quite, not finally, but leading off to an upper world just like this one – a plateau-top of grass and trees and maybe roads, creeks and fences.

'Looks easy,' said Fred.

'You are a big mouth,' said Buckler.

They stuffed a knapsack with food, tightened their laces, stamped their feet, pulled their hats down over their foreheads, and started bush-bashing. It took an hour to reach the foot of the cliffs where Buckler stood watching and Fred started climbing.

That night, the last before heading up to Sydney and school, Fred was exhausted. His knees were grazed and his fingertips sore from scrabbling for handholds. But he'd gone to the top – he would always remember that, actions matched to boast; it was his way of perfection and he was finding it, with Buckler's moonface gleaming from below, urging him on. Buckler was the man who denied him nothing but withheld that admission: the definition of a father, may be, who led from behind.

As Fred came bounding and slithering back down to where Buckler stood he'd taken the applause. Then they'd come here, to another small town, and a pub called the Five Alls.

Around midnight Fred woke and Buckler still hadn't come to bed, so he walked out onto the wide verandah in his pyjamas and leaned over the wrought-iron balcony into the night. The streets of Isabel Junction were quiet except for the bellow of livestock in the railway yards. Two men were sitting on a park bench under a peppercorn tree on a road divider, lit by a yellow streetlamp. One of them yawned loudly, bellowed, like a reply to the cattle. No need to guess who that was.

The other man talked in a loud plummy voice while peering back up at the hotel verandah where Fred lurked: 'Traditionally pub names have a pictorial representation. All are welcome under the sign. The Five Alls are the king who governs all, the bishop who prays for all, the lawyer who pleads for all, the soldier who fights for all and the peasant who works for all. Isn't that just the thing? It sums it all up. Order in society.'

Fred pulled back into the shadows.

'Oh, the sign is peeled off, how shoddy, frankly it's typical of the present publican.'

There was a pause in the conversation, then this: 'Where is our young friend tonight?' said Buckler. For a moment Fred thought that was him.

'Not so young anymore, Major.'

Fred heard the hostility and malice. 'Our eternally *childish* friend, Major, it gives me no pleasure to tell you, cavorts with a woman called The Crow, wife of a communist who couldn't care less if she rutted with a goat.'

Buckler stood and flicked a cigarette butt away sending sparks skidding across the road.

'On that generous note of animal engagement, it's goodnight, Randolph.'

Back in the room Buckler couldn't stop groaning and laughing.

'Now I've heard it all, five divisions of everything under the sign of the squeaky tin. He'd like it if we had tournaments and jousting competitions, lutes, madrigals and folderol. It's medieval. There's goats and kings – Freddy, I know you're awake.'

'You've still got one sock on,' Fred said. 'Your nightshirt's inside out.'

'I saw you up there eavesdropping.'

'You woke me up. It sounded like drunks fighting.'

'Tomorrow you go to barracks and I won't get any more cheek. But here's a tradition for you. The condemned man gives a breakfast order, he gets anything he likes.'

Buckler made himself comfortable on his lumpy mattress. Fred would have baked beans, tomatoes, bacon, sausage, kidneys and a chop.

'Who's your childish friend?' said Fred after a dozy minute.

'On the grounds that the eavesdropper hears no praise of himself, was it you, do you ask?'

'It wasn't *me*,' said Fred.

Buckler said nothing more, until: 'Still awake?'

Last thing, he told stories. Fred groaned in resistance and said, 'Get on with it.'

'The old campaigner came in for supplies,' said Buckler, 'whiskers like wire, eyes beady as bottle bottoms. Reported he'd found a corner of dirt in the Top End and fancied to take up a station there. I argued him back: "Cattle go mad, horses fall to the staggers, sheep have nothing to drink, only camels and blackfellows smile over the spoils. Decent gentlemen go starkers or get religion. You'll end up selling it cheap to a Chink," said I. "Don't stop me dreamin'," said the old campaigner. "'Cool Wells', I'll call it." "Obstacles inflame pioneering," I supposed with an affectionate growl. But I warned him, seeing that I was getting nowhere, "It's bad luck to change a name." "What – do I leave it as it wuz?" "What was that, old chum?" "Desperation Creek," he mumbled into his honest whiskers.'

TEN

THE BIG MEN OF NORMIE Powell's childhood lived on winding dirt roads following the Isabel River upstream to its source. Their acres were given over to fine-woolled sheep. The 1950s were good years and it seemed the new decade now upon them would match. The main men were Knoxes, and Randolph Knox the controlling influence over his elderly father and younger brother, Tim, who was the same age as Normie. In their long breaks back from uni, the two eighteen-year-olds showed up at rugby practice. The coach was Kingsley Colts, who said, when they stood and biffed each other, 'Get down off your hind legs, you animals, this is a game.'

'The game played in heaven,' was how Normie's father, still turning out for the team at forty-one, described it. He would soon have reason to know.

In the previous century on the Upper Isabel, churches were built on steep clay ridges where preachers came on allotted Sundays. Nearby were graveyards arranged by denominations and separated by fences matted with windblown grass. Inside those weatherboard temples mud-nesting swallows and blow-flies left traces requiring work with straw brooms and buckets of hot water and cakes of carbolic soap to clean out the gunk. Normie worshipped out of duty to his father's wishes. He never knew what to pray. Suggesting what it was, by observation, made nature Normie's subject in the same streak of questioning that turned his father to God when he was the age Normie was now. Silence and nature ruled under rafters in the weeks between services and Normie sitting in a pew while his father preached thought about that.

Vince Powell had been a naval officer in the war, then a chemistry teacher and now a muscular Christian with something to prove who loaded hay and drove trucks helping the big men out. His loudest sermon asked, 'What Makes a Man?' and the answer was hardest to give, involving the Trinity and Apostles' Creed and mental gymnastics (and bending your back and taking the blows of your mates). Normie tried hard, but found it a game of words.

'A game?' said Vince. 'It is real.'

It embarrassed Normie the way his father swaggered with the blokes on the footy field, or in summer hit the lucerne paddock and bit crown seals from beer bottles after the hot work was done. That his father would take only approximately half a glass of beer or a small cut-glass goblet of sherry never escaped Normie's absorbing gaze. The son didn't want to see the father drunk but you didn't nibble at fire, you took the burn. A man could never be hero enough, on the Isabel, unless he was dead. Either you suffered or not, and Normie wished there'd been a real fire on HMAS *Thursday* such as other men had in their ships and planes, to burn off half a handsome face.

News of the burning Holden came firsthand from Claude Bonney and Eddie Slim when Normie was a kid and he never forgot the day. Claude Bonney was his friend, guide, nature-lover. They'd stayed in touch. Normie had the same professors now and they knew Claude as one of their best, except he'd never finished his degree. What did he need to learn that he couldn't find out when it came time to learn it? The famous Holden crash had the power to grow in the mind and haunt from the corners of sleep. Life was a blaze, the essence of carbon flung to its farthest intelligence in one moment, reduced to ash the next. That the doomed men in the car were sailors made Normie resent his father for being alive in one of those atavistic attacks of emotion devoid of reason that bedevil a son's mind. Tim Knox had the unspeakable satisfaction of having a dead brother to whom he owed his existence.

Vince Powell talked of mercy but the Upper Isabel men had an unforgiving streak. They never saw mercy required of themselves while seeking contrition from others. Normie flinched under the so-called humorous cuff of Randolph Knox's palm when Randolph called him useless in the hayfield. The bachelor seemed the ultimate representative of a truth that was force. So supreme were Knoxes in the nation's ideal of itself they supplied members of parliament from their family tree, judges, bishops and soldiers in two world wars. Lieutenant Sandy Knox had a memorial stone dedicated on a hilltop granite boulder overlooking the farm, and the elderlies with Randolph, when Tim was eleven, had made a pilgrimage to Greece to visit his grave.

Hard rations were good news for sheep on the Upper Isabel. That was the boast. It stretched to people as the Knoxes' erosion gullies displayed the ruthlessness of a struggle for dominance. Normie eyed this with a survival theorist's eye, a blue Pelican paperback of Marxist biology his Bible of choice. Those valued animals met the challenge of eating grass down to the nub; the harder they grazed the finer their wool became, or so Randolph claimed in his highest excitements in a conundrum explaining the desolation and wealth of the land. Knox flocks resembled dismal maggots crossing the hills but turned a profit enabling Knoxes to take their sea voyages and Randolph to drive a Jaguar two-seater regularly traded in for the latest model.

Randolph's singleness of mind precluded marriage in favour of work. There'd been women who'd tried unbuttoning his duds, but no dice. The person who broke with Randolph and his rule was that lean stick of a sporting bloke who was said by Randolph to have formulated his animal experience on goats. Their feud was vituperative and humorous and entertained the town. Colts worked for Careful Bob Hooke and Randolph walked out the swing doors of the agency if Colts walked in. Randolph retreated to Homegrove while Colts stayed on in Woodbox Gully, in the cottage they'd shared when younger. Colts drove in every direction called upon by Careful Bob, buying and selling rams, and was said by Randolph to be a scabby ram himself, having a sheila in every half-arsed town primed and ready to be served without respect. Randolph couldn't stand it: the rougher Colts lived, the fussier Randolph became, the more outwardly respectable the more Colts reserved his morals to himself. Randolph wore cravats and used a shooting stick when watching the game on Saturday afternoons on the Isabel Junction Oval.

Scalded as they were, bare as they were, the Knox hills were wild and beautiful in their bleakness. They were bordered by cold forests of eucalyptus extending from peaks rarely trodden. Sometimes Normie trod them, a lone walker and rock climber. The organ pipes and flatiron slabs of the Isabel Walls drew him. Nobody else ever went there. From the trig, its pile of stones a kind of fort, the ranges marched away east in folds of blue-smoked haze to the distant sea and west in darker ramparts to the Great Divide. The older male Knoxes despised these eastern reaches as mere cattle runs and barely saw them against the needs of fencing, dogging, rabbit eradication and soil erosion repairs relating to sheep. It was in the overstocked, hard-bitten hills and down to the sparkling river flats they found beauty most, in irrigated paddocks given over to lucerne, deep-rooted and hardy, in drought years lit jade against the dried-up rapids of the Isabel. There Randolph conditioned his rams with the big jaws he called royal.

During haymaking Normie rode with his father from before daylight until after dark, spiralling the paddocks while men on casual rates of pay hurled rectangular bales onto the flat top. Normie would have to say that he and Tim Knox were not so much friends but rather observers of each other's pitifulness by going as hard as they could. Tim was paid nothing being a Knox and Norman paid nix alongside his father. He didn't see his father being used up, that his energy was a flame consuming itself to a purer burn. He thought that way of himself, and his poor mother saw that was right for his age, not Vince's.

Jenny Powell had never wanted to be a vicar's wife but once loved a sailor in a roll-necked sweater, Sub-Lieutenant Powell, RANVR, and said she would voyage with him anywhere. Lately when mail arrived she knew there were limits.

For Vince started tearing up correspondence, often before he'd even come down from the post office verandah, looking around for a bin. It was a lucky day when he found a bin smouldering and already alight. To see the mail flaring and turning to ash worked like a Bex on Vince. Silently he thanked Tub Maguire, the figure in the torn black overcoat who kept the town's rubbish alight with crafty cigarette butts and furtively cupped matches.

Vince walked under low sticky peppercorns remembered from his youth. Down the next street plane trees reached across the white dust road, almost touching. Roses thrived in gardens watered by tea dregs and washing-up slops. St Aidan's came into view, its belltower copied from an original in East Anglia and paid for by Knoxes in 1878. The forecourt of the churchyard had enraptured Vince at the age of five, a pattern of herringbone bricks. If he ever wrote his own story, his spiritual account, it would be those old red bricks with their crumbled edges and stubborn dry remnants of rosemary that would get credit for swaying him towards God.

If he said God lived in the stones and late after turning off lights and locking doors fell to his knees and prayed on them, who would know? His wife wrote to their son at St Paul's College expressing alarm. Normie wrote back with the opinion it was par for the course, but he'd be home next weekend.

Around a corner Tub Maguire lurched from the shadows, the tails of his overcoat flapping.

'If only two days was the same,' the metho drinker slurred, tilting a hat brim chewed by mice.

'Too right, Tub,' said the man of the cloth, hearing the rattle of matches as Tub limped away.

Up near the stone quarry a fire burned, eating dry under-brush in a jaggedy line and harmless in winter.

In the ministers' fraternal of country towns it was said that Anglican clergy did not have a hard road to the pulpit. Rather too easy it was for them to slip on the gaudy vestments and gesture towards the choir stalls for a bit of tra-la-la. Presbyterians did higher degrees in New Testament Greek, Cattle Ticks had the celibacy row to hoe, but after the navy Vince had been a high school teacher one year and a preacher the next. QED as they said in the science staff room, that was the whisper, it was all too quick, but ask Vince and he might tell you differently if only he could find the words to describe his appetite for change and the pressure of attaining it.

Back during teaching Vince had almost exploded test tubes in thought, watching sulphur and silicone bubble. There was a part of him convinced despite physical laws that reality was a deception requiring less than acid, heat or sugars to melt the division between spirit and material. His son, a materialist, might see it in an electron microscope if only he looked hard enough. There was no division, there was never a void beyond, Vince said, when he and Normie debated. 'Wordless harmony a condition of matter,' said a sermon card being drafted. It was Vince's innermost syllabus, which he'd protected from his pupils in the state system but always wanted to teach Norm. The ring around the atom: inwards was where Vince headed when the time came – surrendering his superannuation and sure climb up the Departmental ladder, pinning the gold cross of the bush padre to his shirt collar.

Sceptics and hard-bitten refusers – even Normie, you might say – had Vince's understanding more than fellow clergy who branded this reverend rather too sporty, therefore thick, as he settled into the outdoor Christian role that winter by getting out with Colts on cross-countries. He'd turned forty-two, Colts was thirty-seven.

Scoring a try Vince flew with horizontal momentum, man of the flashbulbed moment on the sports' page of the *Isabel Gazette*, ploughing into the churned earth under the goalposts with his arms held up until the very last moment when he slammed the ball down. Every time Vince got back on his feet he was glad to be alive, and unwillingly, oh so diffidently, saw admiration (a love of the game) gripping Norman.

Vince's sermons, crafted and filed away, often praised by Jen as more than just fine, felt wooden, he told his son. It was why he'd lately abandoned sermons and improvised from a book of Psalm interpretation. It was certainly a gain. Heads snapped from slumber and ecstasy glowed in men's faces and more or less as usual in women's when Vince hit his tonsils hard. The choir doubled in number and Saturday Evensong became a haven of swaying, trilling chanters, Randolph Knox's the finest voice among them. People travelled from distant towns to experience the rumour. The triumph was Randolph bringing a bunch of blokes down from the Upper Isabel.

During Evensong Normie and Tim Knox slipped away, took a Dally Messenger across to the town oval and played force 'em backs with high punts until darkness fell and each claimed a win and came back covered in mud to prove it.

Vince with fifty pounds cash went to Hooke & Hooke and paid six months' rental on the Buffalo Hall, a 1920s fibrolite job lying empty. There in a khaki shirt with the sleeves torn out and wearing footy shorts and sandshoes without socks, he set up trestle tables and accepted donations of food, helping the poor who joined the ranks of his acolytes calling him the best good bloke ever.

This was all very well and interested the bishop, who came to inquire why his letters drew blanks. Excess enthusiasm rather showed other men up. Allowances were made for the phase in any man's life when the scriptures needed living out. 'We all went through it,' said the bishop, smilingly over his athletic colleague's lapse, 'except never as pronounced as Vince.' Contingency plans were made for the next move for an errant vicar – sideslip Vince into the practical side of the Anglican show, second him to a property management working party.

'Not me, I've something to prove.' Vince tore up the letter.

The part of Vince's mind presiding over his being was a relentless taskmaster. He talked about suffering – about being nailed to the wood – but did not talk this way to the bishop. That would not be wise, said Vince, with a strained, crafty laugh.

Jenny felt this invading from where it shouldn't, right into their lives from the holiness plane. Cooling from Vince's enthusiasms she took sides with those parishioners who felt their leader was ignoring them after years of faithful attendance and social contentment as stalwarts. They were the ones who put money into the collection plate and maintained the paintwork and churchyard rose beds after all. The evangelical style made a mockery of their devotion.

Garbage fires burned where Tub Maguire and his relations lived in tin humpies. Going back to childhood any boil or infected cut experienced by Normie was traceable, according to Jenny, to the times her son rode with his father into the dark people's camp. Most of those times Normie stayed in the car, holding germ-free to the doorhandle while kids jumped on the running board, streaking their noses on the window glass, while Vince conducted the Gum Tree Sunday School. It was not very Christian of Jenny to knock these folk but a cold, congealed feeling in Normie's stomach came from her and there was no breaking out of a mother's way of being. The others Normie's age had mostly left school and, though he'd played cowboys and Indians with them when they were younger and dragged billycarts in the dirt, they were strangers now who lowered their eyes greeting Normie back from uni with a low howdy passing through town.

'That woman is back,' said Jenny. No need to ask who. Normie knew it, she'd been on the train.

Kingsley Colts drove her to the cottage the Slims had bought after Jack's transfer to Sydney so that Eddie could stay on. Eddie had long finished school and left, but his mother kept returning. 'Our Colts is paying attention to Mrs Slim,' said Vince. Colts left the house after midnight – was reported as a tomcat in the darkened streets. Now when Vince drove her Pamela sat in the car without speaking and he sat white-knuckled at the wheel. Normie knew all about it without having ever experienced it or even knowing such jealousy existed – in this way, at this age, in their position – the upheaval of vituperation in his father never clearer than when Normie saw Mrs Slim reach over and touch his father's hand; there was no great meaning in it, but saw his father's fingers grip hold and hang on. Saw the *please* on his lips.

Saw the absurd knowledge, the *no* in The Crow's whole body as she stiffened, drew back and said *Thank you, Vince*, and closed the door when they dropped her off; saw the heaviness in his father's eye dragging his gaze after her.

'What's eating you, son?' his father said as they drove away.

'Nothin'.'

And it would be nothing too, but not quite yet. A nothing as fathomless as the depths of the longing heart. Just you wait Vince Powell in the frost-gardens of the Isabel, in this rugby season, when a man past sensible age plays second row in a game beloved of Heaven for the reason of grace descending in the trajectory of a leather ball.

For here is Vince now turning out for training on the shortest day of the year. His steady brilliance in the scrum and sudden, powerful passes from the forwards way out to the winger mark him best and fairest. The boys, Normie and Tim, are with him in their striped, shrunken, hand-me-down jerseys and aluminium-cleated boots, which they love to crackle on the concrete apron of the grandstand. Here is their lanky coach, Kingsley Colts, more willing than the broad run of men to do his bit; the consoler of grass widows leading them in slow breathy circuits of the oval under the bare branches of elm, now semaphoring his arms down to his toes with rapid scissoring ease, now up over his woolly-haired head. A couple of lonely floodlights press against the high, cold dusk.

All week Norman has blocked his father's attempts at pleasantry.

'Put that to use in footy practice,' Vince declares.

With a scowl Normie takes him up on the Tuesday, when the forwards have done with the scrum machine and the backs are finished at callisthenics and Colts calls for the scratch game to begin, seven a side.

Normie is a nimble player who doesn't mind getting hurt.

This evening he's wearing an armour of defiance and might do anything. Tim Knox joins him in the spirit of opposition and the two make coordinated attacks every time Vince gets possession. Away the boys go, getting nowhere, Vince flinging them off like fleas from a dog's back and laughing as he does in an argument about faith, where he is the Chosen One of an inflated leather ball. They attack him on either side but shepherding, Colts calls it, whistling the two back and corkscrewing his heel in the turf. The rule Colts applies amuses a couple of visiting players, big happy men, one a lesser cousin of the Knoxes from up Boorowa way, the other a New Zealander on a study tour of Upper Isabel studs, world famous to those who know about them, but looking like ruins to those who don't. The moment comes when the boys stand back panting and what they merely attempt is resolved. Harvey and Maltman are the names of the vengeful comedians. They capture Vince, still powering in their arms, and oblivious to the sound of Colts calling a halt with his trilling whistle they restrain Vince like a slippery bean and rotate him arse in the air and bring him down headfirst, breaking his neck.

Not a twitch, nor a stab of pain did Vince Powell feel after his body settled around him. A last cockatoo squawked in the trees. He was to speak of it later, describing a woozy feeling ushering in a life sentence. A beetle crawled in his ear and he couldn't scratch it. Just for that moment the whole field ran on and left him alone contemplating the first star. 'Don't move him,' somebody shouted after the pack wheeled and returned standing over him.

'Can't yer walk?' Maltman and Harvey asked.

Something broke in his son pushing through – 'It's me, Dad, Norman. I'm here, I'm the one!'

The one what, it was interesting to wonder, as Normie didn't know which one himself, in cold panic he was, unless he meant the one who loved his father more than words could say, better, realer than the son of God who wasn't there for this.

Colts restrained his anger at the two attacking players. He clutched the offending whistle, tore the string from his neck and stamped the whistle into the mud.

'It wasn't anyone's fault,' was being said in the back ranks, where Harvey and Maltman lingered, kicking at grass with appalling unease. It was the game young men of good family played in New South Wales and put above themselves. Sometimes the worst knock only defined rugby's brilliance.

Young Dr Macintosh came thrashing through the muddy gates of the oval in his Mini Minor. There were those who said he couldn't do enough and those who said he never did anything much. Answering no questions Mac unlaced Vince's boots, pinched his toes, examined his eyeballs with a pencil torch, arranged a blanket over him and placed a hand on his brow until the lights of the ambulance appeared. Next day Mac travelled to Sydney with Vince by plane, getting him seen by the best available at Royal North Shore, a brilliant orthopod whose secret was he walked the hard mile beside the stretchers of the disabled and about a year to eighteen months later farewelled his quadriplegics from rehab into a cessation of progress.

Somewhere in the scriptures the sick were told to take up their beds and walk. The halt and the lame to throw away their sticks, Jesus of Galilee walked upon water. There by the side of the road He tended the injured, the defiled, and from a few loaves and fishes fed the five thousand. A theology was founded on the idea of burdens being removed, it spread through history the antithesis of evil and spoke of itself 1,963 years later in Vince Powell's bedsores, in his problems with ventilators and nights of neglect when nobody checked his terrors.

*

Home on the Isabel they make an interesting pair: Vince Powell and Tub Maguire, the paralysed and the paralytic. Hardly a day passes without Tub nosing through the shrubbery along the back wall of the District Hospital and fooling the nurses with birdcalls, tawny frogmouth booms and Australian owlet-nightjar trills, and with imitations of Doc Macintosh's nasal orders. Swift as a stinko rat kicking the chocks from under the wheels of Vince's chair, Tub pulls him out of the place and goes racing, head lowered and bootsoles flapping. They drop down the hill into town at unsafe speed.

One day rattling over the forecourt of the church Vince is jolted clear of the seat and tumbles uselessly on the bricks, his head twisted sideways and his nose aligned with the cracks where weeds and ant mounds flourish. Another day he chokes in the coils of smoke that rise from Tub's fires.

On a scorching day during a phase of Vince's overstretched lifetime the two men take to the river.

Normie taking a break from writing up his PhD thesis, blazing achiever at twenty-two, fishing under ribbon gums on the opposite bank, head full of contesting theories relating to the everyday, sees them, the ugly wooden chair tilted on the grass and what Normie takes to be an apparition rising from the bank. *What the Jesus fuck*, he wonders.

It is Tub holding the wasted Vince Powell of football fame in his drunken arms with the intention, Normie is absolutely certain, of drowning him. They slither the gravel bend of the Isabel and sink into a deep, clear pool laughing. Tub drunkenly dunks his burden, noisily swearing, and Normie with cold certainty wills his father to die. It would be better.

But Tub is washing Vince, getting the shit off him, and that is all it is. Would that Normie knew what it meant. The thought hits him with the intimacies involved, the hairy bumcrack flashing and the flaccid balls of the man so bloody senseless. He doesn't understand his father and never will, and as for his being the face of courage, defiance, the badge of heroism carried for the burning sailors of the Indian Ocean, forget it.

Normie packs his fishing gear before he is seen. Another five pages before nightfall on the entotic lungfish theory. How they heard the dry land calling.

There comes a flailing, gasping sound and Normie turns to see his father swimming – spouting water like a fountain and restored to his sporting life.

Normie watches for a long while taking it in. Too bloody late, old man. Then he gathers his things and goes.

Not yet, nor for a long time yet, is Normie aware of his father's happiness inhabiting him. During Vince's sermons, so studiously ignored, Normie had no idea. Through the games with their hard-won advances and peerless, territory-gaining punts and faces in the mud tackles something snapped off. It grew another stalk. It learned to play and display on water. Now when lifting a leaf, following animal tracks, slicing through a bed of ants or watching a mob of kangaroos reclining on a hillside, notating their stand-up fights and leaps of mating ritual cross-referenced on graph paper tables, or advancing the lungfish theory, his recent insight, Normie knows how it happens. Through every small opening in life, through the tiniest, most restricted nerve ends, through rips and tears and tatters, life pours.

ELEVEN

FROM THE ROAD THE FOOD was carried up to the climbers' camp site by Normie Powell and Claude Bonney in Mountain Mule packs weighing fifty to sixty pounds each – cheese, smoked oysters, chops, tinned meatballs, tinned spaghetti, red wine, Scotch whisky. These blokes were – Claude Bonney was – legendary for doing it hard. Fred Donovan could not believe it. There were plum puddings and powdered custard mixes. There was raisin loaf heavy as stone. There was camera gear and coils of rope and metallic climbing equipment. Some was carried by girls. Fred, wearing a rainbow headband, had carried none of it; he'd pranced along, leading the way. What he'd remembered as a brief scramble to the foot of the cliffs as a thirteen-year-old turned out twelve years later to be a mass of successive ridges, each steeper than the last and scattered with immense boulders among thickets of tea-tree, lomandra and prickly bush.

All Fred had was an army surplus haversack slung crosswise on his hip holding brown rice, nuts, dried fruit and a jar of gritty wheat sprouts. It was made to impress, Spartan being the word for going bush imparted on those occasions, somewhat mythical in their power being so few, when Buckler and Fred − permission for contact granted − had packed blanket rolls and taken their long drive south from the Near Far West, beaten their way through this same lump of bush to these same rocks rearing like pagan shrines east of the Great Divide.

That was back when Isabel Walls had no name, that anyone much used, but had a feeling about them, stately, beckoning, as the old man reported the first time he saw them − when he'd passed under their shadow on a winding dirt track, on his way home to Mrs B − saying he had something to show him.

Now these cliffs were known as a stash of hard pitches in the dripping clouds of mountaineering legend. Here you came to make a name for yourself.

Germans had come to the Walls, men who'd scaled the North Face of the Eiger and slogged up Carstensz Pyramid in Irian Jaya. They'd camped with Claude Bonney and made a fretwork of arrogant first ascents recorded in an exercise book placed in a tin box held down by rocks on a trig point. One of them, Wolfie Keuper, had stayed, becoming a wild-eyed, stringy-sinewed New Australian cherry orchardist on one of the lower ridges of the dirt road leading back towards the Junction. Bonney cursed him for not being where he'd said he'd be and when. The haughty alpinist had offered to set up fixed ropes. Claude wanted to show him off: a true curiosity of the human species. Game, these Krauts had insisted on eating, believing Australians made no sense leaving marsupials off the menu, which was where Dr Normie Powell had provided, with his zoology dissecting skills, cuts of small slope-shouldered, pot-bellied wallabies that abounded in the thickets, butchering them on a flat rock where you could still conjure a dark lichen of blood.

A blazing camp fire lit the overhang of the Isabel Walls Hilton.

Normie said, 'What are you looking at, Freddo?'

Excess food was spread on the flat rock.

'I'll admit, I'm starving.'

'Take whatever you like, then.'

'What's that sausage there next to the cheese?'

'Salami,' said Normie.

'How do you cook it?'

'Cook it?' said Normie, unsheathing a knife with a heavy curved blade and a serrated spine for sawing bone and gristle. 'You grill it. See here – take a slice, make it thick.'

'Do I leave the skin on?'

'Take it off or it won't swell, now get a stick, pin the salami to the end of the stick and hold it over the flames, not too close.'

'Like this?'

Fred crouched over the smoking fire with a stick in his hands and watched the disc of meat sweating in the dim light. He had an audience of glowing grins around the fireplace stones.

'You'll know it's ready when it starts swelling,' said Normie. 'When it gets to the size of a golf ball, take it out of the flame, blow to cool, pop it in your mouth, swallow.'

Fred watched the meat shrivel and char and burn away. He mimed a gigantic tear over missing his tucker.

Before dark the still incomplete party, ten in number – eight men, two women – stood out from the overhang with their backs to tree ferns and the valley already inked by night and crisscrossed by gliding, carolling currawongs. Tipping their heads back they watched sunset withdraw from the vertical rock face, a fading blush. They ate and drank and talked as darkness thickened. Some planned the routes they'd take in the morning, who'd lead, who'd belay. The cameraman and his assistant drank rum and looked sullen. Their job would be to hang from fixed ropes in bosun's chairs while Claude and Normie found plant and animal curiosities in clefts and crevices, holding them to the lens. Fred watched a girl sidelong, Erica Molinari, who said she would stay in her sleeping bag. Morning mists were ferocious along the range, smeared thick as sheep's wool leaving a treacherous damp on the rocks until the sun burned through. Fred might even stay cocooned there himself, one eye on this Erica with her short blonde hair.

He asked, as they filled their tin cups at the spring, 'You've been here before?'

'No, Claude talked me in to coming. You have?'

Fred nodded, a little glumly, so Erica was on with Claude? Earlier when the party collected Fred from the all-stations at Lone Gum siding nothing seemed sorted between the sexes. Or that was Fred's hopeful impression, at least.

'Yes, and I've climbed them,' he said, adding, to belittle the greats who were gathering: 'On my own, solo.'

'Gee.'

'I was thirteen,' he said, telling her how he'd nimbled crosswise for the whole three hundred feet of vertical knobbly conglomerate to the top terraced ledge, where there were snow gums and a view back over the district wide as a fabled kingdom, Dunc Buckler the witness, that stocky old boast with his hands on his hips, watching wordlessly and shrinking away below until from Fred's perspective he was just a round hat with two feet poking out.

'God,' said Erica. 'Jesus. How could he bear to watch?'

'He's like that. He won't say what he expects of you. But you feel it all right.'

Fred pointed to the gully where he'd come glissading down, to the spot where treetop to branch to ledge to sandy pile of leaves he'd swung himself down acrobatically to get the old man's nod. Later they were all drinking and milling about and he saw Erica staring at him across the fire, wondering as to his truth, no doubt. He worked his way back beside her with animal watchfulness.

There was something keen, a jolt in that look of hers, unguarded. It left Fred wondering what she wanted from him. Then he saw that she shot an even more open glance at Claude. So maybe it would be on tonight between Claude and her, maybe that was the tension, in that strong man, knobbly-nosed and handsome, who left a gap when they sat together, even when Erica gave him what might have been a come-on whack with her hip – as if they had a conspiracy building, only to be gained by a mating ritual played off against a third-party bystander.

'So you're an actor, Fred?'

'Sometimes.'

'That whole thing with the salami was brilliant, the way you set Normie up.'

'But I didn't know,' said Fred.

'That's even smarter, then, to hold your own, and get a laugh.'

'It got a laugh,' he agreed.

'You've no idea how great that is.'

Her hand touched his knee as she talked, but she kept her grey-blue eyes on Claude and his movements around the fire. 'Have you heard of the Southside Players? They're famous for doing elaborate big-time productions – *Kiss Me Kate*, *Annie Get Your Gun*, along those lines – actually, something more ambitious now – *West Side Story*.'

'Hmmm?' said Fred.

'I tried for Maria, and guess who I got? Consuelo, Shark girl with dyed blonde hair, Pepe's girl.' She tugged a lock. 'This isn't my real colour.'

'It suits you but,' croaked Fred. 'Starlet of the amateur stage.'

'I'm not sure how to take that.'

He was sorry he'd said it – implying a loose interest in attraction, reciprocal without too much bargaining, something he'd found that had broken his heart last year (and might again). There was no personal judgement in it, who could blame longing, anyone's, but he couldn't hide knocking musicals and suburban drama groups for their predictable repertoire and synchronised group actions (dances, duets) dedicated to the frothing up of solidarity, a part for everyone who wanted their hour before footlights. There was no place in it for the absolute cry of lone transcendence that was the actor in Fred or maybe the architect, his other vocational urge.

'We had devon at home,' he said, 'wurst or fritz they called it in some places. I lived in pubs, the permanents made their own lunches on Sundays, sandwiches, they had the run of the kitchen. There was always cold meat and sausage. The worst – that's not a pun – was made from donkey meat and sweepings from abattoir floors. That was salami, or so I was told. I never ate it. That's where Normie had me, all I knew was it was raw and what's raw gets cooked.'

He could hardly see her face, then a flame would lick, a flash-bulb puff when someone threw dry bracken on the fire. He felt his breathing rasp, his sinuses thicken. He wanted to throw himself on her.

'More I'm an architect,' he said, 'but I do that tour, Shake-speare for Schools, you might have heard of us, bringing culture to the backblocks. Next stop: Woop Woop.'

'More you're an architect?' she threw his words back at him. She would have heard, perhaps, that he worked as a station assist-ant at Central Railway, the lowest rung of worker wearing the monogrammed belt buckle, tie, waistcoat and enamelled badge of the ARU unionist on the basic wage.

'Architect, architecture – well, I studied architecture but failed third year after repeating second, when funds dried up. Help was denied me for my own good. Where money comes from's always a struggle: it comes, when it does, mostly from my father's wife, who blocks her ears to my existence but holds sway over me via the dole even though we've never met and never will if she can help it.'

'Poor orphan Fred.'

'I do have a mother,' he said. 'Rusty, you'd like her.'

Erica sucked her lower lip as Claude came around the fire towards them, filling tin mugs with Four Crowns claret, frothing it purple with a low laugh, pouring Erica's, pouring Fred's, then moving away again with steady geniality.

'He doesn't know I exist,' said Erica.

'But he stood on your toe,' said Fred.

'You noticed that?' said Erica. 'I'm showing all this interest in you. You haven't asked me too many questions about myself, Fred Donovan.'

'I know you're something at the museum with Norm.'

'I'm totally and completely slave to Norm.'

Fred took his chances: 'So where does Claude fit in?'

'Norm offered me to Claude after hours. Lent me, gave me, threw me in his way. Now Claude wants me to stay with him. I have to decide.'

Fred looked at her. There was a sting of pleasure in the rhythm of her complaint. She couldn't mean what she said, the way it sounded – threw? lent? gave? – a starlet of the amateur stage wearing out the stairs to the Public Health Officer's rooms as the gon was a notifiable infection? Could that be her, like last year's girl slamming him around in a KO sequence of punches to the aorta before moving on to the next bloke?

'I'm an illustrator, a naturalist–illustrator,' said Erica. 'Claude's got a book, a documentary film and a TV series coming up – educational, with the ABC. He draws, outline of animal postures, and they're good, alive, you should see his mating kangaroos.'

'I have.'

'But more is needed and he can't do it all. I'm not sure I love

175

nature as much as I'm meant to. As much as he needs me to. Or even if I love drawing for that matter.'

'I'll bet you're good.'

'I'm slow. Claude's always moving on to the next thing, all go, he's driven. I'm not sure I can keep up. All night in the dark-room's par for the course for Claude. As for Norm, lab work, field trips, writing it up, analysing on two or three fronts with the Barrier Reef thrown in, that's just lifeblood for Norm. He's the youngest PhD they have. If he leaves the museum it will be for a university chair. He's the next Alec Chisholm or Ronald Strahan, the next Jock Marshall or whoever. Everyone says so. Everyone loves him. Then there's little me. I'm just very, very ordinary.'

'You're beautiful,' said Fred.

She said nothing, then said, 'Thank you.'

Firelight softened and mingled the shapes of figures around the rocks. Erica sat on her rock with a stringbag as a cushion, wearing a sleeveless bush shirt, khaki shorts, her knees together, her elbows on her knees, her strong chin cupped in her hands and her eyes inadvertently shining.

'I drink with them on Thursdays at the Gladstone Hotel,' said Fred. 'Fast rounds. It's always schooners. Claude's told me every-thing I didn't know about anything I don't, but I've forgotten it already,' he trailed off.

'Like what for example?' said Erica, as if this might be about her, or someone else, a rival he was told not to mention. He wished it was. Claude had the dilemma of a Shakespearean king – he had the queen; but other men wanted to murder him.

'Sugar gliders,' Fred said, caught in a situation where – but this was Fred – he was fundamental to the drama but irrelevant to the climax.

'Sugar gliders, I love them. Petaurus, rope-dancers, lovely things.'

'Rope-dancers,' Fred saw the word, and Consuelo jiving with Pepe like a lovely snake.

'Girls don't get asked on Thursdays – have you noticed? The boys come round to the flat later, drunk, throwing pebbles at the windows, begging to be let in.'

'Do they get let in?'

'It's against the rules.'

That was the Hen House, then, on Burton Street – nurses, students, typists under the hammer of a baritone landlady with a five o'clock shadow and bulging, blue-veined biceps. It was a legend among blokes after a few chugalugs wondering where to go next. Fred saw the curtains twitch, the hand withdrawn. He saw himself, in some future scene, bellowing from the gutter:

> *Those girls of Italy, take heed of them;*
> *They say our French lack language to deny,*
> *If they demand; beware of being captives*
> *Before you serve.*

Unhappily in love was Fred's testament of personal authenticity – Act II, Scene I of what he was fitfully memorising for the next schools' tour, if the roster clerks at Central allowed his leave without pay.

'Monday nights they're back from the bush,' said Erica, 'tired, starving. We all go out together. It's greasy spoon night – William Street. They can be scathing about everything outside their work, but they're not like workers, desperate workers, my lot: what they do doesn't kill them. They love it over everything else.'

People were drifting off to their sleeping possies.

'Goodnight, Mister Fred.' She stood and dusted her knees.

A while later he saw her standing patiently by Claude Bonney till he finished a sentence. Then they were all spread out along the cliff-line in their unknowable alignments of sleeping bags and food sacks distributed for guarding against bush rats. Fred found a sandy slit just in from under the stars with a billion tons of rock over his head.

At twenty-five, older than the brilliant Normie, closer in age to the brilliantly unpredictable Claude, both country-born boys like him but who'd got on brilliantly, Fred worked at a dead-end job stowing parcels vans on mail trains and sorting freight and waiting to hear if he'd ever be let back in to uni. Anything with wheels they rode up and down the platform before packing it in – bikes, pedal cars, pogo sticks. It was ineffably wasteful, the life of the working man: they drank stolen beer, ate purloined oysters, smoked pilfered cigarettes while sitting on their heels through-out the eight-hour day arguing philosophy and politics with trembly refugees, former professors from the Captive Nations and head cases known only by their nicknames, which, if used, drove them to murderous rages.

Station assistant left time for learning lines and scribbling in a Spirax notebook while riding a rattling goods van out towards Macdonaldtown, sometimes for hours in a kind of dream as the trains were assembled for their night runs into the vast country. One day his old headmaster, Mr Hewan, had seen him, and let his eyes glaze over out of consideration for a Cranbrook boy fallen low. Another time Buckler ran for the Illawarra express and Fred hid behind a pillar. High above the station concourse a fat neon monk, brown-robed and chubby-cheeked, dropped iridescent grapes into a wineglass advertising McWilliams Sherry. Something deficient in the visual effect seemed perfect: the way if a grape dropped down the mind twisted the image and it shot out of the glass and went flying up into the grape cluster again.

The pitiful scrapings of Fred's working day – his bludger's picnic – did not mean he was one with Buckler on the social-ism racket, the equality dream being Buckler's idea of poison to men's relations. When a union rep came round, with pre-war memories, Fred heard stories of unmarked cars from the other side, of men in suits with waddy-dongers who descended from the North Shore into Surry Hills in the 1930s with all the pompous cruelty of unwritten law and lèse-majesté. Fred knew, from reading Buckler's articles, that Buckler had been one of them, a would-be leader of the pack, who in his peevish retirement was sidelined from everything the century had hammered into him, and his inheritors, for better or worse, owned the day. Curiously they included Fred, his consolation prize.

When Rusty came down from the country she shouted Fred tea in the Station Dining Room and she seemed to know better than he did what was ahead of him, that it was great: but then of course she loved him and believed in him. In terms of being believed in, Fred looked for a love equal to that. At twenty-five – quarter of a century old! – he felt as old as he would ever get. It seemed old enough to have done what he hadn't done, as yet, which depressed him. Fred grubbed his way into his sleeping bag and adjusted his hip in a hollow of hard sand, placed his hands under his cheek and peered out at the stars.

Just for tonight Fred invested Erica Molinari with loving perfection, getting for her what Rusty never had, seeing them sitting up late at a kitchen table swapping stories, married with children (a boy and a girl). Like children themselves hardly able to keep their eyes open they stumbled off, shedding their pyjamas into a hot pile on the bedroom floor. But Claude Bonney kept intruding. The phone rang and it was Claude. He saw Claude attached to high windows by suction caps and shining a dazzling white light into the room. Awake, abruptly, it must have been around two a.m. and slugged by sleep he saw it – a light that rode in the sky, dazzling Fred as it faded and he fell back into his hip-hole again. Somebody with a spotlight. Up in the sky. How very strange.

TWELVE

MORNING AROUND THE COOKING FIRE, Fred stirred his lumpy grains and chewed his dried apricots softened by overnight soaking in spring water. An early mist drained off through the treetops. Erica looked numb, shivering beside the fire wearing a man's moth-eaten pullover. 'I could have done with another hour,' she grumbled.

'Had a rough night?' Fred wanted to say, but didn't. Without any rights in a matter he could still feel stung, and it showed.

'Dig in,' he announced in general, swivelling around on his heel, holding out an aluminium dish.

This offer for anyone to share his seeds rang a bit hollow. Erica took some and flicked a dollop onto Claude's plate. They sat hip to hip, a little bit dazed, both of them. Just to confirm the dissolute impression she turned to Claude as if Fred wasn't standing beside them and gave Claude the unmistakably dazzling smile of a woman awakening into love. Claude gave her cheek a slow brush with the back of his hand. What a shithead, what a seducer. Oh, don't you know Claude Bonney that you are fated to reckon with others when there's winning to be done?

Fred thought of the light he'd seen in the middle of the night – mysterious, hovering, dazzling – and then gone back into a thick muck of sleep. Resentment claimed that brilliance: a surge of longing for Erica, insatiable as a moth's ache. Just off the fire a cast-iron pan held bacon, scrambled eggs, baked beans. A two-gallon billy held strong black tea with floating sticks. Others swooped but Fred ignored plenty on the grounds of pride. His stocky, greedy frame had needs distinct from his mind's elevation, however, and when there was still some left he turned his back on Claude in particular and shovelled it in.

'Fred? Freddo?'

Odd man out has feelings, so wait, was the message neoned across Fred's stocky shoulders. Then, having pulsed his sour grapes back up into their bunch, he turned around.

Erica picked the floating sticks from a mug of tea and handed it to him. 'I'm sorry if I bitched a bit last night,' she said. 'You were terribly sweet. How did you sleep?'

'Like a pig.'

'Did you see the light? At two in the morning the whole sky lit up. Everyone's talking about it.'

'It woke me but I have a habit of thinking things like that are just in my head.'

'Oh, they sometimes aren't,' she said, 'surely not everything is,' leaving Fred to wonder if he really wanted to be confused by her, just in order to hope. Her physical proximity gave an answer – skin of dull gold, a perfect stillness in the way she stood with her knees a little awry and her pearly toenails grubby from campsite dirt and showing through the straps of her leather sandals.

'You could get bitten by a snake in those,' he said.

The subject of the Sydney Rockclimbers was UFOs, but Normie and Claude debated propensities of light, atmospheric lensing effects, temperature inversions dimming and enlarging distant pinpricks of light – headlights on the Dividing Range, refracted landing lights of small planes below the horizon, or, listen to this, a small plane piloted by a maniac they knew, Gilbert Dalrymple, with a gravel airstrip on his family's hardscrabble farm. They'd gone to school with him – a skinny, freckled ratbag grown into a handsome, copper-haired Robert Redford look-alike in a bomber jacket with a turned-up fur-trim collar.

'But what about aliens?' said one of the other party. 'UFOs.'

Normie gave a high laugh, his trademark of intellectual contempt. 'UFOs,' he said. 'U bloody fucking F fucking Os – I've never heard so much crap in three letters. Put it the other way around,' he challenged the Sydney Rockclimbers, hazarding aliens scouting the earth for landing sites because humankind was sending out all sorts of crisis alarm signals: 'Scrap UFOs. Make it OFUs – O, object, F, flying, U, unidentified – would you be so convinced what it was? No, you wouldn't. And you'd have it perfectly described as a natural phenomenon. An OFU. "Must be a natural effect".'

'But what?' came the peevish reply from the girl in the Rock-climbers' party.

'Do your science,' said Normie. 'It's what it's for.'

The camp site was like Pitt Street. Somebody shouted there were horsemen coming. Everyone peered back down. There they were, riders head to tail in the vertiginous valley of the Isabel, ascending a fire trail in sheriff's posse formation, sparks flying from hoofs. 'They'll be that hairy wool tie brigade, the Knoxes,' said Claude. 'They never come up here, but they'll want us to know it's private land and warn us off trespassing.'

'If it's Tim Knox I'll talk him round, no problem,' said Normie. 'Don't mention it, though,' he added, going around to each of the small group of core mates (Fred included) – meaning don't mention it was private land to the cameraman, Bob Flitch, and his offsider, the sound recordist, who were already feeling conned over putting their lives at risk, being asked to dangle from ropes while operating camera and mike. It wasn't in their contract (verbal, with Claude), but then neither was staying in their swags past breakfast with hangovers, said Claude, while the rest of them kicked their heels waiting.

When Claude went to them, two grubs on the dirt, and banged a spoon on a saucepan, Flitch barked without getting up that they could have stayed at the pub in the Junction and still got to the Walls in time. 'He's been spewing,' Claude said when he came back to the others. 'There are half-digested onion rings on the bursaria thorns.' It was Claude's first venture into documentaries. He was feeling the strain. His eye for detail was hungry, but dyspeptic.

Two soldiers arrived for the climb, a senior Australian officer, Chook Hovell, and a former commando adventurer, Gideon Pugh. The commando was the one who'd put an ice-axe through the skull of his best friend during a delirium episode in Antarctica. This information was impressive, otherwise two soldiers were the same as everyone else – no braver, no less afeared of gravity waiting on a whim of crumbling rock. Yet the knowledge they were soldiers kept them apart and a whiff of competition drifted on the breeze. Chook Hovell (of Hovell Mills, the flour-milling dynasty) had risen through the promotion ranks since winning the MC as a captain in Korea, doing it hard in barracks and jungle command posts when he could have lived the country life like his cousins, the polo players and Royal Easter Show grandees, the Pullingsvale Frizells. He was now a brigadier.

They'd made a separate camp in the night, now they came up to the overhang, ready for the day. Their arrival motivated Flitch into getting his camera out and starting work with a will. No longer a young man, he'd been a photographer with the 2/1st Battalion in Crete, escaping to Egypt in an open boat and navigating with a map of the Med torn from *Pix* magazine. The story was deemed unlikely by Claude, but Hovell vouched for this gloomy dog of a man who looked like death and could not find work in the film and television business despite having shot footage with Charles and Elsa Chauvel and taken flattering stills of Chips Rafferty, who was not a handsome man. In the code of Claude Bonney all were equal on the slopes, but what Fred liked was the underlying elitism and the way it couldn't be suppressed. As in acting you could be the best but still had to wait for the role to allow you. In that there was no call on democracy, architecture was the same – hold to the structural vision, ignore the rest – and just on this point Fred agreed with Buckler. The hand of authority surpassed consensus.

Looking up at the Isabel Walls in the changed light of morning, Fred had trouble working out where it was he'd scooted vertically as a boy. He'd been surer last night, on arrival. Now he began to have doubts over whether this was even the same place. An amble around the cliff-line would tell him, but before he could start there were groupings to be sorted. The Hovell Foundation was paying Claude's film and photographic costs and Erica's wages if she decided to join him. Hovell, who was well past forty, had never climbed. He was peerlessly willing, nonetheless. The commando Pugh was one of Claude's toughs from the Carstensz Pyramid – an ice climber, a former Royal Marine who'd mixed it on the heights with ex-Nazis.

'Meet Fred Donovan,' said Claude, doing the introductions. Fred gave Hovell the sardonically friendly salute he sometimes gave Buckler, and something about the way Fred slung him the fingers made Hovell look at him twice.

'You must be the architect,' he said, giving Fred the satisfaction of having been talked about, and having been talked about in the shape of the most idealised conception of himself, beloved of both Rusty and Buckler – 'architect' – of which ambition in his life so far he had fallen short, a role that might nonetheless leave behind at curtain-fall something more enduring than just the shimmer of an effect.

Chook Hovell and his commando had an air of having seen things, done things, that necessarily made them sad, proud and ashamed. (Fred, of all people, could guess: he was a reader of seared emotions.) They were recently back from Malaya and Indochina, now doing higher duties at the Royal Military College, Duntroon, and needed the dry crackle of the Australian bush in their ears, Hovell said, and the whiff of Australian dust in their nostrils to know what they stood for. They held back, checking and re-checking their ironmongery of karabiners and pitons. The commando, Pugh, was a short, square man, of the sort that was said never to get on well on rock, with legs like barrels. It showed how you could be wrong. Chook was almost freakishly tall and thin. He was well over six feet with a narrow protuberance of chest bones that crowded up towards his throat and made him look suspended in the act of swallowing, even while talking. His face was narrow, his nose beaked and his jaw was angular, off-centre, and he had a strange need, every few minutes while eating, to lay down his spoon, take hold of his jaw with both hands and crack it back into line. His eyes were something else altogether: they offered trust.

Shakespeare for Schools last year was a medley of scenes from the history plays. Mentally Fred opened the script to lines that weren't his, but he knew all too well:

> Say Warwick was our anchor; what of that?
> And Montague our top-mast; what of him?
> Our slaught'red friends the tackles; what of these?
> Why, is not Oxford here another anchor?
> And Somerset another goodly mast?
> The friends of France our shrouds and tacklings?

Among others, in a varied cameo, Fred had been France on the tour and the Queen Margaret speaking these lines his intense (heart-punching) girlfriend of a lifetime's hopes condensed to a mere week of backblock hotel iron bedsteads; and, he supposed, with jealousy so intense it tattooed strain lines on his face, the list of lords she recited and threw that lord *France* at him (while he was louring off-stage) were her past, present or proposed conquests. If women's hurts were big enough to fill every bucket of tears in the world, men's were a bucket of shameful want.

Shame unassimilable, to use a Buckler phrase on the murderous possibilities of the battlefront and the frontier life of his youth. That was Fred, battered but going forward, and he saw it in Hovell and the commando. It seemed to dust them with under-standing equivalent to something that either could not be put into words, or if words were possible, they'd be from the Bard.

Fred found himself standing next to them when lots were being drawn on climbing teams, and he saw Claude distinctly shuffling the list, so that, to his surprise, it was: 'Fred, you're army.'

While Claude and Normie and the others planned routes, and the soldiers got ready, and the cameraman screwed and unscrewed lenses, and the sound man counted to four, and again to four, as he played himself back, Fred scooted around the cliff-line to a starting point. The Sydney Rockclimbers were already on their way, having elected to do something impossible for which they were likely to be remembered in thirty or forty years' time. Fred clambered around them and watched as the first and then the second (including their curly-topped, skinny, flat-chested girl) winkled handholds from a narrow crevice, which they all went speedily up.

Fred moved around the corner out of sight. Somewhere like this was what he remembered, a clean wall with deep-fissured cracks with gum trees growing out from them. He remembered when he came with Buckler the way the Walls' rock sprang straight up from under the ground, clean as a cut, as if it had happened yesterday and not two hundred million years ago. It was Fred's primal playground revived on a grander scale, home of the Superboy-cloaked Petaurus breviceps, short-headed rope-dancer, ribbon in the rock, emotion set in stone. Here at Isabel Walls it had proved to be so – Erica stepping from that imprisonment, driving Fred a little insane before stepping back. Rock's hard and rock's permeable aspects remained true to a conundrum: you were given in total what you could not have.

Across to the left was an exposed curve profiled with backlit handholds, and Fred decided on a quick warm-up before his name was called. So he extended a hand experimentally and flexed his toes in his Dunlop Volleys, then slipped and slithered, gouging grip into his footsoles until he reached a place where the handholds were knobbly, and he could start moving up confidently instead of low and along. The rock was sandstone conglomerate, an old seabed quitted of its storms and thrust inland over the millennia. Just above tree height it became more vertical, but the going was easier, almost laughably like climbing a ladder, a laced fretwork of choices that sped him, before he knew it, onto a ledge that he remembered so clearly and plainly and personally now. It was a true part of himself. Snow gums. Outlook. Half the world under his feet.

But this was shocking. It was where he'd reached for the sky, sure enough, and looked down at Buckler with his feet poking out from under his hat. It was where he'd remembered his triumph and gained his great sense of himself at the age of thirteen. And it was not very high at all, perhaps only thirty or forty feet out of the available three hundred. It was only about one-tenth of the way up the flatirons, snub-nosed slabs that took a step back from there, then continued soaring, stack after stack after stack. On his right was the gully where he went slithering down to Buckler's nod. So the most boasted part of that day, its pinnacle, so to speak, which had brought him back here yesterday, dancing ahead of his mates, was a lie.

Fred stepped to the edge and looked down. In a clearing out from the overhang appeared the party of riders, men and women, with Normie Powell moving among them, talking. There was shouting – maybe a conflict brewing – but there was laughter. Fred made his way slowly a bit higher, to get a better look and check out routes as best he could, being careful to be sure he could work his way back to the ledge again. His legs were going nervous on him, beginning to shake. Everything vertical had gone vertical beyond belief. Diagonally higher, the Sydney Rockclimbers were stopped in their progress, belting in expansion bolts with ringing blows. Was Fred expected to go up there? He next heard cheering from below. Faces all looking up. At him? It was likely if he made it so, so he posed, King Kong – X of clammy fur at right-angle to the up.

'Catch!' someone yelled.

Fred looked up and saw a face far above and an arm holding a coil of rope. Catch pronounced *kotch*.

A cascade of nylon came whipping down. The Sydney Rockclimbers peered across from their neighbouring pitches where they were busy copyrighting their names in slow motion.

The rope floated uncoiling until it speeded dramatically and struck Fred's ledge like a whip, doubled, tripled, quadrupled, pouring into a pile on the flat stones at his feet. Then, way above, a figure stepped out into the void and came abseiling down, bounding, cursing, talking to itself – yodelling the descent, stopping every now and again to wrench at bushes hurled away over a shoulder.

'Filthy Cooper,' he named himself, or seemed to, as he landed. Wolfie Keuper: he wore boots like blocks of brown wood, bristling long socks up to his knees and leather half-trousers held up by braces, a checked shirt and a Tyrolean hat. He had a pencil-thin moustache and eyeballs like black beads that stared at Fred as if he wanted to destroy him. 'Bloody Aussies,' he challenged, with flecks of white foam on his lips.

A wedge-tailed eagle soared, eyeing the crawling humans.

The sound was like the beating of a lumpy carpet or a coarse pillowcase, a whooshing, swiping, dragging flutter of calico against threads and hard knots. The wrist action was somehow sports-like, a golf stroke by a lone player meeting with clumsy rebuttals all the time, coming up hard against the stalks and needles and woody stems of acacia and hakea, banksia and bottlebrush and whatever else lived in suspension in the semi-sky of the Isabel Walls.

Fred, lashed to a rock, belayed Claude from above, adjusting slack while Claude did work for the camera. If Claude fell he'd be safe thanks to Fred. On a higher ledge Chook Hovell held Fred in turn. Major Gideon Pugh called Erica a tasty bit of cheese. Erica, whooping with laughter, was swung aloft in a bosun's chair to show the cameramen it was easy. A sprite of a girl could do it. Spring into the empty air and propel herself along the cliff-edge by the toes. This was the party now. A great success with Claude away on his new career.

Into Claude's calico specimen bag fell spirals of wiry blossom, gingery streaks of pollen and sticky extrusions taken from beaten plant-life, where insects dwelt at this time of day, on this particular slab of cliff: a selection of creeping, crawling, buzzing, fluttering specks enlarged for the small screen as the hefty Arriflex whirred. Flitch sweated and held the camera grip to his shoulder. Claude put his nose in the bag, grazed his eyes over the haul. When he turned the bag inside-out over a fist and sucked on the tube – the 'pooter' – whisking selections into the capturing chamber, he was the wickedly intelligent boy outclassing his classmates in a town too small for his brain. 'This is me,' he seemed to say. 'It's what I do. And I've only just started.'

The horseriders far below, far from raving, greeted Claude and Normie as prodigal sons of the soil. They watched through pocket binoculars the camera pair being lowered to change film and batteries. Then the whole universe seemed activated, magnetised as the hum of an aircraft was heard; and an ugly low-winged monoplane with a narrow, high cockpit emerged between hills and plugged along the cliff-line throttled back with its wingflaps lowered like dunny doors. The pilot waved. Suspended in lazy time he hung there intent on an object, on a moving fleck on the Walls, on a person, on Erica – dusty-gold girl in a green T-shirt and shorts, *fresh as a blossoming gumnut flower*, thought Fred, sourly, as the pilot backfired the agricultural Auster in a firecracker sequence, pinning her to admiring echoes.

'Oh, dear God,' said Erica. 'Dalrymple.'

'Who?' said Fred.

'Gilbert Dalrymple,' said Claude.

'There's never excitement like this in a town unless Shakespeare for Schools gets the call,' said Fred, wrenching attention onto himself. 'Then it's Gertie get your pants off.'

'The old town was never a hotbed of wild ideas,' said Claude. 'My old man and a schoolteacher, Jack Slim, were on the outer and proud of it. Old man Dalrymple was a nut case. My father, the level-crossing keeper, was the hammer, the sickle of intellectual Bolshevism was Slim.'

'*Jack* Slim?' said Fred. The name had mythical overtones.

'My best friend was Eddie Slim, the son, we had a wake the night Stalin died, smoked ourselves silly, saw things we shouldn't

191

have. I cheated for Slim in exams, wrote up his formulas. He's gone on to geology, I suppose it's not that hard.'

They joined Chook Hovell who used army binoculars on the bunch way below.

'Who is that one?' he said from his perch on the next ledge up.

'Which one?'

'The bloke on the grey, ten o'clock from the woman in the red scarf.'

Claude said, 'It's Edwina Knox in the scarf, the dowager queen. Next to her's Tim, her youngest, who's Normie's mate. On the grey? That's Kingsley Colts, the referee when Normie's father was made a quad.'

'A damaging sort of a bloke, then,' said Hovell. Not a question, more a pronouncement.

'He's the last one anyone blames,' said Claude.

'Kingsley Colts,' said Fred. 'Good name for a man on a horse. He should wear a crown.'

'Colts,' said Hovell with a tight, sick smile. He put his binoculars away and noisily cleared his throat. He tilted his head and gave it a couple of hard shakes until his jaw gave a loud click.

Fred watched him from the side.

You are the strangest-faced, freakiest old scarecrow I've ever had the pleasure of looking at, thought Fred.

A little later Fred found himself alone with Hovell, their backs to the rock wall and their knees pulled tight to their chins.

'Architecture,' said Hovell, with a gift of encouragement in his voice. 'Tell me about your architecture, Fred.'

Fred found himself spilling it out.

One day, he improvises – leaping over the obstacles of Central Railway workdays and a non-existent university degree, and indeed leaping over his acting hopes and what they might mean

– one day he won't do any designing at all, just lead clients to rock shelters and give them an etiquette for sewage control. Let them feel the wind curve around the bones of their fore-heads – the first verandah. Let them pound a stone – the first kitchen. When Fred talks this way he gets a nod of understand-ing. He remembers, he says, his childhood. It was all up trees and chimney-like crevices. Architecture and the tree. The cave. The shelter. 'The world is a house,' Fred declares.

'Well put,' says Hovell. 'But a troubled house.'

'I'm one of the lucky ones,' Fred blurts. 'Our house had forty rooms, each with a numbered door, cooks, waiters, maids with brooms and a yardman with an old Ford truck loaded with beer barrels that I got to ride round the town before I could practi-cally walk.'

'You're still a big kid?'

Fred laughs. For sure. But he doesn't mean that. He just means lucky. Hovell draws it out of him. Because why Fred should be lucky or say he's lucky beats him. Just when he's had his heart hammered, squared off and packed down under a billion tons of sedimentary rock. Just when he's turned twenty-five, his quarter century (ye gods) of non-achievement.

Without quite realising how it was done, except in a kind of daytime dream, Fred finds himself three hundred feet up, at the pinnacle of the Isabel Walls, where climbers are able to step off onto somewhat flat ground. It is a geographical surprise up there. A lost kingdom. Fred likens it to getting to the top of a steep escalator and gliding off onto a lumpy level floor, with a low forest of scattered white-trunked gum trees and a rutted two-wheeled track running through. Here is Wolfie Keuper's Kombi Van in a glade. Here the Isabel Walls lean their praying hands on the cheek of the rusting Buddha, Mt Knox, a head of dry grass and scattered sub-alpine mallees.

One by one, the others arrive. Fred props his satchel against a tree and reclines in the shade, looking out for Erica.

Normie's boots tom-tom an old log bridge soil-covered after years, with gaps showing a clear stream running underneath. 'Water!' yells Normie Powell.

All the elements of Normie's world are at hand – sustenance at the root and out to the tip the motto. Happiness, he remembers, climbed from water where it found its time to live in arduous circumstances. Urey and Miller had shown it in 1952. Look them up, he has no time to tell you. Normie himself saw, eleven years later, in a river swimming hole, a space where solid matter slid into air, and water diverted to earth creating life: where a done man breathed and splashed. Normie and Chook Hovell converse animatedly, then Claude cries, 'Action!' and Normie turns to the camera and explains interconnectedness to which he gives the name ecology. The acting is bad, the technique could be improved. Normie is awful, Claude is better, but Normie is the great teacher now.

And again, it is Fred who knows all this. Sees Chook Hovell taking in the words while Gideon Pugh looks bad-tempered, kneeling, sorting through ironmongery and ropes. It appears that Pugh had words with Erica; he wants her, like a toad wants a juicy bug. He might put an ice axe through her if she spurns him. She will need protection. How does Fred know this? Doesn't have to be told. Clumping, ordinary old Fred with his mental flashes. Or so he casts himself, hero of the hour, bearer and preventer of lusts bedevilling a woman he'll love until he dies, but in all probability never have.

Claude Bonney, Chook Hovell, Normie Powell and Gideon Pugh slither around the bridge and slide down a peaty mass of wet roots. At their feet is a gravelly ledge where clear spring water spills into a bowl of rock. They gulp down water. It is hot now in the midafternoon. Erica stripes a hand up through her hair, dippers cool water behind her ears and feels a pair of eyes on her neck. Must wonder lightly if it's any one of them, but no, it's Fred. She's a little away from the rest. He's holding wattle blossom and presents a sprig with a gruff line: 'Churl, upon thy eyes I throw all the power this charm doth owe.'

'Act two, scene two. Beautiful,' she twirls the blossom, then hands it back to him. 'But I'm just a bit allergic to this stuff.'

'You seem like one of those people who studied a play once. Carved it up in sections.' Fred parks the offering in a bush. 'Layered it into yourself. And never forgot.'

'My Intermediate year,' she nods. 'Correspondence school in a kangaroo shooter's caravan at Byrock. Just me and my dad, Silvio.'

'It can't have been all that long ago,' Fred tries a little harder.

Claude, on his knees, intones for the camera, 'This is just great! *Drosera peltata* – don't step on it.'

The others are drinking their fill and don't even think about what he means – a swathe of glistening sundews higher up the bank, light catching on their sticky insect-trapping tentacles. Flitch says Claude's continuity is up shit creek.

'Well, fuck continuity,' says Claude.

'You can't do that,' says Fred, looking over Flitch's shoulder. Fred is a film festival habitué and director manqué. He's every-thing and nothing in all of his contexts.

Erica sits rubbing her knees – they have begun to ache on the climb – and watches Fred ripping into a tin of sardines. Churl indeed. Now he's made that swipe she can't take her eyes from him, the way when crossing an open paddock she keeps eye contact with the bull. Sullen-eyed, Pugh has backed off.

'Anyone want some?' Fred's arm goes back, he's about to fling the empty away. Then shamefacedly he crushes the can under his boots, wraps it in newspaper and drops it back into his pack. It wasn't even his. It came from the communal haul. Tonight he'll burn, bash and bury. This for Erica's sake. A fiery sanction to a bushland queen.

'I've tried explaining to Silvio, my dad, what Claude and Normie do, how it's important and worthwhile, but he can't understand it. Not when it's not about survival the way he understands survival. Why do they have to go all those places and find the little kangaroos? He can give them all the big roos they want.'

Fred leans back, pulls his hat over his eyes and takes a five-minute smoko. After an interval of resistance a woman finds herself open to persuasion, and why not? Because it happens. Blink awake Erica Molinari and be in love.

Claude and Normie carry on that everything hasn't been got the first go. It'll be another day tomorrow. Flitch is exhausted, exasperated, and it falls to Fred to explain the need for close-ups and cutaways a little more carefully to Claude, who until he learns to use a movie camera will obstinately hold that a movie gets made by the simple expedient of sweeping the lens like a fire hose back and forth over whatever is being looked at.

Down they go abseiling to the bottom of the cliffs again to get ready for another try. Again, it's Fred with his rehearsed wisdom who shines light into the day. Trees, rocks, pathways – beams of sunlight blessing them like pilgrims – flats of lomandra awaiting a bushfire's torch, a flash of a rust-pelted animal – dingo? The tracks say yes, but nobody believes the evidence of their eyes. Something has torn open the sack hanging in a tree holding perishables. Maybe a brown dog run loose from a bush camp and genetically turned back to something finer. Too wonderful to be true if so.

And on that score take a long smooth wall of stained granite the Sydney Rockclimbers have moved their camp under – it must be twenty feet high, set out from the great cliff-line from where it fell, eons ago, with gnarled snow gums and strange mallees fringing its out-of-reach top. Their eyes tell them it's a geological formation, but their hearts cry out, 'It's a monastery wall!' and behind its shelter not the click of insects they hear but the hum of prayer wheels and the chant of saffron-robed monks.

That night by the camp fire Fred recites a one-man show of bushland tales: how his father, a miner, as he describes him, a famous old fart, took him camping and cooked a vomitous mix of nut meat and sweet potato. Fred would rather have starved, so tipped his plate behind bushes, coming back at his father with a wide grin.

Well, some of that is invented. Not all of it, though. The camping bit, the two of them all alone. It happened.

'There was a tree I remember,' Fred begins, then goes vague again. To admit that a man who was a First World War survivor fathered him in a goat's old age might age him too much. Precocious wisdom's all right but not wearing an old man's trousers.

Others take up themes: one of the Sydney Rockclimbers, Jim, is Greek. Sitting in the sidestreet outside his father's Marrickville fruit shop, leaning on his schoolbag against the wall, doing homework on the footpath because it's easier than in the house, he goes on to become a lawyer.

'I like Greeks,' says Fred.

'How do you know any?' asks Jim.

'Well, there's the milk bar, the fish and chips. "The Greeks".'

'Careful what you say.'

'I had a Greek stepfather.'

But that is not true. Fred hardly knew his mother's manfriend with the waxed moustache.

Erica for some reason confesses her first boyfriend, who wore a three-piece suit that made her feel safe as he drove his car up a side road in Dubbo. It also made her laugh, which was her 'downfall'. And still is, she smiles at Fred, without saying it, though Fred gets it, as if it's addressed to him uniquely, for his own sour delectation. He after all has a great sense of humour. He can be the butt of a joke. He can love and surrender his love. He can tumble in the torrent of life, appearing and disappearing in the foam.

'Where's Fred?' chortles Jim, remembering another story he wants to tell that most appreciative of sponges.

But Fred is nowhere to be seen. Odd man out has feelings.

They are fuzzy from the pleasure of drinking wine under the stars, good wine cooled in the spring, firelight reflected in a bright circle against the black, owl-hooting, animal-crashing night. The camera team has bush-bashed and then driven into the Five Alls for cold beers on a clean-wiped bar and the promise of a feather bed.

Fred stands out beyond the ring of fire and pursues the fingernail moon. She loves me, she loves me not. Time to cast the die, except an imponderably weepy part of himself knows the die is already cast. For the last half hour he's been crassly positioning himself so that when Erica chooses between him and Claude – he has the shabby dream of a partner-switch – she'll find his shoulder handy to lean her sleeping head upon. Some quest.

It leads him to the base of a vast old tree. There is a noise in the tree – a scrabble of claws. *What's going on up there?* he wonders, in those shattered branches and late-shooting eucalyptus buds? He shines the narrow beam of his torch and sees a pair of enormous eyes and a damp, pink nose – squirrel glider! Why does this fill his heart? Why does he breathe the words, 'You've come back'?

When he returns to the camp Claude's head is in Erica's lap, and she's stroking his hair, oh so predictably sweet, and the whole damned lot of them are singing 'Yellow Submarine'.

Conclusion: Fred is the odd man out for life. But the feeling suddenly isn't bad – quite the opposite, really, except for brushing away a tear – and Fred comes into the firelight noisily, heavily, commanding. 'The iron tongue of midnight hath told twelve. Lovers, to bed; 'tis almost fairy time. This palpable gross play hath well beguil'd the heavy gait of night.'

'Amen,' say the voices by the fire.

The next day climbing, Fred declares he's giving up acting. He's going to write a book. Architecture? Ditto for the shove. A book to draw the elements of his half-created life into a place between two covers, sewn, glued and stamped with gold lettering.

But nobody believes him and he doesn't believe it himself, because slumped by the trackside fatigued and guzzling water he gets the idea for the part he's auditioned for lately, but spurned – Estragon in *Godot*.

It's not coming. It's not going. It's a railway platform. It's a situation in the bush, under a cliff-line, in the natural way of things. That's what he knows and it makes him sit up, look around – this architecture of the world's stage. It's somewhere here in the crumbling socket of a tree. There's a tree in that play onstage throughout. God knows what it means but it's Fred's tree anyway, by which he was found just in time somehow, and yet so trustingly, when the iron tongue of midnight struck.

THIRTEEN

KINGSLEY COLTS SAT IN THE town park smoking and staring at cracks in the concrete between his boots. It was a Saturday afternoon. Roars of hope and disappointment came from the football ground where he'd mistimed his ref's whistle and allowed two giants their moment of destruction. The event was long-remembered but nobody blamed Colts the way he blamed himself. There he sat through the one afternoon of the week when he'd lost himself in the game, and lost some part of his will or drive as a consequence.

Isabel Junction was a town of rusting metal roofs and termite-eaten verandah posts emblematic of the Australian scene. Tragedy came from shadows of clouds, wind in the hills' puffy cheeks brought it on – drive your car into a tree, fry yourself on an overhead line, drown in your bath, allow two giants their moment of destruction. The Greeks had a name for it: goat-song. You had to laugh. It might have been you next time but wasn't. If you started a grassfire when your slasher hit rocks, throwing sparks, or made some other sort of trivial error, soon rectified, you were never forgiven by Randolph Knox. In Colts's case the misdemeanour, so huge it cleft his life into before and after, was not talked about, not even by Randolph except to his cat: Vince Powell's injury in the match Colts had controlled, or rather had not controlled in the moment that counted.

Frosty with knowingness Randolph was not exempt from joining the general populace on the point. Colts was a lonely wonder, great as a statue cracked by lightning and dripping with marble tears. Randolph would always remember with a shudder of complicity that a lesser Knox cousin had struck half the blow, leaving Vince Powell paralysed. It bound him to Colts with canny possessiveness. Together they memorialised a moment of legendary life. It could never be taken away.

Shambling up the hill on his way to the game, wearing a green trilby, a red MacFarlane clan scarf and carrying a shooting stick, Randolph came to where Colts sat in Pioneers Park rolling a smoke.

They talked as if there'd been no years of sustained almost-silence. Colts licked the dry glue of the Tally-Ho with the tip of his tongue.

'They've kicked off,' said Randolph looking down at his shoes. Then he looked up and met Colts's troubled eyes.

Colts angled his head to indicate he'd heard, and at the same time, low by his pocket, extracted a match from a matchbox with the fingers of one hand and struck a flame.

'You're not coming?'

'There's goats and kings,' said Colts, sucking in smoke. 'Or have you forgotten?'

'No need for that,' said Randolph. '"Kings are earth's gods, in vice their law's their will, and if Jove stray, who dares say, Jove doth ill?"'

'Do say,' said Colts. 'I'm impressed.' There was a long pause then. 'Suppose I should say thanks,' he added, not quite understanding, or rather, not understanding quite what Randolph meant, except it was pretentious yet seemed to be a statement of something he ought to attach importance to, possibly respect.

There was a tour of Shakespeare for Schools that week, with Randolph sitting in the front row leading the applause for the young cast, just as he had at Stratford in the '50s when he saw Larry and Vivien, as he called the Oliviers with strained familiarity.

'Come to the play tonight.'

'I don't think so,' said Colts.

Randolph had seen it twice.

'Well, then, afterwards, meet them in the Lounge Bar.'

It's forgotten the glittering comets that roared across rural skies bringing utmost sophistication and unbridled bad behaviour to country towns: a cast of men and girls in their twenties, priapic young egomaniacs playing the poet–prince and cutting a swathe through loveliness with its legs in the air.

Drinks were on Randolph as he introduced Colts to the lead, Fred Donovan, who played Richard III, Bottom and Malvolio in an anthology of scenes, and still had smudged kohl-eyes after dashing from school hall to bar. 'He's only twenty-seven,' Randolph said. 'Tremendously close to genius.' Later he said, 'They're university students. He's doing architecture, final year. He holds the Lady Margaret Hovell Scholarship for Promising Design, quite a coup. They say he'll get the University Medal after a rocky start. He went to Cranbrook.'

That was a school of a better sort down the hill from their old school overlooking Sydney Harbour. During their estrangement Randolph had missed the pleasure of uniting elements of Colts's early life with the way he lived now. It was something Colts was unable to do himself, Randolph believed, a matter of laying gifts of understanding at Colts's feet, he was the sphinx of provocation.

Soon the cast went out of control with jugs of Reschs and crushed packets of crisps strewn underfoot, bare-legged girls sitting on the knees of shearers and stagehands plucking noisy guitars. Randolph was left forgotten except for his wallet. Colts saw Donovan, a stocky young man, leaning a young woman from the cast against a backstairs wall and shoving his hands up her dress.

Colts wandered out the back where timber offcuts burned in a forty-four gallon drum. The blaze lit faces. One of them was Alan Hooke's, seen dancing with that reckless girl, Barbara, to the thump of 'Satisfaction' played from a portable gramophone on the tailgate of a ute. Most of the time Colts was numb, but here like this he could let himself go. Far older than this crowd (Hooke was barely eighteen) Colts rock-and-rolled like an ape, laughter showing his teeth. Everyone became a shadow at midnight; they mingled as one. In the mornings he'd remember little, till the return of creeping shame. Sunday mornings: Vince Powell would be sitting in the front row pew at St Aidan's, strapped to his chair with leather belts holding down his convulsions. Alan Hooke would be in the choir.

Randolph Knox was away most weekends but that hardly mattered over what he knew. See how Colts tripped from Lounge Bar to Public Bar and back again and out to the yard. Know how a clean, lean bloke fell into habits so fast he seemed since the year of Vince Powell's mauling to belong to their shape – stumbling into the night with Tub Maguire and other humans long stripped of shame around port wine and proof spirits.

Vince Powell's funeral was conducted by the bishop, attended by half the synod. Maguires came from all over the country, rolling up in old cars held together by hope and binder twine. A former ship's bosun piped the coffin home. Pamela Slim wearing black was one of the women comforting Jenny Powell. She came over from the tragic side of town: some thought The

Crow had never left it, the way she appeared at the end of that street, leading to the town common, where nobody went except the garbage lorry attended by garbage men and kids who never went to school.

When the cortege arrived at the cemetery, its tail end was still crowding the herringbone brick pathways of St Aidan's. On Cemetery Hill, in sight of swimming hole and rugby field, Normie Powell came forward at a prearranged moment and kicked a football into the grave. Randolph disliked the gesture as it seemed foreign to the restraint required of custom as old as the worn earth itself: ashes to ashes, dust to dust. What made it worse was it was done with a showy drop-kick, greeted by applause.

There were wakes all over the town. Total strangers cried. Colts's reprobate companions included Randolph's younger brother, Tim. Then came a bunch of Tim's friends renting a farm-house and outbuildings along an eroded creek sixteen kilometres from town. They seemed to be part of a criminal class at the same time as they wrote their PhDs. It was a time of disintegration, disrespect, disenchantment, disaccord.

The effect of the times on Colts, as far as Randolph could tell, was to spoil his appearance. He grew his hair long. It looked like a horror show dangling around his cadaverous stock agent's skinny frame. The times were childish with their idiot games of skinny-dipping and gold-capped mushroom hunts. Acting your age was a test of character. Randolph went all out for culture in cravat and suede shoes. Ted Merrington, the scrap-metal merchant with a private school background and a noisy basso profundo, praised Randolph as a man of taste and Randolph lapped up the flattery, seating Merrington at dinner parties near the traymobile handy to the wine and advising him on live-stock and land values on the Isabel.

A name worth collecting came up: Veronica Buckler.

'You want?' said Randolph, high on gin and bitter lemon.

'A wink is as good as a nod to a blind horse, Randy.'

All was small gains, but 'be thankful for small mercies' was Randolph's motto around the restored friendship with Colts. Summers without Colts at cricket, winters without him at rugby. This was how life was now, they were used to it. The bung-lunged cross-country athlete was gone. The sportsman Colts, the great sheep-classer Colts – protégé of Captain Oakeshott, equal of Otway Falkiner and Basil Clapham – the genial recounter of episodes in New Guinea coastwatching, had left town leaving a slurred cheerio.

The man remaining had the same name, same face, same genial consideration, same bellows-wheeze after effort. But still with that forsaken and preoccupied, faraway look a boy had on Eureka. Colts did the same work but never as peerlessly as once. You couldn't help liking him still. You called him Kings, and he was royal like that. You felt helpless to watch. He just needed a bloody haircut and the stuffing put back in him.

There were explanations, deeds, actions and amends. By the late '70s, Colts was Alan Hooke's baby daughters' childhood Uncle Kingsley. Alan had married the reckless Barbara. Colts was Tim Knox and Pepita Wolmsley's boozy, wiser older friend. They too had children. Randolph marched on Anzac Day, wearing his older brother Sandy's medals. Colts, a returned man, did not.

Colts was on Pamela Slim's visiting list after all this time. They were, though the word was not used, lovers. Still rootin' was the descriptive phrase applied to the situation.

Pamela caught the slow train down from Sydney, doing embroidery and reading hefty novels. Lost in thought she turned a page with a licked finger and looked out the window. On the historical side, reading taught her opposites combined, leaving nothing to argue about. Small towns obeyed the conventions of empires, curtains drawn between acts. Lonely sidings with eucalyptus trees and dusty roads leading out at right angles had a Chekhovian precedence: the epitome of provincial summer afternoons with their muffled couplings in tin-roofed homesteads.

Talk of an affair in past years between stock agent ('randy as a goat') and schoolteacher's wife ('can't get enough of it') was condensed down to the reality of the everyday. Nobody gossiped anymore on who collected whom from the train, where they went or what they did banging the headboards in Woodbox Gully till dogs along the creek bank throttled themselves barking at the end of their chains past midnight. Not even Randolph Knox.

The only one messing it up was Eddie Slim, a dream of bad conscience. Nothing explained him. His mother was at a loss. Dialectical materialism had no answers. Theology might have an answer with its talk of original sin. Ever since Eddie did over the town's milk money on a moonlit night there'd been galloping disappointment. He would be, in a novel, the spoiler returning to make an impossible gripe: con man, card sharp, petty thief, pretender to the throne. At seventeen the Institute for Industrial Psychology in Hunter Street did a test, ranking him capable. And he was. But badness was a virus undetectable in any test.

Pamela was a middle-aged woman now, thicker of figure but moving with her weight balanced like a dancer, showing grace and fine beauty in a pair of tailored slacks and a linen blouse unbuttoned at the throat. If it seemed inexplicable that she would give herself to a man like Colts, remember her themes were pity and disappointment as well as a somewhat anti-doctrinaire contrariness, hammered on the anvil of her married life. 'A woman's natural mission was to find where she was most appreciated and the point was to find out where that was' – this from another of her hefty novels. Well, she had tried.

'Shine a light into yourself,' she'd said to Colts, on more than one occasion doing his thinking for him around what he needed to do, in a woman's way; but as well ask him to wield a crowbar and crack himself open or blow his brains out.

He couldn't, though he knew what she meant. Just sometimes the openings asked of a man came good, but hardly long enough to count, and life at the best of times was a camera lens jammed hardly wider than a slit. Everything that counted had happened in his early life, even before he was born. He could not be, and never would be, what he was meant to be, what he'd been told he would be when a man: Kingsley Colts, son of the late Colonel Colts, the father he'd never known, ward of such legacy as worlds were made from, to become 'Dunc Buckler's kid'. He was a particular reason why a great war had been fought, why a continent was planted with homesteads and fenced, in opposition to desolation. But sometimes Colts woke in the mornings and took in the full gush of light. Then it was good, and the world was ready for him. He smiled, and looked at Pamela wonderingly.

She had learned what few knew: that Colts was a naturally generous man. Hard working, unambitious, helpful. With all that there was the bafflement a woman liked teasing out. She had come knocking at his door when Eddie was a boy. Jack was ill that winter and she'd sought the name of a yardman to get firewood for the classroom and school residence stoves. Colts had no idea of his own best side: within half a day he had the places stacked with logs and trucks arriving with more. He'd done all the splitting and stacking himself and Jack never had to work the woodpile again. A man was not himself unless he excelled himself. Nothing in nature was. She saw it in Colts. She heard Colts drawing raspy breath and was moved by the effort taken. When Colts placed his hand on her head, strangely like a blessing, or watched her moving around the room, picking up her sewing, or standing at the window looking at the alabaster white of frost in the yard, and he smiled at her, rather hesitantly, as in a dream intractable to understanding, she felt a great peacefulness completely irrelevant to the torment of the century (which Jack marched to) or her personal life (where her direct pain was set). Most people had to reach up in life in order to make themselves. Colts was an example of someone who'd needed to reduce or detract from himself in order to get down to what mattered in himself, the contained seed of himself always just out of reach in the soup of failure.

Pamela sat up on the pillows and Colts brought her a pot of tea. He made her laugh by pouring it from high above the cup. She had a rush of feeling, so grateful she was for such moments. 'I have to say,' she said, 'that I could get used to this.'

This was strange of her, as they'd had something like it over the years. The routine of the teapot. The routine of the buttered toast. Always reliable. Always the same. Never varying, a Craven A on the bedside ashtray ready. Nothing more ever asked.

'What do you mean,' Colts looked away as he spoke, '"get used"?'

'Well, Kings,' said Pamela, a bit tensely, a bit searchingly and penetratingly defensive. 'I might even learn what it's like to be truly loved.'

Staggered, Colts thought, *This can't be me.*

There would already have been phone calls starting at six a.m., Hooke & Hooke clients dictating his day. He'd be leaving the house around seven. That was enough for her, and what she returned for, what she found in their adulterous friendship: his gaze on parting or arrival, looking out from a settled world where nothing ever changed if he could help it. She'd never asked what it was for him beyond the craving of touch. Colts never wrote inviting her, it was she who made the choice of when to come. To pick up a telephone or send a telegram was unthinkable on his part. Patterns of nature, seasons and other people's needs besides theirs were involved. Advised by mail, he'd be at the station to greet her, or not, depending on his work movements all over the countryside. She would go to his house then and tidy it up. There was never much to do. Colts would live, if need be, from a cardboard carton or a Globite suitcase. And had.

Later she'd walk to the wrong side of town and visit the Maguires. He'd return to find her sitting on the verandah marking her place at around page nine hundred. 'Oh, Kings, there you are – just listen to this.'

He'd gaze at her while she read him a passage, giving his fullest attention, then he'd go in and put the kettle on. There was no incessant twitter of the intellectual sort, where nothing was ever resolved. He'd taken her on train-droving trips where they'd travelled through pastoral landscapes, where it was hardly believable they weren't on a rattling ride through paradise. His acceptance was profound.

Although Pamela never said a word against her husband or son, she took that gaze of Colts's back with her to be with them. Kings never took a stand on anything much, compared with the stands lives of principle demanded – hers, Jack's. There was none of that old-time rancour of the right – Buckler's – left for Kings to work, except he sometimes said, when election day came round, that he inoculated himself against the bile of Hooke & Hooke clients by sheltering his pencil in his elbow in the voting booth and voting for whoever he damned well liked. There were years when he did that, he said, against the best interests of the rural rump royal: he meant Randolph, a Country Party somebody. Pamela alone of all Colts's friends and acquaintances

210

– save Randolph – knew the impulse related to Buckler more than anyone, to maintaining the true life he'd made for himself over against Buckler's tremendous influence on him as a boy. After the war Buckler had stepped back onto the earth as an extraordinary aged ape, he was now in his eighties, but in Colts's dreams still drove an old finger-slapper grader with clusters of lightning bolts sparking from the blade. Colts was in animated suspension in regard to the passing of the years – his friends seemed to get younger and younger – lucky Colts, perhaps.

Jack Slim bent every rule in the book to keep Eddie from having convictions recorded against his name. Pamela likewise had never said no to their son, but argued it would teach Eddie nothing to fight it out for him through one or other of the QCs of the left who did Jack's bidding. Colts spoke of farming equipment wheeled from sheds, with cars and tractors flogged not by Eddie perhaps but by a suspected bunch whose names along with Eddie's stained the fledgling records of Isabel Junction Intermediate High.

Jack's way won, the QCs won, and Eddie free as a bird swindled a mining partner in Western Australia and was back east driving a new Land Cruiser.

'Not all that glitters is gold,' said Pamela.

Eddie just stared at her, giving his mother that worst feeling, a son's contempt of her as a woman.

'Say I know what I know, not all gold's dinkum, either,' he said.

Jack was tinny too – like father, like son – but you had to be clever to see the switch from Jack's better side – blasé about the affairs he had with his acolytes' mothers in the suburb of grimy houses where they lived. Pamela was sick of catching him out, a weary habit, a tired game. She had her revenge with Colts. The country seemed to be where they had left their idealism, where she returned to find it. Jack had stayed in the CPA throughout.

His consistency was finally questionable, overrated as a principle. The Battle of Stalingrad, Uncle Joe presiding, had taken place as far back as when he chewed sand in the deserts with Dunc Buckler. He had fused into an attitude – resistant to 1956 and 1968 and progressivist disillusion. The left and the right meeting up in a turned circle that seemed to be of her making: the worst came when Pamela destroyed the milky glass paperweight impervious to outside light, souvenir of a Moscow delegation, that he'd picked up and thrown at her when she'd said, 'Jack, we might have been wrong.'

One day Randolph put his revived friendship with Colts to the test. He was not sure what overcame him. He supposed it was to see if their lives were in harmony, which was to say that if two lives were in harmony two men could quarrel, say anything they liked to each other, and the upshot would be they would still remain friends. The inspiration for the test was the gesture Randolph made decades ago when Colts returned from his postwar travels ready to settle down, a gesture of the lingering hand that had seemed to ruin their friendship. But only seemed.

'Now who's that up ahead bleak on the skyline like a scarecrow in the wind, hat brim blown back flat against his forehead?'

Colts. Eleven in the morning parked in a cold paddock corner, counting wethers jumping through a gate – Randolph surprised him in action – stood back admiringly, not interrupting, but mentally, automatically doing the count himself, as a sheep man did without knowing, whenever a mob started jumping.

'Run them through again,' said Randolph, coming up from behind. Colts gave a start. He was nine out from three hundred – no good.

Randolph stood at the door of Colts's ute awaiting the re-count and happened to look down onto the seat to see a half-empty whisky bottle lying there, leaking its consolation to the floor.

'Look here,' said Randolph. 'This is no good.'

He took over, finished the job. They were another man's sheep and he saw them through. It was all quietly done, but with the effect of a bomb.

Randolph waited by the phone, by the letterbox to see if his bomb had result. To learn if taking a stand concerning Colts's workaday drinking 'marked the test'. He stood outside Hooke & Hooke in the stupendous winter cold of Gograndli Street and waited to learn if he'd made a mistake. If he had, it would be like a death, as in death experienced as ultimate act of bravery.

It was all right, though. Colts came to Randolph and said that if he ever wanted to own a house in town there was a property on the books with a stone cottage and a five-acre orchard on the side of the creek where he remembered Randolph saying, years ago, that a man could live out his days wearing a panama hat and tending his roses. Randolph was shy of that age but smiled as he took out his chequebook, thanked Colts for the tip, and wrote out the deposit.

That was the year the drought cut in worse than ever. Buckler turned eighty-seven. Rainfall was six inches, arid zone figures. As a benefit to his peace of mind, not to his Homegrove pastures, Randolph swore drought years were an expression of essential existence. Gaps opened in distances, leaves of gum forests thinned, winter cold came deep as a dry well. A lamb's skeleton loomed on a bare hill larger than a mastodon but wool on Randolph's prize flock grew fine as spun copper. Locusts ate leaves from fig trees on his town five acres and ate the washing from lines across the backyards and out across the plateau of the Upper Isabel where summer pastures, such as they were, withered. In shearing sheds locusts lodged in the wool of sheep waiting to be shorn. On blasted hillsides foxes were seen making spiral leaps to catch as many kick-leg mouthfuls as they could. Hooke did well buying irrigated lucerne bales from rare corners of the state where flushes of green were still to be found. Colts did time at the wheel of the agency semitrailer and took on those men of the Isabel, mean as cut snakes who had money to pay, but said it was robbery, the prices Hooke charged. Colts fined them a little extra by allowing a few bales gratis to the strugglers of Woodbox Gully. It was not something that Randolph would ever know through Colts telling him about it or anyone else telling him for that matter. Just something he knew.

Here it came again. Randolph kept a book on the cycles. Dry, dry, dry, wet, dry, dry. The rhythm was the click of a grass-hopper's legs on a hot afternoon. It was the rumble of rubber tyres on dusty corrugations. It was the rattle of dry lightning on the rusted heights of the Isabel Walls. Those cycles were Colts's, but also Randolph's own. There were days and weeks of dust parching the teeth. From the South Australian side it came – dust – as if Eureka Station (to give an example always in mind) picked itself up like a rippling carpet and was hurled a thousand miles east to pour over the cold plateau in galah colours. Feeder roads were impassable with dunes piling over fence posts. Tractors with buckets and council graders worked overtime clearing a way.

Crawling under a wattle bush on the drunks' common near the Isabel River railway bridge – seeing the bridge's rail line riding through cloud – a man was in the full cry of life expe-rienced at its most calamitous extreme, existence concentrated to a limbless, armless ball of defeated energy still able to pass through solid earth to the condition of a worm flexing through the burial place of hopes.

Randolph went to AA meetings and took Colts along. Colts admitted AA had something to say about his shortcomings, but it

214

had requirements a man couldn't meet. Later under the stars he tipped back his throat. The gargle of firewater was stupendous. Colts read in the small book he was given to take home:

> *In desperate and hopeless conflict, a man stands very near to the gods, in a strength that may have its source in the utter absence of hope.*
>
> *– Anonymous*

That was it exactly. He knew the words in his bones. Talk about shining a light. Colts had read these lines in typescript on the banks of the Darling River when he was a boy. Now to come back to them with understanding was strange. A man's battles were a longer test than a warfront's, more insidious, more grinding you might say without death flicking you off. You could swill the word hope around on your tongue and throw it full to the back of your throat. Full, what a word. Then swallow and choke time.

Colts put a bottle on the table. Crash. Took a glass from the sink. Crash. Poured brandy and drank it neat, then tipped back the kitchen chair, keeping his balance with his hands locked behind his head and staring at the ceiling of knotted white cypress. He was angry with Pamela. Disappointed. Disillusioned. Whichever way he interpreted Pamela's words they meant the same thing. They closed in on him. Weighed him down. Everything changed.

Randolph, an AA veteran who believed he was impervious to regression, was complacent that Buckler's writings were gaining currency enough to save a few alcoholics without the vanity of acknowledgement. They'd never been out of touch. Since their first meeting at Eureka and subsequent correspondence on usage and abusage of written English, Randolph and Buckler had been allies in tackling the problem of Colts from opposite ends of the same struggle. It was, indeed, the motto under which they had met on Buckler's terms. The problem had been Buckler's – passing Colts along. The problem Randolph's – what to do with him since: the two bound as one. The inadmissible faced with the inexplicable, you might say.

It was like working the land itself, a great big bloody challenging hardship getting successively worn down to the bones of gullies and sagging fence lines, the form not the substance the only reward.

Buckler wrote back thanking Randolph, and cursing the government to the grave and perdition. Politically Randolph and Buckler were of the same cloth, concurring that men of the right were beleaguered by the economics of working men (peasants, was Randolph's clandestine word) holding employers to ransom. There was more, as Randolph revived lines of connection that had lain dormant too long. He sent Christmas cards to Faye, Colts's sister, and to Colts's stepmother, Veronica. They were his shadow in-laws and he always wanted their liking.

In replies addressed to Randolph as reliable, implying that her brother his friend was not, Faye wrote from outposts of the Great Sandy Desert where she taught black children in the smoke of campfires, under bough shelters thatched in spinifex. She and Boy Dunlap had thrown in their lot with a bunch of communistic blackfellows – infamous as such – Faye as teacher, Dunlap as linguist, dictionary-maker and self-taught expert on dryblower mining machinery and prices on the rare-metals market. Although Dunlap was a Red without question, Buckler helped out when passing on desert forays, putting pragmatism ahead of principle and giving of the opinion that if you couldn't improve a blackfellow you could at least have a good laugh with him. Dunlap apparently never forgave Buckler's writing in old magazines that missionaries were meddling fools, he (Dunlap) the original poodle-fakir, but having long since resigned from the ministry disillusioned with missions, didn't fulminate overmuch when Buckler raved at him, a diamond-eyed dog growling at his toecaps and anthropological blowflies buzzing around him. Buckler was an old age campaigner of a sort made in Australia. The country ground them up and spat them out; they'd had to work out everything for themselves, and took on strange shapes doing it; mad hatters, misplaced geniuses, authentic ratbags. Veronica's visits couldn't have happened without Buckler providing the transport. It was worth it seeing how Faye enjoyed visits from Veronica. They came every second or third year. Each one felt like the last but wasn't. Randolph waited for Colts to suggest a visit – two men in a truck camping out. None was forthcoming.

Colts helped a single mother, Janelle Pattison, find a house, helped her move in, and on his empty Saturday afternoons started going around to the house and cleaning out the yard.

Janelle's son, Damon, attached himself to Colts. He was a sturdy, sullen twelve-year-old with black curly hair. He had trouble at school, and Colts imagined what it would be like to have a family, this family. As far as he could go with the thought it included a boy lost and lonely, being brought out of himself by the example of a man. Bowling him bouncers did no good, Damon hurled the bat into a hawthorn bush, but archery lit him up when he struck a sparrow. He showed Colts a picture of a crossbow that could be bought by mail order from a hunting magazine: it looked harmless enough.

Janelle, almost a generation younger than Colts, had little contact with Cud Langley, Damon's father. The boy didn't share

Cud's name. But apparently Janelle had been back together with Cud a few times and longed for a full reconciliation, in fact spoke of marriage, but she never spoke of this to Colts.

Janelle had an effect on Colts, a heat flush when he looked at her or thought of her; it would come to no good. At night he dreamed of her, spirit and flesh. There she was, the young mother with red hair and white skin, her baby's fists in the way as Colts slid around to get a better look. He'd been on the run. His dreams were of trains, the fixed rails of destination, what couldn't be reached expressed in the doppler shift of lamplit platforms. When he looked in from the night she stared back and he left his seat and stood in a corridor feeling beaten. Sixteen or sixty, it was just the same.

On a stinking-hot day Janelle came to the door wearing a T-shirt and undies and he was thrown by her casual impression of him as what, a capon? Women her generation sunbathed naked in backyards and swam topless in rivers. Colts's better self had a whim to take care of her, to put an arm around her and draw her in. Parental, he told himself it might be, as he looked around and saw other men his age were grandfathers while he wallowed in shock–effect fascination. The effect on his pocket could hardly be ignored when he decided to buy the house Janelle lived in and rent it back to her for whatever she could afford. The effect on his appearance could hardly be ignored when he trimmed his hair (definitely an improvement), grew a moustache and swapped his moleskins for a pair of flared jeans, not an improvement so much as a wistful pose. Coming up her path he heard the songs of Leonard Cohen droning out from her speakers with such persistence that the mood of them leaked from his heart. 'Suzanne Takes You Down', 'So Long, Marianne', 'One of Us Cannot Be Wrong'. Suppressing a smile at his new look, Janelle drew him to her, what did that mean, and they took a few stumbling dance-steps around the verandah boards after which Colts felt stunned. It was words and music, that was all, but he was left slain, butchered and broken open, while Janelle hardly seemed to notice what she'd done as she grabbed a mop and got on with her cleaning.

Janelle had a way of looking dismayed if not depressed, which stirred Colts's feelings as he stood at the front gate of the plain old weatherboard house extending his goodbyes before he went up to the Five Alls to slake his thirst. The house purchase, when she learned of it, distanced her. She felt uncomfortable with it. The crossbow arrived and Colts sat at home putting it together, putting it on top of a cupboard. The moustache came off and the moleskins went back on.

Interest rates climbed that year, bank managers looked grim; and Colts needed to trade something to keep hold of the mortgage and did, getting offered money for something he owned thanks to Randolph as go-between. It was the painting: *Goats*.

A man wanted a Veronica Buckler, said Randolph – regarded it as a rare prize: 'Yours is a period piece, in its own strange way.'

Well, so it is, thought Colts, experiencing sulky over-familiarity with the '40s style that Randolph carried on about. 'Take it away,' he said. Damon Pattison was there to hear the summation as Colts looked at *Goats* for the last time.

Colts was no connoisseur when it came to styles but knew the decade for its harsh light; its hot, thin shade, through which he sometimes still stumbled, angry and dismayed, drinking from a fibrous waterbag. There he was. All prophesied. Now for his year of changes.

The buyer was Randolph's loud friend Ted Merrington, who trawled through the ranges impressing the wizened with largesse, calling on his monkey-faced twin sons with their crane-equipped ten-tonner to haul out old tractors and whatever else they could seize from under blackberry bushes and from garbage gullies and ship to Red China. Merrington played the game of old-school tie with bullying self-interest. Randolph loved that game in the sheep-bitten hills.

In Colts's Woodbox Gully cottage the absence of *Goats*, a pale rectangle on the wall, made Colts see it clearer. As soon as he pocketed the cheque he felt a door open in the sky. If he'd felt like pleasing Randolph and driving through the desert in a truck with swags and billies, as Randolph kept urging him, he didn't now. This was a release, as if he'd come somewhere to find the vision that drew him. It was an airy openness of release, a deep-drawn clean breath.

His reply to a note from Pamela saying she'd be down on the seventeenth was unusual in that he replied at all. Their habit was that she told him and she came. Not this time, however. Never again.

There were a number of possible reactions to what she'd said when she said she knew what it was like to be truly loved, or something like it. Colts might indeed have asked her what she'd meant, but didn't. Just felt strangled when he felt her asking for more. So he wrote to her for a change.

Blunt, humiliated, stung and goodbye were Colts's astounding words, his expressed feelings in a Lettergram responding to her proposed seventeenth arrival – a Lettergram being a pre-stamped piece of dismal cardboard post-office stationery available at less than the price of a standard stamp as long as no extra pages were included.

Colts's outburst was a surprise, and over and done in his few scratched lines. Lack of any earnest point, but a buried strength, a presence, was what had drawn Pamela to him in the year of changes when they began. Now she found him diminished. This blow was ungenerous of him. His letter hurt.

'Truly loved.' What did that mean? She'd meant that she loved him, couldn't the old fool see it, however undeserving he might think that was. It had come out otherwise. And now this.

Now she wasn't so sure. But that didn't stop her crying into her pillow for what seemed like weeks, before she dried her eyes and resumed her visits to the Junction, staying down the other end of town and managing to avoid Colts just as Randolph had in a previous cycle of withdrawal and known to all. Here were two more strangers to each other in the puzzle of life.

Shakespeare in Schools arrived every September, Randolph its local patron. There was never a season like the first nor an actor as promising as Fred Donovan. Randolph 'followed' Donovan, keeping track of his name on Sydney playbills and architectural write-ups until he was told he was gone overseas.

'Wonderful,' said Randolph. 'To the RSC?'

'No, to New Zealand. Building mountain huts.'

Randolph suggested they see the show in its new configuration and Colts surprised him by agreeing. He was apparently prepared to brave a school hall if Damon would like to come. Violent swordplay appealed to the boy, as stage competed with film for an audience, Shakespeare being the Sam Peckinpah of the 1600s according to roneographed Teachers' Notes placed on each chair. Colts leafed through them uncomprehendingly. Damon sat between Colts and Randolph, the latter explaining plot points in bad breath. Afterwards Randolph took Damon onto the stage to finger the gore of blue jelly where Cornwall gouged out Gloucester's eye.

As if to prove that Colts's intentions with Janelle were honourable he woke one morning in the arms of a woman named Sylvie. They had their own bar stools in the Five Alls where the bar dog-legged into a corner. Colts liked Sylvie's close-set gimlet eyes and thin lips, her complaining directness over getting what she wanted. Sylvie brought out in Colts a variation of lust matched to her country shirts and skinny jeans all somewhat suggestive of Janelle. Married men never had such selfish luxury as Colts took for a bachelor's reward with Sylvie. And get this, Pamela Slim: the word 'bachelor' was out of date as the result of women taking men on, relieving them of choice. Colts lay back, scratching his chest hair and ruminating on existence. Love with Pamela had never had much to do with sex, a side dish. With Sylvie it was the whole saddle of mutton.

On Christmas Day that year Colts drove down to Veronica and Buckler's place on the Isabel Estuary, supplying farm-cured ham from a pig fattened in a compound built of corrugated iron and star pickets, erected at the far end of Alan Hooke's house paddock on the edge of town. He took Janelle and Damon with him. They sang 'Old MacDonald Had a Farm' and Damon counted all the dead animals on the road with exact arithmetic.

Janelle teased Colts frankly: 'You and Sylvie – do you actually do it?'

'Do what?'

'You know, "it".'

'What do you think?'

'I think – uh oh.' She laughed.

With Janelle realising that Colts might not be too old for a rumpty-pump, her manner changed. She was full of affectionate, joshing humour. She felt safer with him and leaned on his shoulder. It made no sense to Colts, except it was what he was trying to say to Janelle through his dealings with Sylvie, when he paraded them to her.

Janelle gave Colts an expensive fine-weave print shirt in an American size and boxed in cellophane. Colts crackled the packaging in his large hands, feeling tides of emotion he was unable to comprehend. Janelle advised him he was wasting his time with Sylvie, which baffled his hopes yet again.

They wore paper hats, blew whistles, spoke to Faye and Boy Dunlap by radio telephone hook-up. After the gigantic reality of childhood there was always the lesson of ordinariness to be borne on Christmas Day. Buckler was eighty-nine that year, you'd never know it. His old-time physical vigour was pouched and belted slacker, but not by much. He'd always worn his trousers above his navel like Tweedledum and his flannel slippers had cuts in the sides like fishes' gills, to protect his bunions. Gone deaf, he shouted as if his head was in a bucket, so it was better to let him monologue his way along than get a word in. Driving the brown Bedford, stamping the clutch, he kept his arms, solar plexus and thighs strong over thousands of miles of bush-bashing every other northern dry season. Next time he'd take the Land Rover. All his old mates were dead. Next dead was the next lot: Hammond Pringle was dead, de Grey, the foreigner Abe and so on. Buckler still wore the old felt hat. He still wore the stained neckerchief against dust and sweat. He still appeared in Colts's dreams, hung on his bones like a giant. His daytime power was long since reduced to a bunch of stories, repetitively told. For these, Colts had been thrown down and left to make his way on the earth among a bunch of rural live-alikes.

Colts went outside for a smoke and a look at the stars. From away over behind the dunes he could hear the surf thumping. He supposed Janelle saw him in Cuban heels and tight blue jeans, wearing a Stetson: so let her, he smiled. He changed into his new shirt. In April there'd be the ride in memory of Edwina Knox, and Tim Knox urging Colts to saddle up for old times' sake. Janelle would be coming along. When Colts came back into the room he'd missed taking out pins and a cardboard collar stiffener, which made them all laugh. Janelle took them out for him.

Janelle came from the horse world at Pullingsvale where polo and polocrosse, rival codes, ruled the calendar year only just holding off from open warfare in mutual derision. As a young girl she'd been seduced to the polocrosse side from pony club with her cousins, the Frizells, sticking to polo. Cud Langley was in the campdrafting, country-and-western corner chasing calves through narrow posts with masterly disdain on ponies just a little bit undersized for his frame. Cud was national campdraft champion and attended by a succession of girl stablehands among whom Janelle had won first place after sitting on a railing fence with six others, waiting to be chosen just nine months before Damon was born.

Damon proved a willing disciple as Buckler turned the pages of the *Illustrated History of the Great War*, describing the firepower of dreadnoughts and the deadly exactness of sniper fire. Then it was all off to bed. Colts woke from dreamlessness to see Buckler in striped pyjamas, standing out in the kikuyu grass emptying his bladder and coughing like a loose crankshaft.

Afterwards, Colts could not sleep and turned on the reading lamp. In the sleep-out Buckler had shelves of books, papers, maps and photographs, tumbling onto the bed and out across the floor. Colts found a pamphlet, *Shakespeare for Schools*, with a section written by Randolph's star, Fred Donovan. Colts frowned, he was never a reader, but read this much and fell asleep at the end.

A king went along separating himself from his kingdom, thrown up in a flood of clods of soil and tufts of grasses ripped from fields of Britain.

Lear was giving his rule away, wishing cares and business from his old age, conferring interest of territory on younger strengths in desire to crawl unburdened toward death.

He promised his first daughter, Goneril, shadowy forests and champains riched, plenteous rivers and wide-skirted meadows. His second daughter, Regan, was promised an ample third, no less in space, validity and pleasure than that conferred on

Goneril. They answered beautifully to his foolishness, the pair
of them rhyming doves of flattery. But when he asked his
youngest, sweetest daughter, Cordelia, for her pledge of love to
draw a third share more opulent than her sisters', she baulked
with nothing to say. Nothing!

Nothing would come of nothing, said Lear, and asked
Cordelia to speak again. When she spoke, it was to regret her
inability to heave her heart into her mouth.

For some reason, when Colts woke, a memory or the expression of a memory was what he had. Never had he heaved his heart into his mouth. He knew he loved Janelle, but she was many years his junior and the idea felt tragic and naive. He'd paid a price in being ungenerous to Pamela. She wrote, finally, and told him so: 'How dare you,' etc. 'It was all going so nicely,' etc. 'I don't understand,' etc.

Shimmering off into the square of Colts's fading dream was the emptied frame of *Goats*. He was anxious that Veronica not ask about it. As far as Veronica knew, *Goats* remained in pride of place on his walls in Woodbox Gully.

Veronica described Limestone Hills to Janelle. 'This man, your friend, was a peerlessly lovely boy. He lived in a place where dryness pulled moisture from the soil and dust exploded in mares' tails on white dirt roads.' She was describing her own painting of course, her favoured colours and textures. Colts clamped his eyes shut, praying she wouldn't name the name, *Goats*.

'Do you ever go back there?' asked Janelle. 'To Limestone Hills?'

'It's in the hands of a sharefarmer,' said Veronica. 'Paddocks, machinery, the lot. Dunc takes his rent, except for a few fenced acres, the graveyard, under separate title.'

The both of them, for some reason, looked at Colts when Veronica said that.

Outside Colts's childhood window, in that sweep of lime-stone country belched by drought, trees died in thousands in the 1940s in patterns like old worn carpet. Veronica had stitched them to canvas with rapid jabs of her brush. He'd set his face to the future, whatever it would bring.

FOURTEEN

ON A COOL DESERT MORNING in the bloom of great age after Buckler had eaten his breakfast of oaten bran, nut mix and chopped dried fruit on a gritty tin plate, swilled tea from an enamelled mug, cleaned his teeth with a shredded twig, and gone for a good healthy bog in the dunes, he cranked the Land Rover, waved his hat from the driver's window and charged off.

It was for his usual circuit of the minerals' map, Geiger counter crackling, radio direction-finder turning as he rotated its small black handle through a hole in the vehicle roof.

At four that afternoon Veronica, a decade younger than he was, a stringy old bird, active physically and mentally sharp, banged off the shot letting Buckler know she was impatient for her canvases to be bundled and the camp ordered for the night – water drawn, wood fetched – these being their after-noon routines on their desert forays, all of which she was mostly capable of continuing on her own except their bargain was otherwise. She made coffee and waited, the quart pot simmer-ing in the ashes. It wasn't the .410 gauge bird gun gifted from her father she used; it was the heavy centre-fire rifle of American make that Buckler employed against bull camels entering the camp. She lugged it between rocks, holding the butt against a buried stone and boomed the signal in the direction he'd gone. The fat, dangerous slug rose Sputnikwards.

No return, the shot brought only intensification of wind, loneliness, sand whispering over wheeltracks. There was no messenger of Buckler's daily schedule – no sign of his dog, that scabby-coated emblem of man trotting into the camp before him.

A wind came up even stronger, cold and bleak as ever they blew in desert winters, lifting the sand like a floating bedsheet, stinging the embers from the fire around Veronica's ankles as she scanned the dark. There was a radio schedule due at nine next morning and nothing to be done till then except wait. Sitting up in her swag, she later told Colts, sleepless, peering at every shape.

On her return east she gave her account and Colts wondered, was the gap in the stars Buckler standing watching, the moan in the wind his crate returning, the voice in the wind the conversation interrupted in a man's life, fractured and never quite smashed, never quite suspended and never quite finished in its demand for an ear lent?

Colts had a recurring dream of Buckler telling him to pull up his socks. It seemed that death and disappearance restored his old power.

It showed in his face, Veronica giving him a long considering stare: 'It's not over yet for you, is it, poor boy . . .'

The boy as referred to, Colts, had turned fifty-eight that year.

Next day the wind blew even stronger, Veronica said, and a promised plane was heard but not seen. A full sixty hours after the alarm went out, the Cessna from Marble Bar landed and the search party started. The police wanted to know if Buckler had listened to forecasts, as you'd need to be an idiot not to know what was coming in the way of windstorms. Anyone wanting to cover their tracks could not have chosen a better time. The search was extended but Buckler's truck was not found and the man's dog likewise.

Talk about ghosts and their whimsical power of growth and destruction – Buckler's disappearance was more than unsettling. It broke a way of thinking over Colts's brain like a jug of iced water. It shook him out of unmastered routines. Strange to say, he stopped drinking.

At the memorial service at Scots Church, Macquarie Street, six months after the event, Colts's eyes wrenched around expecting the doorhandles to be banged open and the man alive to walk in. Veronica seemed to have the same feeling but not about Buckler. 'There are some people,' she said, 'who might try and take advantage of my grief.' Colts had no idea what she meant. Among the scattering of twenty or thirty people, he knew few there. The minister read Psalm 23. A piper played 'Flowers O' the Forest'. The congregation sang 'Abide With Me'. A bunch of old soldiers tottered under the load of their George V medals. Lucky there was no pallbearer detail to challenge brittle bones. Yet with no coffin people hardly knew where to look. Then a stocky, balding man of around forty, wearing a yellow-striped seersucker suit and a sporty bow tie, came from the back of the church carrying a small twist of flowers, went forward, bent to one knee at the communion rail, placed his offering next to Veronica's wreath on centre stage and departed up past the pulpit and out the vestry door without turning around. Veronica sighed, almost a hiss but maybe a sigh of relief. 'Who was that?' said Colts. There was something about the angle of shoulders that gave his memory a tug, a drinker's shadowy recall.

'Never met him,' said Veronica.

Afterwards Colts felt Veronica's fingers firm on his elbow, steering him away from certain people, and planting him in front of others – not before he'd seen the card on that twist of bushland blooms: 'Rusty', just the one word inscribed.

Everywhere Colts went the year after Buckler disappeared he saw the cars men left when they made a break in their lives. Trees grew through them or they were tipped on their sides, rolled over, wheel-less, hubs in the air, axles gaunt, burned clean, left bullet-riddled or painted with warnings. These men's existences ended in boarding houses or in paupers' graves without any memorial except for their vehicles not quite abandoned of feeling.

Sylvie let it be known that she met other blokes. She attracted a distinct bunch, younger, who materialised around sunset at the takeaway counter of the Central Café before they wandered up to the Five Alls for a schooner. Colts she referred to as her desperation policy, not directly to him, but to a woman, who told a man, and the man got the dig in while asking Colts if he liked old coats. It hardly disturbed Colts's feelings. She took pity on him sometimes, he allowed that, hooking her finger into his belt and giving it a friendly tug. She hated to be alone.

'A last-lighter,' Gilbert Dalrymple called Colts, seeing him ambling past Sylvie's fence, hoping for seconds or some such humiliation of the sort slighted men laid upon themselves.

Last-lighters were dumb buggers as defined by Dalrymple – those who squeezed into luck at the final moment of wishfulness, just as Dalrymple did at Mt Stony strip after a day's supering, and the mist came in, and he was lucky to be alive, kissing the dirt.

Acceptance was the times' theme and Colts, a half-generation older than Dalrymple, who had film-star golden locks and various definitions of cool, caught the tail end of it – casting himself as an observer of other men's ruin. Excepting Dalrymple was married, Colts felt a tinge of jealousy around him relating to Janelle.

Dalrymple and Cud were friends. Dalrymple urged Cud to wake up to himself, that he had the best little woman in the world standing by in Janelle if he wanted her. Colts cringed hearing the words. It was from Dalrymple (not through the agency) that Colts learned that Cud had bought Wirra-ding, a district gem: it was a plain brick homestead on a gentle bend of the river with five hundred acres of lucerne flats and hilly country behind. Colts waited to hear what Janelle thought of Cud moving to the town, gracing its horse-talk with his name. Dalrymple seemed to know the answer, but held off supplying it. Anyway it was obvious. Janelle had never looked happier.

Colts's rivals lining up at Sylvie's ramshackle cottage were on a bachelors' honeymoon having glimpsed the solution to the problem that burnt others up – empty desire, nights of frustration, blank incomprehension, the pattern of blokes. Their hair was tied back in ponytails after the after-work shower. Their idea of elegance was the Indian shirt. They wore loose trousers, sandalled feet. They were wispy-bearded, sex-war veterans and used aromatic oils.

They were all a bunch of miserable duds of the male persuasion, in the words of Janelle. 'You're not like them,' she told Colts. So it was revealed to him through these words that he still had a chance with her. She was pleased that he'd given up the grog, taking it as a personal compliment, and asked him to drop his washing around. She seemed to know he was smitten, still, that her name rode above him like the moon in a cloud, never touching the physical elements except in this way of dealing with each other, through his dirty moleskins in a pile and his shyly affectionate readiness to help where he could. If Colts

231

didn't think about Cud and didn't see him around, and if Janelle didn't mention his name, then Colts was happy.

Damon was now eighteen. Janelle, pretty in her flower-sprigged frock, bangles jangling up her arms – more like a sister than a mother to Damon – said he'd come a long way for a boy who tore the wings from flies, upset teapots and bit her friends' fingers and thumbs. They'd gone on a picnic, to bare acres on Duck Creek; it almost seemed romantic until Damon appeared in neighbouring paddocks toting a .22 and shooting back dangerously in their direction.

'He needs a tight rein,' said Colts, holding on to his hat.

'Cud will see to him,' said Janelle, a statement that chilled Colts more than being shot at.

After this Colts took long, apparently aimless, drives through the long summer evenings as if he hadn't already spent more than half his life behind the wheel. The road towards Wirra-ding made him feel as if Janelle was imprisoned there but unwilling to be sprung from its stones. Dalrymple said he'd flown low over, and seen Cud out riding with her.

Colts turned off at Duck Creek, going up into the hills at a right-angled intersection taken on impulse. He felt an unsource-able excitement, a mixture of hope and despair, but where it came from was all around him. A desperation landscape made the heart feel glad concurrently with dragging him down. Hills and gullies were moods and emotions to him, part of his inex-pressible being. He told Alan Hooke he was looking for a place where a pool emerged under ferns and trout rose greedy to a fly rod. Hooke himself had such a place in the hills: The Bullock Run. Hooke went there and stood still. It wasn't Colts's style, he did not fish, and the creeks were all puddles of dry, but it was the feeling he was after, of ripples spreading, lapping banks of dragonfly hum and bee-sting. Nothing in Colts's behaviour on his lone drives squared with his long years of quietly plugging along visiting farms for Hooke and buying and selling sheep and dispatching rams to the butcher and promoting new lines. On a whim he started breeding up a small flock, just enough to cover costs and enter a fleece in the local show. Taking an interest-only loan from the Banque Nationale de Paris, who were offering money to all-comers that year, he bought the Duck Creek acres but now wool bottomed and debt loomed.

It was the outward and visible sign of disturbance, stupidity with money. Dalrymple's father, Oliver, had owned the land in the 1960s and lost it through happy-hooligan spending sprees. He'd bought an Auster tail-dragger, presenting it to his son, stereo sets that wouldn't fit in the lounge and an Indian Chief motorbike immaculately ducoed slime green.

'Lower your landing gear,' said Dalrymple. 'Get a grip.'

Colts hardly cared what he meant.

Bare distances were revealed to Colts through the wooded gaps of the ranges as an unsealed road went through. They offered glimpses of wide-open space where all things could happen. Dunc Buckler was in Colts's mind every time he steered round a bend and saw an old car chassis. Buckler's Land Rover must have run into a wind-scoured gully and been covered, poor bastard, in one of those soil shifts where half the continent lifted in a roar and dumped itself on another. Buckler never stopped coming back, here was chassis after chassis after chassis of scrap metal looking lively, before Merrington and Sons dragged it away and crushed it in giant calipers.

Up on the eastern rises of the Isabel hills, Colts found the rusting VW used by the cherry orchardist Wolfie Keuper. The Isabel Walls threw their teetering shadow on the pop-top.

The seats were gone, the engine was gone, the window glass crazed milky white. Grass grew through rust holes. The VW had a metal frame jutting from the back with strips of tattered webbing made into a seat. It was a spotlighter's perch and Colts instinctively jumped when he saw it. He'd seen Keuper spread-eagled on the beetling Walls in 1967, an ex-Nazi superman. Neglected cherry trees against a wall of gums stood like a man in camouflage greens with branches on his back. A ghost man of the Isabel persuasion, Wolfie had warned trespassers with shots and the mountain still had that feeling of sights aligned. It was how the migrant was seen patrolling during the four days cherries were in season come December, mad as a meat axe in his adopted homeland, although considered quite sane when revisiting the fatherland, from all accounts.

As Colts mooched along he ate a handful of sour bird-pecked cherries and spat the seeds out the side window. Of course, he remembered himself as a teenager, blocking, strutting, unapproachable in cast-off military tatters and spouting bits of talk memorised from Dunc Buckler rants. When Damon was thirteen or fourteen Colts had found him tormenting a sparrow with a stick, and when he objected the boy skewered the sparrow dead. 'Happy now?' It went on from there. 'Kingsley Colts, king shit,' said Damon when Colts had advice for him. Damon's crowing intelligence wiped the teaching staff of Isabel Intermediate High out of the reckoning when it came to useful knowledge. What Damon didn't know he could work out, or learn in ten minutes, hunched over a book while tapping his foot and darting around glances like a trapped foe. Colts heard Cud had put him on a horse and Damon looked for the throttle, a phrase offending to horsemen. Maybe the reason for Janelle getting together with Cud wasn't working, but Colts heard that Janelle was happy.

A band of men peaking with male thirst at the Five Alls claimed the non-drinking Colts as their accomplice as they nursed a nightcap (or three) when the blinds were drawn after ten in the saloon bar, and the coppers up the road turned a blind eye. Colts polished a bar stool or stepped behind the bar as a publican's favour, pulling beers. Just now and then, when

Dalrymple came in, he allowed himself an Islay malt and a dash of tankwater – it had to be late.

Colts was skilled at interpreting what men told him in his line of work. This ram over that ewe. That wool beribboned over this. Prices, margins, futures, stockpiling, marketing. They were more than farm economics to the one who listened. They were the poetry of blokes in pursuit of souls twisted from ideal shapes never entirely lost under the hammer of the seasons. Alan Hooke said that only a sheep man could have such quiet, disconcerting wisdom, born of work in the yards that could only be called self-effacing compared with the galloping, loud manners of cattle men with their burst facial blood vessels from bug-eyed confrontations with horned bellowers.

A long-term game with Colts was whipping Randolph into impotent fury by adopting wayward enthusiasms Randolph couldn't relate to this at all. Unusually for a sheep man Colts was the original bull terrier breeder on the Isabel. He'd borrowed the sire, Grabber, from Buckler.

There was a reason for this passing along of breeds: friendship. Colts felt for Alan Hooke, whose home acreage on the eastern edge of the Junction was besieged by town dogs allowed to stray. Hooke needed an animal more threatening than most in order to bail up owners and their dogs at the same time, to convincingly bellow he'd tear their bloody throats out if they didn't use a chain and protect his rams and Christmas pigs.

Colts bred from Grabber and gave Hooke the best of the litters – coincidentally when Hooke's first marriage, to that wild girl, Barbara, was breaking up, starting lone man with biter as a motif on the Isabel from the day Hooke walked home along the crown of the road and single mothers wished him good huntin' as they took bets on how long he would last without a woman in the house (not long).

Colts and Hooke liked getting into barking fights with clients, which agents needed to show they weren't creatures without self-respect, then turning around and swapping conspirators' grins while their dogs pawed each other and slobbered out by the fertiliser sacks and hay bales where their water dishes were.

Papa was the name of a dog Colts gave to Wolfie Keuper some years back. Low slung with muscular shoulders and a barrel-shaped body supported by wide, stumpy legs, every move Papa made parodied sexuality without any need for an opposite sex. Just material to plunge into would do, crouching over a trembling quarry with rheumy-eyed functionalism, planting seed in flesh and burying fangs in a pumping aorta.

The sole of Wolfie's shoe came away from the uppers flippety-flap as he nurtured his anger through the final burn-out. Papa was in a steel mesh yard at the back, servicing a bitch Melody, whose pups Wolfie gave to men with the same idea as his, which was to make a statement with their lives for once and for good and bloody all. The inheritance of Dunc Buckler via Colts spread into places Buckler never considered and a gone man stayed around barking.

That old VW still startled Colts every time he came around the corner. Its de-glassed headlamps caught the sun and bounced it away to wherever the next car wreck waited to pass it along. Wolfie left a perceptible trail, departing the district on a pushbike, muttering imprecations. It was some years since he was last sighted rootling about in a tidy bin, outside a doughnut shop in the city.

Yet even after all this time the VW looked as if a thumb on the starter and a foot on the gas would make it leap alive. Colts had the impulse to give it a try – why not, a man named Percy Perceval did so with a wrecked passenger bus and it fired. Percy marked the end of a succession of derro characters on Colts's list of callers, a merry, prattling man who made something positive and somehow musical out of the rhythms of a careless life.

That rainbow-painted twenty-eight-seater had come out along Perceval's road, slithered to the verges abandoned, and he got it going again, driving farther along the track, up through the peppermint forests on the southern slopes, through a cleft in the mountainside and into a clearing high above the coastal ranges that were wild as the Owen Stanleys, where Colts had posed with an Owen gun at nineteen for a photograph that he sent to Randolph, and Randolph had glued in his album where it still was.

Smoke drifted through a clearing at ground level, creating skeins of diaphanous grey. It reached into Colts's throat and tightened his bronchus. Percy Perceval was a charcoal burner. It seemed improbable when the old crafts were all gone. Somebody came and carted the sacks away to the city, where they were used in charcoal chicken shops. The wood ovens were dinosaur cara-paces, curved sheets of iron set into the ground, smouldering. Percy worked hard at turning beautiful logs into chunks of pitch-darkness, retaining their beauty in whorls of grain and pressure elbows like photographic negatives. Of all the roads Colts took Veronica down in her old age, this one most attracted her.

On the trackside she collected finger-sized sticks of charcoal that she used for drawing on lavish spreads of paper. It was a country of wounded trees up there along the escarpment where Colts drove that woman, taking in the light.

The eucalypts had the colourings of salves and greases – rust, verdigris, zinc. Eucalyptus rossii was silver frosted, with light lifting the colour tones. Flushes of red, bunches of black, trunks pillar-ing from the shaly ground. Veronica pointed them out, showing Colts how to look closer, always closer without her explanations annoying him, as they had as a boy. So he looked. Possibly for the first time deeply. And she was gratified. She still had him, this man of carapaces who never wanted her to visit his house in Woodbox Gully.

*

Talk of men over the bartop the one night per week when Colts came in and worked for a few dollars was incessant with his friend Dalrymple, whose crop dusting was built on men's dreams more than most, on Dalrymple himself shedding the bonds of earth, serving graziers on the receiving end, men in love with fairy dust, i.e. superphosphate, raining down. In this respect old Oliver Dalrymple had been a dreamer only to a slightly more exaggerated extent than average, just to the level of being held in a straitjacket to quieten the worst of him with a hypodermic syringe.

'All we are, are dreamers,' said Dalrymple, as a kind of benediction over his old man, which Colts denied in his practical life. But now he was silent.

'Men's monologues are streams of photons spraying from personal spaceships spinning beyond the asteroid belt somewhere,' said Dalrymple.

'You'd know,' Colts merely added.

Dalrymple was a talker. Forget the rules of society, wisdom chapping his cheeks like slipstream, he watched from the Five Alls and the best he could say was that a hot meat pie with gravy, peas, mashed potato and sliced carrot served as bar food through the paint-chipped kitchen hatch, along with a whisky's coppery shine, was the limit of the flame to which men owed existence.

Besides which, the Five Alls had a pull taking decisions out of a bloke's hands. A certain slant of the bar, a drum of footsteps not yours on the outside verandah, you were bound to follow. It made blokes smirk in recognition of their fate. You didn't have to live it to know it. Now whose old lady was this coming to give a bloke curry? It was Erica Molinari, Mrs Gilbert Dalrymple, coming into the bar as quietly and as softly as she was able, and after drinking a shandy taking the yammering Gil Dalrymple home.

Colts went along the counter with a Chux Superwipe, making it gleam.

Two men met at the Five Alls for the counter lunch every Friday, almost without fail. Colts came up from the agency and took his place at a dining table and someone brought their drinks. Their talk was gapped by long silences. Randolph never breasted the bar when he wanted another, as every other drinker did, but raised a finger for his fizzy gins (while Colts held to lemon squashes). Randolph was onto being a controlled drinker, having parted with AA. He maintained a fiction that the Five Alls was a hostelry with drink waiters, worthy of his high ideals. You could hear every word he said in the room. People listened.

'I've been reading about courtesy titles. What do you know about them, Kings?'

'Zilch. Nothing. Nought. Zero.'

'Courtesy means manners of the court, civility, politeness, the refinement of the age. The courtesy title of the eldest son of a duke is marquis. Of a marquis is earl. Of an earl is viscount. Younger sons of dukes and marquises are styled lord followed by Christian name and surname.'

'Get away with you.'

'Similarly all daughters of dukes, marquises and earls are styled lady. Sons and daughters of viscounts and barons and younger sons of earls are styled the honourable. None of these titles carry the right to sit in the House of Lords.'

'Is that so?'

Of the two, Colts politely and patiently contributed nothing to the flow of talk and made no move to terminate the lunch until Randolph reached for his hat, paid, and it was time to go. Except that Colts said once a year, 'It's the season,' and Randolph knew there'd be no lunch the following Friday, because of the reasons Colts found to go riding the fire trails downstream on the Isabel River, Tim wearing his cabbage-tree hat, cantering ahead on his seahorse-headed Prancer, waving Colts up on thundering Old Bill.

Colts knew that Janelle would be along. Cud would not be.

They loaded packhorses and rode to the top of the escarpment. To the east the Tasman Sea shone blue as ice. They could see rusty coastal ships and offshore reefs through pocket binoculars. Under their bootcaps were the serpentines of river after it spilled from the escarpment. It was a dream to plunge into, the lower reaches of that river flashing a signal as the sun passed over, home to eels, platypuses, wrens, red-bellied black snakes, kingfishers, goannas. Shallow widths of golden river, waterworn stones, groves of casuarina. They were the backdrop to Veronica Buckler's childhood coastal home, the ramparts of her late-age canvases. Colts imagined he could see her tin roof gleaming.

Tim Knox said it was the West that counted in the dreams of men, 'Out where the bones of the dead men lie,' and he gestured inland from the mountain top like the squatter in the engraving on the walls of Hooke & Hooke.

'I felt that once,' said Colts, seeing himself setting off in a wartime train, full of a boy's longing and expectation. 'Then it's gone.'

'Wake up again,' said Tim.

He wanted to go droving like Randolph had in wartime and never stopped talking about. He really would. Up to Alice Springs, across the Canning Stock Route, on into Kimberley gorges, romanced by red rock and pandanus groves. He would not be helpless like other blokes. He would actually do it. He would not be a spectator to male frustration, like Colts, he said. He'd take his wife and his kids with him.

Colts raised, then lowered, his eyebrows. They were wiry with sprouts of grey tangled in black patches. Hairs sprouted from his ears and could be seen lurking up his nostrils. There was nobody in his life to tell him to get out the nose scissors.

'Give up on Janelle,' said Tim. 'It's stupid.'

Northwest of Eureka Station in a cradle of red sandhills was a camp long-established in Colts's mind. A swag, a collapsible table, an absence of society he remembered and a door – something like a door, at least, a star-framed passageway – which he, Colts, passed through at the age of eighteen as he left Oakeshott's graveside the day of his burial and travelled to Adelaide where he enlisted in the army, his childhood finished in his head.

Janelle sang to her horses. They were Cud's horses.

They camped at a pool. Wattle blossom floated on the water where swimmers broke through, slicked hair and bright eyes in the evening light, wrists and backs sending out ripples. There was a theme of alcohol lapping into play. A whiff of marijuana. The horses munched their nosebags in the shade, the riders drank whisky from a plastic flask and wine cooled in rapids while Colts busied himself turning damper off the camp fire and keeping coals restricted from getting away. Overhead, a scorching wind bent the treetops; red-bellied black snakes slithered the river stones; lace-patterned goannas clawed tree trunks and stared down from steady eyes; beetles and bugs burrowed into swags; cicada and mud-eye carapaces crunched underfoot. An electric-blue kingfisher left expanding rings of contact on the water. Life seemed a great endowment then.

'Kings, I've got something to tell you. Last Friday. In Pullingsvale. Cud and I were married in the registry office. You should have seen Damon's face, it glowed.'

*

241

A month later at the Jockey Club ball, Colts watched Janelle's hair fly loose.

'How are you?'

He wasn't drinking. It amazed him. He wasn't drinking yet.

'I'm good enough,' he said.

The feeling was a small boy's numbness of incomprehension carried by a man with an acorn for a heart.

'Your turn,' she invited him onto the floor. She wore a black taffeta skirt that whipped against him as they danced. When the tempo of the music slowed he extended his hand for the moment to continue but Janelle only smiled and returned to where Cud held her drink. Colts had turned sixty he reminded himself – he ought to know better. But this was terrible. His hand trembled, he went outside and smoked and looked at the stars.

Cud came out and tapped him on the shoulder with a coldie. 'You look like a big wombat sitting there.'

'Eats roots and leaves,' Colts threw the rejoinder automatically and opened the can of Mountain Maid sparkling apple juice so thoughtfully selected by a woman's husband, rapped the metal to his teeth and let it spill in. Janelle came out and took Colts's arm, settling beside him. His stomach lurched at the sound of her bangles. He wondered why men were unable to count their blessings.

Months later he passed Janelle on the road. She barely raised a finger in greeting from the cab of the six-wheeled horse transporter she drove, looking embattled, determined. Another day, she rode a cantankerous mare forty kilometres along the mountain-road verges, mastering its skittering and bolting. Colts heard about this from people he didn't know. It was her business of matching her life to Cud's while reports said Damon was in fist fights with him. Colts heard Janelle sang 'Danny Boy' as she rode. Where was Cud? Following behind in his ute, listening to country tapes, drinking cold cans, keeping his eye on her to be sure she was doing all right. They were lucky and it grieved Colts to say so.

Colts was getting petrol one day when he saw an unusual vehicle half-shadowed in the workshop doorway of the service station. At first he thought he was looking at the back of a specially outfitted lorry. Then he saw it was engineless – a four-wheeled, horse-drawn wagonette. There, around the corner, tethered to verandah posts, were two draught horses and a seventeen-hand stockhorse known to Colts as a rider. A dog growled at Colts while he stared, knelt and offered his fingers to chew.

The scene needed no interpretation. Tim Knox and his wife came swinging down the lane with their arms around each other.

'It's something we always planned to do together, drift across country like you and Randolph did when you were young,' said Pepita. 'Along the Darling, down from the Cooper.'

'It was just Randolph,' said Colts.

'Was it?' said Pepita. 'He gives such a picture of you, Kings, you're always in the camp.'

'Now it's our turn,' said Tim.

Pepita looked absorbingly at Tim. 'Most men can't face their own dreams without a push.'

'Really,' said Colts.

'They say it's quaint,' said Tim, lifting his hat to a passer-by. Having much older brothers, one successfully dead, the other emotionally dead but financially and studwise alive, Tim chose the third way always. Defending the advantages of hay-burning propulsion, he made living on nothing seem a triumph inevitable as defeat.

Randolph still owed them payments.

'He's your friend,' Pepita said. 'Your best friend.'

'That's a stretch,' said Colts.

Word was that Randolph would do anything for Colts if Colts asked him, but there had to be the question.

'You go round getting money out of people for Hooke. Can't you do something about Randolph? We're skint.'

'I'm skint,' said Colts.

'But you're on your own,' said Pepita. 'You don't have family expenses. You've always kept to yourself. You are lucky as tumbleweed, living from a suitcase, driving a company car. You have the luxury of the single life, you don't realise how everything multiplies, not two by two but by some sort of weird algebra as a family grows – where there's a tap in your bank account and it all gets siphoned out.'

Colts reeled back at this summary, questioning his right to a life of his own.

Before heading west, Tim took the wagon for a test run through the Junction with the kids waving to their friends out the back. The draught horses stamped and snuffled, their hairy pasterns sweeping the bitumen surface of the road. Pepita, wiping her eyes with the corner of an apron, stood on the running board suppressing her pride. Love was the window to the soul. Only sometimes the shutters came down, the blinds were drawn, the lamps extinguished and the rheumy whiteness of a blind man's eyeballs common currency. Janelle presented them with a Spangled Hamburg layer. The hen must have come from Wirrading as Janelle had no chooks of her own. Tim tied its leg with string and placed it between the kids who held tightly to the stiff wing feathers as the horses began a ponderous gallop up the last rise from town.

Colts sat at home scraping the label from a flask of Corio whisky, 325-ml size. If he managed to tear the label cleanly off he would reward himself by finishing the bottle: that was the vow. It was sacred, a pledge to the heavens above. The glue was viciously strong. A small nip every half hour was the reward of effort, a result that seemed intolerable after five minutes and which Colts overcame by using his pocketknife and getting the label off just on dark. With blurred vision he counted the sticky moons of paper on the formica tabletop. They added up to the years of his life. A man on his own. What to do now? Up to the Five Alls seemed a pretty good answer, so he went.

FIFTEEN

Now that Colts had his driver's licence suspended and a large fine to pay, with more penalties to come if he so much as climbed behind the wheel of a vehicle for the next eighteen months, Alan Hooke found himself getting out of the office dealing with clients more.

Hooke spent the whole wet afternoon with Ted Merrington walking cows and calves down narrow gullies to a set of yards and drafting them out. It was miserable weather but satisfying work for men. Angry with Colts for backsliding, Hooke saw the day coming, and soon, when Colts would be sacked. But he'd said it before – been saying it on and off for twenty-five years, and Careful Bob before him. He was reminded by everyone who knew them. Colts's life savings were wasted, the weather-board house in Woodbox Gully was sold, the rental house was gone, movable assets all cashed, and God only knew where the money had gone. Down the hatch, obviously. The hundred acres Colts briefly owned on Duck Creek disappeared back into the landscape. Colts lived in a rented ruin Hooke found for him in a thistly paddock on the town creek. Hooke reflected that if he put him off he'd still look after him. That was a proven habit. The cost to his pocket would hardly exceed the cost to his feelings so far.

Hooke, a man surrounded by women – wife, daughters, sisters, mother, aunts – needed male friendships to balance women's utter convictions of how life should be lived. A vestige of this was Colts turning up for work each day with smiling, trembly-handed concentration, wafting an air of shamed cunning, blocking Hooke's every attempt to understand him with stubborn pretence that nothing was wrong.

Hooke and Merrington had opposite styles of doing the required job – Hooke being a quiet, effective prodder whereas Merrington swore and whacked animals' rumps with a length of plastic pipe to get them moving. If a beast proved stubborn, craning its neck, red-eyed across a bony shoulder, Merrington took it personally while Hooke whistled and waited.

Rain slanted from the south and ran over their hat brims and down their noses to their chins. Alan Hooke was a lean, light-complexioned man with a narrow, intelligent face and a flattened nose from boxing. In his youth he'd won the regional light heavyweight belt and few ever forgot that.

Merrington was a big, jokey sort of a man, used to getting his own way, and when he didn't, enforcing it. He was physi-cally, naturally strong, but a bit slabbily overweight with a plum-coloured complexion, and gave his opinions freely. He was known to Hooke, and now Hooke was getting to know him better. Merrington had located this chunk of land while scouring the landscape for scrap steel with his sons and was in the business of turning himself into one of the types he'd bought from – a squatter of the Upper Isabel persuasion, semi-retired while his sons took over the running of the firm and dealing with scrap iron-hungry China.

When a cow lurched heavily through the wrong gate, banging it sideways, splintering a panel, Merrington squatted in a puddle and belted mud with his polypipe, swearing in a rhythm of frustration and sending splats of wet manure all over himself.

Alan Hooke had never quite seen that kind of thing before.

When they got the cows away Merrington switched in the middle of a rant and turned to Hooke, raising a wild eyebrow: 'Shall we take horses next time? Do you ride?'

No answer needed to that. Hooke was raised in dealing stock for a family living, scouring the gullies of the Dividing Range from early youth with a hard-headed father on an irascible fat-bellied pony kept for the muster. There didn't seem much point in taking horses when a walk along a ridge-top with a cattle dog was effective. But if Merrington wanted some galloping fun he'd oblige.

Why Merrington had this effect on him Hooke couldn't say. The divorce from Colts was part of the explanation. The man was well past fifty but like a spoiled child. It was the charm of the cheeky kid making demands, Hooke supposed – you might want to kick them but they made you grin, made you feel you could get them what nobody else could. Maybe that was the key to Merrington's success in scrap, whittling down offers to the point of being begged to take it.

Merrington looked for trouble on the simplest pretext.

'You don't always have to please me, Alan.'

'I like to try.'

'I don't have to please you, though.' Merrington threw a piratical grin. 'Use your agent as a floor mop, as the old saying goes.'

Hooke enjoyed the banter, the game of words. Merrington brought matters chin to chin and then swerved away with opposite meanings. So many of Hooke's clients were hard-dealing men with no imagination to be otherwise. Judge Frederick Knox, who'd sold Merrington his house and land, was an example. Merrington's fancy, it appeared, was to be in the Knox class. Tussock barons, Hooke's father had called them, with never as much cash as acres since the 1950s but with resources to answer higher callings by virtue of being born to rule.

Six months before, on auction day (Hooke wielding the hammer), Merrington won the homestead block excised from a larger spread. It offered barely a basic living in the chewed-out hills, but the riverbank house was a famous pile, a Professor Leslie Wilkinson design from 1923, and Merrington bragged the acreage would yield an impressive costs-to-income potential through his adroitness in beating the arse off a Knox.

Except Merrington was a mere trier in the poverty stakes, really – Hooke's rare contact with an owner who wasn't an authentic hard case but wanted to be seen as one. The money he'd paid for plant and equipment after the auction was way above what anyone else in the district wanted to give. It reversed a trend of gentlemanly conduct when Merrington wrote a cheque without much haggling. It was always Hooke's precaution, Dunn and Brad-street-wise, to bite silver back to the source. This time no need for that – Merrington Metals was solid – but Hooke's question was why Merrington had this almost wheedling need to be seen as someone he wasn't. It turned out that Merrington had something to hide. Hooke learned he was the son of the madam, Betty Truegood, who made a fortune during the Second World War by converting terrace houses at the back of Victoria Street, Potts Point, into flashy brothels for American servicemen. A ringleted eight-year-old boy, Edward Truegood, being debouched from a limousine at the gates of Cranbrook School was photographed in *Pix* magazine in 1950: this was this same florid Ted Merrington now transplanted to the Upper Isabel.

Merrington wore a pair of stiff leather leggings found in a shed. Draped around his shoulders was an oilskin cape left hanging on a peg since the 1940s. He brought to mind a squatter from the Joliffe cartoons in *Pix* – a comical geezer with galahs in the corn and a Bugatti in the woolshed. Hooke calculated bringing Merrington up to date from the workwear side of the agency. He felt warm about his ironical client in the cold rain, catching a glint in Merrington's eye that seemed to suggest Merrington reading Hooke's thoughts and finding them tartly agreeable. They might even become friends. Hooke had reached a stage of life of wanting more zest from his usual cronies, denizens of the Apex Club and the Five Alls Hotel Galloping Wombats Polocrosse Squad, with Merrington a stiff breeze battering up from where housing estates crowded the boundaries of his scrap-metal yard and former farm acres.

'That's the way, Ted,' said Hooke, with the calves jammed black and glistening in the race, smelling of panic. 'You've got them sitting pretty.'

Merrington accepted the tribute with a twisted smile.

'You're limping,' Hooke observed.

'It's from a rodeo fall years ago.'

'No kidding?'

Merrington gave a toss of the head: 'I went jackarooing up Wanaaring way, in the school hols. Stayed with the Jacky Whites, entered the bullock ride as a dare. I was a stupid young booger and now the sciatica stabs like a knife. Our generation needed a war but didn't get it – cracked ribs and a fractured pelvis, they're my battle scars while your old man got his medals at Tobruk, I understand.'

'We had Vietnam,' countered Hooke.

'You believe so?' Merrington's neck elongated and his head wove like a alarmed snake's, arrested in exaggerated surprise. 'You were in that?' He steadied and stared hard. It was possible that Merrington's slum-terrace inheritance was revived for the R and R traffic of the 1960s and '70s and Merrington a beneficiary.

'I was in the lottery but my number never came up,' said Hooke.

'Would you have gone if it had?'

Hooke barely understood the question. Of course he would have gone. That was the deal offered, just as it was when Careful Bob went to North Africa to fight the Eyeties and then to Ambon against the Nips. Only later he might have seen things differently.

'I was a tad too old for that game of marbles,' said Merrington, giving his polypipe a flick on the rails to clear it of muck. 'So I wasn't given the privilege to serve.'

An almost sneer accompanied the words, again leaving Hooke wondering what Merrington meant. That Hooke should have enlisted anyway? That he was, on the contrary, wrong to have even taken his chances?

A phone call came. Merrington's wife, Dominique, relayed information from under an umbrella at the side garden gate. The semitrailer Hooke promised was delayed past dark.

Merrington said, 'Well!' and shot an intense glare at the agent.

Hooke said, 'Easy does it,' and reminded him that nine calves were not a full semi load, and the driver was doing the rounds of the district, so might he just be patient like everyone else? Thus reprimanded Merrington became almost timid and asked Hooke down to the house.

With double whiskies replenished twice over they awaited the semi. It arrived past seven in the sodden winter dark. Half sloshed by then they loaded the stock by headlights, the driver using an electric prod and scampering terrified calves up the race in the rain. Merrington took the prod and tried it, liking the feel. 'This is more humane than people make out,' he said, jolting a poor animal more than was warranted. Then with a reckless leer he reached around behind his back and gave himself a wallop of volts in the left rear buttock.

'Whoa baby! Order me one in the morning!' he yelled.

'Done.'

They took more drinks afterwards to re-warm their saturated bones. Dominique Merrington attentively plied them with *potage velouté aux champignons* and home-baked baps as they sat at the kitchen table, telling Hooke he must bring his wife next time. Hooke then rang Liz to explain his lateness and heard the arch humour in her voice, the note of interested surprise over who was getting him plastered. 'Ted came to the school on Careers' Day,' she said, 'with a stack of slides, and talked to Year Twelve about import–export. They thought he was funny.'

'As in?' said Hooke guardedly.

'Ha-ha. They all want to make their fortunes now selling junk to China.'

'You've met my Lizzie, then,' said Hooke when he came off the phone.

Merrington shot Hooke an empty glance, grinding his bottom jaw sideways as if about to spit.

'Have I?'

'She's a teacher.'

'Oh, delightful. The little English one with plaits?'

'Yes, she's a Pom,' acknowledged Hooke.

'We liked her, didn't we, Dom?'

Merrington's wife turned from the stove ready to agree with him, but then catching herself and laughing and putting a finger to her chin, and saying, 'No-ooh,' that she hadn't actually met Liz yet.

The two men moved into the expansive living room with dogs on the rugs and a fire of red gum in the grate. Hooke talked about his children – his own twin daughters by his first marriage and Lizzie's two boys, Matt and Johnny, by hers. The twins lived with their mother, Barbara, in Sydney, in their second last year at St Catherine's, and visited their home town irregularly. It broke

Hooke's heart missing them through their growing years, and now when they came it was only for a few days at a time because there was too much else going on for them in the 'smoke.

'How old are the girls?'

'Sixteen.'

'I understand that age,' said Merrington in a tone that implied, mysteriously, that Hooke didn't. 'They should come and visit some time.'

'Visit?'

'Look around.'

Merrington gestured about the room, indicating the rooms branching from rooms, to the boot room, the billiard room, the boiler room, to the north and south wings, the attic staircase, the attic rooms, the architectural legend of the Knox House by Leslie Wilkinson on the fabled Isabel. Dozens of paintings hung in the semi-gloom from the ceiling down to the backs of sideboards and couches, ornate frames, historical scenes of sailing ships and artic inlets, willow-lined creeks and standing cattle, blocky abstract squares, carnival clowns and botanical illustrations all mixed in together. The whole thing would mean little to the girls but the offer felt friendly.

'This one's called *Springtime*,' said Merrington.

Above the fireplace a painting of female figures gave an impression of half-circles overlapping. Merrington stood beside it with a look of shy cunning, inviting a response. There were small floating leaves like mini-bikinis covering the obvious bits. Hooke peered close and recognised the signature.

'I'll be blowed,' he said.

'Yes, you've found me out, Al, I don't just deal in rubbish, I dabble with the brush.'

He seemed genuinely humbled by the admission, by the revelation of a side of himself that he might possibly disdain revealing, the little ringleted boy with an artistic blush.

Dominique took Merrington's arm and looked at him admiringly. She was French, angular and graceful, and as tall as he was. 'We met in a galleree,' she said, 'by good chance. I had no idea who he was, rough-and-ready he wandered in from the demolition site next door. After that, well . . .'

She shrugged. He leered.

Hooke liked her. She was wife number three. New life, new wife, new spread, new friendships – it was a pattern in country purchases, newly emerging, a counter to drought-shrinkage.

'I never know what to make of art,' said Hooke, looking around at the pictures, all by known names, he supposed, and worth plenty. 'But I like Norman Lindsay,' he said, recognising a nude with plenty of chest.

He was unable to square the wispiness of the one over the fireplace with the bluff man who'd produced it. 'Around Liz and the twins it's a different story, they'd have lots to say.'

'They could sit for me.'

'Sit?'

Merrington made a scribbling motion with his hand on an invisible easel. 'Twins pay double,' he said, in a bargaining tone.

Hooke said, 'For doing nothing?'

'He's a lightning *croquis*,' said Dominique. 'A fast worker.'

She meant sketcher. The double meaning escaped her. Merrington caught Hooke's eye.

'There would be no funny stuff,' he pouted, 'I can assure you of that' – making Hooke feel he'd had an unworthy thought, when really he was just giving the man his due, reflecting warmly, through a haze of whisky and wine, how there were more ways of skinning a cat than were dreamed up in his little corner.

'Think of it this way,' said Merrington. 'Get the beast right and you never have to feed it or shift it around or call the vet when it gets the staggers.'

'Agreed,' said Hooke.

'Doddery means dollars in the art game.'

'Ha, ha, I'm with you,' said Hooke.

He stood, yawned, stretched, patted the dogs and said he'd better be going. The thought of Lizzie and the life they had was a magnet in the night – her warm toes pulling him over to her side of the bed when he came in, and the way they slept in each other's arms until the early rooster crowed and they woke holding hands as trustingly as children.

'It's still early,' taunted Merrington. 'She's got you by the short and curlies.'

'Maybe so.' Hooke grinned.

'Dear me, Edooward,' chided Dominique, joining the fare-wells at the door, 'I imagine Alung doesn't have the luxury of sleeping in like you do, *dormir comme un loir.*'

Feeling blindly towards his car, Hooke heard Merrington's voice answering her back. It seemed the new wife was being paid out for verbal slips. But why shouldn't a man sleep late if he could? Give Hooke the chance, he told himself, he'd sleep past noon every break he got. Merrington, thought Hooke, was lucky in not having to show up at daylight at yet another set of frosty yards, running through the same whiskery old palaver every day of his life for the sake of the national debt and carrying staff members effectively on the sorry list.

Although not every day really. For there were times mid-month or early in the week previous to cattle sales' Fridays when Alan Hooke's phone fell silent for up to an hour and the winter sunshine poured across the oiled boards of the agency. Then Hooke went around wiping dust from old photographs and chasing blowflies with a ruler. Then he gave the indispensable Jenny Garlick the morning off to visit her mother in the elderlies' wing of the district hospital; and sent Henry Tuck on hourly rates delivering hardware around town from the back of the old Bedford while Colts sidled off at noon to the Five Alls and didn't come back.

Then Hooke was ready for visitors to his alcove under the stairs, the green-stained electric kettle ready on the boil, instant coffee spooned from a jar and a packet of Chocolate Wheatens ripped open and available to anyone who wanted to grab. And intermittently in they came and grabbed – old graziers on their stick-assisted rounds, former loyal clients of Hooke & Hooke, bygone strong men of the Isabel diminished in their bones and down from their outlying acres and wind-rattled pioneer home-steads for good. For the betterment of their old age, and the pleasure of their wives, they'd bought brick-veneer bungalows in town with decent plumbing and cement driveways painted green. Randolph Knox, the odd man out in this sequence, had restored his stone cottage with a walled rose garden, justly famed.

'Up at the Fives,' thumbed Hooke when Randolph came in looking for Colts like an old tortoise wrinkly-necked escaped from his shell.

Hooke knew what was coming when the oldsters nudged him in the ribs and told him another one about Careful Bob, and the one time Careful Bob had got the better of them, the cunning old rat of Tobruk. Except Hooke knew it wasn't just the one time because his father had taken the long view always.

The best example of this was the Bullock Run. It started with those thousand acres bought from the Homegrove Knoxes in the late 1940s. Along the rim of the Dividing Range were more parcels of land Bob had bought for barely the cost of a packet of fags in the '50s and '60s at mortgagees' auctions, deceased estate clearances and the like. Once a scattered mosaic intersected by logging tracks, by the '70s the paddocks passed to Hooke amal-gamated whole. Now with the millennium looming they were a treasure.

The Bullock Run, four thousand acres of mountain fastness, responded to years of aerial supering and low stocking rates, whereas on Hooke's home block, his rocky three hundred acres just out of town (the house within sightline of St Aidan's bell-tower) Hooke ran fine wool merinos until they nibbled the ground almost bare, a choice little flock biding time and building up numbers among the wild turnip and saffron thistle. Hooke guarded their increase from marauding town dogs with a policy of once warned, never reminded. The sheep would remain a mere sideline until wool improved and Hollywood Boy III paid his way handsomely serving ewes. Meantime on the Bullock Run a herd of Black Angus covered the twins' maintenance and education expenses and left change for a red MGB – or some such whim of nature – that Hooke planned wheeling in for Liz's fortieth birthday surprise.

Then there was the time, the old men cackled, competing for Hooke's attention, when Alan was too young to remember, so they said, when Careful Bob had driven warily around the corner near the Catholic church (back postwar when the roads in town were still rough dirt) and the passenger door flipped open and infant Alan rolled out on the gravel.

'You wouldn't remember. You sat there like a little king direct-ing the traffic, covered in dust.'

'Did I just.' Hooke smiled.

'Yeah, till Bob in the Saloon Bar of the Five Alls bought you a raspberry syrup and looked around wonderin' where you was.'

So he had the old men. But since that evening with Ted Merrington, Hooke came back to a thought – opening the door to the street and advancing his indefinable understanding towards that peppery man. It was what he wanted, and why this should be so Hooke wondered. There had been no sighting of Merrington since the night of the big headache when Hooke had driven home seeing double all the way. At the end of that week the monthly statements had gone out as usual, including Merrington's with a few necessary adjustments.

One day it snowed down to the thousand-metre contour line. Colts stayed home with pleurisy and Hooke went round and mixed him a whisky and lemon. In a distant gap of steely-grey clouds Hooke saw the Bullock Run dappled through the state forest. He imagined the black cattle with snow striping their spines and lacing their sturdy haunches. *Get me up there*, he vowed.

Suddenly there was Merrington, haggard and huddled in houndstooth sportscoat and Jaeger scarf, crossing windswept, deserted, inhumanly bitter-cold Gograndli Street and meeting Hooke face to face.

'Hello, bud,' he wheezed through his teeth.

'Ted, good to see you.'

Merrington's tongue, white as limewash, rattled as he shaped his words. Hooke had the feeling he'd forgotten his name, though not his function, as he grabbed him by the jumper and drew him close.

'Where's my cattle prod?'

'Wasn't that a joke?' said Hooke, grinning because Merrington had that effect on him, and he was glad.

'That says a lot.'

'Ted, I'll get you one.'

Merrington bit again: 'The statement you sent me was a fine piece of work. My wonderful price for calves wasn't so great after you cut it to ribbons with your costs and deductions and whatever else you chose to whittle it down with.'

'Just trying to help you, Ted.'

There'd been a load of hardwood planks, Hooke reminded

his client, six twenty-kilo bags of Lucky Dog and a galvanised steel wheelbarrow with a pneumatic tyre, top of the range, for which Merrington had overlooked paying since auction day and which Hooke, after the three-month allowance for terms ran out, had taken care of, as Careful Bob used to say, till now.

'Sharp,' said Merrington, without the trace of a grin.

'I don't like being touched, Ted.'

Best to make that clear to a man who was hard as they came. Whose sons, it was said, did his bidding or else.

Merrington rocked back on his heels and gave a small uncertain laugh. There came again that almost apologetic appeal in the collapsed body language – the retreat into meekness Hooke remembered after reprimanding him in the yards.

It needed to be said, but made the friendly side of Alan Hooke feel sick and sorry. 'Come over to the shop for a cuppa?'

'The legendary old men's club.'

'Is that what they call it?'

'Oh, crafty. As if there's something you don't know. It was the first thing I heard when I came onto the Isabel. That you weren't anybody till you'd got pissed with Colts and been tested by Hooke.'

'Tested?'

'My flaming oath.'

A car went past, separating them, and when Hooke stepped back onto the road he saw Merrington making his way uphill towards the post office, waving farewell as if nothing uneasy had passed between them, as if soon enough – although not today – he would drop in for that hot drink and friendly yarn.

A fact Hooke knew about people who headed up the hill as if to the post office was that up there, just over the rise, Kinloch United Sandison & Ball pitched for business, no matter how small it was. Could be that Merrington was already taking trade to Kinloch the Farmer's Friend, as the franchiser, new to town, called himself, fitting out the staff in akubras and issuing mono-grammed cotton shirts and moleskin trousers to both sexes.

Liz said there must be only one farmer using that lot because of where they put the apostrophe. Hooke liked her loyalty, but noticed his cashflow wobble a bit through the year.

Hooke walked down through the backroom storage shelves and went to the dim windows facing out into the lane. There he coiled cobwebs with his finger and gazed up into the hills at the far end of town. He knew every twist of track and crooked boundary line disputed and argued over since Careful Bob first piggybacked him through the kangaroo grass and showed him the place. A shaft of sunlight passed along the range and the snow showers melted from the far-distant slopes almost as he watched. In the good years of the decade now ending, when snow happened there was constantly the smell of spring in the air, rich and clean, well-watered. Not far off was the excitement of a good flush of feed translating itself into people's wellbeing, interest-only loans, extensions of credit. The depressive cycles of drought were peaked in manic forgetfulness.

There were no cattle prods in stock but Hooke ordered one by express post. As soon as it arrived he threw it on the passenger seat of the Fairlane and drove the fifty minutes to Merrington's Burnside. Walled ivy and attic window crenellations gave the place a lonely touch, as if it could never be brought to life and never had been. Flagstones on the long rose walk echoed in the morning stillness. Nobody was home. Even the dogs were gone. A small flush of green in the driveway wheeltracks showed there'd been nobody home for possibly a week.

When Hooke drove around the back of the house to check the sheds a bunch of cows galloped along the fenceline towards him, just that little bit hungry and wanting a bale of hay. There was hay in the shed though, and Hooke wondered where Merrington had bought it, who he'd bought it from. Seventeen cows meant that Merrington had bought an extra five from somewhere, and paid good money, too, because they weren't cheap anywhere. They hadn't come through Hooke & Hooke, and that thought justified Hooke's taking liberties to find out more.

So with the parcel tucked under his arm he walked down the side of the house looking for a place to leave it, tried the back door, and entered the kitchen with its pots and pans hanging from the ceiling and cricket-pitch length Aga stove and deep square stone washing-up tubs. It was not how Hooke usually did business – donating a long drive to one client alone – unless the favour owed was considerable, and in this case the favour was hardly more than a niggle raised to vague importance. Nor was it like Alan Hooke to go walking through an empty house uninvited. But on he went, nose weaving like a ferret's.

Entering the next room on from the kitchen, a sunroom with southern light, he was drawn to the distinct aroma of turps and oils. The door gave a groan on its hinges. So this was Merrington's retreat, where he dabbled and daubed. A row of cobwebbed skylights revealed racing clouds. An unfinished canvas, perhaps of tree branches, or of skeletonised fingers, or was it bare ribs – it was – stood in the corner. Hooke closed the door on the privacy of what he had seen, a naked someone, still arguing with himself for his boldness. 'He owes me for the drive,' the calculating part of Hooke rationalised, always a ledger there in the back of the mind. But another thought was that Liz wouldn't stand for being excluded from anything he saw, if it was going to be interesting. The living room walls crammed with those framed oils had Liz wanting to look over the Merringtons' collection in full, the other rooms boasted about and the crates awaiting cracking open from storage. Hooke wouldn't want her excluded, either, as that was a principle of life, and so in his head a small competitive argument with Merrington began. Who was the better man?

Passing another door, he looked in, he found *Goats*.

So here was the answer to a question from a while back – as to where that painting had gone, leaving the pale square on Colts's shabby wall, and who'd had the money to pay for it. In the end, Hooke smiled, Hooke always found out. He had Colts. Now he had Merrington. Or almost.

That question was certainly in the air with Merrington – 'to be tested by Hooke' – and had been since the auction, when Merrington bid up to prove his worth and overpriced himself against the district norms. Tracing it back, Hooke identified the question separating Merrington out from his other clients – the source of attraction. Merrington didn't have to be like other people if he didn't want to be. It wasn't the evident wealth that gave him the freedom, though maybe the possible source of it, way back, in brothel earnings, helped cut an edge. Anything bad that could be said about him had been said all his life since he was a boy in ringlets wearing a private school blazer and attracting the gutter press.

By contrast Hooke spent his entire life matching himself to others' needs up to a finely judged pitch of acceptance. Who was more impartial than the auctioneer tenor-throating animals and merchandise to their inherent market worth? He got through by cultivating an air of absolute equality, hard won.

Merrington was more than he seemed, Hooke already knew that. His painting room was more than Merrington, pointing to a truth Hooke had always known in the blustery world around him, but hadn't ever quite focused on to see so brilliantly. For Alan Hooke was at a point in life when he wanted not just to have passed through the world but to have whatever was true in the world passed through him.

There was always that seeking part of Hooke, wanting that little bit more. He felt a nibble of it now, its promise. It gave him pluck in the amateur ring, when younger, and was there in his singing when he was a bit older, one of Rev. Vince Powell's revivalist choristers, in a longing for spiritual moments uncorrupted by second thoughts. But what, Hooke asked himself, was truly, widely and generously amazing about him at all? He was in the groove as successor to Careful Bob down the years. That defined him locally, and still did. That Liz found him remarkable, a cause for praise, was the definition of her loving him. What about the rest?

Something was left over for Hooke as a man that he was faced dealing with as a man. It rose into his understanding as a drive to line up with sex and the providing instinct. Nothing more than that, but it seemed more elevated and he could only express it as a question: where was the room equivalent to Merrington's where Hooke himself kept a few reflections of his aspiring self, ready for show? If a man didn't have one, he surely needed one. The glimpse of *Goats* told him that. Colts was a man whose whole life had shrunk down from something too amazing for him to handle. Hooke wasn't going to have it that way for himself.

Up on the mountain was the best fattening country Careful Bob had ever stumbled across, those crafted, exemplary paddocks surrounded by untouched forest, tall timber shedding long clattering strips of bark, the acreage that the sheep-grazing Knoxes hadn't valued, to Randolph Knox's bitter regret. Could be those acres were Hooke's amazing room, ceiling open to the sky, walls wide.

Hooke kept the wonders of the Bullock Run in the family as a rule. It was his workaday mental refuge, the place he went at weekends and on long summer evenings when the day's dealing was done – just twenty minutes' drive from the agency door to

264

the locked gate. He used to go up with Colts, but no longer. Now he decided to ask Merrington up there.

Let him see something wild after a man's heart, Hooke resolved. Let them make a full day of it as he used to, with Colts. He would bring Liz's boys, Matt and Johnny, who followed his every move; they would ride farm bikes while Hooke and Merrington took to the ridges on horseback, and Liz and Dominique, that graceful Burgundian, spread a picnic lunch on the creekbank near the waterfall. If the arrangement fell at the right time the twins might come, should their Sydney social diaries permit, a bonus for Hooke's feelings and a chance for Merrington to meet them and even possibly for them to decide about the sitting he'd offered, twins paying double.

That year was a hectic one in Hooke and Liz's life. Liz carried a full teaching load with extra marking at night. Hooke ranged wide looking for stock, embarking on long drives and conducting his life via car phone out to the Riverina and north to the Hunter, skirting Sydney where on the horizon construction cranes wavered like long-legged mosquitoes as the city was made over for the Olympics. Several times passing he called his daughters to arrange a coffee or a Chinese meal, but it rarely worked out.

Hooke's was an old problem: offering clients the best-priced animals while securing top dollar when they moved through to the selling end, which, livestock being what it was, came in the same market moment. 'Hooke A Winner' was the slogan current since Careful Bob was a boy in shorts, with a logo of Hooke in trout-fishing waders landing a sheep – but still only as good as the most recent sale. Wool, by comparison, was in a trough and so Hooke had the leisure to acquire, for the two or three concerns that cared enough to try, a line of fine wool breeders challenging his own in readiness for when the industry looked up. Colts's sheepclassing reputation, formerly a Hooke & Hooke cachet, had fallen off. Hooke stood ready to drive Colts around and use his eye from the passenger seat without needing to roll down the window, if need be, to revive and resuscitate the one-lunged man from his drowning breath.

Almost when the details seemed too hard to arrange the twins phoned to set a date mid-term for their seventeenth birthday dinner 'at home', as Hooke liked to say – except the farmhouse on the town boundary of Isabel Junction where they'd started their lives had long since ceased being their centre. Once they'd ridden small bicycles with ribbons flying from the handlegrips past the hayshed and out into the ordinary backstreets leading down to the primary school. Hooke had an enduring image of them wobbling all over the road as he drove slowly behind them, making sure they were safe.

Now when they phoned there was the same feeling of protec-tiveness but he felt wrong-footed, intrusive: 'Why not come Friday evening and go back Sunday night?'

Objecting, they said they would rather travel on the train, arriving early Saturday afternoon and returning late the next morning.

'I don't see the point of such a short stay,' Hooke insisted. 'Less than twenty-four hours!'

He couldn't keep the edge of complaint from his voice, making him seem all obstinate fatherhood to his daughters, whereas to others, including Liz, nothing impossible was his motto and geniality plus his reputation.

'Dad, can we do it our way for once?'

Hooke handed the phone to Liz feeling that they always did.

Hooke's definition of being a man in a family of women was

containment of feeling while the women expressed theirs every way they could. They seemed to have extra lines open to each other while the men's emotional exchange barely connected. Maybe Hooke wanted it that way, liked it better, except sometimes it bothered him, and when it did it seemed more important than anything.

Liz learned how the twins were sacrificing a Saturday night party with their Sydney friends, for which a Friday night party was to be substituted. So a Saturday arrival it would be, no choice.

'You sympathised with them,' said Hooke, as she put the phone down.

'I was young once.'

'So was I, but I paid my dues.'

'Alan, your mother told me you were abominable – never at home, driving hundreds of miles to parties and dances and leaving her dangling when she longed to know who you were interested in.'

'Not at sixteen, seventeen. I was a lot older. Besides, it's their birthday, I'm their father,' said Hooke flatly.

'You don't understand a thing,' she assured him. 'Seventeen is older than it was. Darling, they love you to bits, you're the anchor in their lives.'

Except when he up-anchored that once, he thought, creating uncertainty in their lives of which they might never know the end.

Hooke stood on the platform, his heart full. His daughters stepped from the train – freckle-faced Abbey with a head of flossy red hair wound up in a bandana; Tina with short blonde spiky ends (whereas last time Abbey was blonde and Tina red).

After kissing him they turned to Liz, hugging her to the count of ten. 'No other luggage?' he said as they shouldered their backpacks. They had large paper bags but wouldn't let him take even them. He knew of course how skilled they were at packing minimal luggage after a childhood of shuttle domesticity. They skipped ahead arm-linked with Liz, leaving Hooke with the familiar emotion of wanting more than they could give. In the car he drove with a tolerant half-smile, just holding the wheel and being of service.

'Where's Kingsley?' they said, looking up and down Gograndli Street. There were times in the past when he'd been there to greet them, Uncle Kings, close as family.

Hooke said nothing.

'Oh, I get it,' said Tina. 'He's back on the slops, he's been frozen out.'

At the house Matt and Johnny came running to the car and dragged the girls to the dog kennels to muss the border collie's coat, then to the basketball hoop clamped to the hayshed where the boys shot baskets to the girls' applause until called for afternoon tea. On the verandah Hooke asked them about school marks and they said they'd already told him, but he couldn't remember being told, so they patiently spelt it out.

'Tell them how they look,' whispered Liz.

'Ah, by the way,' he fidgeted with his teaspoon, 'you girls look sensational.' He smiled the easy, loafing smile his clients liked.

'Do you think so, Dad? Really?'

'Yes, smashin',' he confirmed, appropriating one of Liz's North Londonisms.

They were pleased.

Then they were back with Liz, the three of them flinging dresses on beds and pooling jewellery. Hooke went to swab the concrete floor of the ram shed and waited for them to come over. As the sun sank lower he calculated that if they rushed they had time to reach the Bullock Run for a dose of country feel before they scrubbed up for the restaurant. When he went back to the house and put the question to Liz she said she'd never heard anything so absurd in all her life. The girls were in the bathroom with steam coming out from under the door in volcanic folds.

At dinner at the Pizza Heaven they announced, 'No speeches!'

And this left Hooke with a lump in his throat because he wanted to say something tipsily profound over the remains of the garlic bread and a demolished Mexican Special. What was it again?

'I've always been glad I had daughters because sons might clock me and run me down on their motorbikes.'

Matt and Johnny with their wet, slicked-back hair and spotted bow ties gave him the grin.

'Definitely a speech,' groaned Abbey.

'So we're less of a threat,' said Tina with a martial-arts scowl, 'because we're weak?'

'You don't understand. I always had the fantasy of a togetherness thing. That we'd go to concerts in Milan or sample vineyards in, ah, Burgundy. You'd link arms with me like you do with Liz – heads would turn and people would say, "*sacre bleu*, they're incredible *jeune filles*, and they're his daughters".'

'Name the day,' said Tina with a downward lilt to her voice. Everyone knew that Hooke was hard to uproot from his working life, his typical holiday being an expenses-paid trip around New Zealand glaciers as a reward for selling drenches.

'Look,' said Hooke, producing two felt-covered jewellery cases from his jacket pocket and shuffling them like a conjurer. 'Whose is which?'

It was an old birthday routine. Whichever they received, gold wrist bracelet or silver ankle bracelet, they would swap perpetually, everything interchangeable in their lives; their friendship with each other, Hooke felt, a safety net they had when he wasn't around. Once he'd tried to say this to them and hadn't been understood – or only too fully understood, he didn't quite know. If you offered perceptions and got a prickly response, was the message through?

They came around the table, hugged and kissed him, and smiled conspiratorially at Liz because they knew she'd had a hand in pushing him to get what they wanted and in steering him to the jewellery store.

Hooke had them now. But there was still a gap. Their twinship, their life in the city with their mother – an intimacy sealed from Hooke – their girls' web of secrets, their casting of him as cranky and contradictory when he often was not, all this left him feeling excluded as a matter of course, even unloved at bedrock when he considered how much he gave and how little flowed back of what he wanted, and would be only too simple to give.

But what difference did it make really? He loved them. He underwrote their lives without question, and always would. If there was ever a mortal threat to them he would stand before them, sword and shield warding off danger. Frankly he would die for them, though with a lament on his lips: Farewell dear Lizzie, my love, I must leave thee now.

'Dad, you're drunk!'

'What did I say?'

'You were humming some old "choral" item or other.'

Liz squeezed his hand under the table.

Hooke ordered another bottle of red and watched it go straight into three out-thrust tumblers and so went for another. At the bar it was one friendly drunk after another wanting a part of him. Colts was there in the payment line, swaying on his feet, and Hooke stood blocking him from seeing that the girls were home. Colts had a strand of cheesy onion stuck on his lip and promised through pungent breath he'd be at the agency at seven Monday morning to rake out the yard. 'You'd better be,' said Hooke, returning to the table to find the next round of pizzas arrived and everyone tucking in.

'What a strange, jokey, great big bear of a man,' said Abbey, looking back over her shoulder. Hooke for a moment thought she meant Colts, their childhood's tall Uncle Kings, and was shamed.

But it was Ted Merrington disappearing through the flywire door into the dark street with Dominique elegantly blowing kisses a few paces behind him.

'As if it was our fault there weren't any tables,' said Tina.

'What do you mean?'

'Your friend did a routine for us,' said Liz. 'The disgruntled pop-eyed blimp who doesn't get what he wants but charms the children. I thought his wife looked embarrassed. She gave me a rather sweet desperation smile.'

'Look what he did,' said Abbey, flourishing a paper napkin holding a lightning sketch in black biro of a nest of hair and two bright eyes over a strong small chin.

'She called it *croquis, la foudre*.'

'He made me prettier than I am.'

'You are pretty,' said Hooke.

'Oh, he perked up when he saw these two,' said Liz.

'He invited us for dinner,' said Tina.

'When?'

'Tomorrow night if we want to come.'

They stared Hooke down and watched his discomfited surprise.

'You'd cancel your train for that?'

'Would we?' The girls consulted, then looked across at Hooke, holding the moment teasingly.

'Your father's been wangling that invite for months,' said Liz.

271

'Hardly,' said Hooke.

It amused her, Liz said, that Hooke went on advancing his sought-after friendship while the friendship itself, as far as she could tell, existed mostly in Hooke's imagination. But she was encouraged having laid eyes on madame.

Hooke told them about his plans for a full day out on the Bullock Run.

'Oh, that Bullock Run,' said Abbey, raising her eyes to the ceiling.

Liz turned to the girls. 'When your dad and I first met he took me there paddock by paddock over time. Then we came at last to the old mustering hut. That was where I loved my new country and your Alan Hooke in the same breath.' She leaned her head on her husband's shoulder. 'The Bullock Run symbolises the life we made from our broken halves. The hut showed what we could do together. Once it was all bits and pieces. We nailed up board and batten, re-floored it in native pine, and installed the iron stove and unrolled the Egyptian-pattern rug.'

'That Bullock Run,' groaned Abbey to her sister, 'was where I lost my thongs, remember? The iridescent ones with the electric daisies?'

'Have you got proper toilet facilities yet, Dad?' said Tina. 'Or is it still the mattock and the Sorbent roll?'

'I'm not saying we'd camp out.'

'I can see that Mr Merrington squatting on his haunches,' said Abbey, 'being jabbed by a prickle.'

'Do I cancel the idea?'

'Well, darling, I'm for it,' said Liz, before adding, 'You should wait until they have us up there to Burnside as promised. Then we can ask them back.'

*

Hooke relished Sundays, the one day of the week when he slept past five and the phone didn't start ringing at daylight. There was a clattering in the kitchen, and a lot of hushed whispering, so he pulled a pillow over his ears and went back to dreaming. When he reached across for Lizzie she wasn't there, and a while later she came back to bed. 'Where have you been?' he said. No answer, or if there was one he missed it as he drifted off again with her fingers stroking his back, a motion interrupted as she turned a fresh page of her book, and he waited, his body craving the resumption of touch like a fish getting closer to the surface of water and blazing. Remarkable it was to be the happiest man alive.

There was a knock at the door. Abbey and Tina entered with breakfast trays.

'What's this?' Hooke sat up.

'Nothing much,' said Tina.

'Only all those outrageous luxuries they wouldn't let you carry at the station,' said Liz.

Humbled, Hooke glanced out the window into the bright early day, fighting back sudden tears while breakfast was attentively laid out on the bedspread. The window framed granite boulders and pale, bare soil. A straggle of wrinkle-backed ewes filed across the corner of the view. Merinos were always such sad-sacks. The blue shadow of poplars elongated on the ground. When Hooke looked back into the room and bit a square of toast dripping with butter and Vegemite he felt that if he died at that moment, and that was all he ever had, it would be enough.

Abbey buttered a croissant and spread it with strawberry jam, then put it on a small china plate and handed it to him. What antennae these girls had, smiling into his eyes, their hearts unerringly picking up what was right. Even when the faintest signal came in they felt its force.

*

One day soon afterwards the agency door rattled the way Hooke expected – a bit demandingly, a bit overdone. He didn't need to raise his head to know the touch.

'Look what the cat dragged in,' said Jenny Garlick.

'Mind the phone,' Hooke told her, seeing Merrington's barging outline ripple through the double glass doors.

Hooke strode to the front of the shop and made a heartfelt greeting: 'Good morning to you!'

Merrington looked pink-cheeked and fresh. *Off the grog*, thought Hooke, taking a punch to the shoulder delivered with a hard man's pugilistic reach. A token of friendship perhaps, it would leave a bruise.

'I'll have that legendary cuppa I've heard about.'

'Name your poison, Ted.'

Merrington looked along the shelf. 'Could I have a Milo?' he play-actingly whimpered.

'Good choice.'

'Strong, two sugars.'

'Coming up.'

'Ouch!' Merrington mimed as they sat down in the swivel wing chairs under the stairs.

'Sciatica still troubling you?'

'I had a fall. Galloped the paddock crosswise and connected a chukka, but then my pony – not mine, lent by Frizell – chose its moment to belly-flop. Flattened out like the bejeezus. Actually, Hooke, I found myself forking up and stepping off. But I was jolted and the old trouble's back. Limped around using my polo mallet as a walking stick. Not much sympathy from Frizell.'

'You mean Lionel Frizell?' said Hooke.

'Kit, the son. He's a bit of a lad.'

As if Hooke didn't know it. The Frizells lived at Pullingsvale a hundred kilometres away where the high, tumbled country of the Isabel flattened to grass plains, and horsebreeding and the polo calendar dictated the year. The grandparent Frizells, now pushing up capeweed in the family plot, had been valued clients of Careful Bob in the distant past, whereas Lionel and Kit rarely paid without a summons and Hooke had long since stopped their account. But sometimes they met at cattle sales, and when eye contact was made a cheque would be scribbled and passed over with an air of largesse, putting Hooke on the drip-feed till next time.

Merrington took a deep breath through flaring nostrils. 'Polo is my game,' he declared. 'I'm less than useful, though Kit says he'll try me as "B" reserve player one day, so I must be doing something right.'

'You certainly must be. At your age.'

'There's life in the old dog yet. If it doesn't work out there's always the Galloping Wombats, if they'll take me on.' He flashed an inquiring grin.

Hooke ignored it and busied himself with the electric jug. Obviously Merrington knew that he played polocrosse some-times; knew it, too, as a game for tradesmen and pony clubbers in polo parlance.

Hooke said dryly, 'The Wombats have their standards. But you wield a mean length of plastic pipe, Ted, I've noticed, with a classy wrist action.'

'Touché,' said Merrington, giving his Milo a slurp. 'By the way, Kit and Annabelle are coming for dinner on Saturday night. Why don't you and your good wife join us?'

So there it was, the invitation after all this time, rather offhand and at short notice.

Merrington peered at Hooke over the rim of his mug with a twinkly expectation. It occurred to Hooke to beg off, make an excuse, let the whole thing drop.

'Bring your daughters,' said Merrington. 'Abbey the carroty one and Tina the little blonde.'

Offhand, just like that.

Hooke stared at him, trying to make something of it.

Merrington grabbed a copy of *The Land* and read out the long-range forecast.

'El bloody Niño strikes again. This has happened to me before, Hooke, every time I take up a new piece of country – rain to the north, rain to the south, but wherever I happen to throw down my swag there's bugger-all.'

'It's a dry,' agreed Hooke, amused at the way Merrington talked himself up.

'Your bumph said "safe district". I should have allowed for the bullshit factor.'

That Merrington blamed Hooke for long-term weather patterns was a pretty good joke. It raised the stock agent to the level of a god and made every humorous bite a supplication. For this reason, whatever Merrington wanted Hooke was ready to give to him at that moment, except he still had to know what it was.

'This is Australia,' said Hooke. 'Safe means divide by two and take away the number you first thought of. Anyone with half a brain knows that.'

Merrington pulled a small, defeated face.

'I'll remember it next time you build my hopes.'

The point was obvious and Hooke came to it: 'Short of feed, Ted?'

Merrington squirmed in his chair.

'It's not only that, it's the feeding out. I can't even hoist a bale without feeling as if my knuckles have been torn from their sockets.'

'Where did you get your hay?' said Hooke.

Merrington blinked in puzzlement.

'You mean because I didn't buy it from you?'

'Yes.'

'I had a shedful back on the old place after I de-stocked. I trucked it down when they settled, and I had my five other cows there too. Now I've got too many – bad timing. I hear it's pissing down at the old place, has been for weeks.'

Hooke leaned back in his chair, his smile changing from a jagged slit in galvanised iron to something cosier, more forgiving. Better men than Merrington made mistakes on a larger scale.

He made a decision: 'Look, Ted, have you got an hour or two?'

'Right now? I'm stuck while Tinkers do a drive shaft on the Merc.'

'Okay, let's go.' Hooke grabbed his hat. 'I want to take you somewhere.'

SIXTEEN

NOTHING MUCH WAS SAID when they came to the locked gate where the yards were. Nothing much needed to be said as they got under way and started climbing the high, sparkling ridges of the Bullock Run.

Merrington just asked, 'This paddock yours?' And then at the next vista – 'This one, too?'

Each time Hooke nodded and Merrington took it in.

The late-afternoon light played its part compounding impressions, speaking for abundance, coming in thick, golden slabs from around steep corners and through old forest eucalypts parted in bars of shadow on the track. Surely, thought Hooke, this was a picture.

Merrington sat with his shoulder jolting against the passenger door. He seldom spoke but Hooke could almost hear the cogs in that gnarly brain. Light shone across into the heart of the mountain, purple against the tightly massed trees, the eucalypts giving out their oils and mists of oils, blue growth tips among the red growth tips achieving the mixture of colour. An artist would know that without being told. A dabbler would feel a twinge. A scrap man might look at it that way, rust being red-gold. It was human to look for beauty and sustenance in the fragile growth. It held the Australian eye.

The Toyota climbed the winding gravel track, its tyres spitting stones into gullies of fern. Up higher, more exposed, were ridges of silver-topped ash with conical ant hills like mud-built houses and native reeds among the dry stones. Hooke said that he often imagined all of Australia in these four thousand acres, the walloping variety of the country from the southeast forests to the outcrops of the Kimberley, the distillation of abundant space in a wagtail balanced on a blade of grass, nipping at ripe seed heads. He'd seen them in both places, cousins across a line endless on the diagonal.

While the agent waxed lyrical Merrington's mind was on the material part.

'Four thousand, you say?'

'More or less.'

'All this your timber?' he grunted. The ash was sieberi, a eucalypt prized for hardwood house frames.

'Yep.'

'Why don't you mill them?'

'Would you?'

'I might. Then again I might not.'

Merrington started talking about the geology up there. It emerged he knew a lot. It turned out he'd had mining interests, all gone bust thanks to a partnership with the redoubtable Eddie Slim. Through those interests he'd learned his geology, though. Each gully of the main creek had a story to tell that Hooke had never heard better told, dramatised with a commentary that might have been lifted from the Nature Channel. As Merrington spoke, Hooke saw changes to the landscape speeded up, the patterns of erosion at work. Where the creek cut terraces over the years, thick with tussock and reed, mazed by cattle pads, Merrington aged trees. Hooke realised that on the lower terraces there was no tree older than when Careful Bob first brought him there. It showed that at least since then there had been limited ravages, no landslips and mini Grand Canyons as on the Mundays' dismal overcleared subdivision lower down, where entire creekbanks floated into neighbours' paddocks when it rained, carrying grass, rocks and cowpats – chunks of country like wedges of cake flipped from the main plate.

Hooke interpreted all this as Merrington praised him personally, giving him points.

But then Merrington snapped. 'Why are you doing this, Al? Do you think I'm that loaded?'

Hooke laughed. 'You are. But I'm not selling it.'

'No?'

'Never. It's for my kids and their kids. I think of myself as holding it in trust.'

'Noble sentiment,' said Merrington.

'If they don't want it I'd rather give it back to the blacks.'

'If you mean that,' Merrington angled a look, 'I could introduce you to someone.'

'Let's wait and see.'

'So what's the deal?'

'I'm offering you a respite, Ted, a place to spell your cows and build them up, leave you with grass at home.'

'Really? Truly?'

It was odd and rather touching that Merrington hadn't understood this. He spent so much time working around behind people he missed the obvious open palm. Nobody else had grass and until this moment Hooke hadn't been thinking of letting anyone in.

'What's your agistment rate, then?'

'I don't want money for this.'

281

'What do you want?'

Hooke hadn't thought of it. Now he thought of it. 'A painting.'

Merrington said, with too much complacent cleverness for his own good, 'One of mine?'

'I was thinking of higher up your walls.'

'Were you indeed.'

Nothing more was said. Anyway, thought Hooke, it was preferable to wait until Liz made the pick. Then, depending on value, Hooke could decide to let Merrington have more if it was worth more.

Liz didn't take long to make her pick.

'That picture is worthless,' said Merrington.

It was on the Saturday night, Liz clutching her welcoming G & T, her eyes settling on a tiny portrait – it had passed Hooke by – a woman of around forty, plain as a plank of wood, but with a look of sharp authenticity staring from a paint-peeling frame.

'That's strong,' she said.

'Everyone says so.' Merrington gestured at other pictures with his whisky tumbler. 'Can't you be less predictable?'

'But I like it. Who is she?'

'Who is she? She's an old domestic who did mopping and cooking. The joke is that she looked in the mirror and painted herself up. She must have had tickets on herself to get herself up so ugly, don't you think?'

'Truth is beauty,' said Liz.

'Do say.'

Liz ticked off a few famous names with excited pedantry as Merrington led her around, then came back to the tiny portrait.

'Who painted it?'

'Hand unknown.'

'I like it as much as anything in the house. I love the character shining through. It's an unusual, soft palette, all those browns and pinks.'

'Up the value or I won't get my grass. Come on, pick something worth dollars.'

There was some kind of secret burning him. Anger was the key. Why didn't he like it when people liked him and, particularly in the case of Alan, those who liked him a lot? What did he hate in himself like poison?

Liz thought, *This must be his mother. It's a treasure. I won't force it.*

Merrington drifted back to the drinks table, stunning himself with spirits before the wine started flowing.

'Your walls are such a living embodiment of art history,' said Liz, rather gauchely as it wasn't all good.

Merrington gave no reaction, but brightened when Liz added, 'The twins asked me to tell you they appreciated your offer of conversation.'

'And the sitting,' Merrington reminded her, 'don't forget the sitting at going rates, times *twa*.'

They heard a car outside.

Kit Frizell and the young Annabelle were an hour late and were welcomed effusively by Merrington, even though he had fumed about their tardiness over drinks.

Annabelle was hardly older than the twins – early twenties at most. During introductions she held Liz's eye and smiled in a friendly, inquisitive way, as if to say, *Won't this be fun, but watch out*. There was a painting of her in the studio almost finished that Merrington was insisting on as a late wedding present, the sort of gift that would be a burden. It had that washed-out look, swirling blues and greens, and Liz's summation whispered to Hooke was that it lacked both character and accuracy, and that was the main difference from Merrington himself, who was overdosed on definition.

The male hug was new to country manners that year, but Frizell gave Hooke a clumsy one, and when the others weren't watching took a crumpled cheque from his pocket.

'How does a grand affect you?' he confidently grinned.

'It'll do for now.'

Over dinner Merrington raised topics from the head of the table.

'Anyone heard of Cam Whitten?'

Nobody had except Hooke. Whitten was a pugnacious radio broadcaster at the stock exchange end of the dial. Apparently Merrington hated him, had a thing about him. They were very alike. You might guess Whitten had hit him with a Pig Iron Bob stab, on account of profiting with North Asians. Merrington said Whitten took his holidays in Manila and bought underage girls from their starving mothers for a few cheap dollars. Had this on good authority: heard it in Manila.

Jumping up, knocking his chair back with a vigorous clatter, Merrington described a plan he had of coming up behind the broadcaster and giving him a thumping on a dark night, teaching him a lesson he would never forget for the sake of those poor Lolitas, crippling the man's larynx with a rabbit-chop, disabling him for the microphone and breaking his legs with an iron bar and putting him in a wheelchair for life.

'For life!' agreed Hooke, tossing back his wine.

'Struth,' said Kit, grinning.

'What sort of evidence do you have?' said Annabelle. 'I mean, this is serious stuff.'

'My 'usband, right or wrong, is a terrific "card",' said Dominique, with aloof, rather razor-like concision of wit. You could see it was early days in their marriage and there were things to be learned about Merrington that might not be welcome.

Dominique roused the admiration of the table, going through the entire evening on one small cut-glass goblet of shiraz, eating a small but highly considered portion of each dish.

Merrington scuttled around the table waving a new bottle and topping up glasses.

Liz asked in a change of subject: 'Who can define the word "jackaroo"? Alan gives me a different answer every time.'

Annabelle shot straight back, 'Young man of good family paid peanuts to slave in hope of advancement.'

'Oh, I like that!'

'It's certainly not a holiday job,' said Hooke, remembering Merrington's boast that he'd jackarooed in the school holidays many years ago. The judgement was out before he realised.

'Beg yours?'

'Well, remember you told me – '

Merrington snorted. 'Of course I remember what I told you! Want to see my X-rays, or do you want to step outside?'

Frizell touched Hooke's elbow and winked, 'Don't stay past midnight. Fun till then.'

Merrington tapped his fork on the edge of the dinner service. When Hooke looked up a pair of hooded, hawkish eyes met his. Too late already.

'Do you want to put a price on that mountain grazing, Al, or just leave it to your wife to bargain me in over some dross on my walls?'

'Not if she's a loved one,' said Liz.

'Loved one, my arse,' said Merrington.

'I'd rather leave it to Lizzie,' said Hooke. 'What do I know about art? Anyway, it's a private arrangement, price not the most important factor, and I'd rather not discuss it in front of these people anyway.'

'You've lost me,' said Frizell, raising his hands in goofy surrender.

At this moment Dominique left for the kitchen with an armload of plates, sending a glance at her husband fearful with appeasement.

Hooke felt cold and humourless. To have given, and to have hoped – well, that was past attempting.

Merrington turned to Annabelle almost coaxingly. 'What should I do, young one? Let go the one she wants?'

'You're asking me?' Annabelle pointed a finger at herself, leaned forward and laughed, then tossed her long blonde hair back over her slim shoulders. 'It depends what you want to do,' she said with quick clarity.

Hooke interrupted, his voice blowing through the silenced room like a dry wind clearing a way for itself as it went.

'I made a gesture of friendship, Ted. That's all it was. But if you want me to tell you, I will. The grazing's worth lots. Take it or leave it. Otherwise, believe me, you're out of the game and the RSPCA will slap a writ on you for starving your herd.'

'I'll choose another picture,' said Liz.

'Can't have that,' said Hooke. 'It's the one, or the offer is zilch.'

There was a long, uncertain silence and then Merrington made a loud mock yelp of pain.

'Done!'

He brought the painting around a few days later, insisting on finding the best place in the house to hang it – 'Where she'll feel at home,' he quipped. Liz was wary of him at first, then enjoyed the visit and was moved when Merrington stood in front of the picture and said his goodbyes, folding his hands in front of himself ceremonially meek, like a chastened small boy, the ring-leted cherub of yesteryear, addressing a few words to the face.

'Wherever you are in outer space, look down on us kindly for our sins.'

'Amen,' said Liz with a sense of having softened Merrington almost to the point of confession.

They took tea on the verandah corner overlooking the ram paddock. It was where Hooke sat with his shotgun on wild nights, waiting for town dogs to try their worst. 'Your husband's a tough cookie,' he said, 'drives a hard bargain.'

'He sees that in you,' said Liz.

Merrington asked were Abbey and Tina interested in coming up to Burnside.

'I believe they are,' said Liz. 'They're on a savings junket for the overseas experience.'

Liz had, besides, on the absolute q.t., made a phone call to Annabelle Frizell to ask if there'd been anything out of order when she sat for Merrington – men with paintbrushes being what they were in the moustache-twirling department.

'Not a jot,' Annabelle confirmed, 'not a whisper of anything untoward. You heard him, he hates all that. Though I did unbutton my shirt when he asked.' Then she paused to express something perhaps she knew, but couldn't quite be said. 'I think I scared him, but aren't your girls quite strong? Anyway, Dominique's there in the next room cooking up a storm. She's super-duper.'

So Abbey came down three weeks later because Tina had found work at Just Jeans and she hadn't. She stayed the weekend at the Merrington house, starting early, finishing late.

'What was it like?' Hooke said as he drove her back to the station.

'It was all right. Plenty of hours but a bit boring. You try and sit without moving for days on end. He asked me to come again the weekend after next.'

'Will you?'

'I have to, don't I, if I want the trip?'

'I'm matching your earnings dollar for dollar,' said Hooke.

'I know that, Dad. He asked lots of questions about you – how you got your land cheap, how Grandpa did. He thinks you're smarter than most.'

'Does he indeed. Then that's all right, then.'

But Hooke was over Merrington pretty much.

It was Liz who collected Abbey after the next weekend of sittings – Abbey collapsed in tears, hunched in the passenger seat almost as soon as they drove from the Merrington front yard. What she told Liz shocked her, but Abbey, shrieking, made her promise not to tell anyone. Liz said she would have to tell Alan.

'No, not Dad. I handled it all right, didn't I? I told him to stop, and he stopped it.'

'You were brilliant in the circumstances.'

'Dad'll only do something about it. He'll say something. He'll tell people. He'll go to the police. Oh, my God. He'll make a mess.'

She sat huddled against the car window.

'That's what really has to happen,' said Liz.

'He said it was our secret and "don't tell Al".'

Liz felt sick.

She waited until Abbey had left on the train and then she went home and told Hooke. 'Abbey wants to handle this herself,' she said when she'd done. She doubted if Hooke heard her.

*

Later that night Hooke sat on the verandah waiting for dogs to come slinking around his sheep. It was when they came, full moon, the shadows of poplars shortening and the hare in the moon sitting up, ears twitching amid the craters and seas of white.

Hooke's anger poured through his thoughts unstoppably. It didn't feel like his own emotion, strangely, but like something drawn down from a poisonous sac Merrington knew better than he did. How could he have been such a fool as to miss what was going on? All those occasions when Merrington needled him and it was hatred, parasitic, harmful.

He didn't think of himself though, but of Abbey and Tina. He remembered all those times following their bikes through the sparkling mornings, keeping them safe until school. The feeling had never left him.

It was mostly newcomers' dogs Hooke caught, their owners never believing their animals had it in them – claiming their dogs weren't sheep killers, believing they'd never hurt anyone. They kept those arguments to the end, when confronted. Dogs loved sheep with a madman's fetish. They bailed them frightened in corners and savaged them helpless. Only the ram stood ground with a line of courage when Hooke strode to the rescue, nights when he came upon Hollywood Boy III hurling dogs from his bloodied shoulders and meeting their return rush like a hardwood plank tufted with fibre.

Intoxicated with discovery, the dogs returned to their owners' knees and bestowed aroused gazes. He could guess the welcome: 'What have you been up to, rascal?'

Pretty soon Hooke would make a phone call. 'I'm sorry, but it can't happen again.'

'Can't? Who are you to say that?'

'I'm Hooke the stock agent.'

If he saw the owners in town he eyed them over. No longer

did Hooke seem the genial and pleasant bloke they'd heard about. They went around to see where the damage was done, down near the farm boundary fence where a laneway ran between poor weatherboard houses with roofs of rusting tin. Across the end was well-strained ringlock with strands of barb on top and below. There was a sign painted on a steel drum filled with concrete: Loose Dogs Will Be Shot. They hadn't seen it before, or if they had, thought it was just graffiti.

On nights when wind sucked and rain blew they listened as sounds were carried. Was that a distant wild yelping, was it their imaginations, was it the thud of a shotgun blast muted by storm? It made the hairs on the back of the neck stand up.

It was a misty dawn a few days later when stock trucks arrived at a side fence of Merrington's Burnside, well away from the grand house. Boltcutters were used. A fence swiftly parted, wire rolled back and trucks backed in. Merrington woke late hearing confused bellows and went up the hill to find his herd returned to him. Placed under the verandah eaves away from the drizzle was the painting of his mother, the madam, so full of the outrageousness of life and unfairness of life captured by an unknown hand.

One afternoon as shadows deepened Hooke drove to the Bullock Run. Time had passed but there wasn't a moment when his anger abated. Just the appeal of Abbey stayed his reaction. She wanted to follow it through and couldn't say what she would do or how she would do it or when – and so they let the matter stay between them, always waiting. It had been like this for quite a while now, as Hooke bent to the rule of women but assessed suitable planks that would do for a man. He stashed them in various places ready for a change of policy and always carried an iron bar in the car in case he met Merrington on a lonely road somewhere, just the two of them, no witnesses, and he couldn't help himself, God help him.

Cresting the last ridge, Hooke just made the overlook in time to see his sleek beasts like ghosts standing in the rye and sharing the pasture with kangaroos. Big greys too, major eaters, but he didn't shoot them. If he had a painter's skill, he thought, he would take a lifetime to get them down – the way they spread alarmed across the far slope hopping like fleas, or else the one standing fast, the big buck chest-growling, head cocked sideways, protecting his females with troubled integrity.

What else could Hooke do up there except sculpt the gullies with hoe and backpack spray against burr and thistle, keeping them clean for abundance? Sometimes he waited on a high ridge with a Winchester .44-40 cradled, ready for a file of marauding pigs to appear, and when they came, busy tuskers rambling and snouting on short legs, turning the pasture over with the wastefulness of fools, he sent them spinning with well-placed rounds of snap and rapid. Apart from fencing and drenching, there was nothing much else to do and then it was time to get back to his sheep.

Cattle were easier than sheep by far. But sheep were more the measure of a man in the world Hooke loved. He must talk about this to Colts. It was a wisdom Hooke puzzled over as he drove back to town listening to the sound of his tyres spitting gravel: how a wreck and a failure might be the distillation of meaning waiting to be learned.

SEVENTEEN

AFTER THE 1990S CAME THAT whirling run of zeroes, with age unbidden the theme of men who'd leapfrogged decades barely remembered in a stretch of work and forgetfulness watered by booze.

Dalrymple stopped the car at a familiar road junction and made a call he didn't like making. It was to an official with an office on the Isabel where a dam was proposed, augmenting the capital's water, nobody knew when, or even how as the Isabel was a weedy drain most seasons. The good years were gone. Dalrymple, once intrinsically of those parts, requested, almost cravenly begged permission to park his car at a padlocked gate and walk to a deserted location.

'We don't normally allow access.'

But this was Dalrymple, mate, Gil Dalrymple. He didn't have germs on his shoes. Around about spread paddocks once owned by his father. There was an Oliver Dalrymple Lane in a subdivision. 'The Flying Saucer Road, river to the stars, those of us that lived here celebrate the sky.'

A considered blank at the other end of the line. 'Don't know you, fella.'

Dalrymple chanced a last passport of sorts.

'I'm a mate of Colts's,' and a trace of suspicion slipped from the man's voice.

'Phone me again on the way out.'

'Shall do.'

'And say g'day to Kings. How is he, the old fart?'

'Battling.'

Dalrymple palmed the phone into the glove box and nosed north along the dusty farm road. It used to be lots busier as he came barrelling down, averting head-ons on the blind crests with his kids yelling in the back, belting each other around the ear-lugs with their schoolbags. Now Dalrymple crept along in memory, tracking the cold, alienated landscape in a battered Honda Civic, a scroll of dust flattening behind, limp grey hair, formerly golden, tousled in the wind, blue-washed eyes narrowed.

It had taken him a few years to make the return to the Isabel, promised himself since he couldn't remember when. No planning involved, just a hung left from the highway as he followed the tilted signpost on a whim: Duck Creek 13 km. All other times across the severed years he'd gone straight on, making whistling-bys with a no thanks, another time'll do. Such a bunch of crooks and misfits spraying thistles, herding sheep into broken-wired yards, his mates, confidants and customers calling for fairy dust, it made Dalrymple grin.

Having seen Colts go down, Dalrymple's chances hadn't been good. All those saloon bar discussions canvassing world politics, livestock, rugby, flying, women and ghosts. Now Colts was a ghost of his former self – a ghost of a ghost – being nursed in Sandstone Cottage by Randolph Knox of decent persuasion. Word was that Randolph rationed Colts whisky and Colts painted the cottage as thanks, teetering up a ladder and wavering along a plank half shickered at seventy-five.

Arriving at the highest ridgeline the Duck Creek road ribboned ahead, empty and familiar. Life was a matter of avoiding then meeting fates as a product of avoidance. In an Isabel Junction cottage Dalrymple's ex-wife, Erica, was making a new life for herself. A sixty-year-old man in a gaudy bow tie was courting her. His name: Fred Donovan.

Claude Bonney had put a biologist's slant on it, trying to make Dalrymple feel better, saying it was a phenomenon of human sex display that second-string boyfriends from decades past came back into women's lives offering new beginnings and statistically women went for them.

'She'd never mentioned him. He's an architect?'

'Back in the Hen House days he was a failed student railway worker pinching stuff and filling his head with big ideas. She hardly noticed him, to be honest.'

Bonney was the one who'd won her first, but not for long before Dalrymple made his bid and after a whirlwind romance they married. As Bonney's next-door neighbours, out on the Duck, Dalrymple flew while Erica remained the zoological illustrator doing the best, most exquisite work in the country, but only at approximately the rate of one or two finished plates per year, the proofs of which she passed over the boundary fence of their adjoining properties for Claude's wondering and exasperated appreciation.

Very strange, hummed Dalrymple, this place of lives lived now gone. A man was given for the sake of convenience a name, while littered behind him were occupations, identities, marriages, mistakes. It seemed like a summary of existence to slither the gravel, a moment of shedding skins should anyone ask for a definition. Was it the man himself or the life he lived doing the moulting? A hunch that was encouraging said the life, while those inclined to find fault blamed the man.

Dalrymple best knew the drainage system of the Isabel from the air. At a thousand feet, trimmed level after dumping super, tracking past Duck Creek heading for Mt Stony, he'd habitually glanced down on the house he owned, gaunt paddocks and a carpet of pines along the creek, the old meat-house like a matchbox where carcases hung in winter, cased in fat for a week, colder than any fridge.

The frost hollows shaded purple always told Dalrymple there were eighteen minutes left to set down on the Mt Stony strip, and God help him if a ground mist came in.

Dunno why, that thought always made him smile. Now he'd never fly again. Too risky-disky.

Large hands on the steering wheel, quick glance in the rearview mirror – an inner voice playing mental radio, bits of old songs nasally hummed, conversations with a blowfly Dalrymple couldn't get out of the car.

'You are my sunshine, my only sunshine' – *thwack!*

The vehicle swerved on the dry grass verges. Leaning from the window Dalrymple followed energetic gyrations of paired lorikeets braiding and sweeping a fence line, making cries of metallic music as they flipped and went.

'Come back, return, I'm yours, goodbye.'

Every phrase so plaintively familiar. But where did that voice come from, apparently dictating one's existence? Was it Dalrymple's own, or shared?

The ghost of himself, it was, he reflected, as he re-engaged gear and drove on. Talking to that fellow back there certainly had the feeling. Jamboree of ghost men on the Isabel.

Dalrymple glanced at his knuckles on the steering wheel. *Very solid my friend, you are*, he told himself. The contours of bare hills and broken clay cuttings and their absence of obvious beauty were part of him. Ditto yellowed grass the pelt of a lion. Mentally he reached for morning mists and mugs of tea awaiting the sun's melt-off. There behind the hangar he stood emptying his bladder into the shaggily frosted gullies.

A man's best moments came when he stumbled upon himself accidentally complete. If life had a purpose, was that what it was?

Maybe that's why a crash, a charred dab in a golden paddock, had seemed the best awaiting Dalrymple, an enlarged full stop. Then there would have been no way to say he was somewhere he wasn't, someone he wasn't.

The crash came, but it wasn't the flying sort. Erica handled the non-flying sort better because it wasn't a tease of imagination or dirty fuel or metal fatigue, but a manageable life event – whereas Dalrymple thought: better the Bureau of Air Safety investigation, widow in the anteroom, than a lawyer's office, the marriage counsellor or the certified shrink's itchy couch, or (in the case of Kingsley Colts) the Napoleon couch in the corner of a sunny sitting room, a plaid blanket over the knees, in a centrally heated, convict-era cottage watching five-day Test matches on satellite TV.

Dalrymple was ageing by the calendar's reckoning and felt it in his bones – although not too much yet, just a painful knee, a sore shoulder, a stiff neck creaking and catching when he turned his head too far. Ticker in the danger zone, however, and Dalrymple didn't think about that, nor of his hands trembling when he lifted a coffee cup to supercharge waking. Single malt was always Dalrymple's comfort, the pure refined version of heartland for someone homesick for unreachable places. Randolph Knox blamed Dalrymple for getting Colts back on the stuff, but to be honest, Dalrymple had riposted, Colts wasn't choosy round spirits.

Clouds raced over, blue and hectic. It was dry, always dry out the plateau road, but cloudy with a buffeting wind. So many crosswind landings wrestled and won, they said Dalrymple could land backwards on a skewed tailwheel if he chose.

Now scuds of vapour formed over low hills, granite boulders, thistly paddocks and dead trees. There was a whole twenty-four months once when rain was condensed mist droplets. Sandhills blocked the road and Duck Creek got fully six inches, arid zone figures.

That was the year Dalrymple stared at the sky from the end of a crowbar building fences and Erica went to work cleaning the toilet block in the Isabel Junction caravan park. It was when Janelle Pattison went for him with a knife on behalf of the sisterhood, a key moment in Dalrymple's marriage tale, just as it was for Janelle, but the other way around, for it was when she joined lives with Cud and they'd since been solid.

'Here we go, buddy-boy.'

Dalrymple parked, walked a few paces, clambered over a padlocked gate and thump landed on the other side in a bare, bare paddock. He'd seen a bloke send his thigh bone into his pelvis doing that. The Duck Creek home track, re-routed years ago, no longer entered the old way to reveal the sweep of the landholding – a matter of pride when Dalrymple and Erica bought from the front gate. That was on the 17th of October, 1981, after spring rain – well known as the mugs' date for rural real estate on the Isabel, according to Colts's information, singularly wry – poplars smelling of honey, clover frothing and rye grass imprinting rivers of wind, lambs almost grown out, their mothers matronly. It wouldn't have mattered, as Duck Creek was a piece of land as close as Dalrymple could come to buying back what his father had wasted. Then he, the son, was the wastrel.

Now Dalrymple sneaked in like a thief, alarming staggy wethers. There were new owners under the hills, the larger runs subdivided except for Cud and Janelle Pattison-Langley's Wirra-ding, and Claude and Jacquie Bonney's Duck Creek Wetlands, their boundaries lapping up to what was called the environmental exclusion zone of the projected dam.

Dalrymple shaded his eyes and realised there was more than a kilometre to walk before he even joined with the old track. For this way in he could not see the shearing shed under the old bark-peeling viminalis and the various improved paddocks once revealed from an elevated angle as workable and worth the price; those dreams that were no longer on show, for which Dalrymple and Erica had busted a gut to pay, grading a strip on the ridge above the house and building a hangar with the words Dalrymple Aviation painted on galvo ribs.

The homestead itself never showed itself until the last moment. So Dalrymple didn't expect it yet. What puzzled him was a plantation of pines wedged across the middle distance and showing a stiff green wall of treetops at the top of a rise he walked along. Could not remember for a minute which paddock he was in – a neighbour's?

Dalrymple's navigational sense was better in the air than in walking shoes. The track upon which he trudged sliced east between granite tors casting sheets of speckled exfoliation. In crevices safe from stock a leaseholder had jammed rolls of barbed wire now rusted. They were taken from a demolished fence that Dalrymple had built with his own hands. Which way had it run? He could no longer tell. All boundaries were melted.

And the pines, those pines – he came back to them – who'd planted them?

Of course, now that he thought himself into spatial order and mentally joined the new track to the old, *he* had – last seen in driving rain with thousands of feathery-topped seedlings unloaded from a tractor-trailer. He turned into an alleyway of trees where the trunks were solid and dirty-horned rams got up on beds of brown needles under a radiata canopy sheltered from wind.

Things were quiet at the Duck Creek crossing where cars and dogs and shrieking children once splashed through. There came

Dalrymple throwing a long shadow. So quiet at the crossing these days that a wombat had set up residence, burrowing under a chunk of reinforced concrete loosened in a flood. How that water had torrented! Milk chocolate churned to foam, sky laid down as a river, flattened, wetted the grass for miles around the year Polly was born.

The pump shed Dalrymple built that year still stood, ditto old tin sheets lying in a ditch, which he'd always meant to move. It was a shabbier, more condensed, grittier and more disposable place than he remembered, for it was leached of dreams and therefore with the feeling of mere wasteland stumbled upon.

And yet there was the house, with the question storming as Dalrymple stumbled up to a bedroom window with a flap of torn insect screen scratching in the wind. Who was this being standing so intently still as to feel himself disappear? A man back on the other side, making a choice the way a ghost did, whether to haunt, or to toss all that and come out alive.

Dalrymple had loved entering the gauzed front bedroom and closing the door against houselights, standing with his nose to the window netting and watching freeze-frames of lightning in the dark.

'Gil?' her voice called him.

A thunderclap pretended he didn't hear. He was a youngish man in that phase of his unfolding, in which he was spared knowing himself. The rolling plateau of granite rocks and wind-blown tussocks gave a sense of being alone on the planet. He liked that, and never wondered why, or what it would lead to.

Out of the darkness came the rumble of hoofs. A strike of white fire and Erica's mare skidded, lit up where Dalrymple had started scooping a tank before his dozer threw its tracks. In the next loud crack Cosma came at the gallop between trunks of glistening snow gums – seemingly motionless, tail erect, loudly snorting. It meant there was a gate left open or a gate knocked open in the squall. No point in rushing out, nothing to be done, but Dalrymple hoped the mare wouldn't spike herself on a Telecom star picket he'd meant to remove. Should have the day before, or really the week before when the cable layers finished and Dalrymple took them beers, a carton of Tooheys hefted high on a generous shoulder.

Back in the town of his birth Dalrymple had been a boy standing at the window of an electrical store and looking at the blank screen of a television set before he'd ever seen a TV picture or there'd ever been reception in the area. Fragments of streetlights and passing cars had the excitement of a good flick.

Erica opened the door behind him, admitting a shaft of light.

'Gil, are you in there? I wish you'd answer me. The kids are frightened and they need you. Don't be unavailable when you're needed.'

An edge to that word, used by Erica when Dalrymple took jobs away from home, brooded, took long walks or went to the Five Alls until way after closing time and drove home blind as a bat. Unavailable, a word taken from a book about men and used to hobble him, he argued, whereas unavailable in Dalrymple's vocab meant something else – appetite defined as perfectly strange and perfectly beyond understanding. Unavailable to himself, which didn't mean don't try perfectly grasping.

Why Erica with her beautiful wisdom would need any self-help had raised a tricky question, troublemaking, a bad sign between them.

'Cosma's in the home paddock,' he said.

'I'm more worried about the kids just now.'

'She's your horse, honey-hearts. But there's that steel post, y'know.'

Her silence told him she knew all about the picket. A lesser woman would have rolled her eyes, but Erica had an implacable way, she made a monument to justice and stood there waiting. Somehow she knew the horse was safe while at the same time Dalrymple was already responsible for its death.

He couldn't say it having lied, having made a false promise to lapse his commercials and stop risking her breadwinner – but during a storm he was up there with his great wings flung around. Erica once called him the eagle who'd won her, clawed her from the rock of the Isabel Walls where he'd backfired his Auster and drawn her eyes up: expecting dunno what from his need to soar – abundance? What she loved in him first she blamed him for later. That was the mystery of marriage, and it beat them.

'You can't just disappear, Gil. It's teatime.'

There was a dull flash, an echo of weak thunder. The storm had moved too far away to be interesting. Dalrymple led the way back to the kitchen.

'The kids are okay,' he said as they went in. 'It's you who's frightened. You don't like saying what rattles you, that's the pits. And they pick up on it.'

'Rattled, scared, you can say that again,' she allowed.

But brave too – with the fatalism of a soldier, he had to acknowledge. He wasn't as brave as her himself because not as fearful. She never missed a parent–teacher night and would visit old people in hospital, those she'd met at her humble jobs, or on the road befriended when their cars broke down, stuck by their steaming radiators with reptile calm. She lent money to people in trouble and gave too much, cutting the household back to neck chops and suchlike, and it seemed to please her, that Dalrymple and the kids risked breaking their teeth on bone fragments.

Erica's father, Silvio, had been a tough old bastard. He took her from school and used her roo shooting as a child at Byrock, where they'd kept a refrigerated trailer. She'd aimed the spot while he took them out – big reds and fully grown greys – a nightly killing for pet food suppliers until the day came when Erica stood up to old Silvio and she rocked from home.

She'd missed so much school and then caught up. They'd sparked, ignited, at Claude's Duck Creek Wetlands Open Day when Claude and Normie Powell raised money for quadriplegic research and Dalrymple offered loop-the-loops.

Erica still shot for the dogs, drawing a bead in the creek paddock at twilight, going forward with the skinning knife. He'd find her kneeling, splashed with blood, hacking through sinews, because old Silvio had started something that might be described as a battle against whatever it was that limited a woman.

Dalrymple knew her secret and it confounded him. Unlike other people who were good at shutting things off, Erica had no way of stopping what started in her head. Silvio had behaved towards her as he might to a son, and that was all right, lots of girls rose to that expectation in the bush and it made them. But Erica made it an attitude about everything when she was older. She just had to do it. For that reason she had rock climbed with the Bonney crowd. She'd lived with Claude attempting to match his pace, and he was not a bad bloke – just wasn't up to her, though he always believed he was better.

'We cannot, will not, are not seeking another cent from the bank,' she'd said when Dalrymple came to her with the scheme for the interest-only loan that would set them back on their feet. A French bank too, which seemed a cracker of an idea to him – Banque Nationale de Paris. They were the best rates on offer. *Bon chance*. Everyone on the Isabel had been onto them.

A grave woman, in short. There was medication in the pantry and Erica used it, but she liked the fags and vodka greyhounds best, two or three biggies at the end of the day, and sat for hours when the kids were asleep with a sketchbook in her lap. Bloody tense, that meant, at the work of living. Yet Dalrymple loved that grey-eyed tiredness of hers, with the downturned smile and the prominent vein in her forehead that swelled sometimes, and the bare curve of her neck, which he stroked while holding her, calming her, getting her to trust him again and twisting her hair and coiling it to the top of her head.

'Nice, nice,' she'd murmur.

'I want the chance to make you happy.'

These words Dalrymple used when he first loved her. She gave him that chance. Then they were living it.

In the kitchen Erica took Polly's braids and made them tight as licorice twists. Polly was seven, then, precursor of wide-foreheaded beauty, holding her feelings glassily open, which meant an element of judgement visible in her mother's favour. Kim had a pale, five-year-old freckled country-boy face, and he and Dalrymple were like two dented, dusty scones, the pair of them. Already they had a conspiracy of blokes going between them.

The kids ate their baked beans on toast with mounds of steamed spinach on the side, sprinkled with grated cheese. They had white moustaches from drinking milk and Dalrymple tousled their hair with one hand on each submissive, grateful head.

'Don't you know you're safe in the house? It's your castle,' he said.

'The lightbulb went on and off,' said Polly. 'It sort of sizzled.'

'That's normal,' said Dalrymple.

'She said it was going to blast,' said Kim, looking up defiantly.

'That would never, ever happen,' said Dalrymple.

They got it from Erica. She was unable to touch a slack powercord unplugged from a wall without wondering if it still had electricity in it. Old Silvio covered every practicality in her education except her mind. They'd only had Coleman lamps out west, the light of camp fires and Lighthouse candles.

Dalrymple said, 'I saw a fireball once.'

'Not now,' warned Erica.

'Hey, but it was quite something. It was down on the Isabel Estuary, on the coast. Came through the lounge window and danced round the kitchen, soft as fairy floss. Everyone laughed, but their hair stood on end and their fingertips glowed purple.'

'Did it blow up?' said Kim.

'I just said what it was – harmless.'

After they cleaned their teeth they went to Erica for a story.

Dalrymple stepped to the door and reported a clear sky.

'The stars are out. Here comes Mr Moon. Hey Kimmy, let's go to the top of the hill and check that horse.'

'Can I, Mum?'

'Fine,' sighed Erica, releasing an arm from around her son's waist. He ran to Dalrymple and launched himself at him, and Dalrymple lifted him to his shoulders.

They walked up the hill and the mare came from shadows and followed through the gate.

The boy smelled of damp grass and fresh wind, muddy earth and a whiff of horse from stroking Cosma. The very essence of Dalrymple, he was. No way to see him as a semi-professional League player with a head like a concrete potato, one who slips Dalrymple cash, two or three hunnerd dollar notes at a time, withholding condemnation. Ghosts have power but only in the shape of chronology shredded, never to the letter of outlines fixed.

Later that night Erica told Dalrymple she didn't like him interrupting their story time. Polly was a great little reader and Kim wouldn't get hooked if Dalrymple kept tempting him off.

'It's important a kid goes free,' said Dalrymple.

'Whatever that means,' said Erica. She rolled over. 'Hold me,' she said.

Dalrymple waited until he heard her quiet breathing, then turned his back, looked out the window into the sparkling, rain-washed night. He imagined he was a battle-tank commander. The enemy came from the direction of town. Dalrymple had them bailed up in a gully of rocks. Tracer bullets lit the sky and he picked off small, dark, scurrying figures as they scattered. He did it wing-over and screaming down, the Gatling pouring hot lead like a garden hose.

One day Dalrymple rang home and heard his own voice on the answering machine. Leaving himself a message he knew he'd be first back to savour its curiosity.

That was the day he knew he needed to run. He didn't like who he heard – 'You're goanna die,' he told himself, so many parts of himself flown, so much held back unfinished.

Dalrymple goes to the rocky hilltop above the house, outlook wide, dusk not far off in the sparkling winter light. He makes a fire of bark and twigs before the time comes and he will have to face retracing his authorised steps to his car. He can see the car parked away and away, winking like a heliograph in the last reflected sunlight, and knows it will be star-dark before he stumbles back. On the main highway fifteen kilometres away cars already have their headlights on, so far off that as the minutes pass their lights go piling into each other in a continuous animated pulp of diamonds.

Once before there was something like it, along a pipeline big enough for a monkey's motorbike to ride through, travelling two thousand kilometres into mountain gullies from a gas field under the inland sky.

Dalrymple had known nothing about it until Colts told him. Taking a long back road out of ample curiosity, Colts took a wrong turn and went for miles in the direction of sunset over bare hills.

Almost on dark it was a camp of a sort Dalrymple came to. He had never seen anything like it – boom gates and mesh trackways leading between brightly lit bunkrooms. Climbing from the car that day was like arriving by flying saucer on the planet Earth still wrapped in its strangeness. A million bucks minimum in transportable comforts, there was no other way of describing it to Erica that expressed his decision fully, that there would be bankable cheques if he could get an in. Thus did a man immerse himself in a new dimension of revelation apologised for as money for the family purse.

It was one of those infrastructure projects you didn't read about in the papers anymore. When Dalrymple was a kid they were launched by prime ministers and relayed on national radio while explosives plungers were pushed and the earth shook. Now they were only written up in the financial pages. It was like receiving what he never counted on, but somehow always did, just in the nick of time – call it grace.

Dalrymple ignored Keep Out signs and investigated the facilities. He fell into conversation with a bloke who told him a lot in the short walk they took from car park to poolroom. In a mess hall he ate lasagna and salad after getting a meal ticket from a cook who welcomed him. Then there was Eddie Slim. They greeted each other like long-lost brothers, which was hardly the case: as boys, Slim had smashed Dalrymple's balsawood glider without saying sorry, and Slim's father pawed Dalrymple's mother after making promises laughed at in retrospect, when she was publicly called hysterical.

They settled into the wet canteen, bringing up names. Normie Powell had flown with Dalrymple last year on contract, mapping wetlands across the Top End and doing loops and wing-overs for the hell of it between thunderheads.

'So he's the great man now,' said Slim. Everyone he'd ever known had played a game of keeping him on the outer.

It was the ideal job and Dalrymple hadn't even known it was coming. On the phone he painted it to Erica as more or less local, home every weekend, but Australasian Gas Reach was the company name and Dalrymple reached indeed, wearing a monogrammed cap under the blue sky, filling a barcoded niche with his photograph laminated on plastic, occupation – Pilot Observer, Line Inspection Group – stamped in red letters. Home again, Erica laughed sideways and said he looked bought up. Only one word was needed to renew their conflict, and that was the one.

After the first time it was a month before he was back home again – Erica talking about the charge it gave his balls, same as if it had been a woman, she said, the corners of her mouth tensing. Sometimes he was poised within sight of the sea, other times found himself with red dust between his teeth on the farthest fling of the pipeline west. His boy and his girl loved the presents he brought them, Barbie dolls and GI Joes from old-time cluttered general stores, last-minute grabbed.

Erica incessantly asked what his feeling was, and if only he could articulate the feeling he could do anything, go anywhere, make free with their lives, she implied. The word summarising it for Dalrymple was waste, but how could he say it? Waste so intrinsically part of him it was beyond expression. She might think he meant his life was wasted with her, but no not that. Waste as defined by a process of nature, the wearing down of hills to the distant sea that he talked about with Eddie Slim as they sat in the purple dusk drinking themselves silly. Dalrymple ached being part of it although hills didn't have feelings, only Dalrymple did.

Of course a female was involved: a battered beauty sitting at the end of a dirt strip. Dalrymple ran his hands over the Maule taildragger's fuselage and wrestled mockingly with the prop as if he were enlivening a living depressive. When he took her up, snarling along ridges in late afternoon light, holding to steep low circles with G-forces dragging his cheeks, he knew he was ready to die. But he didn't or wouldn't die, readiness being a condition of life now for Dalrymple.

The task was to talk into a mike, interpreting and observing. He snarled the Maule over rocks and gullies in pursuit of its own dancing shadow a bare one hundred feet below. A spotter of broken fences, scrub fires, wild pigs, mobs of kangaroos and emus by the hundreds, camels and horses, of tracked intrusions into no-go zones, Dalrymple was paid to think aloud, a connoisseur of himself. It was dollars for dreaming, he declared on the quiet in case he spoiled his luck. Anyone who wanted to go for a spin he took them. Often it was Eddie, that schoolteacher's metal-struck boy from years past, who talked about going back, buying a piece of land on the Isabel with goldmining water races overgrown with trees and delving for gold.

West of a dusty railhead there was a week when Erica came with the kids in the school holidays, the Honda loaded with camping gear. 'We apologise for our interruption,' she said, unable to make any utterance free from bitterness until Dalrymple came home. They couldn't touch, or meet eyes really, yet had a treaty going when Dalrymple flew, Erica settling something inside herself alongside of him, allowing her fate was all his for the skyborne duration.

It was gold-bearing, semi-desert country where mines opened in good years when the exchange rate was favourable and closed in the bad; an expanse of quartzy ridges, scarred watercourses, cold winds over the saltbush plains. It excited Slim in the passenger seat. The gas field itself was another five or six horizons north-west and Dalrymple was thinking of nothing when a wink of mellow light came from a scraped arena during a lazy turn. He applied power and around he went again, noting the landmarks. Slim said nothing.

Over cold beers leaving Olympic rings of condensation on a formica tabletop, Slim told Dalrymple how gas-bearing strata was mined. Down a borehole thousands of metres deep a gel mixed with ball bearings was pumped under extreme pressure until a cap of rock was shattered and the gas released from that was taken off.

'Exciting stuff,' said Dalrymple.

It was, said Slim, but not the same as gold, that mythical magma of the soul, and he gave Dalrymple a smile that seemed to say he was on to him.

Next day Slim and Dalrymple set off in Slim's Toyota, taking Kim, Polly and Rachel, Slim's fourteen-year-old, Dalrymple asking them to keep their eyes peeled across particular claypans he remembered from the sky.

'For what?' said Slim with that same amused although calculating sidelong glance he'd give a bloke to make him wonder.

Dalrymple had a feeling of heavy excitement, a gambler's certainty. Astonishingly that same glint he'd seen from the air answered him on the flat. Implying no special reason for asking, he asked Slim to turn one-eighty degrees. Slim's kid, Rachel, picked up on it although all Dalrymple said was he saw a flash, as from broken glass.

The vehicle stopped, the kids jumped out and started racing.

It was in the papers, the legal wrangle, ownership hanging on when the word – gold – was spoken in relation to the glint, and by whom, to whom. For it had not been Dalrymple who spoke it, said the judge, but the geologist Slim's precocious daughter – never Dalrymple to whom gold must henceforth be described as having no earthly function or use, merely a product of time rolling its planetary weight over him and excreting under pressure the essence of something lived. In a word, waste.

Or so Erica, who pursued the Slims in court, earned the right to think.

For Slim's Rachel reached the nugget, shouted her claim to Slim and squealingly attacked the soon to be celebrated lump, while the others watched, standing back as if from the heat of a blaze. Slim got around behind his girl and the pair wrenched it loose, quite unable to hold the prize, grasping its slippery lugs, clods of earth falling from pitted hollows of tremendous weight as they wheezed.

The nugget was called the Slim Find and displayed in the foyer of the Chifley Building flanked by armed security guards, an object of extravagant disbelief worth dollars in multiples of hundreds of thousands on the gold market, but to a pair of competing billionaires, bidding for the nugget intact, worth much more. Slim dealt with them, whatever it did to his soul, and the Dalrymple claimants were awarded just enough, after costs, for Erica's three-bedroom cottage mortgage-free after their separation. There she lived to this day in Railway Street, Isabel Junction. Dalrymple kept the Honda.

Reaching into his backpack Dalrymple drew out the bottle of Islay malt he'd carefully but self-deludingly stashed and refrained from telling himself he had the whole damn day long. How beautiful that spirit looked through its warps of glass when held to the last of light. A goblet, he called the Pyrex tumbler he carried for the purpose of civilised enjoyment.

By the time Dalrymple mixed his drink among the reeds of Duck Creek a torrent of cold air descended to nose level. High, dark banks guided him to the north-west. He calculated two drinks would bring him to a point where striking up from the bank would bring him onto the road. Rather than a blundering return through his own former paddocks he would follow the road back to his car. The route would take him through the bottom of Cud Langley's land, then Tim Knox's land, then he would reach Claude Bonney's land.

On the creekbank horizon line the lights of Bonney's house winked through frosty air as Dalrymple navigated closer. He was almost to the end of his second drink, mentally juggling the idea of a third, when a voice exploded from the creek ahead of him.

'Fuck! Fuckin' water! Fuckin' barbed wire!'

It was Damon Pattison. Dalrymple cowered against the bank, amazed. The sound of grunts and splashes came from a mere twenty metres away when he'd felt alone in the universe. As he wriggled to the top of the bank, a flume of shotgun-fire sparked red across the gully and a shot rang out.

A second voice yelled, 'Anyone there? Is that you, Damon?'

It was Claude Bonney.

Lying prone, tasting gravel, heart thumping, Dalrymple awaited the next shot. He heard the raspy breathing of his fellow night-marauder crouched below in the reeds: Damon Pattison scouting around the night paddocks looking for thrills, defining himself away from Wirra-ding and its set routines. Whatever was happening made Dalrymple's presence an excess of one. At that moment the ghost of himself detached itself from his company without even the politeness of a farewell. He rolled, scrambled to his knees and ran off.

Later that night he appeared at Erica's door, arguing his way in. 'Just for tonight,' she said. God knew why she bothered, but something about Dalrymple made her reverse a previous stand

– grass sticks in his hair, seedily drunk, that was expected, but a light that had often disturbed her gone from his eyes. It wouldn't do to tell him that something was gone, doused, drained. He wouldn't know what to put in its place. Nor would he have to try. She showed him to the spare room and told him to take a hot bath and sleep in if that's what he needed. But to be gone by late morning.

Then she went back through the house collecting her car keys and a few belongings and headed out the north-western road, to a high rocky knoll where there was once a one-teacher school. A new life was beginning. The three-acre block had languished on Education Department inventories since the school was closed down. The titles were deemed to have been locked up in bureaucracy, but Fred Donovan had dusted them off during a file search and closed a deal. Such a deal had eluded Eddie Slim for years. Donovan was clever like that. Slim was furious. Served him right for taking what wasn't his, a great big chunk of happiness by the name of gold. All that remained of the teacher's residence and schoolroom was the bell-strut jammed stiff, rusted supports on a splintery hardwood pole. Back out of sight of the road was an area scraped clean of old bricks and twisted plumbing where a house would rise from the earth, built of earth.

Donovan was in daily contact with Erica by email or phone. He'd drawn her into his world, his way of seeing things, through a phenomenal bout of finding no-one to equal her over the years and getting in touch after her divorce from Gil. She conceded her life was a dream. She would give him that.

Blink awake Erica and be in love – F. Donovan. *What thou seest when thou dost wake, do it for thy true-love take* – Wm. Shakespeare.

All right, she would. From her high vantage point overlooking misty riverflats and hazy humpy ranges, she watched car lights shifting along the district roads until one broke free of the rest and commenced its steady, brightening progress up towards her.

EIGHTEEN

CLAUDE BONNEY FOUND THE FRESH footprint on the steep side of the creekbank a few hundred metres from his house. It was the mark of a boot with a ridged sole, showing distinctly on a step of eroded clay.

Bonney had never before seen such an intricate pattern except in fossiliferous strata, among ferns and podocarps before there was anything human on the face of the Earth. The print belonged to no-one he knew, indeed who came down to this tangle-rooted, steep location except Bonney himself? There was Tim Knox and Cud Langley but the rest of the neighbours along the Duck and Isabel bends were gone, and this end of the district was stripped of working farms. Farther back towards town, farmland was carved into smaller and smaller blocks to make what were once called hobby farms, but now were called rural acreage, as if they needed to be put to no other use except to be framed in tight fences and given their house, shed, dam and For Sale sign.

The print was heavy-pressed two metres below him, a mark etched by the spring water oozing out around it, as distinct as a freshly revealed husk or glistening half-tide shell. It bespoke the full weight of a person standing motionless, the presence of an intruder.

Bonney looked around. Pathways led through the dry reeds and juvenile willows, but they were made by animals – waterbirds, foxes, stray sheep. Nowhere could Bonney see the blundering signs of breakage indicating a human going through.

Claude Bonney, photographer and botanical illustrator, when working his wetlands wore green rubberised waders up to his armpits and moved in drugged, silent fashion along banks and through swamps with his camera and collecting gear around his neck, his freed hands repositioning each bent reed and betrayal of his retreat as if he were gently rowing.

He slithered down for a closer look, clutching poplar roots for handles as his heels gouged into the clay. He stood parallel to the mark, twisting himself to face the direction of whoever had stood there before. Slowly and deliberately raising his head, Bonney found himself staring through grass a few hundred metres in a direct line to the windows of his house. He tapped his pockets and withdrew the small folding binoculars he routinely carried and found himself looking directly into his bedroom. He saw Jacquie lean from a window flapping a rug. The dogs leapt at her and he heard her shrieks of laughter as she encouraged their antics.

That night he saw him, the shadowy cut-out of a man making his way up the creekbed after dark, a torchbeam flashing in the frost, on and off, on and off, ice-shine up the poplars for a hundred feet. 'Fuck! Fuckin' water! Fuckin' barbed wire!' Then nothing except silence and darkness.

Bonney recognised the voice. *What's the silly bastard doing?* he thought. *I'll give him a scare.*

Above the creek, Bonney stood on a rocky knoll holding his shotgun, barely breathing. He fired into the silence, the butt of the .12 gauge kicking against his shoulder, a concentrated hard flash igniting the lower night.

The sound echoed away. 'Anyone there?' shouted Bonney. A stupid question. Then after a long wait, hissed, 'Come on up, Damon, I know it's you.'

Throughout this lonely, star-dark end of the district there had been a spate of robberies lately. Stud sheep mustered from roadside paddocks after midnight, bales of wool rolled from shearing sheds at two in the morning, diesel drained from overhead tanks at dawn, fine wool lambs scooped from paddocks by organised gangs running silently, swiftly over the frost, gathering weaners under their arms the way the wind gathered fallen leaves. Knox was done over. Cud Langley ditto.

Bonney hadn't suspected Damon Pattison before.

'Was it you?' demanded Bonney the next day.

Damon Pattison chortled, 'Would I do that to a mate?'

'Do what?' said Bonney.

'Pinch his stuff.'

Bonney looked at the younger man sideways. 'Well, that's interesting, I didn't say anything about "stuff". Just was it you in the creek, mate?'

'I'm not stupid. The way people look at me in this place . . .'

'Drunk or stoned in the paddocks,' said Bonney. 'Cutting across country. I was out there with a gun.'

'It's a free country.'

'I decided to give them a scare. I could have killed whoever it was.'

'I would have shook your hand,' said Pattison. He continued carving a lump of wood while Bonney watched him, a hawk escaping his big-handed attempts. The sadness, the disappointment was there.

They seemed to have an understanding after this. Damon Pattison started attaching himself to Bonney's world, appearing unannounced every day or so, chopping wood for Jacquie, mending the roof, teasing the younger girls and not saying a word to the older ones, except looking forlorn. The broken artistry of existence longed for connection.

'Give me a look at your boots,' said Bonney one day.

'Like them?' said Damon, hopping around on one leg.

They were the ones. They both knew it.

'Wait'll I get you aligned in *my* sights,' said Damon.

'You'd be lucky, I'm bulletproof,' said Bonney, who'd had poachers after him in Zambia and raskols leaping from the undergrowth in PNG, bites from a brown snake and a near-fatal sea-stinger attack.

Normie Powell wasn't so lucky. Bonney was called to the phone to hear the worst.

Normie, these days, was all heart but medically speaking weak-hearted. He would have been safer in an Edwardian novel where he'd wear a solar topee, a white linen suit, take sea voyages, excite ageing spinsters, outlive the strong. Instead he was all man, kept working, half killed himself in cardio stress tests, had a family of five to support and the memory of a father who was only fully himself in water, and just for that memorable once.

Normie was not religious but the son lives out what the father only attempts, evolutionary theory insists, otherwise no evolution, and that was Normie, with his gift of knowledge that had arrived that day. The vision of spouting water told him all he needed to know of life. His father was tied to a clumsy pushcart but Norm never would be. If bonds ever bound him he would die in preference to having himself strapped down. Never say die, say, 'Fuck 'em.'

The academy had a research station on the coast where Normie exhausted himself skindiving. In the rugby season he wore an electronic heart monitor on the sidelines. Nobody went as hard at living as that. Life was a scrum heaving and straining, the ball in there somewhere and coach Normie screaming over the sportsfield, 'Get it out! Get it out, you bastards!'

Almost single-handedly Normie Powell worked on rule changes at the national and international level of the game, minimising neck and spinal injuries until they became the standard.

But now to this day when Bonney received a call with bad news half expressed and he was asked to hold the line.

Waiting, phone in hand, he pictured the Dividing Range hills from Norman's wide, clean office window. They rose beyond the shaved edge of the parade ground, massive and sheep-cropped like low poured glass, with sometimes a flash of silver as a plane made its approach or took off. Bonney gave an imagined glance inside the room. No asepsis there – a cigarette spiralling smoke from an ashtray, a half-eaten white bread roll containing low-cholesterol spread and salami, a mug of black coffee steaming on the edge of the desk, briefly abandoned. Periodic tables and molecular models like a child's toys. There was no tricking with fate in Normie Powell's way of things.

Then, at last, Bonney imagined Normie's footsteps in the corridor hurrying back, drawn towards the sound of the ringing phone, the waiting illicit cigarette, the heart-cheering caffeine, footsteps coming too fast, beating, pounding their way down the corridor, blood gathering from the veins too quickly, too urgently, the veins becoming congested and the pressure rising intolerably.

It was no good. Bonney drew a line through waiting as he always did, leaving it to others to attend to what was needed.

That night he drove in. Darkness star-shining still. Fog in the hollows. A man lay writhing on a hospital bed, drip-feed tubes in his nose, Normie Powell dumped on his side as if hurled from a height, dropped on his head, you might say, his life knocking itself out. A man younger than Bonney, but not by much, as they got older, a shiner from Isabel Junction Intermediate High, gold on the honour board, clammy, half naked under the sheets, gasping like something held under water, an aquatic ape learning it can swim only briefly on the surface of time, and only too briefly, oh so briefly, on the evolutionary scale.

'Don't bother me, I am working, I am concentrating, hell, it's hard, it's a problem, it's killing me! It's my life, my life's work to see this question through.'

Bonney came to tell him he loved him. It could not be said in words. A group of them had gathered. Eddie Slim flew in from Bali, the most lost of any of them attempting to claw his way back to meaning through various lavish lifestyles and this way of saying sorry to someone he'd maliciously maligned when he could. Men without religion praying through dry lips, trembling with fear of life, too much of it unexpected, the way it unrolled from a bloke's bare hands even when he kept his fists clenched tight.

Normie's eyes were closed, he was breathing so fast, no sportsman had ever had so little oxygen available, no drowning diver, no aquatic ape nor Anglican priest galvanised to walk again, his lips white, pinched in the struggle, devoid of words, devoid of thought, existing maybe in the willed light of prayer but that was all. It had begun with a heart attack. Then a stroke. Then came pneumonia. Now it was all-in TV wrestling in a coma. Sisters and wardsmen rolled him over. Bonney made jokes over his struggle to friends who were there, strangers and friends, foretelling recovery, how Norm was to take it easy again, no arguments, the golden handshake and the leisurely tome by the banks of the trout-fishing river.

Outside in the frost after the announcement a certain tearless elation. Vengeance of the survivor. Coffee at someone's house.

Then, well past midnight, the long drive back into the country. Bonney alone, headlights picking through the starry night, Bonney going carefully to avoid kangaroos and wombats on the road, not wanting another death tonight, no, not of any

kind whatsoever, large or small, no extinguishing of consciousness or dreadful moment of Jacquie lifting a telephone in the
sleeping house, getting the news. Then stopping for a breather on
the top of the Divide, absolutely no other headlights anywhere
for a hundred kilometres around. Black night, charmed world,
amazing room the world was. Smoke from ice in the grass. The
Milky Way crammed with stars. The Southern Cross tilted hard
up against Asia at the perpendicular of deep winter.

Where was the road leading home from here, leading in?
Where did it go? Get me onto it demanded Bonney with
resolution.

The gravedigger edged closer on his Kubota front-end loader,
checking his watch, moving into overtime while the sun went
down between the sheep-bitten hills. Long shadows departed
across the gravestones of Isabel Junction cemetery, the crowd
moved away.

Normie's colleagues from distant universities in their expensive three-piece suits, paunches and Ray-Ban sunglasses, so
prosperous and weighty, thinking, *who next?* There goes the first
of their generation to get a chair. Normie's old supporter Chook
Hovell would never have such an insouciant intelligence, such a
wise-thinking sidekick to stimulate his liberalism again. There he
was tossing a handful of dirt into the bitter earth.

There was Eddie Slim avoiding Gil Dalrymple, because of
greed for gold that transcended decency; there was Tub Maguire's
seven surviving kids out of eleven weeping at the memory of a
good man's good son gone; there was Kingsley Colts in a suit a
few sizes too large, rumpled necktie and loose collar, keen to get
to the bar at the Five Alls before the tab ran out, arriving late at
the back-end of the crowd, leaving early.

Doors of expensive grey hire cars caught the light, clicked shut on the ashen-faced wife and grown children, this death a rough divorce for them, Normie old mate, rougher than for you, being unasked for, rougher than anything they the living might create for themselves. Dad. Why?

The unearthly vibration of female vocal chords sang 'Ave Maria' as the clods of oblivion thudded. The Catholic anthem beloved of a lapsed Anglican, a lover of natural history, a lover of life proclaiming life.

Earth was dumped on you, Normie, when all but two went home. May you have a bunch of it in your fist to mound for a place kick now.

Bonney stayed and took photographs, finding Tim Knox in tears, sitting on a pioneer stone, somehow trying to say he'd sort of never really clicked with Normie, but Jesus Christ he'd loved him.

Driving home from the airport one night Claude Bonney was exhausted. He was back from the Okavango Delta after thirty-six hours of delays. The film team he'd hired had been good, he'd hardly been needed. His profession felt empty without Normie its outrider, grief and despair had the better of him. He saw shapes in the headlights that were not there, turned the stereo full volume, surrendered to a rush of feeling. Why, Bonney, with nine lives to be lived and lived? Wasn't he happy? Couldn't he just hold the happiness like a reverberating chord, the road unribboning into a river of stars? All his life observing nature and now subject to its cuts. The hiving off of friends. The way existence was real as dirt, but provisional as snowflakes.

Raging hammer of brakes and pelting gravel. Trunk of a tree

in shuddering headlights. Bonney shakes himself awake after the microsleep that kills, draws breath, drives on.

Outside the Lone Gum Garage a broken neon sizzled, steam billowed from a kitchen exhaust. The highway patrol were eating hamburgers and doing paperwork. Bonney could see the naval piping of the burned sailors' uniforms on the old road behind the hill.

Properly awake now, driving fast, Bonney wove through the all-night transports and accelerated, taking the Isabel turn-off near the travelling stock reserve where Normie had catalogued every native grass, reptile and rare carnivorous marsupial. The road emptied and became his alone – passed in an hour at the wheel of a Volvo the distance Bonney had cycled in two days as a boy. Mournful Lone Gum lights sucked away, driven back into space, the speakers dying in his ears, the huge curves and unimpeded ascent of the Dividing Range unfolding ahead. He ought to be home.

Coldness came on Claude Bonney like a river. Two in the morning and late, very late now, across the river and up the Flying Saucer Road, a ribbon of white dust in night-time paddocks bare as the moon. Here Tim Knox stopped to let UFOs sweep towards him over barbed-wire fences, their windows illuminated from within smearing into the watery constituents of light, showing rows of heads turned staring in his direction, he said. Then he said, putting rationality back into what he saw, 'It was light, just light.'

Light was the wonder.

Bonney was fully awake now, warm bed in his mind, Jacquie making room for him, Bonney a stranger to her through his various tempers in a lifetime marriage but that to be made right.

*

323

On a back hollow before moonrise a rusted ute lurked, waiting. Three o'clock in the dead cold Isabel plateau morning. Minus eleven degrees and still. Drought cold, Antarctic valley deep. Dead rabbits and a small black wallaby draped on the tailgate, and Damon Pattison with a bumper glowing in a cupped hand thinking, *What's old Claude Bonney doing coming in so late, where's he been? Never known such an all-round, self-contained, do-it-yourself merchant. Always thinking. Working it out.*

What if I hit him with the spot, parted a slug through his hair? Wouldn't that make him wonder? Jesus, would I laugh. And old Bonney, he'd piss his trousers.

Damon Pattison flipped his butt away into the frosty grass, where it fizzed.

Blaze of white light – OFU?

The shot ran through the night. As windscreen glass shattered, Bonney was stunned by a thought, the last he would ever have: *I'm on the receiving end.*

It hasn't hurt yet, then it begins. The shock of it coming through in waves and waves and waves. Scrabble of claws running out the full length of a chain and never arriving. Just those poplars and fragments of fountains touching the stars.

NINETEEN

Spot fires tracked roads leaping towards ridgetop estates with tongues of flame pacing Major General Wayne Hovell's slowly moving car from kilometres away. Helicopters thudded in smoke, taking turns dropping water into crazed balls of heat and banking steeply off. At an arranged rendezvous an escort tanker appeared from a side road leading the car on, emergency lights flashing in the daylight dark. Three hundred metres altitude up from the railway line the Friendly House, restored to its greatness by Fred Donovan, burned to the ground.

Wearing a maroon beret tugged low on a weathered forehead, Wayne Hovell followed the tanker with the same quick attention he gave to everything in his late age, a bit careful on steep corners with smoke stinging his eyes but otherwise doing all right. At the last road barrier he unfolded himself from the Subaru like an intelligently designed but slightly rusted all-purpose pocketknife, and looked around for a known face.

They brought Damon Pattison forward, a cop at each elbow steering him up from a gully. Ever since Pattison's release after serving eight years of a twelve-year sentence, Hovell was the one called when the poor bugger's name appeared in police files cross-referenced to serial pests. If it hadn't been for a contact in the force there were three, maybe four occasions when Pattison's refusal to explain himself would have landed him in court for break and enter or arson – crimes inspired by the basic needs of food and warmth, it might be argued, but in Pattison's case no margin for excuses allowed as a lifer on early release.

An odd case, Pattison, having pleaded homicide when manslaughter was more the act he'd bungled when Claude Bonney was shot dead, a poor joke gone wrong – everyone seeing it, even the afternoon editors – all except the judge who underwrote Pattison's self-condemnation and gave him twelve years. After his time in the slammer he'd emerged a stubborn survivor with terminal unwillingness to explain himself, like a rock or a tree, just being in the world and resisting by nature. Bonney's widow and family wanted nothing to do with him, but he was still in character as an agent of fate and was just as bent on making amends as he'd been former bent. Just give him his chance.

After leaving the army Wayne Hovell had spent the next twenty years in public service – with the UN in Africa and then with natural disaster and firefighting coordination teams at home and interstate. He was called to Sydney from beach holidays almost every January and February as New South Wales either flash-flooded or burned. Supporting campaigns for the homeless, the vagrant, the outcast, the friendless and destitute without any fanfare, at least, that he generated himself, was Wayne Hovell's way. A few times each year he spoke from the pulpit of St Stephen's Uniting Church in Macquarie Street, giving the lunchtime sermon. Whatever the text, his theme came back to courage in action, how there was no giving without forsaking. 'Renounce the Hidden', 2 Corinthians 4:2. It was something easier to encourage in others than to apply to himself. He was one of those finished products of a respected value system, the best a society could offer back to itself. What was his lack, then, his hidden? It was time at the age of eighty-three to bring it out.

Come Anzac Day Hovell marched with a breastful of ribbon at the head of a limping column. Defence planners and those he'd commanded sought him for guidance on the principle that anyone who'd commanded a platoon and a division had something worth saying on anything. Every three months meetings of the Lady Margaret Hovell Trust in an office high above Martin Place called for his judgement as money was portioned to community organisations fallen between government cutbacks and financial oblivion. A particular interest was prisoner rehabilitation but the net spread wider. On committee days Hovell quizzed investment advisers and chided his sons, in their fifties, about the contents of their portfolios and the degree of ethical consideration going into their share parcels – bluntly, never enough.

A late-flowering interest was art. Hovell attended painting appreciation classes encouraged by Tabitha, his wife, and developed that dimension of being, the privately intuitive, he'd underplayed in the name of the service-collective.

Since beginning prison visits a few years back Hovell thought that if the distorted energy Damon Pattison generated could be put to use the world might be a better place. This was after the example of Hovell himself, but so blindingly obviously so that he was for long years unaware of its origins in an episode of schoolboy bullying and the complex fractured jaw that jammed on him, sometimes hourly. That moment, sixty-eight years ago, awaited an act of redress for which Hovell's distinguished military career had been merely a diversion. It was no coincidence that Hovell's old quadrangle bully, Colts, had played a role in Pattison's teenage years but hardly decisive. When Pattison spoke of Colts, Hovell had the impulse to better Colts even yet: to break what was broken. It was a vengeful example of the shamefully hidden. But there you were.

Pattison's genius for trouble was astonishing in Hovell's view. Turn it around, face it the other way, what then? At the time the two met, soldier and inmate, Hovell was guest-lecturing at Staff College where he'd developed a few ideas crossing over from the field of battle into managing peace accords. He'd found his ultimate conflict resolution collaborator in the person of Normie Powell looking at competing tendencies in natural communities. Public Health: what a great category heading that was, symbolical of more than sewerage works and anti-malarial fog machines. It allowed viral opposites to join in the name of unforeseen solutions. There was no point kidding yourself dealing with rabbits when your subject was snakes, Normie liked saying. Then he illustrated the sadness factor by dropping off the map when best loved, most appreciated.

'I've got a question for you, Damon,' said Hovell.

'What's new?' grunted his passenger.

'How'd you get into this particular scrape?'

Pattison held off answering while they drove through cross-roads where people stood at their gates in weird yellow light, gazing north at smoke climbing into the stratosphere. The long ridge was once farmland, with the Friendly House used as a hayshed when it fell into ruin.

'I was up the road, on the housing estate, helping a bloke who does garages. You get the slab in first, then Mike rolls up. You hold one end of a rod while Mike bolts the other. You look for the missing packet of screws – they come in plastic bags with numbers. I was up at the shops getting smokes, standing outside watching the Friendly House burn.'

'That's all, Damon, just watching?'

'I dropped a match.'

'Intelligent,' Hovell sighed, unable to help himself.

'A dead one,' Pattison said.

Hovell pictured Pattison, the self-appointed deus ex machina catching the eye of a watchful emergency worker or cop, flame feathering his fingertips – Pattison going to the edge of self-destruction on the wildest day of the year, extinguishing the provocation almost too late, only when it was interesting to do so by scraping backwards with a boot heel, perhaps.

'You think I did it. Why'd I go and do a thing like that? Stuff a few leaves up their drainpipe, break a window, let the sparks fly in on all them beautiful Veronica Buckler originals gone up in smoke.'

There'd been a Buckler Retrospective in the restored Friendly House. It had opened a month before the fires.

'I know one that's safe,' said Hovell. He swallowed, picturing the gawky truth of his appearance. 'It's called *The Chook*.'

Tabitha had bubble-wrapped *The Chook*, sending it off to the National Portrait Gallery, an exhibition on loan from various sources ('Those Who Made Us').

'That makes two,' said Pattison, surprising Hovell with his information. 'Two that's safe.'

Being wise to never pushing, Hovell said nothing but waited to be told. He sensed a change in Pattison equivalent to something Hovell often hoped for, it came about in men, God alone knew how.

They turned off the main road heading south. Pattison rolled down the window, inhaling thinning smoke. 'Next stop Isabel Junction,' he said.

Last time from the St Stephen's pulpit Hovell looked into the scattered congregation and saw Pattison trying not to draw attention to himself by sitting in the back pew. Grizzled head bent, grubby hands steepled and covering his eyes like a small, vulnerable yet hopeful child's bedtime petition. *I can help you,* decided Hovell. *You shall allow it.*

Now it felt like the other way around as Pattison angled in his seat, staring at Hovell from the side. He'd seen Hovell palming tablets into his mouth, swigging on water. Via peripheral vision Hovell looked back at the mat of orange whiskers and the glint of saliva on cracked lips – leave to the imagination the sullen weight of Pattison's reproachful, mudfish eyes.

'You're skinnier than you were, John Wayne.'

'I don't think so.'

'You're sick, you're crook – and you still pester me.'

This was a kind of praise.

'Everyone's on medication at my age, Damon. It's a given.'

'I've got a question.'

'That makes a change,' said the old man.

'You'll say yes?'

Hovell adjusted his grip on the wheel.

'I mean you'll have to,' said Pattison, betraying uncertainty for once.

'Is it about me?' Hovell asked.

'You're so bloody good, what's your problem.'

'Spit it out, then.'

'This car's got a roof rack,' he reached a hand up, feeling the fittings.

'Surprise me with what you mean,' said Hovell.

'It's that painting – *Goats,*' said Pattison. 'I was a complete arsehole, don't ask me why, and Colts bought our house for us. Saved my mum's life. Used his last dollar and sold *Goats* to a bastard of a man, Ted Merrington, who let his son Harald serve time for him in Goulburn Gaol.'

'The goat meant tragedy in ancient Greece,' said Hovell. 'In

Ireland a goat king was crowned every year. When I was there I heard of a goat being caught in Ulster and stopped from being taken south.'

'I want to do something for him,' said Pattison. 'For Kingsley Colts.'

This answered a prayer for Pattison's wellbeing that Hovell had made, but only in a certain direction. 'Lord,' he said to himself, 'does it have to be Colts?'

They drove along humpbacked gravel roads where the air thinned with increasing altitude and tussock grasses bloomed insect hordes in the late-afternoon light. Pattison directed the way while Hovell's thoughts bore down on the next few days of his life. He could do without this diversion. A decision needed to be made on the purchasing policy of the small but useful lending library in a backroom of the old goldmining township where he and Tabitha raised Belted Galloways and kept bees. A fishing holiday in Alaska involving float plane connections needed finalising – it would be his last. Visits to grandchildren and great-grandchildren were called for – he'd made those a strong habit this year. The kids loved him for the presents he gave and for the interest he showed in whatever was happening in their lives, from a problem in recorder class with the youngest to an act of drug-using self-destructiveness with an older one. Hovell withheld judgement and was loved with devotion that was to remain a gift in the lives of those kids for a good long time. Light shone through his pink blood-vesselled cheeks like a torch held under a blanket recalling the deepest and most secure childhood moments.

Colts wasn't good in the mornings but by dusk he was all right, tootling along with his fox terrier, Pat, angling the square blocks of the Junction on a favourite walk, banging up to the Five Alls to surprise himself with a nip.

The bar crowd was mostly kids new out of school, tattooed, singleted, bottle-blonded boys and girls, some of them calling Colts Kings or Old Kings to show they were in the know about a legendary old fart. 'Good on ya, Kings, have one on us . . .' Buying Colts a snort was like throwing a dog a bone, no trouble. Girls said Pat was so sweet they could eat her alive as they nuzzled her wet nose.

Colts went through the Five Alls and came out the other side pleasantly cheery, only reeking a little of brandy fumes. Last week, finding him stinking-trousered in Pioneers Park under a photinia bush, Randolph had nudged Colts with the tip of his walking stick when he would rather have struck him.

Down the main street greeting strangers with a blurred smile and peering through the smudged glass of the bakery, Colts spotted, between the community notices taped to the window, a man around his own age buying pies.

Didn't like what he saw – a stirring of resentment as he picked the beret-wearer as the superior sort of traveller favouring the Isabel now, history-hopping as they expressed it and feeding from a crushed paper bag. A high court judge or retired governor with that casually cultivated tweedy look, so condescending to failure of the self-willed sort.

From a car Colts was watched in turn.

'There he goes,' said Pattison, hunching down in the passenger seat of the Subaru.

Then it was Hovell's turn, with a surge of revulsion towards a man he thoroughly knew, as part of his bite, swallow and lifelong mechanism of expression: Colts. The sight of that flushed skeleton shook him, that doddery shadow enacting a ghost wish: *He's kneeling as I come up behind him with the offer of a tyre lever, and then, as he knows me, I bring the bar down.*

'Let's get out of here,' said Hovell, dumping the baked goods in Pattison's lap.

Just out of town Hovell apologised and stopped the car, getting the door open even before it rolled to a halt. There to his burning-throated humiliation he barfed his guts out into a bush, wiping his mouth and looking around guardedly, blaming his oncologist for prescribing a stronger dose of cisplatinum.

Recovered, pounding the steering wheel metronomically, a bit overdone, Hovell found he was able to function despite feeling harrowed and drained. You felt one way in military parlance, you fulfilled orders in another. You soldiered on. 'The godhead in us wrings our nobler deeds from our reluctant selves.' That was his code.

Now in a dark pit of himself Colts lay at the bottom, fit to be flayed. Never far from Hovell's thoughts was the parable of the good Samaritan as a yardstick of action, helping decide when to reach a hand for the bloodied figure huddled beaten and lost, to whom Colts, Hovell cautioned his admiring conscience, bore no resemblance at all.

Pattison's idea was to buy back *Goats* and give it to Colts, Hovell to supply the money.

'It's worth a fortune,' said Hovell.

'Depends who you are,' said Pattison, 'as to what a fortune is.'

Pattison looked at him then turned away. A profound, probing silence travelled between them. Hovell knew Pattison would never again touch firearms or express an enraged, extreme opinion likely to ignite any sort of fatal confrontation, the moral equivalent of arms. He was bound, tied and held to a life sentence of self-control. He would sometimes, however, make strange requests.

Pattison gave directions; Hovell, after some thought, obeyed.

They arrived at a homestead on the Upper Isabel, with abandoned cattle yards choked with thistle. A withering season of neglect lay over Ted Merrington's Burnside. He now lived alone, keeping an ear out for cars crunching the side road.

The big ship's bell door-ringer clanged.

'All right, all bloody *right*,' and Merrington wrenched the door open to find himself facing a known identity, the philanthropist big-spender, Chook Hovell.

'Good evening, let me introduce myself, explain myself . . .'

'Not at all, delighted, do come in . . .'

Merrington had never lost an electric effect on men of good judgement: Hovell felt for his sword.

Shortly afterwards Merrington found himself better off than he would have been selling *Goats* through the Macleay Street dealer he had already promised (make that half-promised) a sale. 'If I had started that fire myself, creating a shortage,' his satisfaction implied, 'I could not be more pleased. Add to that the supreme satisfaction of having paid peanuts for the cameo in the first place, from a drunken sot.'

When Hovell and Damon Pattison left, the picture bound in an old blanket and tied with twine to the roof rack, Merrington held the cheque to the light and waved it in the air, fanning his cheeks before placing it under a paperweight. Something else to be done, then, for he felt charged up. There was still sufficient daylight to walk over the hills and gun a bunny, scare a wild pig, slug a mangy fox or disintegrate a wild cat deceiving him through the folds and declivities of the land. He filled a pocket with shells and set off.

After the death of Boy Dunlap, Faye Colts came east and gave a few half days a week as consultant researcher in West Australian languages at the ANU. Sorting Boy's notebooks and transcribing his early ethnographic recordings took much of her time.

Somehow the word got out. Colleagues in the research school loved the idea that the beautiful young model glowing in flower beds and radiating rings of golden bathwater in the lost Buckler masterworks (reproduced now in weekend magazines) was the same authoritative woman in her eighties putting young linguists in their place and arranging the assumptions of anthropologists on the basis of a lifetime of living in bush camps.

Isabel Junction was only two hours away and when she could, Faye drove out to see her brother.

'You can't go on living like this,' she said, resuming a custom of care never quite abandoned on her marriage those years ago, but more intense, as if sisterly closeness could be taken up without question now that she'd got the more interesting claims of her life out of the way – 'saying it was just yesterday you bunked in with Randolph, really!'

'Not exactly "yesterday",' said Colts. 'Not "bunked in", either.'

'All right, darling, but how long has it been, freeloading when you've wasted everything, and I think Randolph would never say so, but Stone Wall Cottage is getting a bit too much for him. It's very unsatisfactory Kings, when you think of it.'

'Only temporary . . .'

Faye trailed off, hating to use the word 'waste', that lascivious theme of the Isabel she had studied long distance – waste in men's lives embraced with more passion than they gave to anything but dogs and sheep and the Five Alls Hotel.

Would somebody please explain to her what it meant? she'd asked, carrying the question into the anthrop tearoom one day. 'And don't start telling me anything specious, as favoured in postgrad speculation, along the lines of men having completed their reproductive function and finding there is nothing left for them so they might as well go off. There's spirit, you know. There's love.'

This from a woman who'd known happiness in her married life, in extreme circumstances of geography and material reward.

She'd believed in love, having fountained that particular emotion through all her days and suffered to prove its truth. Wasn't going to give up on love quite yet, then.

Boy had nosedived the Cessna on the 13th of June, 1991, on his seventieth birthday, stalling on take-off from Nullagine, heading back for the big happy all ready and waiting for him, people coming in from a thousand desert kilometres in all directions, driving all manner of strange contraptions. Never had celebration turned into funeral so abruptly.

Colts waved an unlit cigarette around, then hunched in over it, flicking a lighter peevishly.

'I do give Randolph a hand round the place, don't say I do not.'

The most she'd seen him do was track up through Randolph's olives lifting rocks and getting down on his knees under weed mat looking for a bottle he'd hidden that had probably been smashed by the slasher. Then he came back to the walled garden and his wooden bench, his tobacco tin and transistor radio tuned to rural roundups.

'How long has this been here?' said Faye, shuffling through a pile of mail. She showed Colts a letter, one of dozens that lay around in a mess – she'd forwarded it to him months ago.

'A while.'

'You know what it says, then?'

'Buckler is "in"?'

The chairman of a working party on the Australian Dictionary of Biography advising on subjects for inclusion had recommended that the racist, utterly forgotten, troublesome, egomaniacal, warped but peerlessly brave Major Dunc Buckler, MC (1894–1985?) was worthy of inclusion.

'You were his shadow, his footprint, his little sidekick and pal,' said Faye.

'So I was.'

Colts made something of watching an ant clambering over a splinter of wood on the seat beside him, leg by thin leg.

On her next visit Faye spoke decisively: 'Your friend Kingsley is taking a holiday from the Isabel,' she told Randolph, after working out that although Colts would agree to almost nothing, he would do almost anything, now, if she led.

Randolph sat under a pool of lamplight with the volume a fellow-royalist, Eddie Slim, had given him for Christmas, which he pored over like a studious monk – Prince Charles at Highgrove, a name so like Homegrove it thrilled, a book of organic farming on biodynamic principles, which Randolph loathed as a rule.

It wasn't until the next day, and they were threading into the late afternoon sun on a back stretch after many hours that Colts felt his stomach lurch, and cursed not taking a last look around his hiding places. A line thinner than saliva reached the back of his brain to the last drink he took, two days ago, passed over the dry-stone wall by Gilbert Dalrymple, no longer a partaker but soft landings his wish for the incorrigibly desperational.

'Where are we going?' Colts blinked. So far he'd dozed, cocooned in a mood taking him far back past any beginning of what could sensibly be called his life. He'd assumed they were going to the comfortable flat Faye had been given in University House (above the garden bar), or possibly headed in the opposite direction, to the far South Coast, where Faye proposed visiting the rural cemetery south of Narooma where Veronica was buried.

Instead they swallowed a sun of boiling fire, and came towards nine down a dirt road and then to a recognisable place (whitewashed stone in the headlights) where Faye led Colts by the hand up a gravelled pathway, into a room where there was a bowl of ripe figs, a jug of water with a beaded glass cover, a narrow bed with a cotton bedspread and theatrical posters on the walls, *A Midsummer Night's Dream*, *Richard III*, *Waiting For Godot*. It was a boy's bedroom kept for a boy's return, intensely familiar and old, a cool cellar in the hot night. But Colts wasn't that boy he found himself confusedly thinking. After fumbling with his glasses and beaming the bedside lamp around he saw the name Fred Donovan featured on the old posters.

Because of this room, because of the purple split figs, the deeply recessed windows, the hot night and loud crickets, the stars caught in the angle of narrow window glass, Colts began to understand something about fragments of importance in a life, how they flew apart and kept their distances life-long. How they were that life in the end, such as the stars were, in their cold distances.

He'd never seen Fred Donovan perform but remembered him from the Five Alls — a cheery, voluble, overweight young bloke greeting him with a beer and a whisky chaser. Then Randolph pompously started following Donovan in his next career, that of architect: Donovan's name loudly dropped in company, his prizewinning designs clipped from colour supplements and into the scrapbook with them.

Now Colts remembered Donovan saying he'd grown up in pubs when Colts quipped he'd grown old in one, and so he recalled without the name Donovan ever teasing him before, that Rusty was a name snapped off a branch, and left as a flowered twig at Buckler's memorial service by a half-familiar figure.

She knocked at his door, a thin, sharp-eyed old woman with the light behind her, leaning on a stick, introducing herself.

'Are you comfortable, Mister Colts?'

Thank you, he was, because of this room, because of the

purple split figs, the deeply recessed windows, the hot night and loud crickets, those stars caught in the angle of narrow window glass.

Limestone Hills was her retirement fund, she said, a piece of country living where city people could spend a night or two and explore the local attractions: gold panning, limestone caves, vineyards.

After she left, Colts swept the lamp around the wall and looked again at the tinted features of Fred Donovan, and saw Dunc Buckler written all over them.

Then Colts undressed and, using the towel and washing bowl provided, cleaned himself – face, underarms, chest, everywhere – and lay down on the tight white sheet naked as a corpse. Eyes open, lids peeled back, listening and wondering what he was listening for. Was it a machine breaking the gunpowder rocks, throwing sparks? Was it that?

At breakfast under a net of vines on a white-painted, wrought-iron table they deferred to Colts as if he trailed a dynamite fuse. 'Tea, eggs, orange juice – we squeeze our own . . .'

Faye had been talking. 'Watch him.'

Each day Colts was stronger on grilled cutlets and mashed pumpkin, on cheese pie and shepherd's pie, a style of cooking Rusty brought from her pubs. Up and down the track and into the dry creekbed Colts walked, along the low rocky ridge of hardy plants, scraping their seed-heads in the dust. Of course it wouldn't last, but while it held, this was the life and the definition of the life in Faye's estimation.

These days a sealed road led into town, to a clinic where Colts was treated for the leg ulcers he barely noticed.

They heard the pallid cuckoo calling over paddocks of wheat sown by a sharefarmer who watched the wheat wither to nothing. They turned back time, remembering the first steps they took through the wire gate with the grimy spring that slammed back resisting sheep getting through. It was all Colts remembered, he said. The two of them back together. Entering there.

'No, there was somewhere else . . .' said Faye. 'And you promised to come with me.'

Mornings were bad, evenings a test, Colts dodging the cocktail hour hanging over him. They had pineapple juice topped with cold ginger beer in schooner glasses. A line of foam was left on Colts's upper lip. It looked like the moustache worn by a handsome old Greek café owner, said Rusty. Such a man the last and greatest love of her life.

So Buckler had a son. Faye had tracked him down this far, making the friendship with Rusty. The question was, had Veronica ever known about a family hived off, and the answer was that she had – of course she had – though she did not ever speak of it. Money sorely needed by Rusty at various times of need had come through from Buckler's account. He didn't have a red cent after his mining ventures drained him. So it was all from her.

They talked about 1942–43, when this had begun, the creation of who they were. Buckler had been on a foray when he left Colts at Eureka, some wild notion about investigating mysterious sounds – Faye told the story for Rusty, Colts listened, correcting this fact or that – rumbles of mining machinery reported coming from the broken ranges and long sea inlets away to the north, possibly from Japanese landing parties doing God knew what. Buckler crossed the continent to investigate. But there was nothing there, nobody there except three white people – Buckler's own estranged wife, Veronica, his ward of legacy, Faye, her husband Boy Dunlap – and a headcount of ninety-three blackfellows of supremely doubtful loyalty, as

Buckler characterised them in the report he wrote to the army chiefs who ignored it.

No doubt Buckler always loved Rusty in the stronger way, the wanting way, but she wouldn't have him. Only those visits sometimes, when he saw Fred. How Veronica must have loved him to be satisfied with him beat the two women at the level of reason but not of the wanting heart.

Had he ever come back east, that last time they went bush together? It was a question of interest along the lines of all unsolved disappearances. Faye brought out maps and Rusty perched her magnifiers on the tip of her nose, Colts peering over their shoulders and saying very little. When Buckler left the camp that day, they wondered, had he gone through the deserts to reach Rusty, to see Fred a last time? If so, it would have been an abandonment of Veronica, a piece of old-age nuttiness, inconceivable to consider even in a man attuned to a double-serving life. No, it was not to be considered.

Yet they considered it – the two old magpies, Faye and Rusty, as they gave each other foot massages in the window seat, did the washing up together and went about the droughty garden in the spirit of long-lost sisters.

Fred always said it was possible, reported Rusty – sometimes in the early years between Buckler's visits he said he'd seen him in the flesh when he wasn't supposed to be there. Fred's earliest childhood had been a catalogue of imagined events interspersed with the rare enough too-real ones. Buckler influenced his imag-ination, made him what he was, a show-off loving attention and getting it without going to the extremes Buckler had gone to in two world wars and the contested peace between them. Since turning to architecture putting it into physical shapes, dwellings, shelters.

'No,' said Colts sharply, breaking a silence.

The women looked over at him, to where he stood forgotten

in the room, sorting photographs from old shoeboxes and arranging them for Faye to decide which to paste in an album.

'"No"? What do you mean?'

'No,' he said. 'Buckler never went very far. Look at these.'

They were taken at Boy Dunlap's funeral. Colts fanned the photos over the table. Faye had gone around snapping people she'd known over most of her lifetime, from many far-flung communities, outstations and bush camps, catching them as they came into the place on the flatboards of trucks and clinging to various doorless cars – old men with prophetic beards, jelly-fat women sitting on the ground cross-legged and laughing, kids running up to the camera and splaying out their limbs, pulling faces, throwing wide grins. And there in the background of one of those shots could be seen the chassis of a vintage Land Rover, Buckler's – hauled in from some side road among the trees. Desert oaks Colts imagined, a circle of them, the wind mournful in the needles of the branches but such a wind as would allow a man to tuck his skull under his arm and rise up and ride into the night sky.

Colts was down at the dry creek a day later when a car drove in. Dust billowed over him and drifted away. When he got back to the house a painting hung on the verandah wall. Colts stopped and looked. Indelibly stared, dumbstruck and sober. A corner post was in the painting and it held up the roof of the real house in the actual garden of Limestone Hills where he stood imagining himself back into the painting he'd sold for a song: *Goats*.

'An anonymous benefactor,' said a man wearing a beret, stepping from the shadows of the grape arbour, 'wants you to have it, Mr Colts.'

Colts peered at the visitor, the man with that jarringly dislocated angle of jaw, with that long, sharp, weatherworn face of moral authority, freakishly sharp of nose and protruding chicken-chest, last seen in the street outside a small-town bakery.

'You?' he challenged.

'No, if it was up to me, Colts, me,' the man stepped closer, trembling-lipped, dropping his voice a couple of tones so that what was said would pass only between the two of them, 'I would keep this great picture for myself.'

'Hovell.'

'Colts.'

Faye asked Hovell to drive them in his robust car and insisted on Kings taking the front passenger seat. It was not yet obvious to Faye that for the duration of their drive, which wasn't far, the two men weren't going to talk. Down a rutted road, up a rutted hill. The grave Colts had always believed was far from Limestone Hills was close.

Midafternoon and Hovell's all-wheel drive navigated the track leading out to the abandoned cemetery on the rocky ridge where Faye had seen her mother buried long ago. A brave little girl wearing a seersucker frock, her hair pinned back by tortoise-shell combs, she had taken on so much.

She led Colts to the broken, weed-strewn gravestone, but when he began weeping she stepped back. Goats had been through eating everything. When Kings sat on the gravestone sobbing, kicking the bitter earth, she said nothing but went over to the only tree offering shade, a peppercorn where she unpacked Rusty's picnic hamper and poured tea from a thermos for herself and Hovell.

'He'll be a while yet, I think,' she said.

Author's Note

Early parts of this work appeared in *Best Australian Stories 1999* (Melbourne, 1999); the *Monthly* (September 2005); *Where the Rivers Meet: New Writing from Australia* (*Manoa*, Hawaii, Winter 2006); *Making Waves: Ten Years of the Byron Bay Literary Festival* (2006); the *Bulletin*, Summer Reading Edition (December 2006 – January 2007); *Best Australian Stories 2007* (Melbourne, 2007); and *The O. Henry Prize Stories 2008* (New York, 2008). Acknowledgement is made to the editors concerned: Peter Craven, Frank Stewart, Mark Tredinnick, Marele Day, Ashley Hay, Robert Drewe and Laura Furman. Quotations attributed to Dunc Buckler on pages 7 and 215 are from *Soldier In Battle* (1940) by G.D. Mitchell (1894-1961). Thanks to John and Gwen Bucknall for being part of this story's search for itself in bush camps and conversations over the years; to Bill Gammage for a resonant reference; to Jim Morgan for more than an anecdote; to Trevor Shearston for shining a light on the manuscript when needed most; and to Susie Fisher, with love, for inspiration in, and beyond, these pages.

Roger McDonald was born at Young, New South Wales, and educated at country schools and in Sydney. His novels include *1915*, winner of the *Age* Book of the Year, *Slipstream*, *Rough Wallaby*, *Water Man* and *The Slap*. His account of travelling the outback with a team of New Zealand shearers, *Shearers' Motel*, won the National Book Council Banjo Award for non-fiction. His bestselling novel *Mr Darwin's Shooter* was awarded the New South Wales, Victorian and South Australian Premiers' Literary Awards, and the National Fiction Award at the 2000 Adelaide Writers' Week. *The Ballad of Desmond Kale* won the 2006 Miles Franklin Award and South Australian Festival Prize for Fiction. A long story that became part of *When Colts Ran* was awarded the O. Henry Prize in 2008.